PRAISE FOR BEN

"Here's a near-future space adventure that's as frightening as it is smart. Jeremy Robinson's BENEATH is packed with believable tech, a page-turning story and an alien intelligence so creepy, you'll pray NASA never makes it past the moon." --*J.C. Hutchins, author of PERSONAL EFFECTS: DARK ART and 7ᵗʰ SON: DESCENT*

"Jeremy Robinson hits his stride in BENEATH. His story-telling is as tight as ever, delivering thrills that raise the heart rate and science detail that gets the mind cranking just has hard. An evocative blend of Crichton and Clarke, BE-NEATH is destined to become an instant new media classic." --*Phil Rossi, Best Selling author of CRESCENT, HARVEY, and EDEN*

"Isolation, cold, and the unknown: Like *The Thing*, BENEATH taps into those fears, and a couple more we never know we had. Robinson strips away all that we hold dear, sends us into the deep dark, and dares us to make our way out of it." --*Mur Lafferty, author of PLAYING FOR KEEPS and award-winning podcaster of I SHOULD BE WRITING and the HEAVEN series*

"Robinson grabbed my attention in the first chapter, and kept hold of it. BE-NEATH isn't your run of the mill way distant future fantasy sci-fi. It reads like its real, like it could happen today...but we hope and pray it doesn't." --*Basil Sands, author of 65 BELOW and FAITHFUL WARRIOR*

"Masterful Craftsmanship...a chilling tale that finally answers the question: Are we alone?" --*thenovelblog.com*

PRAISE FOR JEREMY ROBINSON'S JACK SIGLER SERIES

INSTINCT

"If you like thrillers original, unpredictable and chock-full of action, you are going to love Jeremy Robinson's Chess Team. INSTINCT riveted me to my chair."-- *Stephen Coonts, NY Times bestselling author of SAUCER and DEEP BLACK: ARCTIC GOLD*

"Instinct is a jungle fever of raw adrenaline that goes straight for the jugular."-- *Thomas Greanias, NY Times bestselling author of THE ATLANTIS PROPHECY and THE PROMISED WAR*

"Jeremy Robinson is a fresh new face in adventure writing and will make a mark in suspense for years to come." -- *David Lynn Golemon, NY Times Bestselling author of LEGEND and LEVIATAN*

PULSE

"Rocket-boosted action, brilliant speculation, and the recreation of a horror out of the mythologic past, all seamlessly blend into a rollercoaster ride of suspense and adventure." -- *James Rollins, New York Times bestselling author of THE LAST ORACLE*

"There's nothing timid about Robinson as he drops his readers off the cliff without a parachute and somehow manages to catch us an inch or two from doom." -- *Jeff Long, New York Times bestselling author of THE DESCENT and YEAR ZERO*

"Robinson's latest reads like a video game with tons of action and lots of carnage. The combination of mythology, technology, and high-octane action proves irresistible. Gruesome and nasty in a good way, this will appeal to readers of Matthew Reilly." -- *Booklist*

"Raiders of the Lost Ark meets Tom Clancy meets Saturday matinee monster flick with myths, monsters, special ops supermen and more high tech weapons than a Bond flick. Pulse is an over-the-top, bullet-ridden good time." -- *Scott Sigler, New York Times bestselling author of CONTAGIOUS and INFECTED*

"Greek myth and biotechnology collide in Robinson's first in a new thriller series to feature the Chess Team... Robinson will have readers turning the pages..." -- *Publisher's Weekly*

THRESHOLD

"With his new entry in the Jack Sigler series, Jeremy Robinson plants his feet firmly on territory blazed by David Morrell and James Rollins. The perfect blend of mysticism and monsters, both human and otherwise, make THRESHOLD as groundbreaking as it is riveting." – *Jon Land, NY Times bestselling author of STRONG ENOUGH TO DIE*

"Jeremy Robinson's THRESHOLD is one hell of a thriller, wildly imaginative and diabolical, which combines ancient legends and modern science into a non-stop action ride that will keep you turning the pages until the wee hours. Relentlessly gripping from start to finish, don't turn your back on this book!" -- *Douglas Preston, NY Times bestselling author of BLASPHEMY*

"Jeremy Robinson is the next James Rollins" -- *Chris Kuzneski, NY Times bestselling author of THE SECRET CROWN*

"With THRESHOLD Jeremy Robinson goes pedal to the metal into very dark territory. Fast-paced, action-packed and wonderfully creepy! Highly recommended!" --*Jonathan Maberry, NY Times bestselling author of THE KING OF PLAGUES and ROT & RUIN*

BENEATH

JEREMY ROBINSON

BREAKNECK MEDIA

ALSO BY JEREMY ROBINSON

For Walter and Stan

ACKNOWLEDGEMENTS

Because this is a special edition, published by myself, so I don't have the normal group of people to thank. No publisher, agent or designers took part in the creation of this book. I wrote it, laid it out and designed the cover myself.

But that doesn't mean it was created in a vacuum. I must thank the diligent work of my advance readers and spell checkers whose dedication and support made this possible. Karen Cooper, Tara Elly and Dan Boucher – your advance reading comments helped improve the story. You were my editors for this book and I thank you for it. Merrill Allen, your final read and typo fixes were invaluable and kept me from looking like a dolt.

Thanks must also go out to audiobook narrator extraordinaire, Jeffrey Kafer, the voice behind the free podcast novel edition of BENEATH as well as the (not free) audiobooks for PULSE and INSTINCT. You make my text come to life.

Last, and always, I need to thank my infinitely supportive wife, Hilaree and my three adorable and creative children, Aquila, Solomon and Norah.

"If we have learned one thing from the history of invention and discovery, it is that, in the long run - and often in the short one - the most daring prophecies seem laughably conservative."
-- Arthur C. Clarke, *The Exploration of Space*

"It is easy to go down into Hell; night and day, the gates of dark Death stand wide; but to climb back again, to retrace one's steps to the upper air - there's the rub, the task."
-- Virgil, *Aeneid*

"Spaceships and time machines are no escape from the human condition. Let Othello subject Desdemona to a lie-detector test; his jealousy will still blind him to the evidence. Let Oedipus triumph over gravity; he won't triumph over his fate."
-- Arthur Koestler, Writer

"The search for new life, exploration of the world around us, accumulation of global knowledge for the betterment of mankind; no one questions these ideas. They are the fundamentals of world-wide human society and the very basic principles of science. New life forms are discovered every year in the most remote regions of our world, providing unique glimpses of the evolutionary process and delivering incredible advances in medical science, saving countless lives. Seeking out new life should be a tantamount concern to every living soul on Earth..."
-- Dr. Kathy Connelly, Biologist and Oceanographer

"Maybe this world is another planet's hell."
-- Aldous Huxley

PROLOGUE -- COLLISIONS

Glowing dully in the light cast from the distant sun, a spinning chunk of interwoven nickel and iron the size of Khufu's Pyramid, cruised past the outer fringes of our solar system, missing Pluto by a miniscule six hundred thousand miles.

Moving at 75,000 miles per hour, the asteroid sped past the orbits of Uranus, Neptune and Saturn, bringing it deeper into the solar system and on a direct collision course with Earth. But, as often happens with solar intruders, a slight tug, a nagging pull of gravity began to exert its force on the interplanetary projectile. The course of the asteroid was modified and redirected towards the solar system's vacuum cleaner, mighty Jupiter.

Just as the ancient god Jupiter protected the Roman Empire by reaching out and smiting enemies with lightning bolts, so too did the solar system's guardian. Reaching out with its gravity, Jupiter pulled the asteroid toward its surface, threatening to crush it within a high pressure atmosphere of hydrogen, nitrogen, helium and other gases. The asteroid, now on a collision course with the outer atmosphere of Jupiter, began building speed, pulled in faster by Jupiter's influence.

Passing Jupiter's outer moons in rapid succession, the asteroid's fate seemed clear. But a near miss with Callisto, Jupiter's eighth and second-largest moon, altered its course ever so slightly, just enough to cause a premature collision. Noiselessly, the asteroid impacted with the frozen surface of Jupiter's sixth moon, Europa. The surface of the moon exploded with energy created by the impact and massive chunks of ice, launching stone and other materials into space. Some were pulled back by Jupiter's gravitational grip, but other chunks, moving fast enough to escape, tumbled into space and scattered across the solar system like a broken dinner plate across a tile floor.

One object in particular made off like a fleeing prisoner, toward the center of the solar system—toward Earth. The football-field-sized asteroid which once threatened Earth had been replaced by a smaller chunk of Europa, which slowly spun through the solar system, passing through the asteroid belt and the orbit of Mars without incident.

The house-sized object passed the moon and burst into flames as it entered Earth's atmosphere—3,053 years later.

EARTH

1 – IMPACT

Muscles stretched and bones cracked as Michael Peterson twisted his own neck with his hands. His mother had always told him that cracking his own neck would one day paralyze him. But Peterson had stretched his neck to the point where his vertebrae popped every morning since his was a child. He stepped out of the tent and shivered as the frigid air struck his lungs.

If only mom could see me now, he thought as he looked out at the white expanse of the Arctic where he'd come in search of meteorites. Every year, thousands of space rocks made their permanent home on the surface of the Earth, or in this case, the frozen surface of the Arctic Ocean. It wasn't that meteorites were more plentiful at the North Pole, just that they were easier to spot. Black specks on the stark ice usually meant one of two things, a polar bear's snout or a meteorite.

Peterson had the rugged look of a man who ought to be out in a cold expanse, seeking out new-found wonders. His face was covered in stubble, which helped block out the unending cold. His jet black hair had a slight wave to it, but was now covered by a wool cap and parka hood. Some teenagers might consider him old, but he was still ready to take on most any challenge his profession could throw at him. Not that there was much to being an astrogeologist with a specialization in meteorites. If he wasn't collecting rocks from around the world, he was dissecting them in a warm, cozy lab. But it was exciting work. He believed that the evidence for life on other worlds wouldn't be found through monitoring radio waves like the folks at SETI or by finding traces of water on the surface of Mars. No, the proof would come to us, in the form of microorganisms embedded in a meteorite. It only needed to be found.

He was only a child when the news of ALH84001 hit the papers in 1996, but it was one of his sweetest memories. The meteorite had been found on Antarctica in 1984, but wasn't analyzed for years. When it was...it rocked the world with the possibility of extraterrestrial microbial life on Mars. The president addressed the nation about the find. Conversations of life on other worlds ran rampant. Peterson based his school science project on the Martian stone, earning him an A in eighth grade astronomy. He was devastated when the stone was proven to contain no evidence of life, but the flame had already been ignited. Earning his doctorate degree by age twenty-five garnered him the respect of his peers and allowed him to start working on his life's dream at a young age. It was now 2021 and after seven years of searching, he was no closer to his life's goal than he was at the millennium.

Peterson lifted a stone in his gloved hand and let it drop. He watched as the rock hit the snow, creating a small plume of icy dust, and a tiny pockmark. Lifting the stone, Peterson smiled at the mini crater. He had often pictured what it would be like, witnessing a meteorite crashing to Earth; bursting through the atmosphere and crashing to the ground. He'd seen the results when such collisions took place in the civilized world; car engines torn through like a tank had just taken a pot shot, living rooms destroyed, trees severed in half. It was a miracle no one had yet been brained by one of the falling stones. He'd seen it all, but when it happened to him, for all his years of dreaming, he found himself completely unprepared.

The streak overhead caught his attention as he stretched in the early morning, preparing for another long day of scouring the frozen cap of the world. His first thought was that it was a crashing plane, or perhaps a satellite. But something about the way it glowed and broke up told him the object falling across the deep blue sky was not manmade. This was the real thing. An asteroid turned meteorite plummeting to Earth before his eyes.

It fell to the north, disappearing over the horizon. Peterson's eyes widened; he feared the object had been completely disintegrated by Earth's friction filled atmosphere. Perhaps he would find nothing but interstellar ash? Or maybe nothing at all. He was terrified that he would have nothing to show for the most enlightening, most invigorating and satisfying experience of his life. He held his breath.

A second later, he heard a distant thud. The meteorite had struck the ice, and not too far away. His mind spun with the possibilities that came when any meteorite was discovered: proof of extraterrestrial life, new elements, maybe even evidence for the beginning of the universe. The possibilities were endless. This object that just fell into his proverbial backyard could be as old as the universe itself. He stood there for a minute, pondering what he would find, and then suddenly snapped out of his thoughts, sounded the alarm and gathered his crew.

"Benson! Get your ass up!" Peterson shouted as he shook the outside of the sturdy, orange tent.

"I'm awake. I'm awake," came a voice from inside the tent. Seconds later the tent was unzipped from the inside and a tired, bearded face gazed out. "What the hell is so important?"

"A meteorite," Peterson said, with glowing eyes.

Benson was annoyed. "Yeah, we find a lot of those up here, but not at six o'clock in the morning!"

Peterson leaned in close and spoke with a voice that demanded attention, without the use of volume. "You don't understand. It just hit. I saw it hit."

Staring straight forward for a moment, Benson was lost in thought. "You're sure?"

"Saw it with my own eyes," Peterson said. "Wake the others. We're leaving in twenty minutes. And we're not taking any chances, so break out the bio-suits."

"Are you sure that's necessary?" Benson asked with a snicker. "You do realize how improbable it is for us to find life on one of these rocks, don't you?"

"Just do it," Peterson said as he walked away.

Within thirty minutes, they were high above the crash zone, circling a crater the size of a typical backyard swimming pool. Peterson looked out from the side of the helicopter, peering through the clear faceplate of his bio-suit. His heart skipped a beat. There was something at the center of the crater.

Something red.

"Take us down," Peterson said to the pilot, who instantly brought the chopper around. They landed fifty yards away, sending up a blinding plume of snow.

As soon as the chopper came to rest on the ice, Peterson, Benson and three other men, dressed from head to toe in silver biohazard suits, entered the swirling wash of snow and set out toward the meteorite. As though rehearsed, all five men reached the outer perimeter of the crater simultaneously and froze.

"Oh my god," Stewart, one of the interns, said as he gazed into the crater.

Peterson looked at Benson with a smile stretching wider and wider. "You're with me."

Slowly and calmly, Peterson and Benson descended into the crater which was six feet deep and smooth. The ice melted and refroze. It was tricky navigating the steep angle but the bio-suits had been designed for use in the arctic and the built-on crampons bit into the ice. Once at the bottom, Peterson opened his hip pack and took out a small device he had designed specifically for his line of work. He called it a geospectrometer. *Geospeck* for short. The device could scan any object, geological, biological or man-made, and tell you what it was composed of—instantly. What was more important to Peterson was the device's ability to detect the presence of life, or even the residue of life, down to the microscopic. It was the astrogeologist's magic wand. Many finds which would have taken years to scrutinize now took seconds with a degree of error that put human analysis to shame. Every find was valuable, but thus far none had contained even a hint of life.

He looked down at the object. It was the size of a football and deep red in color. *This is definitely something new*, he thought, and then frowned. *Or waste ejected from the space station.*

He held the *Geospeck* over the object and watched as an array of numbers danced across the LCD screen, working calculations and identifying the rock's chemical and physical makeup. The numbers changed to words, listing out all known elements, several of which were common in all meteorites. Then it stopped.

Peterson's eyebrows furrowed deeply. That couldn't be it. Nothing in the list of elements listed on the *Geospeck* could account for the vibrant crimson color. Before he could voice a complaint at the device he had created, a new set of words were displayed on the screen.

Unknown element: classification - 001EL

Unknown element: classification - 002EL

Unknown element: classification - 003 EL

Geologic Analysis: Unknown materials present.

Biologic Analysis: Unknown potential.

Peterson's jaw went slack. Not only had they discovered three new elements, solidifying that this was indeed from another world, the biological analysis came back: *Unknown potential.* This by no means meant that he had discovered life, but something in, or on, this rock had confounded the geospeck. And *that* was something worth getting excited about.

"Unbelievable," Peterson said to himself. He looked back at Benson, Stewart and the others. "We've found something...something...I don't know...."

Stewart's excited eyes widened behind the bio-suit's mask. "Life?"

Peterson smiled. "Maybe."

Stewart looked confused. "Maybe. *Maybe?*"

"That not good enough for you, Stew?" Benson said.

Stewart looked uncomfortable. "Well, I—"

"Try to understand this from our perspective," Peterson said. "We've been coming here and collecting stones from space for how long now?"

"Seven years," Benson said.

"Seven years," Peterson repeated. "And this is the first truly unique meteorite in all that time. It contains something we—something *no one*—has seen before."

Stewart looked pleased again. "So this is big then?"

Peterson chuckled. "Very big."

"Famous big?" Stewart said.

Peterson put his hand on Benson's shoulder. "We'll see."

Stewart leaned over the lip of the crater and peered down at the meteorite, half buried in the ice, its red surface shining in the bright sun. "This...is...awe—" Stewart lost his balance and fell forward. "Whoa!" His arms spun madly, like a penguin trying to fly, but it was no good. Stewart spilled into the crater, tumbled head over heels and began to slide, face first.

Leaping out of the way, Peterson realized that anything falling inside the crater would inexorably be drawn to its center, where the meteorite now lay. Half out of fear for Stewart, half out of concern for their find, Peterson yelled. "Dig in with your crampons! Don't hit the—"

But it was too late. Stewart's forward motion came to an abrupt halt as he smashed face first into the meteorite. Everyone stared at Stewart's motionless body, waiting for something, anything, to signify he was still alive.

"I'm okay!" Stewart shouted with a chuckle. "The facemask absorbed most of the impact." Wearing a wide grin on his face, Stewart rolled over onto his back. "See, I'm fine.... Huh."

After years of working with science minded folks, Peterson had learned that there was a single phrase that always held more meaning among scientists than among the layman. The simple word, "huh," usually predated a significant discovery, observation or in some cases, immediate and approaching danger. Peterson rushed toward Stewart, "What is it?"

Pointing towards his clear mask, Stewart said. "There's a crack in the mask."

Peterson kneeled over Stewart's body, inspecting the mask.

If Stewart came into contact with alien biological material, the effects could range from nothing to instantaneous death. That's why with objects of particular interest, Peterson always had his crew wear bio-suits. When he inspected the crack in Stewart's mask, his anxiety level grew from moderate to severe. He sucked in a quick breath.

Stewart grew instantly nervous. "What?"

Benson knelt down next to Peterson and saw it too. "Some of the meteorite is imbedded in your mask. Can you see it?"

Stewart went cross-eyed, focusing on the inside of his mask. "Yeah, I see it. A little red line. Looks like dust in the crack."

"Is there any on the inside of the mask?" Peterson asked.

Stewart scanned the inside of the mask. "I don't see any. Am I going to— aachoo!" Stewart's head rocketed up with the force of the sneeze and then smashed back down. "Sorry about that, I...I..."

Peterson inspected the crack. The red material was gone. "Oh god." A thin cloud of red dust swirled inside the mask. Stewart inhaled and sucked in the material.

"I...where am I?" Stewart said, his voice sounding sleepy.

Benson shot Peterson a worried look.

Peterson whipped around toward the other men. "Get to the heli! Tell them we need a med-evac over here, right now!"

The men bolted for the chopper and Peterson turned his attention back to Stewart, who was beginning to quiver.

"What's that?" Stewart said fearfully, looking to his left. "Something's over there. And there! No, no, no. Where *am* I?"

"Hang on, Stew. I'm still with you." Peterson said, trying to remain calm.

"Dr. Peterson? I can't see you! Who's that talking? I can't understand?" Stewart shook violently. Benson did his best to hold him still. "My head...in my head...I can hear them talking to me...What are you?"

Stewart became deathly still, sucking in quick breaths. His eyes were wide. Peterson realized he was listening to something. "Stewart, can you hear me?"

"No..." Stewart said.

Peterson was confused by the response. If Stewart couldn't hear him, how did he know a question had been asked? It was when Stewart spoke again that Peterson realized the delirious intern wasn't talking to him.

"You're lying! No...no! Stewart was screaming as his body convulsed violently. His back arched as though an electric shock had ripped through his body. A burst of red foam spewed from his mouth, coating the inside of the mask. He froze in a sickening arched position.

Peterson and Benson knew Stewart was dead. And because he was contaminated there was nothing either man could do to resuscitate him. Peterson slumped back onto the ice, his chest rising and falling quickly as he attempted to catch his breath.

Both men looked from Stewart's dead body, then to each other, then back to the meteorite. Despite feeling sick to his stomach, Peterson realized what Stewart's death meant. It was a tragic loss, but in his death he proved the presence of alien biology.

Deadly biology.

Living biology.

Peterson lay on his back as the sound of the approaching helicopter grew louder. He sighed as he looked up at the bright cobalt sky and said, "All my life..."

2 – LAKE VOSTOK

At -55 degrees Celsius, the air felt cold enough to freeze human lungs solid. Kathy Connolly had first felt the chill more than five years ago when she first arrived at Lake Vostok, deep within the heart of Antarctica. And now, with the outside temperature hovering around -70 degrees, she was ready for the balmy -55 degree weather to return. Of course, technology had improved since her first days at Lake Vostok. What was once several layers of thermal underwear, thick Parkas and rigid gloves had been replaced by super thin fabrics such as Insulite and Protectarol, which kept the body warm and pulled moisture away from the skin. In addition to the thinner materials was the revolutionary Simmer Suit. It circulated hot water through "veins" webbed throughout the quarter inch thick, head-to-toe garment. On top of that was worn a comfortable, wind resistant hooded jacket, light snow pants and sturdy boots—all designed to be functional and eye-catching.

But even with all the high tech gear, the cold still hammered her body. Connelly and Willard were already ten minutes over that mark, and the cold was beginning to seep through.

"Boss, we have to get back inside!" Willard shouted over a gust of wind. Ethan Willard looked like a visitor from another planet. His body was covered in the same outdoor gear as Connelly, but his light blue eyes were concealed behind bug-eyed, mirrored sunglasses.

"I just need one more minute!" Kathy said.

"Another minute and we'll be popsicles! We have to go now!"

Connelly trusted Willard's opinion, but TES was too important. When the winds had picked up, she had known the supports would need to be secured, but she hadn't counted on the drop in temperature. Connelly looked up and took in the massive structure, which she had designed and built, mostly with her own hands. The Thermal Exploratory System (TES), towered fifty feet above Connelly. Its three black diamond shaped panels pointed skywards, enclosing and protecting the delicate innards—a sphere and three cranes—which gave the entire structure the shape of an ominous dark crystal.

"Not yet!" Kathy said. "TES is too important!"

"Important enough to die for?"

Connelly whipped her head to Willard and gave a quick nod.

Willard shook his head. "How am I supposed to keep you safe if you don't listen to me?"

Connelly's fingers flew over a keyboard at the base of one of the TES panels. Work was slowed by having to constantly brush snow from the plastic covered keys and her gloved hands made frequent mistakes. She had delicately tightened the slack on two of the support cables which held TES rigid against the wind, and had just started tightening the third when a loud *twang* filled the air. Connelly shuddered. She knew what that sound meant. One of the cables had snapped loose.

"Shit!" Kathy shouted. "Ethan, secure that line!"

Willard grunted in frustration, but quickly ran for the line, which was being whipped side to side, like a wriggling snake. Willard crept up on the cable, which was as thick as Kielbasa and flexible as a double jointed contortionist. Willard bent down, preparing to pounce.

Before Willard's muscles could snap him into action, the cable swung in his direction and wrapped around his ankle. A strong gust of wind took hold of the cable and pulled. Willard was yanked off his feet and dragged back and forth across the ice like a rag doll. Willard tried to dig into the rough snow and ice, but his gloved fingers simply scraped the surface. Willard's stomach twisted as he was launched skyward and slammed back down again. He coughed as the air was knocked out of him, but he managed to get out a yell, "Some help here!" It was all he could manage before the cable was plucked up by the wind and Willard was airborne was again.

Connelly looked over just as Willard struck the ice. She wanted to help, but couldn't. Not before finishing. She worked the console with a burst of speed, eager to assist her friend. She gave the cable, which was whipping Willard around, some extra slack and prepped the retraction process. Once started, they would have thirty seconds while the system warmed up. After that, the cable would retract and either yank them both skyward, or snap securely into position on a hook braced twenty-five feet within the ice crust.

With her finger hovering over the final key, Connelly prepared herself to run. She pushed the button and sprinted towards Willard, who was now in a sitting position, hanging onto the cable above his feet. Connelly ran to the cable and took hold a few feet above Willard.

"Bout time," Willard said.

"Shut up and get that off your leg!"

14

Willard squinted behind his sunglasses. "Or what?"

"Just do it!"

Connelly imagined that Willard could hear the urgency in her voice, even above the howling wind, because he sprang into action, tugging at the thick cable.

Willard's foot was freed and he grabbed the cable, which ended in a loop. "All set!"

"Get it looped up!" Connelly shouted.

Willard tugged back on the cable, fighting against the wind, and with Connelly's help, was able to pull the slack cable closer to the hook, extending a few inches from the snow.

"Ten seconds!" Kathy shouted.

"Ten seconds until what?"

Connelly didn't answer and Willard didn't press the subject. He dug his heels into the snow and fell back with the cable, pulling it toward the hook with his hands. There were only inches to go, but the wind was putting up a fight.

"Five seconds!"

Willard grunted as he pulled with all his strength. The cable slid over the hook, but looked as though it might slide back off. With all the slack Connelly had given it, the cable thrashed wildly in the wind. But there was no time left.

"Let go!" Connelly shouted as though their lives depended on it. Connelly dropped the cable and dove to the side. Willard rolled away. As Willard flipped onto his back he saw the slack on the cable disappear as the line was sucked into TES like a giant strand of spaghetti. The line snapped taut and would have easily cut a man in half if he'd been standing too close. Willard caught his breath as he stared up at the secure line. They'd done it.

A shadow fell over Willard as Kathy stood above him. "What the hell are we still doing out here?" she asked. "It's freezing!" Willard laughed as Connelly thrust out her gloved hand and helped him to his feet.

15

From above, Lake Vostok was a sheet of monotonous white so plain it looked like God forgot to color a portion of the world. The stark expanse was barren, save for three outposts, the original Russian Vostok Station, which had fallen into disarray over the past forty years and was never used because of contamination and structural hazards. Then there was the Joint Vostok Venture, which rented their facilities out to groups of scientists studying the ice layers and attempting to burrow down to the liquid lake below: of course, in thirty years of trying, no one had yet succeeded. That's why Connelly and her crew were here, to achieve the unachievable. But Connelly insisted on secrecy, insisted on her own facility, and after what she showed those funding her expedition, she got everything she wanted, and then some.

The Vostok TES Observatory stood in stark contrast to the surroundings, with its nine dark gray metallic domes, each pocked with round portals and luminous flood lights. Some of her Vostok neighbors had commented that it looked like a UFO at night. The nine domes where spread out in a circle and were connected by curved tunnels, all of which joined together at the center, where a large dome, the size of a four bedroom house, served as the main living quarters.

Willard and Connelly entered one of the outer tunnels through a thick hatch. Snow exploded into the hallway. Willard closed the heavy door behind them and secured it. After pulling off his hood and Simmer Suit head covering, Willard shook his golden hair with his finger, sprinkling water into the air, and smiled at Connelly. "Geez boss, you're almost as crazy as me."

Connelly smiled in return. Coming from Willard, that was a compliment. She continued to remove her gear, down to her Simmer Suit, as she spoke. "Better get used to it," she said. "Once TES is up and running we're going to be spending every other hour outside, just melting through the ice."

Willard shook his head. "That *is* crazy."

Connelly offered a sarcastic smile and said, "Thanks for your support."

ׁ   ׁ   ׁ   ׁ   ׁ

The main living quarters were composed of separate bedrooms and a multi-function room, which served as kitchen, dining room, living room and most recently, electronics lab. The space was circular and forty feet in diameter, but it was cluttered with computers, spools of wires, soldering equipment, computer chips and other assorted high-tech gizmos. There was a lab for such work, but with only three of them currently stationed at the Vostok TES Observatory, they preferred to spend most of their time together.

Robert Samuels sat alone in the massive room, relaxing with his feet up on a desk as he soldered a small chip to the innards of a tiny cube-shaped device with two metallic connectors on either side. He bent in so close, gazing through his thick glasses, that he didn't notice his scruffy beard was beginning to singe. The rancid smell of smoldering hair hit his nose and he immediately sat back and began to pat the smoking beard out. He attempted to regain his casual composure as the hatch to the living quarters swung open.

Willard entered first with Connelly at his heels. "All I'm saying is that I'm sure, if I were a scientist, which I'm not, thank goodness, I might understand why melting through miles of ice to find some microorganisms is worth risking my life."

Robert turned to Willard and Connelly with a smile on his face. He'd heard this conversation before. "Funny... You say it's not worth risking your life, but alas...here you are."

Willard sat down across from Robert while Kathy put on a fresh pot of coffee. "Yeah, well, someone's got to keep you two alive." His nose crinkled. "What's that smell?"

Robert shrugged and did his best to look innocent. "I don't smell anything."

Willard glanced at the soldering iron still in Robert's hand. "You burned your beard again, didn't you?"

Robert furrowed his eyebrows. "I was concentrating."

Connelly returned from the coffee pot, which was beginning to gurgle to life and playfully rubbed Robert's already messy head of hair. "Don't start, boys." She sat down next to Robert and rolled her neck. "How's it coming?"

Robert held the small cube aloft like it was a prize recovered from a treasure chest. "We now have full BUD capabilities."

"What's BUD?" Willard asked. "Your dog?"

Robert grinned and pushed his glasses higher on his nose, pleased at the opportunity to explain. "BUD was originally a military project for tracking submarines around the globe. It was so sensitive that, when placed underwater, it could hear a dolphin fart a thousand miles away."

Willard smiled. "Dolphins fart?"

Robert ignored the question and continued. "The equipment picked up so much noise that software had to be written that would filter out organic sounds. Even after they removed all the whale calls, struggling fish and barking seals, they had to filter out man-made noises like recreational vehicles and underwater construction. When they were done, they could hear every sub under the water and track them to within a few yards."

"I don't think there are any submarines in Lake Vostok," Willard said.

"Quite true," Robert said. "I've removed all the software."

"Leaving us with one of the most sensitive microphones in the world," Connelly said as she stood and walked back to the coffee maker.

"Right," Willard said, "but how does that help you? You're looking for microorganisms."

"The point is, if there is anything, anything at all, making noise down there, we're going to hear it. Geothermal vents, shifting ice, even the microorganisms themselves. If there is any noise at all, we're going to hear it loud and clear."

"A microscopic symphony," Willard said.

"You got it," Connelly said as she returned with three piping hot mugs of coffee, which she placed on the table.

"OK," Willard said, "that's cool. But I still don't understand the significance of finding anything below the ice or even how you expect something to be alive down there. Like I said before, I'm no scientist—"

"That goes without saying," Robert said with a smile as he raised his steaming mug to his lips.

Willard continued, "—but the pressure must be intense. Not to mention the lack of sunlight and food."

"Ahh," Robert said as he finished taking a sip of the rich Columbian coffee. "Perhaps there's hope for the boy yet. That was actually an intelligent statement." Robert looked at Connelly. "You want to field this one, Kath?"

Connelly nodded, crossed her legs, and after taking a long sip from her mug, she looked at Willard. "Lake Vostok is buried beneath 4,000 meters of ice."

Willard opened his mouth to say something, but Connelly seemed to read his mind. "Roughly 13,000 feet," she said.

Willard closed his mouth and Connelly continued. "This means that any life we find down there has been cut off from the modern world for a million years. This life would most likely be in the form of microbes we call extremophiles.

"Like me," Willard said.

Robert chuckled. "Your penchant for extreme sports is a choice, Mr. Willard. These creatures have no option but to survive, sometimes thrive, in the most inhospitable environments on Earth."

"And the discovery of which," Connelly said, "would give us hints as to the planet's climate going back millions of years. Not only that, but the discovery of new organisms helps us to understand the world and quite often lends to major breakthroughs in other scientific fields."

"Like medicine?" Willard offered.

"Exactly," Connelly said.

"Though even I'll admit that the chance of a new drug being derived from a million year old microbe is unlikely," Robert said.

Willard smelled the aromatic coffee. "This lake...isn't it a closed ecosystem? I've seen enough conservation specials to know that bringing in foreign germs or animals usually wreaks havoc on the ecosystems without defenses. Your million year old microbes might catch the modern flu and be wiped out."

19

"That's two intelligent statements. Watch out, Ethan, you might just change my opinion of you. Though you're correct. That's why TES will be sterilized before melting through the ice."

Connelly chimed in. "And the exterior surface of the TES sphere, and even the TES cable are so hot that any microbes or viruses that the sphere comes in contact with on the way down will be vaporized."

"Huh," Willard said as he sipped from his coffee. "Sounds like you have all your bases covered."

"That's why we're the scientists," Robert said, "and you're the bodyguard."

"Safety specialist."

"Same thing."

"Hey," said Willard, "you two would have died like twenty times already without me here. If there's one thing I've learned about you science types, you've got all the brains in the world and no common sense. Not only do you walk into door frames and microwave metal containers—"

Robert looked over his steaming mug. "That only happened once."

"But you also believe that microbes could survive beneath this ice. You still haven't explained that to me. Your microorganisms are going to have to be beyond extreme to pull that off."

"There is one likely source of energy," Connelly said. "Given the shape of the lake, which is roughly the size of Lake Ontario, but far deeper, it's possible that there are geothermal vents heating the water and providing reduced metals and chemical nutrients. On top of that, the ice above is constantly moving, about four meters—thirteen feet—every year, providing nutrients and perhaps even ancient biological matter to the water. It is the most extreme environment on Earth, to be sure, but anything's possible."

"OK, fine," Willard said. "But why Vostok? Aren't there any other frozen lakes in the world? We're in the middle of nowhere with nothing else to do but freeze our butts off and play solitaire."

"There are seventy lakes under the ice in Antarctica, but most are much smaller than Vostok and probably have frozen solid within the past few thousand years. Vostok's size and depth make it the ideal hunting ground for microorganisms."

Willard placed his mug on the table. "So you're saying there is no other place like this on Earth?"

Connelly thought about the question and then nodded. "Yup, there really is no other place like this on Earth."

"Well, that's cool," Willard said. "But I still think this may be a big waste of time."

Connelly stood and headed toward the coffee maker with an empty mug in her hand. "If we get down there and find nothing, you might just be right."

Willard laughed lightly. "Then what?"

"Then," Connelly said, looking back at Willard as she poured some more coffee, "we're all out of work. Hey, what's this?" Connelly picked up a piece of paper sitting in the tray of the fax machine sitting next to the toaster.

"Sorry," Robert said. "Came in earlier. Haven't got a chance to read it yet."

As Connelly looked over the page, her face fell flat. Robert noticed right away. "What is it?" he asked.

After crumpling the piece of paper and rejoining the men at the table, Connelly said, "The Global Exploration Corporation strikes again."

"Those guys are a pain in the ass," Willard said, shaking his head in frustration at just hearing the name.

"What do they want this time?" Robert asked.

"Seriously," Willard said, "would you have even taken their money if you knew how many strings were attached? They want you to fly out there again?"

Connelly looked Willard in the eyes, her expression dull, as though she were living in a surreal world where what she had just read made no sense at all. "Not just me," she said. "They want all three of us... Tomorrow."

3 – GLOBAL EXPLORATION CORPORATION

Michael Peterson found the lower hallways of the Global Exploration Corporation to be sterile. They had made an effort to soften their image on the floors above. The tourists, visiting on a daily basis, always 'oohed' and 'aahed' at the elaborate murals of Mars' surface, the ocean floor and the view from Mount Everest. But those floors contained gallery displays of the functional labs hidden below. The corporate offices were on the top floors. They were bright and full of green plants and seascapes.

Peterson chuckled to himself. Here he was, about to embark on an amazing adventure and he couldn't get his mind off the lower level decorations, or lack thereof. The floors were squeaky clean linoleum and the walls were white concrete. The only color came in the form of arrows pointing towards various departments; geology, astronomy, oceanography, biology—experts on almost every kind of "ology" could be found within the confines of these barren walls. The GEC made up for its lack of decor by housing some of the most colorful minds on Earth. Peterson was often proud that he belonged to such an astounding group, but felt even more pride at the fact that his past discovery and potential future discoveries were on the top of the GEC's to-do list.

Stepping into the cavernous elevator, Peterson sighed with relief for the privacy and the fact that he would soon be out of the windowless lab area and striding through the upper halls of the corporate offices. He hit the button for the tenth floor and then leaned against the back wall of the elevator. He closed his eyes and smiled as he imagined what the future might hold. Then the elevator stopped.

Peterson opened his eyes and looked at the control panel. He was stopped at the eighth floor. He'd reached the corporate levels, but not quite high enough. He leaned forward to push the buttons for the tenth floor again when the doors slid open. Standing on the other side of the opening doors stood a woman who looked like a strict school teacher, but her kind smile offset her bunned red hair, steel gray-blue eyes and tight-fitting power suit. She was easily fifty, pushing fifty-five but she held herself like a thirty year old. She looked at her watch and said, "Ahh, Dr. Peterson. Right on time, as usual."

Peterson smiled. "Miss Heintz. I thought we were meeting in your office...We are meeting in your office, right?"

"Call me Nancy, Dr. Peterson."

Peterson relaxed at the offer of using casual names. It was generally considered a compliment if the higher-ups referred to you by your first name, but even more so if they allowed you to use theirs. "Only if you call me Michael," he said.

"Very well, Michael. I was thinking about a different location for our meeting today." Nancy stepped into the elevator and took out a key card. She waved it in front of a small scanner mounted above the floor buttons. A small green light above the scanner blinked on while the metal beneath the floor buttons slid away, revealing a new button marked with the number eleven. She hit the button. The doors closed and Peterson felt his stomach sink slightly as the elevator began to rise.

"I didn't know there was an eleventh floor," Peterson said.

Nancy smiled. "There's not."

The doors opened to the tenth floor and both waited patiently for the doors to close. Peterson shifted nervously. The doors soon closed and they were pulled upward once again. He watched as the number changed from 10 to 11. He was beginning to feel curious about what he was being invited to see. When the doors opened, it was more than he could have imagined.

Peterson's mouth dropped open as he stepped into the forty-foot tall, football-field sized green house. A large number of well-labeled plant species thrived in the massive space. At the other end of the greenhouse he could see full-sized trees, growing tall. Some bore fruit. Peterson took a deep breath and smelled the sweet and spicy air. *Like an old fashioned apple pie*, he thought. The bright green of the room in contrast with the dark blue, northern California sky was enough to take his breath away. He turned to Nancy. His stunned expression made her laugh. "What *is* this place?" he asked. "You can't see this from the road or parking lot."

"Only from the air," Nancy said. "It's not that we're trying to keep it a complete secret, but many of these plant species are endangered or already extinct. We try to keep exposure to outsiders to a bare minimum." Nancy raised her hand toward one of the tallest trees in the room, which had been trimmed to keep it from bursting through the glass ceiling. "That's a Brazilian Mahogany tree. Ten years ago it was used to make furniture and flooring, so much so that it simply couldn't recover and the best efforts of green organizations couldn't save it. There may be a few trees surviving in what little is left of the rainforests, but for all intents and purposes, the species is extinct, and that...that is the last one. We're hoping to reintroduce them in the next year."

Peterson looked at the tall tree. Its bark was smooth and grey; its leaves a brilliant green. A powerful tree. The fact that this might actually be the last of its kind on Earth made it awe inspiring. Peterson looked at Nancy with wide eyes. "Why did you bring me here?"

"Three reasons," Nancy said. "First, to give you a glimpse of the future. A greenhouse twice this size has been constructed for your mission, only the plants are different. If they're not producing food, they're cleaning the air or some other kind of benefit. Second, look up there." Nancy pointed through the glass ceiling towards the dark blue sky.

Looking up, Peterson could see the moon hovering in the sky above. "It's been fifty-two years since man first walked on the moon and we still look at it as a crowning achievement of mankind. With manned missions to Mars thrown in the trash for various reasons and the more recent moon trips being...redundant, space exploration has been in a slump. We need this to work, Michael."

"Not to worry," Peterson said with confidence. "Everything is on schedule."

"You're sure about that? About everything? I'm meeting with the board tomorrow. They'll give me the final go ahead even with a slim chance of success, but the final say is mine and I don't like slim chances. They haven't worked for any space program thus far and we don't need another failure on our hands. So I'll ask you one last time. Are you absolutely, one hundred percent, without question, sure that you'll find what you're looking for?

"Not a doubt in the world. I've worked my entire life for an opportunity like this. I promise you, we will succeed." Peterson smiled. "I wouldn't be doing this otherwise. I don't like to fail."

"Good," Nancy said. "Neither do I."

A loud ring filled the air. Nancy reached into her coat pocket and pulled out a tiny cell phone. "Director Heintz here."

"Dr. Connelly and her crew are here to see you, Ma'am," came the voice of a receptionist on the other end.

"Direct them to my office," Nancy said, before hanging up the phone. She turned to Peterson, who was looking at the massive greenhouse. "Feel free to stay here as long as you'd like, but don't touch the plants. I'm meeting with the TES crew now. Update me on your progress by the end of the day."

"Will do," Peterson said.

Nancy entered the elevator and disappeared behind its closing doors, leaving Peterson alone in the gargantuan greenhouse. He looked at all the vegetation, some of it otherworldly and then up to the moon. His body shivered with nervous energy. He knew his view from the next greenhouse he'd be standing in was going to be even more impressive.

಼   ಼   ಼   ಼   ಼

Connelly stretched and touched her toes, which felt awkward in the formal business suit she was wearing, but the three flights it had taken to get them from Antarctica to northern California had been cramped. Flights were much faster than they used to be, but more people than ever were flying. After landing in San Francisco it had taken them another three hours to drive to the Global Exploration Corporation's headquarters, which was situated in a forty acre portion of prime landscape. The grounds were impeccably maintained. The lush green grass was as trim as a marine's hair. A brook ran perpendicular to the main entrance at the front of the building. The compound could have been mistaken for a national park, if not for the expansive parking lot, barbed wire fences and large marble sign which read: Global Exploration Corporation.

Overall, visiting the site was a relaxing experience and Connelly could understand why so many scientists clambered to get research space within the facility, but coming here was never a good thing for her.

The GEC had been funding her project for the past five years and in the last year alone, her funding had quadrupled. She wasn't sure why the money was increased, and she never asked. It allowed her to finish work on TES three years ahead of schedule. Upon arriving at the front door of the GEC headquarters, they were ushered in like celebrities, offered drinks and muffins, and had been waiting quite comfortably for twenty minutes when a pretty, young receptionist strode into the lobby and flashed a smile.

"Director Heintz is ready to see you now," the receptionist said. "Please, follow me."

Connelly stood with Robert and Willard at her side and followed the receptionist to the elevator. The doors opened and the receptionist motioned for them to enter. Once all three were in, the receptionist joined them, hit the button for the tenth floor and then stepped back out. "Take a right out of the elevator. Director Heintz's office is the last door on the left." With that, the doors closed and the three were left alone.

"Do they pay them to act cheery?" Willard said with a grin. "I think that girl ate Happy Flakes for breakfast."

"Corporate complexes like this tend to be imposing," Robert said, "even to the employees. It helps to a see a happy face, even if it's fake."

"'Imposing' is an understatement," Connelly said. "And I have a long list of questions that need answers."

Robert played with his beard. "Like why they pulled us out two days before our first full test."

Kathy nodded. "Or the urgency behind the trip. Next day air from Antarctica isn't standard procedure."

"Or," Willard started, "why we're being treated like royalty. They were practically shoving those muffins down our throats."

"Fattening the goose," Robert said.

"And I take it you've never been picked up at the airport by a limo before?" Willard said.

Connelly shook her head, no. "Just another in a long line of questions we need answered. This better not be a waste of time."

Ding. The doors opened and all three put on phony smiles before exiting the elevator. They turned right and headed down the hallway. The impending sense of doom grew like a tangling vine. Connelly paused at the polished oak door before knocking. "You ready?"

Both men nodded. Connelly knocked.

"Come on in," came Nancy's voice from the other side of the door.

Connelly turned the handle and entered the gleaming office. Connelly squinted as she entered the massive corner office, two walls of which were windows. Nancy was standing by her boomerang shaped desk. Connelly noticed a few family photos on the desktop, but nothing else out of the ordinary. No schematics, no documents or even a laptop that might provide some hint as to why they had been summoned.

Nancy motioned to three plush chairs that faced her desk. "Please, have a seat."

The three silently took their seats and waited for the bomb to drop. Nancy sat across from them, in her own comfortable-looking seat. She leaned back and smiled. "Mr. Willard, I see that your sense of style has not been exaggerated to me by our mutual acquaintances," she said with a grin as she took in Willard's casual blue jeans and green fleece outfit.

Willard turned red and looked at his clothes. He glanced at Connelly, with her business suit, which accentuated her long, firm legs. Then he looked at Robert, who'd at least made an attempt to look professional with his sweater and tweed jacket. Compared to them he looked like a college student. He opened his mouth to speak, but was cut short by Nancy. "Of course, I only jest. Your other, more impressive qualities, have been made clear over the years as well. Your expedition has one of the highest safety ratings of all our expeditions and you're in one of the most inhospitable environments. Well done, Mr. Willard."

Willard smiled, clearly pleased. "Thank you."

Connelly shifted in her seat. Nancy turned to her and said, "I trust your flights were bearable?"

Connelly nodded, "I slept through most of them."

"Well, you must be wondering why we've made such a to-do about you being here?" Nancy said.

"The question has crossed our minds," Connelly said.

Nancy took a deep breath and let it out slowly, as though she were chewing over how to best phrase her next words. Connelly's stomach twisted with nervous tension. She was sure her funding was about to be pulled. "I trust everything is operational? With TES I mean."

"Yes," Connelly said. "We were planning to do our first full run through in two days, but we're positive she's fully functional and ready to go. We'll prep for the test as soon as we get back."

"That won't be necessary," Nancy said. "Kathy...may I call you Kathy? I always prefer talking to my best scientists on a first name basis."

"Of—of course," Kathy said.

"Kathy, how would you feel about continuing your work with TES at another location?"

Connelly raised a skeptical eyebrow. "What do you mean?"

"For the sake of time, I'll put this bluntly," Nancy said. "TES is needed for a more pressing expedition and we'll be transporting her by the end of the week. This is well within our contract agreement and is final. But I need to know if you'll be coming along."

"You can't do that," Connelly said defiantly.

"Look," Nancy said, softening her voice. "I know this is hard to comprehend right now, but the fact is, I had to pull a few strings with the board to keep you on this project."

"This is *my* project!" Connelly gripped her armrests.

Nancy rocked in her chair for a moment and then said, "Not anymore."

Willard interjected before Connelly could stand and start screaming. "Hey," he said, "I just got a natural history lesson from these two so even I know that there is no other place on Earth where there's a frozen lake buried under that much ice. So please enlighten us. Where on Earth, aside from Antarctica, is there a lake buried beneath miles of ice?"

Nancy smiled. "There isn't."

"I don't understand," Connelly said. "Where do you plan on using TES?"

Nancy looked into Connelly's eyes and said, "Not on this planet."

Robert leaned forward with his eyebrows perched high on his wrinkled forehead. "Come again?"

Nancy's smile grew wider. "Not on this planet... As you probably know, NASA had been planning a trip to the sixth moon of Jupiter, Europa, for years. But they ran out of support from the U.S. government. The GEC picked up the tab and have been coordinating our private enterprise with NASA and the U.S. government."

"This is unbelievable," Robert said. "Europa...but I thought they sent a probe there in 2010?"

Nancy nodded. "The Europa Orbiter. After a preliminary scan of the moon's surface, measuring density, temperature and other common elements, the probe was destroyed."

"You mean it crashed," Willard said.

Nancy shook her head. "No, it was destroyed in orbit."

Robert's forehead became even more wrinkled. "As in blown up?"

"Yes," Nancy said. "Just before contact with the probe was lost, it recorded an extreme increase in external energy. NASA believes a massive solar storm caused an overload. The rest is history. However, the mission was not a complete failure. The probe was able to determine that there is, in fact, a vast ocean one mile beneath the ice crust on Europa."

"I sincerely doubt that the existence of water alone is enough evidence to spur a manned mission to the center of our solar system," Robert said.

Nancy leaned forward on her elbows, growing excited. "Last year, a geologist named Michael Peterson, discovered a meteorite in the Arctic. It's been determined that the asteroid originated from Europa. It was the size of a football yet contained biological material swirled among some unknown elements."

Connelly, who had been lost in a sea of anger, snapped to attention, listening to every word Nancy was saying. "Biological?"

"Dead, of course," Nancy said, "destroyed during re-entry, but let there be no doubt, there is life on Europa, and we're going to get a look at it, up close and personal. We want you three to go."

Connelly looked stunned, but her defiance managed to take one last stab. "If we don't?" she said.

Nancy crossed her legs and sat back in the chair. "The project will go on without you and the operation of TES will be given to someone else. Though I'd prefer you on the team; if something were to go wrong I can't think of anyone better qualified to make the repairs. Can you?"

"You're telling me," Connelly started, "that you're sending us into space to search for life...on a moon. And if we don't go, my work, my life's work is going to go without me?"

Nancy nodded.

Connelly's eyes dropped to the floor and she stared at it blankly. Questions flooded her mind. "Am I correct in assuming there isn't even an atmosphere around this moon."

"Actually," Nancy said, "There is. Albeit, very thin, but it does contain small amounts of oxygen. Kathy, I understand how you must be feeling right now, but the possibilities for discovery are beyond anything humanity has ever achieved."

Connelly became suspicious and squinted her eyes. "If we already discovered alien life from this meteorite of yours, why haven't we heard about it? Why isn't it plastered on every newspaper from here to Siberia?"

"That's because," Nancy said, "we haven't told anyone. Various space agencies have made major blunders in the past by going off half cocked and announcing to the world that they've made some major discovery, only to have it proved wrong in full view of the public. The result is a loss of credibility and of funding, governmental or otherwise. So you can see why we're treating this delicately. Failure, right now, means discovering we were wrong and that's it. But if we told the world we had discovered extraterrestrial life, and then, oops, we were wrong... Well, that would set the world's space programs back. And I'm not going to let that happen."

Robert was nodding, "Makes sense."

Connelly sighed and shook her head.

"I'm sorry," Nancy said, "but I really do need an answer."

Connelly looked Nancy in the eyes. "The simple fact that I go where TES goes, means I'm in. But, what you've told us— I never considered that TES might be used for something so foolish. So incredible. The possibility of finding life somewhere else in our solar system is...unbelievable. But I do have one condition."

Nancy nodded, waiting patiently.

"When we get back...when we return, I get TES back. Finding E.T. will be the discovery of a lifetime, but I'm still interested in understanding our own planet."

"Of course," Nancy said. "We will have a second TES unit built for you while you're gone. I'm afraid once TES is deployed, she will remain on the surface of Europa forever.

Connelly looked at Robert and Willard. "Well, boys? Feel like going to Jupiter?"

The best Robert could manage was a slow, stunned nod. Connelly looked beyond Robert to Willard. She was surprised to see his face looking very upset.

"I don't know, boss. It doesn't sound very safe. You on a moon. But you're crazy and likely to get hurt, and you'll need someone to save your butt. I couldn't live with myself if I didn't go, but... Are you kidding? I'm in like sin."

Nancy had to stifle a smile that grew at seeing Willard's excitement. "Excellent," she said. "I'll inform the council that we have the rest of our crew."

Connelly froze. "The rest of our crew?"

"You didn't think you were going into space alone, did you?" Nancy stood. "You'll meet them soon. For now, let's get you settled."

Connelly, Robert and Willard stood from their chairs and onto wobbly legs. They followed after Nancy, who was heading for the door. Willard slapped

Robert on the back. "You know," he said, "I was wrong about you nerds. You guys do get to have fun. I might not die from boredom after all."

4 – THE CREW

Connelly was out of breath when she reached the fifteenth floor of the GEC training facility. She had waited ten minutes for the elevator with no luck, so she had opted for the stairs. As she approached the sixteenth floor, she began doubting her decision to climb twenty-three flights of stairs.

A week had passed since Connelly learned she'd be joining the first manned mission to a moon beyond our own. But right now, the mission was far from her mind. With her armpits growing damp from exertion, she was beginning to worry that the other crew members, whom she would soon be meeting for the first time, would get a bad impression of her. Connelly was in great shape, but even a marathon runner would have had a hard time vaulting up twenty-three flights of steep stairs.

That's what she told herself anyway.

When Connelly rounded the stairwell and headed for the seventeenth floor, she heard panting. She slowed her pace and looked through the bars. A man was standing on the top stair of the next floor, his hands on his knees and his head lowered. From this viewpoint she could see he had well manicured, wavy black hair, and was casually dressed in tan slacks and short sleeves.

Not a scientist, she thought.

She continued forward, trying not to look hurried. "Hi," she said as she began to walk past the man.

The winded man looked up and smiled. Kathy felt a twang inside her stomach as the man's face came into view. His cheeks were covered in rough stubble, which suited him, his eyes were dark brown and his smile was as white as an Antarctic white-wash.

Definitely not a scientist.

"You on the new GEC stairwell exercise plan too, huh?" he said.

Connelly smiled. "Mmm, I find the stairwell paint smell invigorating."

"I hadn't noticed anything invigorating about this stairwell," he said, then flashed a brilliant smile. "Until now."

Ugh, must be from PR, Connelly thought.

She began to move past him, doing her best not to return his smile.

"Sorry," he said. "That was inappropriate."

Connelly paused. He stood straight and extended his hand. "Michael," he said. "I'm in geology."

Connelly inadvertently raised her eyebrows. Trying to hide her surprise, she quickly shook his hand. "Kathy. Oceanography," she said.

"Huh," the man looked surprised.

"What?"

"Just didn't take you for an ologist."

Connelly cringed. *Ologist? Seriously?* "Well...you don't look like a geologist either," she said, looking down at her clothes. She was dressed in jeans and a tight fitting white blouse. *Not* like an 'ologist'.

He smiled. "I guess we're even then. Where you headed?"

"Twenty-third floor."

"Me too. Mind if I keep you company on the way?"

Kathy wasn't sure if she should be excited or annoyed, but saying "no" in either case would seem rude. "Lead the way."

Michael paused at the next flight of stairs. He turned to Connelly and said, "You're not married, are you?"

Kathy stopped on the fifth stair to the top.

Who is this guy? The Don Juan of geologists?

"No," she said. "My line of work doesn't leave much room for romance."

"Ouch," he said, and gave another of his infectious smiles. "Guess we'll have to schedule dinner far in advance, huh?" He continued up the stairs, more slowly now, giving Connelly a chance to keep up.

Is he really asking me out for dinner or is this all a tricky geologist ruse? She pushed the conundrum from her mind. It didn't matter anyway. In three months she'd be standing on the surface of Europa and Michael the geologist would be millions of miles away.

〴   〴   〴   〴   〴

Connelly scoured the door numbers as she walked through the maze of hallways, looking for room 117, where she was scheduled to meet the rest of the Europa crew. Michael the geologist was still with her, apparently unable to find his room as well.

"You been here before?" Connelly asked.

Michael scratched his head. "Once, but never on this floor. It's a maze."

"Maybe it's a test," Kathy said. "Whoever is smart enough to figure out where their room is, is smart enough to be employed by the GEC."

"Looks like we're getting pink slips tonight."

They rounded a corner and were faced with a long hallway. The door to the right was labeled 103. The door to the left was labeled 23. Michael shook his head. "Like driving in Boston."

"You been there?"

"Born and raised. Well, not in Boston, south of Boston. An island off the cape. Martha's Vineyard."

Connelly slid past Michael and checked the door numbers as they moved down the hall. "Ooh, someone grew up with a silver spoon."

"Not everyone on the island is rich."

"Riiight."

"Ooh, I get it now."

"You're from the mainland. Let me guess. The North Shore? Salem?"

Kathy paused and smiled. "Beverly."

"Close enough," Michael said.

Connelly started down the hallway again. "Well it's not where I spend my time now."

"And where might that be?"

"Ass end of the world. Antarctica."

Michael laughed. "Wouldn't you know it? We're polar opposites! I spend most of my time under the skirt of the Arctic Circle. So much for dinner."

Connelly raised an eyebrow as Michael took the lead again, searching the door numbers. "I never said yes."

Michael gave her a skeptical glance.

Connelly ignored it. "What's a geologist doing in the arctic?"

"Looking for meteorites," Michael said.

Connelly squinted. "Meteorites?"

Michael stopped in front of a door. "Ahh," he said. "Here's my stop."

Connelly looked at the door. It was number 117.

Michael smiled. "Shall I open the door for you, Dr. Connelly?"

There was no hiding Connelly's shocked expression.

"Oh, I'm sorry." Michael extended his hand. "Michael Peterson. *Astrogeologist*. I discovered the Europa sample. I'm the geologist on the Europa mission."

Connelly shook his hand for the second time. *Sonofabitch.* "You knew who I was this entire time."

Michael Peterson nodded. "Sorry about that. I couldn't resist. Look at it this way, at least dinner is an option again." Michael opened the door. "Ladies and mission leaders first.

Connelly walked through the open door.

₪   ₪   ₪   ₪   ₪

"Look who's late," Willard said as Connelly entered the room.

She gave Willard a sarcastic smile. After Michael Peterson's ruse, she was in no mood for witty banter. She looked around the room. For a multi-billion dollar corporation, they certainly hadn't put much effort into snazzing up the training facilities. The room reminded her of her third grade classroom at Cove School back in Beverly, minus the plants, toys and schoolbooks. There were five rows of adult sized desks, a white board at the front of the room and a large mirror at the back.

She was tempted to wave to whoever was observing them on the other side of the mirror, but thought better of it.

The room lacked the chalky smell of old classrooms, but more than made up for it with the odor of permanent markers and bleach.

"Who's your friend?" Willard said as Peterson entered the room behind Connelly and shut the door.

"Robert, Ethan, this is Michael Peterson. He's the geologist who discovered the Europa meteorite, and he's going to be our geologist on the mission."

"Hey, Mikey," Willard said as he shook Peterson's hand with a dazzling array of moves ending with a punch of the fists. Michael looked horrified by the end and pulled his hand away quickly.

"Ethan Willard," Peterson said. "Safety specialist...and smart ass."

Robert shook Peterson's hand. "A pleasure," Robert said.

"Robert Samuels, oceanographer and crack shot, self-taught electronics engineer."

"Correct on all counts," Robert said with a smile.

"And I've already had the pleasure of meeting out mission leader, Kathy Connelly, biologist, oceanography and my future dinner date."

Connelly's face flushed with a mixture of embarrassment and anger as she took a seat at one of the desks.

Ethan chuckled. "Boss, things move faster in space, but you're still on the ground."

"One more word," Connelly said. "And you'll have to walk back from Europa." She looked at Michael. "That goes for you too."

Willard leaned over to Peterson, who sat at the next desk over. "She's always testy with men she likes." Willard gave a wink.

"Pack your walking shoes, Ethan," Connelly said without turning around.

ℼ   ℼ   ℼ   ℼ   ℼ

"I don't know," Timothy Harris said as he rubbed his bald head. "I see a lot of potential for tension."

Nancy Heintz stood next to him, watching Connelly, Peterson, Willard and Robert through the back side of a one way mirror. "Would you prefer they be serious science types? Their psychological tests came back fine. A short temper here, a tendency to talk too much there, but nothing serious."

"Still," Harris said, "If you want me commanding this mission, I need to have full faith in my crew, even the scientists. If anything goes wrong out there, we're on our own and I need everyone to be physically and psychologically at the top of their game."

A loud laugh from the other side of the one way mirror brought their attention back to the crew. They were all laughing at something.

Harris turned to Jen Choi, who had been watching the group with an unwavering eye. "What happened?"

Choi turned to Harris, swinging her pony-tailed black hair behind her head. "Willard passed gas."

Harris smiled. He willed himself not to, but he couldn't help it. He turned back to Nancy.

"You see?" she said, also attempting to hide a smile. "The only lethal gas you'll have to worry about while in Europa's orbit is from Mr. Willard."

Harris chuckled. "Fine. But I'm putting them all through the wringer and if they don't come through clean, they're not coming."

Nancy nodded. "Then make sure they all come out clean, because if they don't, none of you will be going."

The smirk on Harris's face disappeared. "Understood." Harris looked back through the one way mirror. Everyone had moved away from Willard. Connelly was waving her hand in front of her nose. Robert had his nose hidden beneath the collar of his shirt. Peterson was standing in the doorway, which was now open, moving the door back and forth to promote air circulation.

Harris's smirk returned. He looked back to Choi. "You ready to get started?"

Choi still wasn't smiling. Harris knew she wouldn't, either. Choi was a South Korean, Center for Disease Control and Prevention specialist turned astronaut. She had everything they needed for this mission and a serious demeanor to boot. Only she, Harris, Nancy and Peterson knew of the potential hazards of this mission and the death in the Arctic. But with Choi along, they were prepared for the worst. She had handled some of the deadliest disease outbreaks in recent history and had a flawless track record. Harris wondered how many strings had to be pulled before the CDC let her go. With everything she had seen, he knew she had reason to be serious, but still found her inability to smile unsettling.

Choi nodded.

"Let's get started then."

As Choi led the way out of the room, Harris glanced back into room 117 and felt a shiver of apprehension crawl across his ribs. This mission would make or break his career. Of course, whether the mission succeeded or failed, he would still be remembered in the history books. But *how* he would be remembered had yet to be determined. Space travel in general was dangerous, but when you take high speed travel, unknown space and an inexperienced crew into consideration, it was downright nuts. He hadn't worked out the odds of success yet—didn't want to—but his gut said they weren't good. That they were more likely to be remembered with a plaque or a statue while their dead bodies floated through space. But avoiding that outcome was his job. And he was ready for it. Determination replaced the apprehension. He would make these scientists into astronauts or die trying.

₪　₪　₪　₪　₪

Connelly had just sat back down at the desk when the door opened and a balding, African-American man walked into the room; his spine held straight, his demeanor friendly. The man was followed by an Asian woman with beautiful tan skin and serious eyes.

"Hello everyone," the man said. "I'm Captain Timothy Harris, your mission commander. This is Jen Choi. She's my second in command, and on this mission, what we say is equal to the word of God."

Choi walked to the front of the room, carrying a handful of file folders. Harris stood behind the desk.

Choi stood in front of them, not relaxing her posture. "We have three months of training to complete. Three months after that, we will be walking on the surface of a moon in orbit around Jupiter. Please pay attention to everything you are taught. Even the smallest detail, while perhaps boring to you now, could save your life or the lives of this crew. Any questions before we get started?"

After a moment of silence, Robert found the guts to speak. "Uh, here to Europa in three months? Isn't that kind of, well, fast?"

"We will be using a new propulsion system in an experimental spacecraft named Surveyor," Choi explained, "which will allow us to reach abnormally high speeds."

"Sounds dangerous," Willard said.

The slightest hint of a turned up smile appeared on Choi's face, but then quickly disappeared. "It is."

"Oh." Willard said. "Well, as long as we're not being pushed through space by a series of nuclear explosions. I saw that in a TV special and...I..." He noticed Harris's sympathetic smile. "Dammit."

Connelly looked at Peterson. "Not that I'm complaining. I realize that you made the original discovery, but why are you on the team? Europa is primarily composed of ice and water, and we're searching for life. Why send a geologist?"

"The meteorite we found in the arctic was composed primarily of extremely dense ice," Peterson said. "But swirled within the ice were veins of unknown elements, which when analyzed in the lab, turned out to be highly energetic. My theory is that the microbial life on Europa survive by somehow absorbing this elemental energy. I'd be happy to show you my data."

"Sounds romantic," Willard said.

Before Connelly could shush Willard, Harris broke in. "All right, folks. Stay focused. You're about to get five years worth of training in three months. You don't learn this stuff, we don't go." Harris looked at Willard. "You following me?"

Willard smiled and gave a salute. "Let's do this."

5 – PREPARATIONS

Glistening stars sparkled in the dark sky above Connelly's head. She had been staring at them for several minutes. As she gazed into the expanse, her chest felt as though it were being compressed, similar to her experiences with deep water diving. Every breath was work and soon she felt her lungs growing tired. Her breath became labored and quick.

Connelly felt as though she would suffocate. She was in no danger of suffocation, but the tightness in her chest squeezed tighter with every passing second. Her thoughts drifted to the cause of this *attack*. The word slammed into her mind and added weight to her chest.

This was an anxiety attack.

It had been many years since Connelly's last anxiety attack, and that had been a minor episode. She had seen a psychologist, had worked through the problem, which had been brought on by witnessing the death of her closest friend, and had only taken meds for half a year. But she remembered the feeling of impending doom, of looming death, like it woke up next to her every morning.

The stars above her became blurred swirls of light that danced in her vision. The lack of oxygen was taking its toll on her mind. She was beginning to hallucinate. She was going to pass out.

Connelly reached back into her mind and plucked from the lessons she had learned on how to deal with anxiety attacks. She concentrated on her breathing first, slowing the rise and fall of her chest, breathing deeply, sucking in air, ignoring the pain. The tightness subsided some and her vision began to clear. The stars came into focus and the atmosphere seemed to cool around her.

Before she could register a physical change, the stars grew closer, larger. She knew it was impossible. Stars were light years away. Traveling to the outer fringes of our own solar system wouldn't increase the size of stars. But these enlarged as she neared them, like they were painted on a flat surface.

Connelly turned her head and looked back. The Earth was below her, floating away. With the realization that she was hovering in space came an incredible coldness that tore through her skin and made her bones feel brittle. She faced forward again and felt her body strike a surface. It was soft, like silk, but firm.

The impact made her gasp, but when she sucked the air into her chest, she inhaled a mouthful of the silky surface. It filled her mouth and oozed into her lungs. Then gravity returned and pulled her body down. The material was yanked from her lungs as she began to fall. Connelly reached out for the surface, searching for a handhold, but her fingers flailed against the smooth ceiling. There was nothing to hold on to.

Spinning her body to face the Earth, Connelly began to think. None of it made sense. It wasn't real.

But it *felt* real.

With the ground approaching rapidly, Connelly's body tensed, bracing for a deadly impact, but her mind was somewhere else. Connelly reached her hands down toward the ground and saw a vision of her arms being disintegrated even before the rest of her body hit. It was her left middle finger that struck first.

Then the rest of her body plunged down—and bounced.

Connelly lay in bed, flat on her back, her body still bouncing from the impact. With the surreal world fading away, Connelly's logic began to take over.

It was all a dream—a stress induced dream—but still just a dream. Connelly stared up at the ceiling and began to wonder about the feeling of impact that she had felt. When she woke, she was very aware that her body had, in fact, felt like she had really fallen. It was so real that even after she was awake, her body was still bouncing.

Memories of past discussions entered her mind. A scientist named Gunthar Holtz worked on the same research vessel as Connolly for a summer. It was a brilliant research ship, equipped with submersibles, shark cages and the best mobile labs she had ever seen. But at night, when the day's work had been finished, there was nothing to do but enjoy the sweet sea air and exchange stories.

It was Gunthar's stories that filled her mind now. He was a staunch believer in telekinetic powers, extra sensory perception, out of body experiences, astral projection, all the powers of the mind beyond the body. Gunthar explained once how he would have recurring dreams of falling; sometimes from an airplane, sometimes from a building, but always falling. Just as his body struck whatever surface he was falling toward, he would awake to find that he had really fallen. He explained that the human mind, while in REM sleep was more open to the hidden powers it possessed. His fear of falling was so great that the anxiety he would feel was strong enough to trigger a telekinetic event—on his own body. When he woke from a dream of falling, the telekinesis was disrupted and he would fall back into his bed.

Connelly had never experienced such a thing, but was now beginning to wonder. As a scientist, she was always interested in exploring new frontiers, but mental powers seemed more in the realm of the paranormal than scientific. It was a subject of hot debate that summer, but she hadn't given much thought since.

Connelly sat up in bed and rubbed her warm hands across her forehead. They felt greasy. She stood and wandered over to the small bathroom attached to the meek quarters provided her by the GEC. The bathroom was small, like the bedroom, but it was functional and modern. She turned on the faucet and let the stainless steel basin fill with cold water. Once full, she plunged her face beneath the water and counted to thirty. She felt the remaining clouds in her mind vanish and her thoughts become clear.

Water poured from Connelly's cheeks as she pulled her face up and glanced in the mirror. She looked tired. *Three months of intense training will do that,* she thought. The rest of the team, with the exception of Jen Choi and Captain Harris, looked just as tired and beaten as she did. As the water dripped away from her eyelids, a wisp of motion caught her attention. The shower curtain behind her had moved ever so slightly, as though a gust of wind had swept through the room, but there were no windows open and her door was locked.

Or was it? Connelly couldn't remember.

Connelly turned to inspect the shower, but before she could even raise her hand to the curtain, it burst open and a figure, dressed in black, stood inside the shower stall.

Staring wide eyed, Connelly was confused and bewildered. Peterson, dressed like a Navy Seal, was standing inside her shower, gazing into her eyes and flashing his perfect smile.

"What the hell are you doing?" Connelly said.

"C'mon, Kath. Don't pretend you're not happy to see me." Peterson's voice had a tone to it that Connelly had never felt before. But Connelly was no longer noticing his voice, or his smile, it was his hands that held her attention. He was wearing tight, black gloves, the kind you see burglars or murderers wearing in made-for-TV movies. Connelly's eyes returned to Peterson's as he stepped out of the shower.

"Try not to fight it, Kath. I'll make it as painless as possible." With that, Peterson leapt forward and gripped Connelly's throat with both hands and squeezed down.

A wave of panic crashed over Connelly's body. Her chest tightened and hurt as though someone had reached through her ribcage and gripped her heart. Orbs of light spun in her vision. She looked up at Peterson's face, which was twisted with rage. His eyes were glazed over. He was drooling. "How's this for telekinesis, Kath?"

What? How did he know? Had he read her mind?

No. That's impossible.

The reality hit her like a fist. Her mind spun madly and her back arched in pain.

Then the tightness was gone, from her chest and her throat. She opened her eyes and blinked in the brightness of the room's bright lights.

"Turn the lights down," a familiar voice said. Robert.

The lights dimmed and a sea of faces came into focus.

"Am I awake?" Connelly asked.

"Yes," someone replied.

She remembered everything now. She had been put into a deep REM sleep so that her psyche could be stress tested. People who passed the test could take a shower, sleep it off, and be back to work the next day. People who failed needed weeks of therapy. It isn't every day that your worst fears, which are secret even from yourself, are revealed to you. Connelly felt the sensors being taken from her forehead and body by unseen hands.

"How did I do?" she asked.

Robert's smiling face filled her vision as he leaned in close. "You, ah, you did great. But you must have had a doozy of a dream there at the end. Your heart rate skyrocketed just before you woke up."

"It was Michael…"

"I was in your dream?"

Connelly held her breath. She forgot that the entire crew watched the reactions of the sleeping subject, so they could see for themselves how the dreamer reacted physically to stress. She turned her head in the direction of Peterson's voice and saw him standing a few feet away. He wasn't angry or drooling, and black gloves were not on his hands.

"Hope I didn't hurt you," he said with a small smile that revealed he knew the dream was bad.

"Actually," Connelly said, "You killed me."

For a brief moment, Peterson looked sad, but a smile quickly replaced the frown. "Still," he said, "it's nice to know you're thinking of me."

ℕ   ℕ   ℕ   ℕ   ℕ

For three months, Connelly and her crew had been subjected to personal interviews that delved into the deepest depths of their psychology, subjected to embarrassing medical exams, endured physical training and evaluation, and all that was before the technical lessons that everyone had to learn…just in case the worst case scenario happened—death of a crewmember—or members. If the captain died, Choi would act as pilot. If Choi died, Connelly was next in line. Thankfully, autopilot could handle just about everything, but the scenario worked in multiple situations. If Connelly died, Robert would take over, then Willard and so on. Death would not end their mission. It would simply reorganize their duties. Too much money was being spent to call it quits for one death or even two, maybe even three. It was their least favorite subject to discuss, but all understood the protocol's necessity.

Connelly felt a chill at the back of her neck as she took in the latest in a slew of technological advances that the world didn't even know existed. She, Willard, Robert and Peterson were standing in a small rounded room with metallic walls and no windows. At the center of the room was a chair that appeared to be molded right into the floor, like a smooth, silver throne.

To either side of the chair stood Harris and Choi. Between them and in front of the chair was a small cage containing a guinea pig. The guinea pig squeaked loudly and Willard tensed visibly.

Robert smiled at Willard. "Afraid of the little pig?"

"I was attacked by one of those things when I was a kid," Willard said. "Nearly bit off my finger…It squeaked like that the whole time."

Harris cleared his throat, asking for their attention. "What you're seeing right now is top secret, brand new technology. Without it, this trip wouldn't be possible."

Willard raised his hand. "Um, it looks like a chair. Mankind has had chairs for like, what, ten thousand years?"

"You've never seen a chair like this," Harris said. "Trust me."

Harris nodded at Choi, who walked around to the front of the chair and knelt down next to the guinea pig cage. She opened the small door, reached in and picked up the squealing rodent. She held the guinea pig up and said, "This is Lucy."

"You named the pig?" Robert said and then looked at Connelly, "They named the pig."

Choi moved back to the side of the chair, still holding Lucy. "This is an impact chair. They are designed to aid the human body in resisting the effects of high speed travel. That includes extreme acceleration that would normally kill a man and massive deceleration that would be equally as damaging."

"Sorry to be the continuous voice of doubt," Willard said, "but how does a chair do all that?"

"Watch." Choi held Lucy out over the chair and placed her on the seat. Lucy sat still for a moment, her tiny chest rising and falling quickly. Then the chair began to move. "Lucy has been through this several times, so she knows not to run or panic," Choi said.

The seat of the chair became like liquid, oozing toward and around Lucy's body. It covered her back, torso and eventually head, until all that was left was a lump in the chair's seat—a lump that was breathing.

Willard's mouth dropped open. "The chair ate Lucy."

"Lucy's just fine," Harris said.

Peterson stepped forward. "I'm sorry. I don't understand. How is it breathing in there?"

"Breathing tubes inserted through the nose," Choi explained. "You'll receive nutrients intravenously. Microshocks will keep your muscles from atrophying. A gel will be secreted between you and the liquid metal, creating a buffer that will minimize the effects of intense acceleration and deceleration on your body."

"You mean the effects of a series of nuclear explosions," Willard muttered.

Harris spoke over him. "On board the Surveyor, each of you will have your own quarters. The rooms on board are very similar to what we have here in the training facility. You'll have your own bed, your own private bathroom and an impact chair. But unlike the bed and bath, you will not be using these chairs while we are in orbit. They are only to be used in transit...for the duration of transit."

Peterson raised his eyebrows. "We're going to be in the impact chairs for three months?"

Harris nodded. "Three months, two days and three hours. Unconscious for the duration. When you wake up you might feel a bit weary and slimy, but otherwise you'll be fine. Not quite the stasis chambers you see in science fiction movies, but they get the job done."

"Will we age?" Robert asked.

"Sure will," Harris said. "Three months out and three months back. We're all about to have six months shaved off our lives. But honestly, anyone who doesn't think loosing six months of their life to get a front row seat of Jupiter is crazy."

Striding quickly, Choi walked to the door, opened it and motioned for the others to leave. "If you don't mind," she said, "we have much more to cover today and a very tight schedule."

Harris headed for the door, followed by Willard and Peterson. Robert lingered behind with Connelly. They looked back at the chair.

"Unbelievable," Robert said before the left.

Sitting alone at the center of the room was the impact chair. A silver hump at the center of the chair continued to rise and fall as Lucy continued to breathe in her liquid metal womb.

ת   ת   ת   ת   ת

Beads of sweat rolled down Connelly's forehead and stung her eyes. She'd been pounding the punching bag for fifteen minutes—her daily routine—and was only now beginning to tire. Her white tank top was wet around the collar and her grey sweatpants clung uncomfortably to the slick skin of her legs.

She'd taken up slugging a punching bag fourteen years ago as a way to relieve stress and anxiety. It made her feel strong, and when she was done, strangely enough, it made her feel more feminine. At the end of every session,

Connelly would build her intensity, swinging harder and faster, unleashing tension she wasn't even aware existed. She was surprised that today's workout was one of her fiercest ever. She wasn't sure why.

The day had been normal enough, as normal as possible. The morning was filled with classes on subjects ranging from astrophysics, to space flight, to preparing space meals. She'd had a quick lunch with Peterson, which was pleasant, and then went through several last minute physicals.

Connelly's punches grew stronger. The bag swung wildly with each hit and her knuckles began to burn. Maybe it was that in two days she was going to be launched into space, travel across the solar system in search of life on a moon where risks were high and chance of a rescue, if something should go wrong, was nil. That would make sense, but Connelly knew something else was eating at her.

With a mighty punch, Connelly hammered the bag, sending it in a long swinging arc. Then the bag stopped in midair—caught. Peterson stepped out from behind the bag. He was shirtless, glistening with sweat and smiling his Michael Peterson smile. "Whoa there, killer. Working out some frustrations?"

"A girl can't stay in shape?"

"You're pretty fierce is all I'm saying. Wouldn't want to be on the receiving end of one of those punches. Can't say I mind your shape though."

Connelly did her best not to smirk. "Keep talking like that and you'll find out what one of my punches feels like." Connelly looked at Peterson's slick torso and chuckled. "You get all oiled up to come talk to me?"

Peterson smiled. "I was running. But you're right, the sweat does bring out some of my better features." Peterson jokingly hung on the punching bag so that the majority of muscles in his upper body flexed.

Connelly raised an eyebrow and smiled.

"So I've been meaning to ask you something."

Connelly tensed at the new tone in his voice.

"Call it a hunch, but I've got the impression you don't necessarily want to be here."

"Good hunch," Connelly said. " Can I be honest with you?"

"I won't tell a soul."

"We're going to a moon, in space, with no atmosphere. The chance of us finding life-forms beyond microbes is remote in the grandest sense. And the chance of any microbes we do find being beneficial to the human race is even slimmer. We should be putting our money and interest into understanding our own planet before going to this moon, simply to satisfy our curiosity."

"You know," Peterson said, "we could have just as easily said that about Antarctica. No one lives there. What could we possibly learn about life as we know it today. What good is biological history anyway?"

Connelly's lips curled up. "Ahh, but you're wrong. Life discovered in Antarctica may be completely foreign to us currently, but they are still *Earth* organisms. They'd provide a glimpse of how life evolved on *our* planet perhaps millions of years ago. Even if we do find life on Europa, it will have evolved under completely different environmental influences. The chances that alien life will have any positive, tangible ramifications on humanity is near impossible. In fact, the true effects may be entirely negative. Sure everyone will be excited that we've discovered alien life. But what if we bring it back, expose people, and later find out that we've brought back the plague of the twenty-first century?"

Peterson's eyes froze for a split second. It was almost imperceptible, but Connelly noticed. He was afraid of that, too. *But why?* She continued with her speech, not wanting him to know she noticed. "You see? There is no real benefit."

"That was a mouthful," he said.

"I just don't want this to end up being a big waste of time."

Peterson relaxed his body. "Somehow, I think you might change your mind when we get out there. Do you know much about our solar system? About Jupiter?"

Connelly shook her head, no. "Only what I learned in high school astronomy, but that was long, long ago."

"Why don't I fill you in over dinner? Maybe we can work on some of that skepticism?"

"I had lunch with you during a break. That was lunch. Between co-workers. What you're asking now is more than that, correct?"

"Yes, Dr. Spock. I do believe it is."

Connelly smiled. "Sorry, not on this trip, Romeo."

With that, Connelly, turned and headed for the women's locker room door. Why had she said no? Despite his arrogance, he was smart, funny and attractive—a rare combination to find in the sciences. But this mission was big. Too big for romance, and she would continue to push her feelings to the wayside, at least until they were all back on Earth.

She could almost feel Peterson's gaze lingering on her back, probably on her butt. She could feel the fabric of her sweatpants riding up, but didn't dare adjust it while he was watching. With a quick turn of the head, Connelly gave one last look back. Peterson waved with a smile and she felt a tightness in her chest, but this wasn't anxiety.

Connelly laughed to herself as she came to a realization. The punching bag wasn't Peterson, but her tension *was* caused by him. The energy she felt now, after speaking to the man for only a few minutes, wasn't going where she wanted it to go. So she was beating the hell out of a punching bag instead.

6 – GOING UP

Rubbing his eyes in the morning sun, Willard looked at the incredible view of the Pacific Ocean. The crew had been flown from the GEC training facility to San Diego where they boarded a GEC research vessel and headed out to sea. By nightfall they were all situated in cramped quarters within the walls of the Naval Auxiliary Landing Facility on San Clemente Island. Sleep came quickly to all, as it had throughout the duration of their grueling training, but an early start was on the schedule for today.

BENEATH

It was seven o'clock in the morning and the CH-46 Sea Knight helicopter's tandem blades sliced loudly through the air. Loud snoring from across the helicopter's interior rumbled along with the chopping blades. Willard frowned and shook his head. Captain Harris sat across from him, sleeping as soundly as a dead man in the grave. Willard wasn't bothered by the sound, just by the fact that Harris could sleep at all.

Willard blinked and felt heavy weights dangling from his eyelids. He turned his attention back out the window to distract himself from his slumber lust. The water of the Pacific was deep blue and the millions of tiny waves reflected glints of yellow from the sun.

But then, something far below caught his eye. A grey shape cut across the ocean. He recognized the shape. "There's an aircraft carrier down there," he said to no one in particular.

Connelly, Robert and Peterson, who had been involved in a scientific discussion of no interest to Willard, immediately moved to the windows adjacent to Willard's, peering down at the ocean. Choi made no move and looked disinterested. Harris remained asleep.

"Is that where we're going?" Robert asked.

"I don't know," Connelly said. She looked at Choi. "Are we landing on the aircraft carrier?"

Choi shook her head, no.

Willard took his eyes off the carrier and looked further out, towards the horizon, where he saw another vessel, and another, and another. He quickly counted fifteen in all, of various shapes and sizes. "Looks like they have a whole fleet out here."

Robert pushed his glasses higher onto his nose and looked at Choi. "Are we launching from sea? Are these ships for our protection?"

Choi rolled her head on her shoulders. "In response to your first question…" As Choi spoke, a loud and constant rumbling grew quickly from behind the helicopter. "The ships below are not for our protection."

The rumbling grew to a deafening level, and then roared past. Willard snapped his head toward the window in time to see three fighter jets.

"*Those* are for our protection." Choi stood and moved to the central window, through which Willard had been gazing. "The ships are protecting *that*."

Willard looked out the window and followed Choi's pointed finger to what looked like an oil platform. Then he saw several more. At the center of the conglomeration of platforms was a massive construction that looked like a floating city. But he knew this was no ordinary city. It had all the bells and whistles of a scientific facility; satellite dishes, multiple antennae, generators, solar panels, and more than anything else, it was clean—gleaming white.

But what stood out most about the gigantic platform was a shimmering blue streak that rose up out of the center and disappeared into the sky. Willard lost view of the line several times as it would momentarily blend in with the blue sky or ocean, but a reflection of sunlight or a white cloud would reveal the line rising into the sky, beyond Willard's vertical view.

Brow furrowed, Willard said, "What the hell is that?"

"I don't understand," Robert said, "Where are we launching from? I don't see a shuttle or a launch pad and I sure haven't heard of a space launch from sea."

"Is that what I think it is?" Peterson said.

"What do you think it is?" Robert asked.

Peterson stepped away from the window and locked his eyes onto Choi. "Is that the space elevator?"

"One of them, yes."

"Space elevator?" Connelly said. "They're for bringing equipment into space, not people. Why are we here? TES is already in orbit."

"OK, now I'm nervous," Robert said. "So let me ask my first question again.... Where are we launching from?"

"We're not launching," Choi said.

Connelly's eyebrows shot to the top of her forehead and her voice became defiant. "What?"

"Your anxiety is misplaced. The mission is continuing as planned."

Connelly's shoulders dropped.

"Tell me we're not taking the space elevator...into space," Robert said.

"I'm afraid I must disappoint you, Dr. Samuels."

Robert sat back, looking pale. "You okay, man?"

"I don't like elevators," Robert replied.

"It will be a quick ride, I'm sure," Willard said.

"This elevator is sixty-two thousand miles high," Choi said.

Willard's face fell flat. "Oh."

Robert lowered his head. Connelly rubbed his back.

"Something going on?" Harris said as he stretched his face and blinked his tired eyes.

Choi turned to him and said, "We're there."

Willard looked back out the window and followed the blue streak from the platform and into the sky. This tiny blue streak would bring them to space, and hopefully, back. Willard smiled. "Intense."

ℕ　ℕ　ℕ　ℕ　ℕ

Robert stood at the base of the world's tallest structure and did his best not to throw up. His eyes followed the blue, micron thin ribbon skyward until his neck couldn't bend any further back. The ribbon disappeared into the sky with no end in sight. Since landing he had learned that this recently constructed space elevator had yet to be revealed to the world. There were three others around the globe, but none as massive as this.

The first three had been built five years ago and were widely publicized. Everyone knew about them. They had been shipping satellites, space station modules, even small spacecraft into space with never an incident and at extremely low costs. The success of the space elevators had single handedly saved the globe's space programs.

But the one thing the elevators couldn't transport was people. Equipment designed for space could be brought into space without survivability concerns. People were a different matter. For years, the Institute for Scientific Research (ISR) had sought to create an elevator that could safely transport human beings into space, to a small space station at the end, where they could dock with spacecraft built in space with parts the other elevators transported.

Robert swallowed with a gulp. They had apparently succeeded.

The behemoth of human engineering he now stood on rose out of the middle of the Pacific Ocean. The original elevators had a three foot wide ribbon that was just a few microns thick and sixty-two thousand miles long. Robert had learned that this ribbon was identical to the other in construction except for being six feet wide. The extra width gave this elevator the ability to lift 110 tons. The added lifting capability allowed the ISR to construct a module capable of sustaining human life, quite comfortably, during transport to and from space. It was complete with plush chairs, grand windows, refreshment bar and all the necessary facilities for keeping a crew of astronauts relatively comfortable while they were transported into space.

But Robert knew that no matter how comfortable the ride was, he'd be a nervous wreck the whole way up; in part because of his fears, but also because he'd managed to hide that fear during his psychological evaluation. He'd prefer being launched in a shuttle with an exploding rocket beneath him over riding for hours in a glorified elevator. The inner workings of the space elevator had been explained to him; the ribbon, constructed of a super strong carbon nanotube composite was held aloft by centrifugal force—it's why all four space elevators were built at the equator where the earth spins fastest. The station at the end of the ribbon served as a counter weight and was held in a perfect geosynchronous orbit. The module clung to the ribbon with a set of rollers which were powered from the ground by a free-electron laser, and could move up the ribbon at a steady pace. All this technology made Robert excited and intrigued, but his old fears were coming back to haunt him.

When Robert was a child, he avoided elevators at all cost. He'd sooner take thirty flights of stairs then ride in an elevator. Things had changed for him ten years ago when he went on a date in Seattle—the first in two years—with a stunning woman who seemed more interested in his mind than in his body, which was a good thing...a very good thing. They had a wonderful dinner—

lobster with shrimp cocktail. For him it was one of those nights you never forget.

To his never ending surprise, she had called him the next day, and invited him out for a surprise. He happily accepted. For twenty minutes they drove around the city, him blindfolded, her behind the wheel. When she parked the car, Robert felt an excitement he had never felt before. His throat was parched. His heart was racing. When she took off the blindfold, all that disappeared. He stood at the base of the Seattle Space Needle and looked up. The blood fled from his face and his mouth dropped open. He began to sweat at the base of his back and felt a pain in his knees.

Mind spinning, he tried to think of an excuse to use the stairs, but couldn't conceive of a way to justify climbing fifty-two stories. Dumbfounded, he couldn't react. She had grabbed him and dragged him forward, racing toward the elevator. He was still looking up when the elevator doors closed behind him and the doorman said, "Next stop, observation deck, five hundred and twenty feet up."

Robert cringed as he remembered the twisting sensation his stomach felt as the elevator surged up. For five seconds, Robert managed to remain calm, but the gentle touch of the woman he had grown so fond of, broke the barriers of fear. He wept, sobbed really, for what seemed like twenty minutes. He spilled out onto the observation deck, terrified. Moving like a scared rabbit, Robert searched for the stairs through blurry eyes. He didn't hear anyone asking to help him. He didn't see the people diving out of his way. His worst fear had been sprung on him before he had a chance to prepare. Robert found the stairs, stumbled all the way down, hailed a cab and went home.

He never heard from her again.

Since that day he resolved to conquer his fear of elevators and had done so with some success. He regularly used elevators now, using a counting technique that no one ever noticed. As long as he kept counting, his fear could never take hold.

The only person he ever told about his fear was Connelly, his closest friend and greatest supporter. She hadn't teased him once since he revealed his secret fear and occasionally, when they rode in elevators together, she would shoot him a reassuring glance. As far as he was concerned, her judgment and understanding where infallible—it's one of the reasons he was willing to follow her into space. Of course, no amount of reassuring glances could ease his fears about *this* elevator ride.

Robert looked up at the blue ribbon reaching up into the sky and wondered how high he would have to count. "How long will it take? To get to the top, I mean."

Harris looked over at Robert. He'd been explaining the beneficial ramifications of the space elevator on space travel and how their mission, if successful, would be the first of many jaunts to the outer reaches of the solar system. He looked at Robert with some sympathy in his eyes. "All day, I'm afraid."

"As in twenty-four hours?"

"Eighteen"

Robert squinted his eyes as he performed some mental calculations. "At one number per second…. Sixty-four thousand, eight hundred. Never counted that high before."

"Excuse me?" Harris looked confused.

Robert shook his head. "Nothing…nothing. When are we leaving?"

"One last debrief and we're boarding," Harris said as he eyeballed Robert's pale face. "You don't look so good."

"I'm, ahh, I'm fine. Really," Robert said, but didn't sound all that convincing. "I'm ok." He looked up at the elevator ribbon and shuddered.

Harris let out a sigh and looked over his shoulder. The rest of the crew were speaking with Choi, well out of ear shot. "Listen, Dr. Samuels…. If you're uncomfortable with enclosed spaces, maybe you should rethink—"

"No," Robert said. "It's not that…just…just elevators."

"You're sure?" Harris asked.

"Been that way all my life," Robert said. "Put me in a coffin, I'm fine. Put me in a coffin in an elevator, not so fine."

Smiling, Harris patted Robert on the shoulder. "You know, we are well funded. You can have a sedative for the duration of the ascent."

Robert's eyes widened. "Seriously?"

"Sure, if you don't mind waking up in space."

Robert again looked up at the elevator ribbon. This time he smiled. "Thank the Lord."

ℼ   ℼ   ℼ   ℼ   ℼ

Willard stretched as he stepped out of the elevator and onto the largest man-made spacecraft ever built. The very long trip in the elevator had gone smoothly and was exciting for the first hour and then time to time when the continents came into view. He'd thumbed through the magazines kept on the module, obviously meant for the more scientifically inclined. After an hour of sitting he was kicking himself for not bringing a good novel along. During the final hours, when all conversations were exhausted, the magazine supply had run out and several of the crew had fallen asleep, Willard took to amusing himself by watching Robert, who had been heavily sedated, twitch in his sleep.

Craning his neck in every direction, Willard gazed at the massive docking bay. The floor was smooth until it reached the curved walls, where massive columns ran from floor to ceiling every five feet. "They look like ribs," Willard said as Connelly entered the bay behind him.

"The belly of the beast," Connelly said.

Peterson stepped out of the elevator module and stood next to Connelly. His eyes went wide as he looked at the bay. The ribbed walls stretched thirty feet high and seventy five feet across. Three large doorways were located on one wall and the opposite wall appeared to be one massive door. In front of the door were three small spacecraft that looked like a cross between jet fighters and tanks. "Wow," he said. "Beast is right. I didn't imagine the ship was this big."

"Beast, nothing. Welcome to the Surveyor, folks. This is the most state-of-the-art spacecraft ever built. It's going to take us to Jupiter and back. She's the first of her kind, and your new home. And she's got all the amenities of home, and then some."

"So this is it, huh? We're in space?" Willard jumped up and down a few times, his footfalls echoing in the massive bay. "Gravity feels real."

"It should," Choi said as she wheeled the still unconscious Robert into the bay. "The World Space Organization spent thirty billion dollars developing the series of spinning superconductors spread throughout the ship. They produce a powerful gravitomagnetic field—artificial gravity—that doesn't require the craft to also be a massive centrifuge."

"That's a lot of money," Willard said, looking around the bay. "They put any of that cash into developing space windows?"

"Sorry, Mr. Willard," Harris said. "We're on a tight schedule. I need you in your quarters in twenty minutes and in your impact chairs in twenty-five."

Nods all around. Willard looked down at Robert who sat unconscious. "What about him?"

"Should we just leave him out? No reason to wake him up, just to put him back to sleep. Let him wake up at Jupiter."

Harris nodded and clapped his hands together. "Let's do it. I'll show you each to your quarters. We'll get Dr. Samuels squared away, then the rest of you can get in the chairs. Choi will do a final inspection before launch."

"What happens if we're not in the chairs by launch?"

Harris frowned. "Be in the chair by launch." With that, he walked away, towards the nearest doorway.

Willard looked at Peterson. "What happens if you're not in the chairs by launch?"

"You'll be a stain on the wall by the time we get to Europa."

"Oh," Willard said. "He could have said that." Willard shouted ahead to Harris, "You could have said that."

න   න   න   න   න

Willard had been in his quarters for five minutes. In the first forty-five seconds he took off all his clothes accept for his boxers. For the remaining four minutes and fifteen seconds he had been pacing in front of his impact chair.

After seeing Lucy the guinea pig eaten by the chair, Willard hadn't given it a second thought. But just minutes ago, after Robert had been stripped and hauled into his chair, he'd witnessed firsthand how the chair consumed a human body. The metal oozed over Robert's flesh like it was alive, swallowing him up. Willard felt his stomach flip flop as the metal slid over Robert's nostrils and eyes and felt a slight queasiness when he saw tubes move up through the silver metal skin and into Robert's nose, mouth and arms.

He was relieved to see Robert's breathing chest rise and fall beneath the metal epidermis, but couldn't help feeling fearful of being encased in a metal tomb. When the process was complete, Robert looked like a worn statue of pharaoh.

The experience left Willard unusually nervous. His extreme attitude was taking a vacation and left him with sweaty palms and a wrinkled forehead. He looked down at his boxers, then back to the chair, imagining how it would feel when the cold liquid metal covered his nether-regions. "No way," he said.

After taking a deep breath and letting it out slowly, Willard inched forward, reaching a hand out to the arm of the chair. "Okay...I can do this."

With a quick burst of motion, Willard put his hand on the armrest. The liquid metal began to cover his fingers. He pulled away quickly. After sliding his boxers to the floor, Willard inhaled and exhaled several times in a row.

"One..."

Willard gripped his fists into tight balls.

"Two..."

Leaning forward, his muscles tensed.

"Thr—"

The door behind him whooshed open and Choi stepped inside. "Why are you not in your chair?" she demanded.

"What the! Hey!" Willard grabbed his boxers and held them up in front of his naked body. "I'm naked here!"

"I can see that," Choi said without a hint of embarrassment, interest or humor. "And you'll be naked *and* dead if you don't get in that chair."

"I know...I know. It's just—"

Choi stepped forward and reached out for Willard.

"What are you doing?" he asked in surprise.

Choi's hands came to rest on Willard temples. "Helping you relax," she said, standing intimately close to Willard's naked body.

Willard looked down and noticed two things—how close Choi was standing to him, and how attractive she looked her tight grey jumpsuit.

"Close your eyes," Choi said in a soft, almost seductive voice.

Willard closed his eyes and couldn't help but smile. His first experience in space was going well and getting better.

"Breathe deep," Choi said. "Listen to the sound of my voice."

Willard couldn't take his mind off the sound of her voice. All his worries and fears were disappearing and being quickly replaced by more primal thoughts. He felt Choi's hands rest gently on his naked shoulder. She squeezed him gently.

"Now then," she said, "there is only one thing left to do."

Willard raised his eyebrows, his smile expanding.

Choi leaned forward and put her lips next to Willard's left ear. "Sweet dreams," she whispered.

Willard felt the pressure on his shoulders intensify for just a second and then felt his body falling backward, pushed by Choi. A cold surface broke Willard's fall and he opened his eyes. Choi was standing above him, smiling slightly.

Willard looked confused. "You smile?"

Choi glanced down and Willard followed her eyes to his lap, which was already covered by liquid metal.

He was sitting in the chair.

Choi stepped forward, put her hand on Willard's forehead and held him back in the chair. He began to complain, but the liquid metal covered his mouth before he had the chance. She turned and left Willard encased in his liquid metal cocoon.

₪   ₪   ₪   ₪   ₪

Twenty-five minutes after the crew had departed the space elevator and Choi confirmed the crew's readiness, the ship's auto pilot took over. Docking clamps released. The massive ship, which looked like a cross between a Navy Destroyer and a Bullet Train with massive amounts of shielding on the front and rear, drifted away from the elevator until it had put a few miles between the two.

A small hatch at the back of the ship opened, jettisoning what was essentially a nuclear warhead. A burst of light that looked like a distant star going super nova exploded from the backside. It was bright enough for Nancy Heintz to see from the rooftop greenhouse atop the GEC headquarters.

When the light had disappeared from the blue sky above, Nancy's phone rang. She held the phone to her ear and listened. "Surveyor is successfully away, ma'am."

"Thank you," she said and then hung up.

Immediately, the phone rang again. Nancy looked at the small display screen that revealed who it was calling. She read the name and answered immediately.

"Mr. President," she said and then listened. "Thank you...yes sir...thank you. I'm sure it will too."

Nancy began to pace. "No sir. No. I wouldn't worry about that yet. Yes, sir, I'm positive that this mission will go smoothly. Our technology is state of the art and if anything should go wrong, the crew is well trained and can handle it...yes sir. Thank you again, sir."

With that, Nancy hung up the phone and turned it off.

"Nothing will go wrong," she said to herself, and then repeated it in her head like a mantra.

But she wasn't entirely convinced.

EUROPA

7 – ORBIT

The view from the surface of Europa had been the same for millions of years. Jupiter always dominated the sky, its yellow, orange and red gases swirling constantly, propelled by storms the size of other planets. Alongside mother Jupiter were the sister moons, Io, Ganymede and Callisto, which glowed dully in orbit alongside Europa, whose icy surface shone brightest of all—unique among her sisters.

But a new spectacle, one never seen from the surface of the ice moon before, arrived with a flash. Like a streak of lightning it burst into the night sky— something foreign arrived. It came from the inner solar system and stopped above the moon, hovering in orbit. For ten minutes it slowly circled the ice orb; its presence revealed by the sun reflecting brightly off its shiny exterior.

A few other objects had arrived in years past, but none so brilliantly or quickly. This was new, larger, more threatening than the others.

And its arrival didn't go unnoticed.

ℕ ℕ ℕ ℕ ℕ

The Surveyor's cameras began recording images. Photos of the jagged ice surface, which was brilliant white mixed with smatterings of light blue. Tall peaks of mountainous ice rose toward space. Deep, round depressions sunk down to a perfectly smooth covering, apparently where an asteroid had long ago hit the ice and broke through to the ocean and refroze. It was one of the first hints mankind found as to the possibility of an ocean beneath the frozen surface.

In stark contrast to the brilliant ice were thousands of crimson cracks etched into the surface of the moon as though by a giant laser. The coloration varied slightly from line to line, some maroon, some ruby, some the color of cherries, but all red. Most scientists still held to the theory that these lines were sediment that rose to the surface, pushed upward by tidal flexing caused by the gravitational pull of Jupiter, or asteroid impacts, or thermal venting. Maybe all three. While mode of transport was still debated, all agreed the markings were massive sediment-filled cracks—but this was all best guesses—speculation. It was one of Europa's secrets the crew hoped to uncover.

The cameras shot several thousand photos, saving each image in the Surveyor's databanks. They'd be used to help determine the best landing zone for the crew and the ideal location for TES to melt through the ice.

Inside the ship, systems were coming online one by one. A single screen in the control center blinked to life. Text scrolled across its screen.

Destination reached...
Life support systems engaged...
Gravity engaged...
Status check in 3...2...1...
Optimal atmosphere...
Optimal pressure...
Optimal gravity...
All systems functional...
Deactivation of impact chairs in 3...2...1...

נ   נ   נ   נ   נ

The silver skin of the lone impact chair began to move as the occupant regained consciousness. Its metallic surface warmed and thinned. The shape of a hand stretched out, pulling the liquid metal. With a sudden burst the hand was free.

Grasping the arm of the chair, the hand flexed and pulled. A face began to form at the top of the chair as the person trapped inside pulled himself free. The metal stretched and turned whitish-grey as it thinned, and then snapped. The tear spread down the surface of the chair. The occupant plunged forward and spilled onto the floor.

Still clinging to his boxers, Willard lay on the floor, shivering and covered in slime. His teeth chattered as he squinted his eyes against the sun-like lights recessed into the ceiling of his quarters.

Willard let out a light groan as he stood to his feet, careful not to slip and fall. He rolled his head on his neck and scanned his quarters. The room was identical to the one he'd had during training. Not much for hominess, but it got the job done. The bed was firm and small, but comfortable. The living space was cramped by American standards, spacious by Japanese, but provided enough room to do pushups and crunches.

Willard turned his attention to the small bathroom. Like everything else, it was small, but functional. The water pressure, at least on earth, had been superb and the hot water was instant and relaxing. Willard thought it was strange that as he thought about the hot shower, his mouth began to water. It was then, he realized, that he was extremely hungry.

But food would have to wait. The slime coating, which was beginning to chill his extremities needed to be washed away. Willard stepped into the small bathroom, dropped his boxers into the sink and slid into the shower. He rested his head on the shower stall wall and sighed.

Reaching down, Willard took hold of the shower knob and turned on just the hot. There was a pause as air was noisily forced from the unused pipes. Willard rolled his eyes and thought about the shower in his Moab, Utah apartment. He'd stayed in Moab for two years, working at a gas station and mountain biking on the weekends. That was the beginning of his love for all things extreme, but no one else in Utah was—

His mind cleared with the realization that he was awake. And that meant he was in orbit around Europa, a moon of Jupiter—in space!

He was about to let out a victory cheer when the telltale pops and gurgling noises of approaching water caught his attention. It burst from the shower head and coated Willard's body.

He let out a scream and struggled to shield himself from the jet of water, shouting, "Cold! Cold!"

₪   ₪   ₪   ₪   ₪

Connelly reclined in her chair positioned on the side of a very long, oval table. The chair, which was vaguely shaped like a clamshell felt strangely comfortable. Peterson and Choi sat across from her, while Robert was to her right and Captain Harris was seated at the head of the table. All were freshly showered and had completed the three month journey in perfect health.

Peterson shifted in his chair. "Should someone go look for him?"

Robert nodded. "Maybe his impact chair malfunctioned?"

"Unlikely," Choi said. "All systems are green across the board. His chair deactivated with the others."

Robert twisted his lips in thought. "Ethan has been known to take long showers."

"Malfunctioning chair or long shower," Harris said, "It doesn't change the fact that we have a schedule to keep."

Connelly sighed. "I'll go find him." Connelly stood and turned to the entryway.

The doors slid open and Willard walked in wearing a blue bathrobe and a white towel wrapped around his head. "Doesn't this billion dollar spaceship have hot water?"

"Of course." Harris said. "Why?"

"I prefer my drinking water ice cold, and my shower molten hot. The showers here—not hot. Very cold." Ethan took the empty seat to the right of Robert.

Connelly sat back down. "Mine was fine."

Choi made eye contact with Willard. "Maybe someone thought you needed a cold shower?" She smiled sarcastically.

"Was that a joke?" Willard said. "You joke? And, by the way, I haven't forgotten that trick you played before we left."

Robert turned to Willard. "What trick?"

Willard took a deep breath. "I was having trouble getting into—"

"Gentlemen." Harris's voice was calm but firm. "We have more important things than cold showers to talk about."

"Right," Willard said. "Europa…. But this doesn't feel any different. Can we see Europa? Jupiter? Is there a window nearby?"

Harris smiled ever so slightly. "Glad you mentioned it. First on our agenda is a quick training on how to access the windows on Surveyor."

"But there are no windows," Willard said.

"Actually," Choi said, "We're surrounded by windows."

Everyone searched the smooth paneled surface of the curved ceiling and walls.

"I don't see any," Robert said. "Are they hidden?"

Harris pulled a small remote control device, the size of a credit card, from his jumpsuit pocket. "In a manner of speaking." Harris put the remote control on the table so that everyone could see it. "Some of you may have noticed a small remote in the desk drawer of your quarters. Additionally, you will find a remote, identical to this one, in every room on board Surveyor that has at least one outer hull wall. You'll also all receive your own personal remote, which you can carry with you at all times."

Peterson took the remote and inspected it. "There's only one button." He looked at Harris. "What does it do?"

"Lights," Harris said to no one in particular. The lights, which streamed up from where the floor met the walls, dimmed until the room was pitch black. "Now point the remote at the ceiling and push the button."

Connelly couldn't see Peterson comply, but after ten second she noticed a change in the ceiling. It began to glow white, gently becoming translucent.

Harris began to speak as whatever was happening to the ceiling, continued. "Several of the hull's interior and exterior panels are made from a new material that becomes transparent when a specific electrical charge is applied. Just point the remote at almost any portion of the outer hull and..."

Within fifteen seconds, the majority of the ceiling had become completely transparent. Connelly gasped.

"...Voila!" Harris said.

Before them was a spectacle no human had ever seen before. Taking up a large portion of the view was Europa, which was bright white, crisscrossed with crimson lines that looked like scars. She could see it so perfectly, so clearly, all her problems with this mission were forgotten. She smiled widely. This was a moon sized Antarctica!

Connelly looked left and gasped again. Jupiter was there, but it wasn't the still shot of Jupiter people are used to seeing. It was fluid and active. Swirls of yellow, orange and red churned over the surface of the planet. Connelly knew that Jupiter was the largest, most powerful of the planets, but to her, from this perspective, it looked fragile.

The conference room glowed light orange from the light reflecting from Jupiter and Europa. Connelly's eyes adjusted, and she could see the rest of the crew, all looking up, mouths open wide.

Robert started to speak. "Oh my... That's, ahh, that's..."

"Incredible," Connelly finished.

Robert nodded.

"I can't believe it," Peterson said, his voice soft with awe. "Jupiter..."

"You're looking at the largest planet in our solar system folks. She's composed of hydrogen, helium, water, nitrogen—swirling around a tiny, super-dense core. She's beautiful, but deadly. Insurmountable pressure and extreme radiation make Jupiter impossible to explore."

Connelly's attention was piqued. "Radiation? Will it affect us?"

Harris took his eyes off the view and turned to Connelly. "The Surveyor, the landers and even TES are protected by electromagnetic shielding. This blocks 99% of the radiation. The shield on TES is powerful enough to cover a two mile circumference and should allow us to set down in an ideal melt zone and close enough to explore one of the red lines."

"Why didn't you tell us this before?" Willard asked, his voice serious, but his eyes still on the view through the ceiling.

"It's a non-issue," Choi said. "The electromagnetic shielding is sufficient."

Willard looked down from the view and met Choi's eyes. "Are there any more non-issues I should know about? Because I can't keep this crew safe if I don't know every possible danger that exists up here."

"You weren't informed because it's not a danger," Choi said.

"Not a danger?" Willard huffed. "What would happen if, in theory, the electromagnetic shield and whatever back-up systems are in place fail? What would happen? In theory?"

Choi looked at Harris, unsure of how to answer.

Willard rolled his eyes. "End result. Don't need the details. How long would we have to live."

Choi looked back at Willard. "Six minutes."

"Six minutes to live. Any ways to avoid being fried by the radiation?" Willard asked as his leg began to bounce beneath the table.

Harris cleared his throat. "We would pilot Surveyor into a stationary position on the far side of Europa, which would block the majority of the radiation, until the problem was fixed."

Connelly sat forward. She could see where Willard was headed. "And if we're on the surface?"

"You have six minutes to get six feet below the ice. That would block the radiation," Harris said.

"Listen," Willard said, "I know you don't think I even need to be here, but I have a track record of keeping people alive, and if you're working against me, I can't do that. I'm not asking, I'm telling you, give every possible worst case scenario before we head to the surface, or we're not going."

Connelly wanted to object to Willard's demand, but she knew he was right. He'd saved her life more than once and she knew it was largely because he was always prepared for anything. "Ethan's right," she said, "give him what he needs, or we're not going."

Harris let out a long sigh. "Choi, see to it that Mr. Willard is fully informed about all possible dangers."

Choi nodded with a grim expression. "Yes, sir. But I think he'll find—"

Willard interrupted. "I think you'll find that danger comes from the unexpected. That thing no one sees coming, is what gets people killed."

A faint glow shimmering on the table top caught Willard's attention. He slowly looked up. "For example, if a shower of glowing spheres were to crash into the outer hull, would we be prepared for it?"

"Fiction is not something we prepare for," Choi said.

Willard looked her straight in the eyes. "Maybe it should be."

Choi looked at him, her eyes reflecting her confusion.

Willard made the most sarcastic face he could manage and then thrust his index finger toward the transparent ceiling.

All eyes went to the ceiling.

"Oh my God," Peterson said.

Connelly's eyes grew wide as she looked up at the view, which minutes ago, was Europa and Jupiter alone. Now there were hundreds, maybe thousands of glowing spheres, the size of golf balls, hurtling towards them. They were beautiful, shimmering like living stars, but caused Connelly's muscles to tense.

This isn't right.

All eyes remained glued to the clear ceiling, watching as the closest of the spheres approached the outer hull. The glowing orb struck the hull and began moving along the side. The brightness of the orb became dazzling for a second and then it exploded with the force of a quarter stick of dynamite.

The room shook and the lights flickered.

Harris leapt to his feet and headed for the door.

"What the hell?" Peterson said.

"What's happening?" Connelly asked.

"I don't know," Harris said as he neared the exit.

Connelly returned her eyes to the transparent ceiling and watched as the cloud of glowing orbs closed in.

This is definitely not right!

Willard shot an evil eye at Choi. "If we live through this, I want to know everything."

Choi nodded, all traces of annoyance gone from her face. Then she bolted after Harris, who had just exited the room.

Willard looked up at the ominous view. "Fiction my ass."

The room shook as a second explosion rocked the hull, then another, and another.

Stumbling across the shaking room, the rest of the crew headed for the door. Connelly looked up at the cloud of shiny bombs headed their way. Instead of wondering how they were going to survive the massive pummeling, her thoughts jumped ahead to the next obvious question.

Where did they come from?

8 – THE ATTACK

The ship's violent shaking reminded Peterson of the time his brothers tricked him into riding his bicycle down a very long staircase. Every jolt shook his body so much that his teeth began to chatter. He clenched his jaw tight to stop the annoyance and set to the task of moving through the ship.

Twenty seconds into the attack, the lights had gone out. They were replaced by dim, red emergency lights. So now, not only did the shaking floor make it hard to walk, but the dull light made it nearly impossible to see.

As he stepped forward, Peterson's feet hit the solid grey floor panels, sometimes too early and too hard, and other times too late. He lurched forward, bumping into Connelly. And she was having just as hard a time walking.

"Sorry," Peterson said, after colliding with Connelly.

"Which way to the control center? I lost sight of Choi!" Connelly shouted over the rumble of the Surveyor's shuddering body.

Peterson flashed the schematics of the massive ship through his mind. It was hard to think with all the noise, but he recalled the data he needed. "That way!" he said, pointing to the left.

Connelly led the way, followed by Peterson, Willard and Robert.

Peterson rounded a corner behind Connelly and looked back. He saw a terrified Robert closing in and Willard behind him. But Willard's face wasn't etched with concern like the rest of them. He looked calm. Peterson couldn't tell if it was an illusion created by the vibrating ship, or if his eyesight was true, but he swore he could see the slightest smile on Willard's face.

Robert passed Peterson without saying a word, too preoccupied with their dilemma to care about Peterson's pit stop. Willard caught up and Peterson could see that the man, who was supposed to be watching out for their safety, appeared to be enjoying the danger.

Not really sure why, Peterson felt infuriated by Willard's lack of concern. "You enjoying this?" Peterson asked as Willard moved past.

Willard looked him in the eyes. His smile grew. "You're not?"

"We could die!" Peterson said.

"But what a way to go, right?"

Peterson nearly choked. *Is he serious?*

"Don't sweat it, Mikey, I always come out on top." Willard patted Peterson on the shoulder and moved past, into the control center.

Peterson followed him into the control center and was greeted by chaos.

He lumbered towards the center of the room, with Connelly, Robert and Willard. They looked like lost sheep in the middle of a lightning storm. Warning lights flashed in a myriad of colors, giving the room a seventies disco feel, and alluding to greater problems around the ship.

Harris and Choi were seated in twin chairs at the front of the control center, which was a pentagon shaped room with two chaired consoles on four of the walls. Peterson noticed that two of the vaulted ceilings panels were transparent. He gasped as he saw a cloud of what looked like millions of the tiny bombs floating in their direction.

"Some kind of charged particles!" It was Choi, screaming over the ambient noise. "The computer can't place them."

"I want to know what the hell we're dealing with here!" Harris shouted.

Choi threw her hands up. "The system is failing! We need to reboot!

Harris gazed up at the approaching cloud and looked unsure as dozens of explosions pounded the ship's hull. Peterson knew time was of the essence and any pause might make their situation more dire. He moved forward, intending to spur the captain on, but Willard beat him to the punch.

"Reboot!" Willard said, squeezing Harris's shoulder. "Do it now!"

Harris nodded. "System reboot in three…two…" Harris looked back at the rest of the crew. "Hold onto something!"

Peterson dove into the chair like a kid playing musical chairs and held onto the armrests with a python grip. Harris opened a small panel and depressed a single yellow button for three seconds.

Everything went black, which accentuated the approaching bombardment. Petersons's mouth slowly opened as the densest portion of the orb cloud grew closer. He jolted as the vents in the walls slammed shut and the hum of electricity cut out.

The only thing he could hear now was the shaking ship and each tiny explosion, as they continued to degrade the integrity of the outer hull. His eyes snapped to a single monitor, which blinked to life. Text scrolled across the screen.

Life support off…
Gravity off…

Peterson felt himself become weightless. A surge of nausea filled his stomach, threatening to make him retch. He moved his hand to his mouth, preparing to block any bile that might escape, but the motion created by his arm was enough to move his entire body up off the chair in the weightless environment. He sucked in a breath and noticed the air becoming stale. He glanced at the computer screen and read the text upside down.

Life support systems off…
System shutdown…

Peterson worried that rebooting the system was a mistake. What if it didn't restart in time? What if it didn't restart at all?

Knowing his life was out of his hands, Peterson concerned himself with the only thing he could do to improve his safety. He pulled himself back toward the chair, but pulled too hard. He slammed into the seat of the chair and felt a pain throb in his side as the armrest pushed into his gut, knocking the wind out of him. Gasping for air, Peterson, righted himself, grabbed the other armrest and pulled himself firmly into the seat's cushion.

When he was finished, he glanced back at the screen and was relieved to see the startup sequence beginning.

System reboot...
Life support systems engaged...
Main electric engaged...

The room filled with a blinding light. Peterson squinted against the harsh glow, but opened his eyes painfully wide when he saw Willard floating ten feet up, clinging to a cargo box.

Robert, who was clinging to a support rail, his body floating horizontal to the floor, noticed Willard as well. "What are you doing?"

Willard had a bewildered look on his face as he spun slowly around in midair. When he returned to facing Robert below, he said, "I thought it was bolted to the floor!"

A beep, which was barely audible over the rumbling ship, drew Peterson's eyes back to the console screen.

Gravity engaged...

Thud! Willard crashed to the floor, as did Robert. Everyone else had made it to a chair and Peterson knew they were feeling just as he did, sick with the sudden return of gravity. But also relief. He looked at the screen and wrung his sweating hands together.

Status check in 3...2...1...
Optimal atmosphere...
Optimal pressure...
Optimal gravity...
All systems functional...

Harris's voice boomed a command. "Take us into higher orbit!"
"Already on it!" Choi said.
Peterson watched through the clear ceiling as the approaching orbs began to move away, heading down. But he knew it wasn't the orbs moving. Surveyor's upward motion just made them look that way. Still, he couldn't help but think the mini-missiles had been aiming for the ship. But it was impossible to prove. It was most likely that they had witnessed a natural phenomenon not yet observed by astronomers.

Astrophysics wasn't Peterson's field, but he knew enough to compile several theories on how the bright spheres had been created and how they were spewed into space. Jupiter alone contained so many mysteries that Peterson felt overwhelmed when he considered them. Of course, theories, while useful, are not conclusive. To really know what the orbs were, he'd have to observe them again and again, until true scientific data could be gathered.

And he knew for a fact that he'd be happy never seeing one of those things again.

Peterson let out a long breath as the rest of the explosive lights disappeared beneath the Surveyor's higher orbit. The shaking ceased. The noise dissipated. Everything, except for a few blinking warning lights, was back to normal.

The crew slowly climbed to their feet. They hovered around Harris and Choi, who were still seated at their consoles, breathing heavily. Choi punched a few keys on the console and switched on the autopilot.

Willard leaned close to Choi. "Did the electromagnetic shields hold?"

A sudden look of concern washed over Choi and she worked the keyboard with fast fingers. A diagnostic flashed onto the screen. Her shoulders sank with relief as she read the text. "A few failures, but the backup system kicked in. Shouldn't be too hard to fix. We're okay."

Peterson noticed that Willard didn't appear too convinced.

Connelly put her hand on the back of Harris's chair, stabilizing herself. "Please," she said, "someone tell me you know what just happened."

Choi looked over her shoulder and spoke, "They were charged particles...very large. Contact with the hull appeared to cause an explosive reaction."

"I know all that," Connelly said. "What I don't know, is *what* they were."

"I'm afraid no one knows that," Harris said, "but you're not going to believe this." Harris turned to his console's screen. "I had the computer analyze the speed and inclination of those particles, so we could know where they came from. There's no doubt about this, folks, they came from Europa's surface."

"No..."

Peterson didn't know who said it. He was too astonished to identify the voice.

He saw Choi's lips move and knew she was speaking.

"Perhaps this same phenomenon disabled the Orbiter in 2010?" Choi said.

Peterson shook his head and cleared his mind. When he finished, he noticed Connelly was staring out the clear ceiling, a smile forming at the side of her mouth. He followed her eyes and noticed a single bright orb, floating past. The sphere's light faded, flickered and disappeared.

When it was gone, he turned to Connelly. Their eyes met and a full fledged smile broke onto her face. "We have to get down there."

But Peterson wasn't so sure he wanted to any more.

With every footfall, Connelly's steps echoed a dull thud through the maze of hallways. She'd been told by her mother on several occasions that she walked on her heels, which created loud thumps when she walked. As a result, she was never good at sneaking up on anyone. The long, empty hallways of the Surveyor accentuated the noise created by her footsteps, so much so that she became annoyed by them.

She adjusted her stride so the sole of her foot struck first. The noise disappeared.

Mom was right.

Connelly looked down at the digital map of the Surveyor's inner workings, which was displayed on a four inch touch-screen. Below the screen were numbers one through eleven, each representing a deck of the Surveyor. The user could move around the map and zoom in and out by dragging a finger, or two, across its surface.

Sighing, Connelly stopped at an intersection and looked in every direction. She looked back at the map, huffed in frustration and took a right. Being an intelligent and self sufficient woman, Connelly was unaccustomed to being lost, but the ship was so new, and so vast, that she had become hopelessly lost after only five minutes.

Connelly picked up her pace in an effort to speed through the maze, knowing she would eventually find something she recognized.

Without looking up from the map, Connelly took a right, using her peripheral vision to guide her forward. Had she been using all her vision, she would have seen Peterson approaching, looking down at his own map.

"Oof!" Connelly collided with Peterson and fell backward.

Connelly let out a slight yelp as she toppled over, but felt a force beneath the small of her back push up and equalize her fall. In seconds she was back on her feet and looking into Peterson's smiling face.

"Is it just me," Peterson said, "or do you swoon every time we're together?"

Connelly pulled away from Peterson's protective arm. She wasn't sure how to respond. He was obviously joking, but she couldn't help but think he really wanted to know. She knew that men thought about sex...or women...all the time, but up here, in orbit around Europa, just a meteorite's throw from Jupiter, and having just survived a completely new extraterrestrial phenomenon, she couldn't fathom Peterson had enough room in his mind for romantic thoughts.

She then realized that since the floating light bulbs nearly killed them all, Peterson had crossed *her* mind once or twice, as well. Her face began to flush, but she put on a straight face and decided to ignore his comment.

"I take it you're lost too?" she said.

Peterson looked down at his map and shook his head. "This thing is useless."

Connelly smiled.

"How long you been at it?" Peterson asked.

Connelly rolled her head around on her shoulder, feeling two of her vertebrate pop. "Too long."

"Well then," Peterson said, as he switched off his map and pocketed it, "I say we explore. It's not like we can get any more lost than we already are, and the best way to learn something is by experience. We'll know our way around this beast in a few hours."

Connelly raised a single eyebrow. His skepticism was clear.

Peterson lowered his gaze. "C'mon. We have two hours before debrief..."

Connelly's expression didn't change. In truth, she was doing all she could to maintain it. She didn't want to show him an iota of above average interest.

"I won't hit on you," he said. "I swear."

A smile crept onto Connelly's face. She reached down, turned her map off and put it in the pocket of her gray jumpsuit.

"That's the spirit," he said.

They continued walking together. It was five minutes before either of them spoke again.

Connelly wracked her brain for a conversation piece. The uncomfortable silence drove her crazy. Anything work related seemed contrived and all personal subjects felt too...personal. She forgot all her concerns when a door label caught her attention. "What's that?" she asked.

"What?"

Connelly pointed her index finger to the text that caught her attention. "Bio-Lab."

Peterson walked to the door, which was labeled, BIO-LAB in bright yellow. "I think I know. They had something like it on the roof of the GEC building."

He pushed a button to the side of the door and it whooshed open. He motioned for Connelly to enter first. "After you."

Connelly wasn't sure they should be entering a laboratory she knew nothing about without the captain's consent, but the idea of returning to the never ending maze of hallways seemed torturous in comparison. She walked through the door and stood still as she took in the view.

The first twenty-five feet of the hundred foot wide room appeared to be a solid metal platform. Along the walls were long black lab tables. Atop each table were several odd looking machines, with solid black, octagonal shaped bases and a glass top that looked like a giant upside-down test tube. They ranged in size from six inches tall to almost six feet. The larger ones sat on the floor in clusters of five. Inside each of the glass cylinders were plants of various species.

But the strange glass containers weren't what captured her attention the most. Connelly thought the room must be as deep as a football field and maybe a hundred feet tall. From the platform to the back wall, which was barely visible, and covering all one hundred feet of width was a jungle. Scores of plant species grew in real soil and reached toward the ceiling. There were fruit trees, a large garden and flowers; brilliant beds of roses, daffodils, tulips and others were in full bloom. Connelly took a deep breath and smiled as the aromatic air swept through her nostrils. "What is this place?"

"A greenhouse. It provides a portion of our food and air." Peterson bent down and picked a deep red rose. He handed it to Connelly. "Amazing, isn't it?"

Connelly took the rose and placed its petals against her nose. She drew in a deep breath and felt her muscles relax.

"How does it smell?" a firm, feminine voice asked.

Connelly turned around and saw Choi standing in the doorway.

She wasn't sure if they were going to be in trouble for invading the bio-lab, but she decided it would be best to play it cool "Wonderful," she said. "But why are there flowers on board?"

Connelly offered the rose to Choi, who took it, smelled it and then handed it back. "Psychological studies have revealed that flowers have a calming effect on people. Long term space missions can be…stressful."

"That's an understatement," Peterson said.

Choi nodded. "Perhaps you'd like a bouquet for your room?"

Peterson chuckled.

Connelly was feeling more comfortable now. Choi seemed to have no problem with them being in the bio-lab. "What are these?" she asked, motioning to the test tube-like devices.

"Plant incubators." Choi walked to one of the larger units. "Watch."

Choi reached into a small pouch that sat atop the nearest table. She pulled out a single, tiny object that Connelly thought looked like a seed. After twisting off the glass top, Choi pushed the seed into the soil that filled the black base of the plant incubator. She replaced the top and flipped a switch on its side.

A mist sprayed into the glass tube, clouding the interior of the incubator. Connelly moved closer, trying to make out what, if anything, was happening inside the contraption. The glass slowly began to clear, like a windshield defrosting.

Peterson leaned in close next to Connelly. "I don't see anything."

"Just wait," Choi said.

The glass cleared and Connelly thought she saw the soil at the bottom twitch. She focused on the soil and saw it again. "It's moving," she said, her voice almost a whisper.

"Where?" Peterson asked.

Connelly pointed to the soil without a word. They watched, spellbound, as a small green sprout emerged from the soil and twisted upwards, growing at an incredible rate. After twenty seconds the sprout had reached three feet in height and had began to grow small branches and leaves. After another twenty seconds the four foot plant was pushing against the glass.

With her face almost mashed against the glass, Connelly gazed at the plant as the first signs of small, green tomatoes began to grow at the end of the nearest branch. Choi reached over and turned the machine off.

"We let the fruit begin to grow, but it has to finish at its normal speed or it spoils," Choi said.

"How…" Connelly stood up slowly. "How did you do that?"

"The plant's atoms are sped up, which causes a chain reaction in the plant's chemistry and cells. I'm not entirely familiar with the science behind them, but as you've seen, they basically make vegetation grow at an accelerated rate."

Connelly shook her head in disbelief.

Choi's expression changed as she looked from Connelly to Peterson and then back again. Connelly became suddenly self aware. She glanced at Peterson and noticed he was standing comfortably close to her. Their hands were almost touching.

"What are you two doing here, anyway?" Choi said, her tone suspicious. Choi looked at her watch. "Debrief is in ten minutes."

A look of shock appeared on Peterson's face. "We got lost."

Choi squinted at them, making no effort to hide her disbelief. "Then you can follow me to the conference room." Choi moved past them and strode to the door.

Peterson leaned over to Connelly. "It was fun while it lasted," he whispered.

Connelly crossed her arms. "You promised."

"So I lied," Peterson said. "Look, in my line of work, when you find something worthwhile, you go after it."

Connelly frowned playfully. "You're comparing me to dirt now?"

Peterson chuckled as he headed for the door. He turned to Connelly looking over his shoulder. "Dirt, no. A nice diorite maybe."

"A diorite," Connelly said, keeping pace behind Peterson, "doesn't sound too bad. What is it?"

"A rock."

Connelly laughed, but then sucked in her breath, not wanting Choi to hear her. As she exited the bio-lab, she glanced back and thought about how much the world around her was changing. Space exploration, extraterrestrial phenomenon, plant incubators. It seemed everything in the solar system was evolving around her.

9 – DEPLOYMENT

There were two things that Choi couldn't stand.

The first: infectious diseases, which she had spent the better part of her adult life battling on the job for the CDC, and personally after being diagnosed with Hepatitis C, which she contracted from her mother at birth—a fact that was kept from her employers at the CDC, and now, at the GEC.

The second was almost as bad: professional adults getting goo-goo eyes for each other, which she had spent all her life avoiding. She could feel the energy from Peterson and Connelly like it was a static charge in the air, and it made her cringe. To Choi, it seemed that the only human diseases that had no cure were lust, desire, love, and a slew of other emotions that made things of importance seem insignificant.

As she led Peterson and Connelly to the conference room from the bio-lab, she listened in on their conversations. Most topics seemed innocent enough, astrogeology, oceanography and extremophiles, but after joining up with the GEC, Choi spent enough time around crush-struck scientists to know that talking science and using big words was the equivalent of talking dirty to the layman. She'd attempted to be patient with them in the bio-lab, even amiable, but her patience was wearing thin.

Ever since making the move from the Center for Disease Control and Prevention, Choi had discovered a new world of annoyances. Six years ago an outbreak of a mutated common flu swept across the globe. Science predicted common illnesses would reemerge as modern plagues, but mankind had ignored the warnings, bathing in antibacterial soaps, popping antibiotics whenever a sore throat struck, and taking vaccines for every ailment imaginable. The resulting super germs were nearly unstoppable and humanity's immune systems—adapted to having antibiotics and vaccines do all the work—were weaker then a newborn baby's fifty years ago. But of all the new strains of germs, bacteria and viruses that cropped up around 2015, the flu was the worst.

The original outbreak started in Omaha, Nebraska and spread across North America, moving with the produce shipments. It had reached both coasts in three days and before anyone realized it was worse than the seasonal flu, it had leapt to every continent on Earth. Choi was relatively new to the CDC, but they recognized her talents immediately and put her on the first response task force.

Choi's work led to the development of a vaccine, which was mass produced and administered globally, saving countless lives. But the result, while a success for Choi, had been a stunning failure for the human race—two million people died from the flu in 2015.

Choi had dedicated her life to stopping illness before it got out of control. She'd become renowned in her field and a celebrity face at the CDC. It was almost on a daily basis that she was approached by a newspaper, magazine, television news show; even the FBI and CIA had tried to recruit her. But the strangest offer she received was from the GEC. She had laughed when Nancy Heintz introduced herself over the phone.

"What does the Global Exploration Corporation need with an infectious disease specialist?" Choi said with a note of sarcasm.

Choi remembered Director Heintz's next words perfectly. They had changed her life. "I am well aware of your achievements Dr. Choi, and I commend your work. The world is a safer place because of you. But new threats arrive at our doorstep every day. The Global Exploration Corporation's work places our staff at the outer reaches of the global frontier. Did you know that over seventy-five percent of new infectious diseases are first encountered by GEC employees?"

Choi had heard of several cases involving the GEC, but had never totaled them, and would have never guessed the percentage to be so high. Her interest was immediately piqued, though still reserved.

Nancy continued, "Working with us will give you first access to these diseases as well as provide a measure of safety for our scientists, who are some of the brightest minds on the planet. We would place you on the forefront, where your talents could be used to stop these diseases before even one human life was lost."

"But the GEC doesn't have the resources I would need to—"

"Dr. Choi, you will have *all* the resources you require. Even more than the CDC provides."

Choi was speechless. She'd been made the best offer anyone had yet to make. And it was from an organization that had nothing to do with infectious disease. Or did they? Choi's mind spun through the possibilities.

"What aren't you telling me?" Choi said.

Nancy was silent on the other end.

"Tell me now, or the answer is no."

What Nancy told her next sealed the deal. The human race was going to other worlds and if life was discovered it would almost certainly first be discovered in the form of microscopic germs, viruses and bacteria. The GEC was exposing the world to a vast spectrum of new dangers, and Choi, it seemed, was their chosen leader in the defense of humanity from the extraterrestrial sniffles.

When Choi found out about the Europa mission and the incident in the Arctic, she insisted on being on the mission. She couldn't sit back and monitor the situation, like she did with Mars. She had to be there at ground zero, because what she saw in the Arctic, at Peterson's discovery, was one of the most unusual, complex life forms she had ever seen. The man, Benson, had been killed in seconds with some kind of virus or poison that had simultaneously affected his mind and body. There was nothing else on Earth like it. She felt it was her position to make sure it stayed that way.

No one argued her point when she volunteered to be the mission's second in command. And now here she was in space, defending the earth from microscopic invaders and listening to a couple of scientists ogle over thermal vents.

The door to the conference room whooshed open. She led Peterson and Connelly inside. She was glad to see Harris, Willard and Robert all waiting inside. "Take your seats and we'll get started with debrief," she said to Peterson and Connelly.

Choi took her seat next to Harris and waited silently for him to speak, attempting to calm herself before the coming barrage of questions and answers.

"Deployment of the TES unit will commence in ten hours." Harris got right to the point. It's one of the reasons Choi agreed to serve under him. "The ground crew will follow one hour after touch down."

Harris took time to look each crew member directly in the eyes. "But before you get your feet wet, we need to get you acquainted with your new space suits."

Choi could see the concerned looks already emerging around the table. She wondered how this crew would handle significant discovery if they were thrown out of sorts by a new space suit.

Harris spoke. "We won't be using the bulky suits you had during training. What we have for you is much better. Your work will go much more quickly in these, moving around will be considerably easier and if the worst should happen, they can withstand the polar opposite pressures of open space and deep ocean waters."

Choi picked up a large metal suitcase that sat on the floor next to her chair. She set it on the table, popped the latches, opened it up and swiveled it around so the crew could see its contents.

Inside the suitcase was a folded up, grayish blue space suit that looked as thin and as smooth as silk, along with a matching helmet. Choi took the suit by the shoulders and lifted it out of the suitcase. It unfolded in her hands, looking like a cross between a biohazard suit and a traditional space suit.

She could see the aghast looks on the crew's faces. Knowing they would soon express their doubts as to how this flimsy suit could protect them from both space and ocean depths, Choi launched right into her prepared speech. "This is a newly designed space suit formally called a Personal Multi-Pressure Space Suit, or simply called a PMS."

Choi paused, giving Willard time to finish chuckling.

"It is much lighter than traditional space suits," Choi continued, "and provides ten times the comfort, safety and maneuverability than the old suits. A small pack on the back provides air filtration, heat and pressurization, all controlled by this small screen on the left wrist."

Choi held the left sleeve out for everyone to see.

Robert started to raise his hand. "How—"

"Before you bombard me with questions, let me finish my briefing," Choi said.

Robert yanked his hand down.

"The PMS is made from a flawless silicon reconstruction of spider's silk, which is the strongest natural fiber in existence, only made stronger by man. They are impossible to tear, cut, or pierce. They aid in protecting the human body from radiation, micrometeorites and in combination with a reinforced honeycombed exoshell, they provide a stable, comfortable, pressurized atmosphere."

Choi waited for the first comment. She didn't have to wait long.

"I hate spiders," Willard said.

Choi resisted the urge to roll her eyes. She knew Willard was attempting to be humorous, but his humor was often ill-timed. If it were not for his perfect record when it came to safety and his accurate prediction of unpredictable circumstances, she would have considered leaving him on board Surveyor during the initial landing, if only to avoid hearing more jokes.

"What about the face mask?" Connelly said. "The suit is impervious, but what about the mask? It looks like it could break pretty easily."

Choi kicked herself for forgetting to explain the mask. "The mask is composed of a self-healing alloy. The masks are shatter resistant, but can be cracked under extreme duress. However, if you simply close your eyes, hold your breath and count to ten, your mask will reseal itself at ninety percent its original strength."

"They've been tested in space and excel beyond all our safety standards," Harris said, standing to his feet. "If you could, just gather around. We have suits for all of you and Choi will help you put them on."

As the group stood and began shuffling towards her, Choi felt some relief. Loss of human life had been her enemy—her nemesis—for years. She looked down at the row of suitcases lined up at her feet. The fact that the crew would be wearing PMSs at least meant that something severe would have to happen for one of them to die.

Choi relaxed as she reached down for Connelly's suitcase. She felt certain the crew would be safe. What could be more severe than the bombardment they had already survived?

ׁ   ׁ   ׁ   ׁ   ׁ

Sitting motionless for ten minutes straight, Connelly found her palms to be unusually sweaty. Her stomach churned like she'd eaten a cup of butter and her mouth was painfully dry. The symptoms, at first, seemed similar to an anxiety attack. But Connelly's past anxiety had been brought on by simple choices. She had once stood in front of the banana display at the grocery store for fifteen minutes, frantically trying to choose which bunch was best. There was one with five bananas, but they were too small, one with four, but they were too big, and the bunch with five that were just the right size, were too green.

Thinking about her current situation, waiting in the command center, killing time until TES was launched, Connelly knew that this was not a banana episode. She decided to chalk it up to nerves and pushed the subject to the recesses of her mind. Wiping her damp hands on her jumpsuit, Kathy sat up straighter and asked, "How much longer?"

Harris spun around in his console chair. A wide grin was stretched across his face. "Deployment is prepped. We're ready if you're ready."

Connelly felt her stomach stir. She tightened her stomach muscles and bit her lip for a moment.

Why am I so nervous? What am I afraid of?

"Ready," Connelly said, and then looked at Robert, who was seated with Peterson and Willard at a six foot, round table at the center of the room. "Ready?"

"Ah, yes...I've been ready for the past ten hours," Robert said with a grin. Connelly noticed his legs were bouncing nervously. Robert saw Connelly's eye on his legs. "I can't help it. I'm nervous."

Right there with you, Connelly thought.

She stood and shook her hands out, willing the nervousness out of her body. She rolled her shoulders and walked to Harris's side. "What are the chances of anything going wrong?"

The question was meant as space filler—something to occupy her mind. But the way Harris's fingers froze over the keyboard and the suddenness with which he held his breath, told Connelly that it was a loaded question. Harris turned to her and sighed. "You really want to know?"

"I—I guess," Connelly said.

"Cause you look nervous," Harris said with a sympathetic glance.

"I do?"

Harris nodded. "Look, I'm the best there is. I wouldn't be here otherwise. If I can't get this baby to set down on the ice without a hitch, no one can."

Connelly forced a smile.

Harris took her hand and squeezed it. "Just sit back and enjoy the show." Harris pulled a remote from his pocket, pointed it at the ceiling and pushed the button. After turning a hazy white, the ceiling became transparent, revealing Europa.

Connelly instantly felt her apprehension fade away, replaced by a sense of wonder she thought could never fade, no matter how many times she saw this view. Connelly took a seat next to Willard.

"Don't worry, boss," Willard said, "There's an extremophile down there with your name on it."

Connelly gave an unsure smile and returned her eyes to the view above, which was in fact, below. "Please, God, let this work."

"On my mark," Harris said to Choi, who was seated at the next console over. He turned his head to the crew, his smile growing. "Launch."

Choi pushed a single button at her console and a dull *thunk* reverberated from somewhere else on the ship. Connelly stared up at the clear ceiling. She realized she was holding her breath when her chest began to burn. She let the air out and sucked in another breath. Then something she had never dreamed could be possible floated into view.

The fifty foot, triple diamond shape of TES eased away from the Surveyor, drifting slowly toward Europa. It looked like a black spinning jewel, like some fantastical magical gem. She imagined that entire nations would have fought and died for TES, and now they were sending her away. Connelly felt a wave of sadness sweep through her, but it was quickly replaced by excitement when a burst of blue flame shot out of TES's exterior.

Connelly gripped the table's edge and opened her mouth. Before she could speak, she clenched her jaw tight, having almost made a fool of herself. The blue flames originated from directional jets installed by the GEC. She had forgot they were there, but quickly remembered what they were. Without them, TES would fall to Europa and crash on impact, destroying her life's work.

TES continued away from the ship, blue jets erupting every now and then, adjusting its course. Occasionally, Connelly would hear Harris or Choi speak some rapid words and work their consoles in a hurry, but her attention was firmly fixed on TES. Connelly broke into a wide smile as TES, which was now the size of a quarter began to open her panels.

She looks like a blooming flower.

The panels opened until they lay out flat, like a defunct radiation symbol. Blue flames burst several times, sending TES into a slight spin as she continued toward the surface. It was soon the size of a dime and in less than a minute, looked like a black speck hovering over the white surface of the moon. Connelly looked away when she could no longer see TES.

"How are we doing?" she asked.

Harris ignored her question and glanced at Choi. "Stabilize."

"On it."

"How are we?"

"A little hot."

"Got it…Altitude."

"Ten."

Ten feet?

"Engage clamps."

"Done."

"Initiate feed."

"Feed is…activated."

"Well done."

Harris and Choi simultaneously leaned back in their chairs, looking very relaxed. Harris glanced up and saw Connelly standing behind him. "Did you say something?"

"Are we? Did you?"

Harris leaned forward, tapped a few keys on his keyboard, and leaned back with a smile. The screen in front of him blinked to life, displaying a white landscape. The sky was dark and covered with stars, the ground was gleaming and in the distance, a patch of red color could be seen. Connelly leaned in close and the rest of the crew gathered around.

Connelly looked back at Robert, who had his hand to his mouth and was chuckling. She looked back at Harris. "Is this?"

Harris cracked his knuckles and let out a slight laugh. "One small step."

Peterson placed his hand on Connelly's shoulder and squeezed. "You did it. Welcome to Europa."

10 – GOING DOWN

Willard stepped forward, hearing only the swishing sounds his freshly donned PMS suit made when he moved. He looked at the door in front of him marked, "Decon," and wondered how the process would feel. Decontamination, other than a steaming hot shower, was not part of his daily routine. Not that he minded. Contamination was one of his primary concerns. He'd taken Choi aside after the last debriefing and grilled her about the possible dangers that would be involved with the crew coming into contact with alien biology.

Standing in the doorway of the conference room, Choi appeared to be hesitant at first, but ensured him that the true danger of biological contamination was human to alien. If life exists outside of Earth, and we step into that ecosystem, we are the invaders—we are the invasive species. It occurred on Earth in the 1800 and 1900's when germs, disease and various sycophants brought to the New World wreaked havoc on ecosystems that had no defense. Only the ecosystems that had highly adaptive defense systems survived.

"That is the danger of humankind," Choi said. "In the past we've sought to protect only ourselves from new environments. Not the other way around. The result was the loss of eighty-five percent of the world's plant and animal species."

Willard felt himself relax around Choi for the first time. She spoke passionately and he could swear a genuine smile was seeping onto her face.

It seems our second in command has a soft side after all, Willard thought, *for germs.*

"But what about the dangers to the crew? If we can infect other species with our germs, what about the other way around?" Willard asked.

"As I mentioned, the human race always protects itself first." Choi leaned against the door frame. "And we're no different. Unlike your typical unintelligent life-form, which develops defenses through millions of years of natural selection, we can prepare for the worst in advance."

Willard nodded.

"The electromagnetic shielding, the PMS suits, decontamination procedures… We're prepared to defend against microbial invaders."

"But how do we know it will work against something new?"

"In theory, we don't."

Willard opened his mouth to speak, but the protest he nearly raised was cut short.

"I designed the decon system myself," Choi said. "I guarantee you, nothing short of a human in a PMS could survive the process."

Willard shifted his weight. "You designed the decon?"

Choi appeared stymied for a moment. Willard wondered if her involvement in the decon system was supposed to be public knowledge.

"I uh, yes. I designed the system."

Willard became more curious. "Forgive me for asking, but what do you know about decontamination? Is that standard astronaut training?"

Choi looked at the floor and then sighed. She returned her eyes to Willard's and took a sudden casual demeanor. "I was with the CDC for a few years before moving to the GEC."

"CDC…" Willard said, letting his mind fill in the full phrase. "You were with the Center for Disease Control?" He didn't hide his rising apprehension.

"My history with the CDC had nothing to do with my qualifications for this mission," Choi said.

Willard wasn't sure whether to believe her or not, but he felt certain he wouldn't get an honest answer if there was more to the story. "A lucky bonus then?"

"Very lucky," Choi said, regaining her relaxed posture. "Their previous decon system had several flaws. The crew and the alien environments will be safer from contamination than ever before."

"How's that?"

"Decon consists of an alcohol solution spray down—three variants, an O2 wash down, an anti-bacterial mist to kill anything that survived the alcohol, a second O2 wash and exposure to low level radiation and extreme heat at the end. We'll be comfortable in our PMS's the entire time. Won't feel a thing.

And anything that survived would also have to withstand the vacuum of space. Nothing, microbe or otherwise, could survive. We pass through decon on the way out for the environment's protection and on the way in for ours."

Willard chewed through the information and came up with only one question. "What about the germs inside the suit? You can't decontaminate our bodies."

Choi's eyebrows rose. "Good for you, Mr. Willard. The solitary remaining risk of contamination lies in the rupture of our PMS suits or face masks. The decompression of the suit will pull air out of the suit, still protecting the suit's wearer from contamination, but exposing the environment to any germs the wearer might be carrying. So as far as crew safety goes, we're in no biologic danger."

Willard wasn't sure if he felt better or not, but she had answered his questions and then some. "Guess it would be bad if any of us had an infectious disease then, huh?"

Willard wasn't expecting the response he got to his off-hand comment. Choi's casual demeanor vanished and was replaced by a steely gaze. "Very bad," she said before turning and walking away.

Standing alone before the decon room, Willard now wondered how well the PMS would protect him. *If it can survive decon*, Willard thought, *it can handle space.* The light above the door flashed green, signaling that Connelly was through decon and the rest of the crew was now waiting on him before they descended to Europa's surface.

The door slid open, revealing a long, dimly lit hallway. A conveyor belt moved slowly forward, leading to four separate compartments separated by hanging sheets of plastic.

Like stepping into the throat of a whale.

"Please step forward," a voice commanded.

Willard had heard the voice several times as the rest of the crew went through decon before him, but it still made him jump. He stepped on to the belt and was pulled into the chamber. The hallway dimmed as the hatch sealed behind him. A loud spraying mist coated his body, killing everything it came into contact with.

ℕ   ℕ   ℕ   ℕ   ℕ

Lander One's hatch craned up, revealing a bright white landscape that reminded Connelly of Antarctica. If it weren't for the way her body floated in Europa's low gravity, she would have felt right at home. Of course the luminous landscape mixed with a starry sky was something she had never seen before. On earth, when the sun was shining, the sky was blue, but here, on a moon with the tiniest of atmospheres, the skyline was perpetually filled with stars.

After an anxious ride on the Lander, which looked like a cross between a Ferrari and a Winnebago, Connelly took her first step into a low gravity environment with a bit too much jump in her step. She soared seven feet out before landing. Smiling wide, she turned around and looked back as the rest of the crew exited the silvery grey Lander.

Robert leaped out of the open hatch and landed next to Connelly. "Amazing." Robert bounced around Connelly, "So strange."

Willard, Peterson and Choi, exited the Lander and quickly adjusted to their low-grav legs. Choi spoke into her headset microphone, knowing that while on the surface, every one of them, and Harris, who was monitoring them from the Surveyor, could hear every word she said. "Everyone check out?"

Nods and yeses all around.

"Peterson and I will be collecting ice samples from the nearby red streak," Choi said. "Connelly, Samuels and Willard, you will begin the melting process. Check in every half hour. Meet back here in two."

"And if anything goes wrong?" Willard asked.

"Head back to Lander One ASAP and let us know on the way. We can evac and be back to the Surveyor quicker than most ambulance trips."

Willard nodded.

"Make sure to switch your com over to your specific crew's frequency," Choi said as she moved to the rear of the lander. She punched a few buttons on a keypad built into the rear of the Lander. "Peterson and I are on Com 1, you three take Com 2. We don't want to hear everyone's conversations at the same time. If you have an emergency, switch to the emergency channel and everyone will hear you."

The rear hatch of the lander slowly opened. Two long tracks slid down to the ice. A large, thick wheeled ATV rolled gently down the tracks and stopped at the bottom. The small vehicle was sleek but sturdy—the SUV of moon rovers. A small, two-wheeled trailer was attached to the back of the ATV, designed to safely transport a wide variety of samples. It had freezers to keep ice frozen, dry tubs for soil samples, even sterile containment units for biological matter.

Connelly couldn't stand the anticipation anymore. She knew the answers they sought were still a long way away, but for the first time ever, she was going to see her creation, TES, in action. Even inside the temperature controlled PMS, she could feel her underarms beginning to perspire. She put her hand on Robert's shoulder. "Ready?"

"You kidding?" Robert said. Both of them turned and took a few steps toward TES, which could be seen as a black splotch on the white plains, one hundred yards away.

Choi took the driver's seat and Peterson climbed on behind her.

"Hey Kathy," Peterson said.

Connelly turned around as she bounced away. She could see Peterson's smiling face behind his PMS suit's mask. "Hope you find what you're looking for."

Connelly waived. "You too."

"I'm switching you off now. See you in two." Tires spun, launching the ATV forward. It cruised easily over the ice with its spiked tread.

Connelly did her best to hide her smile from Robert, who was looking at her with suspicious eyes. Using her right hand to work the control panel on her left wrist, Connelly switched from Com 1 to Com 2. "Can you hear me, Robert?"

"You two a thing now?" Robert asked, not amused.

"I'll take that as a yes." Connelly bounded forward in the low gravity, hoping to avoid the conversation. Luckily for her, Willard wasn't as interested as Robert.

Willard landed next to Connelly after taking a huge leap. "How come we don't get a speedy thingy?"

Robert chuckled. "Probably because you call it a speedy thingy."

It took the three of them ten minutes to bumble their way across the frozen surface of Europa. No one spoke much; they just looked around, admiring the never ending incredible view. Jupiter was directly in front of them. Connelly couldn't get over the planet's size. When Europa's rotation had them facing Jupiter, the king of the solar system took up the entire view. She recalled what it had been like seeing the Grand Canyon for the first time. The sense of dizziness and awe. The Grand Canyon was inconsequential compared to Jupiter.

Of course, Connelly knew that for all of Jupiter's splendor, it also posed one of the greatest mission threats. If the electromagnetic shielding provided by Surveyor, the landers or TES gave out, they'd have six minutes to get the system back online or get six feet beneath the ice.

Connelly took her place behind the TES control panel. The sphere, which was clear on top and solid metal alloy on the bottom, was dangling over the exposed ice at the center of TES. Three cranes, attached to TES in between the three large panels, which now lay flat, held the sphere aloft and provided electricity, heat, air, pressurization and communications. In addition, the cables also contained heating filaments, which kept the melted water from refreezing. Once a hole was melted in the ice, it would fill with water from the ocean beneath. If left alone, it would quickly refreeze and trap the TES sphere below.

Stepping away from the control panel, Connelly approached the sphere and reached out her hand, placing it on its smooth exterior. "Okay, baby, this is it. Show me what you got." Connelly slid her hand off the sphere and took a jump back. She turned to Robert, who had taken her place at the control panel. "Heating coil status?"

Robert glanced at the screen. "A-Okay."

"Support cables?"

"Holding..." Robert smiled. "Kath, we're as ready as we're going to be."

Connelly moved behind the control panel with Robert and Willard. "Guys, I just wanted to say..."

"Boss," Willard said. "Quit stalling and hit the damn button."

Connelly laughed, put her thumb on a button labeled, ENGAGE, and pushed it down. Moments later, wavy distortions of heat could be seen streaming off the metallic bottom of the sphere. After thirty seconds of silence, the sphere began to lower toward the ice.

Watching with the eyes of a hawk, Connelly saw the top layer of ice begin to melt as the sphere descended. Moments later, the sphere made physical contact with the ice. A plume of steam launched into the air, propelled by the great heat of the sphere. Connelly's facemask clouded as the area fogged over.

The entire event was perfectly silent. In the vacuum of space, which they were exposed to on the moon's surface, sound could not exist. But she could hear the loud cheers of Robert, who raised his hands in victory. "There she goes!"

The steam, which had formed a cloud over a fifty foot radius began to cluster and refreeze. The gravity of the moon, while weak, was still strong enough to pull the ice crystals back to the surface. Connelly held her hands out as the newly formed snowflakes descended.

A chill suddenly shook her body when she realized that the snowflakes looked like the explosive charged particles that had nearly destroyed the Surveyor. She began to imagine what would have happened to the ship if they hadn't been able to clear the cloud. But before her mind could fully commit to the subject, her eyes transmitted new information that took precedence over every other thought in Connelly's mind. The snow and steam had cleared enough that she could see the area the TES sphere had been.

The sphere is gone! she thought.

Connelly took a careful step forward, looking into the newly formed, ten foot wide hole in the ice. Inside was a pool of water, perhaps five feet deep, and below that, beneath the shimmering alien liquid, was the TES sphere, moving steadily downward.

She looked back at Robert and Willard, who wore smiles on their faces. "It's working. TES is working."

₪   ₪   ₪   ₪   ₪

On the trip down from the Surveyor to Europa's surface, Peterson had felt a little apprehensive. He remembered what happened to Benson. The fear in his eyes. The voices he heard before dying. Convulsions. Blindness. Bleeding. All of it in just seconds. But once he had set foot on the moon, he became more relaxed. The beauty of the place usurped all his fears.

Until Choi hit the gas. For three minutes now, she'd been weaving back and forth, dodging ice heaves, taking corners at breakneck speeds, and sending the ATV catapulting in the air as the bounced over rises in the ice.

His immediate protest was met with quick, "Testing the limits of the ATV. Just hold on."

As they headed toward a steep rise in the ice, Peterson decided it would be best to close his eyes. He knew the PMS suit couldn't be torn open and the mask could reseal, but that wouldn't stop an impact from breaking his bones. As they neared the rise, Peterson closed his eyes. He could feel the ATV moving. It's rumbling engine silently shook his torso. Then they hit the steep rise, moving up at rollercoaster speed, Peterson prepared to feel the surface of the moon disappear, and then, maybe a minute later, they would crash back down to the ice and tend to their wounds.

But rather than moving up and out, Peterson suddenly felt himself jam forward into Choi's back. He heard her grunt in his headset. Then they were stopped.

Peterson hopped off the ATV and glared at Choi. "What the hell is wrong with you, Choi? First you try to kill us by driving like a madman and then you try to break my neck by hitting the brakes!"

Choi was motionless.

"Hello? I'm talking here…Choi…Choi?" Peterson studied the expression on her face. She looked dumbfounded. "What's wrong?"

Choi's raised her arm and pointed straight out.

Peterson felt a sudden twist in his stomach. Peterson followed Choi's extended finger and found himself gazing out over a wide valley. His mind went blank and he could swear he felt himself floating out of his body. What he was seeing was totally, utterly, unreal.

After an entire minute of staring, he turned to Choi as she turned to him. Their eyes locked.

Choi spoke slowly. "They…they look—"

Peterson finished her thought.

"Alive."

11 – FIELDS OF RED

The agonizing slowness of TES's descent began to drive Robert crazy. He'd been pacing for a half hour and was starting to feel his muscles twitch. He paused his slow motion pace and shook out his arms. "I can't take this," he said. "How much longer?"

"No way to know," Connelly said as she hovered over the TES control panel, watching for the slightest change in the status display. "Not until we break through."

"If there's water at all," Robert said.

Willard looked up from the nearby TES panel, where he'd been lying down, enjoying the view. "What do you mean, *if?*"

Robert felt the urge to adjust his glasses, but they were unreachable behind his mask. "There's, ah, no guarantee we're going to find water. Science says there is water beneath the ice, but science has been wrong before."

"What about all this ice?" Willard asked. "If there's ice there's water."

"Now he's a scientist," Robert said with a chuckle. "Ice, technically speaking, is frozen water. But frozen water cannot support life...as we know it. And since this is a search for life, we need to find water of the non-frozen variety."

"But the guys at the GEC—"

"They're placing bets," Robert said. Robert knew that most scientists were also great gamblers. They pegged a theory, backed it up with original thinking, found proof that supported their hypothesis and then did the leg work, proving the theory correct. They were at the final stage in this process, final proof. Robert looked to Connelly, "You can explain it."

Willard bounced toward them and stopped next to Connelly at the control panel. Connelly took a deep breath and let it out slowly, allowing her first words to merge with her breath half way through. "There are several theories for how water might be warmed beneath the ice of Europa's surface; tidal flexing caused by Jupiter's gravitational pull, thermal venting, a molten core. The list goes on. But until someone drills a hole in the ice and sees the water for themselves, it's all just theory."

"Like the Big Bang," Willard said.

"Precisely," Robert added with a raised finger. "We've found all kinds of evidence that supports the theory, but it has never been more than that."

"Guys..."

Robert was about to launch into the history of the science versus religion debate and didn't even register Connelly's voice. "Now, if you recall—"

"Robert." Connelly's voice was firm this time and captured Robert's attention.

Looking at Connelly, Robert could see her muscles were tense, even through the PMS suit. Her hands held firm grips on the sides of the control panel.

"What is it?" Robert asked as he bumbled toward the panel.

Willard looked over Connelly's shoulder. "Something's coming through."

Robert stopped next to Connelly and looked at the display screen. Numbers were scrolling across the screen as the system analyzed the new information.

"What's it doing?" Willard asked.

"Receiving data," Connelly replied.

"Did it find something?"

Robert looked over at Willard with nervous eyes. "That, or it malfunctioned and is reporting the problem."

All three pairs of eyes were glued to the screen. The text began to transform into words. It displayed one line at a time.

EVENT REPORT
DESCENT CEASED
DEPTH — 01.534 MILES
CAUSE — NEW SURFACE LOCATED
ANALYZING...
ANALYZING...
ANALYZING...
ANALYZING...
TEMPERATURE – 55 DEGREES FARENHEIT
CONFIRMATION – LIQUID WATER DETECTED

    ऱ   ऱ   ऱ   ऱ   ऱ

"Do you realize what this is?" Peterson said, as he bent down at the edge of their earth-shattering discovery. The view before him was one hundred percent alien to Earth, yet Peterson, Choi and a few other GEC employees had seen cell samples taken from a meteorite that crashed in the arctic and killed Benson. He hadn't seen them at full size, but the red coloration and maroon soil was identical.

Choi looked at Peterson, her eyes wide. "Is this..."

Peterson nodded. "This is it. From the meteorite. This is it."

He stood to his feet and took in the unbelievable view for the second time. Spread out before him was a field, an endless field of red, gelatinous cucumber-like plants. Bunched in small groups of three to seven, they stood erect like tight clusters of crimson bowling pins. As though pushed by a nonexistent wind, they slowly danced from side to side, shimmering in the light cast by the distant sun.

Turning his head from side to side, Peterson realized that the entire expanse, which was miles long and hundreds of yards across was covered with the red organisms. They weren't just surviving on the surface of a frozen, radiation-doused moon that had the thinnest imaginable atmosphere, they were thriving!

Peterson hopped to the ATV's trailer and opened a hatch on the back.

"What are you doing?" Choi asked, crossing her arms.

"Getting samples."

"I don't have to remind you what a small amount of this material did to your crew member."

"Benson ingested it; took it into his body. I have no intention of repeating his mistake or allowing anyone else to do the same. You built the fail-safes in the lab yourself." Peterson took a small shovel and a glass canister out of the trailer and headed back to the red field. "This is what we came here for, Choi. It's why you're here."

Choi loosed her crossed arms. "If I sense anything is going wrong, even for a second, we get rid of it."

Peterson paused by the field, prepared to strike the ice. He glanced at Choi briefly, then looked back to the nearest patch of red organisms and raised the shovel up. Before he could swing the shovel down and pierce the ice, Choi had his arm locked in her grip. He starred at her defiantly. "Hey."

"The GEC gave me full authority to pull the plug on this entire mission if I thought there was a risk of infection. You're here to collect and study rocks. You answer to me. Am I clear?" Choi let go of his arm.

Peterson stabbed the shovel into the ice, just in front of the nearest patch of red cucumbers. "Crystal," he said. "Now if you'll give me some room I'd like to—" Peterson pushed down on the handle, raising the shovel up and yanking a portion of the organisms away from the field, snapping what appeared to be roots. The action caused a chain reaction. Like a shockwave, moving out from the fresh wound, the rest of the field bowed in the opposite direction, like ripples on a pond. It happened so quickly that Peterson hardly had time to register what he'd seen. "Did you see that?"

"Are you trying to change the subject?"

"No..." Peterson poured the sample he'd taken into the glass canister, turned back to the field and stabbed the shovel in a second time. Nothing happened.

Peterson pulled the sample up, again snapping the roots. Still nothing happened. Peterson sighed. "Must have been seeing things." Peterson placed the second sample into the canister.

Choi slid the cover onto the canister and sealed it. "I think that's enough."

Peterson smiled. "You should learn how to relax." He picked up the canister and carried it back to the trailer. "I think when the GEC learns what we've discovered, the balance of power is going to shift. No offense. Really. I think you need to be here, but this mission is about one thing and one thing only."

"And what is that?"

Peterson replaced the shovel and locked down the trailer. "Life."

"I suppose then, that the GEC and you should ask the question. Now that alien life has been discovered, what is more valuable?" Choi swept her hand out toward the sea of red. "Alien life, or human life?"

Peterson eyed the passenger's seat with apprehension. He didn't want another roller coaster ride. Moving as quickly as he could, Peterson bounced to the front of the ATV and hopped onto the driver's seat. He looked over at Choi and patted the passenger's seat, motioning for her to get on. She frowned and moved toward the seat.

"Choi," Peterson said. "They're little red cucumbers... If we don't eat or breathe them, what's the worst they could do?"

ᴎ   ᴎ   ᴎ   ᴎ   ᴎ

Connelly felt her knees shaking as she inched towards the edge of the newly formed, mile and a half deep hole in Europa's surface. She peered over the edge. The vertical tunnel stretched down for one-hundred feet where it met the water that rose up from the ocean surface. "Why is the water so high?"

Robert looked over the edge. "It's like a giant straw. The water pressure below is pushing it up until its weight, which is greatly reduced on Europa, balances the force. The same thing happens when you put a straw in a glass of water—the liquid rises higher in the straw. If not for TES's heated cables keeping the water warm, it would have already begun to refreeze and reseal the whole. Wounds in the surface must fill and freeze very quickly."

Connelly felt a wave of dizziness warble through her mind. She leaned away from the edge.

"Careful near that edge, boss." Willard said

Connelly turned to Willard, who was standing a few feet back, checking the time on his wrist display. "Aren't I always?" She wondered if her nervousness showed through her shaky voice. She couldn't tell.

"Astounding," Robert said. He was looking down, into the void, shaking his head. "Can you believe this worked? I mean, I, ah, I knew it would work...but on a moon?"

Connelly knew exactly how he felt. TES had been her life's work and she had always pictured this day, the moment when TES would be deployed, melt through the ice and discover alien life. But she had always pictured it taking place in the Antarctic. They would cheer over some hot chocolate, vid-phone some colleagues and go back to work. But here, on Europa, the sensation was very different. TES, while a true achievement seemed insignificant to their current surroundings. Connelly felt as though her dream now realized had become cheapened by Europa, and while she couldn't deny the stunning success and wonderment of it all, she was beginning to resent Jupiter and all her moons.

"Hate to be the bearer of bad news," Willard said, "but we haven't heard from Choi or Peterson this entire time. Am I wrong, or did she say to check in every half hour?"

Robert's forehead became crinkled. "No...you're right." Robert looked at his wrist display. "And it's been almost two."

"And I think we can all agree," Willard said, "that Choi is not the type to be late."

"Unless they found something incredible," Connelly said.

"Or are unable," Willard said.

"Switch over to Com 1," Connelly said. All three quickly made the switch. "Peterson, Choi, this is Connelly. Can you hear me?"

Connelly and Robert shared a nervous glance. "If you're on Com 1 and can hear me, please respond."

A crackle of static filled their ears for an instant and then disappeared. Then it was replaced by a voice. "an hear you... ait until you...what we discov..."

Connelly felt a surge of panic. It was Peterson's voice, but he was yelling. Was he in pain? Were they in trouble? Connelly spoke louder. "Are you okay? Is anyone hurt?"

"What...No... 're fine."

Connelly relaxed. The message was broken, but clear. "What were you saying before?"

"...found something...t's unbelievable!"

"What? What did you find?"

"ife..."

Connelly felt like ripping PMS suit off, throwing her headset on the ground and smashing it. "Say again? I can barely hear you."

"ife, Connelly. We found life!"

Connelly gasped. Her mind spun. He said *life*. "But...what...Michael, we just finished melting through the surface. TES hasn't performed any tests yet. We haven't found *anything* yet."

"No," Peterson said. "On...surface."

Connelly's eyes went wide. They found life on the surface! Without thinking, Connelly took a step back, but instead of feeling the firm surface of the frozen moon beneath her foot, she felt nothing. Connelly yelped as she began to fall backward, into the chasm. Her arms flailed madly, but only added to her momentum.

Craning her head to the side, Connelly could see she was falling into the pit. She saw the water shimmering one hundred feet below and wondered if she would survive the impact in the low gravity. She imagined she would, and that the PMS suit would keep her from freezing and drowning, but TES would have to be retracted to get her out of the hole and that could take an hour. She felt sure she didn't have enough air left.

A voice shouted in Connelly's ear, so loud it hurt. She didn't make out a single word. Then the voice came again, "Raise your arms!"

Willard.

Connelly had learned to trust that voice. She knew the harsh tone that took over Willard's voice in times of crisis. It meant, *listen to me and you'll live.* She listened to it every time and was alive today because of it. Connelly didn't hesitate. She raised her arms toward space.

Less than a second later, Willard's body sailed into view above her. He was moving fast and had his hands outstretched toward her. Connelly realized that for Willard to already be here, he must have taken action before she had reached a forty five degree angle.

"Take my hands!" Willard shouted.

With outstretched fingers, Connelly reach for Willard's hands as the floated past. Their fingers touched, frantically searching for a grip on the other's hands. Then they connected. In an instant, their hands were locked. Connelly felt a tug on her shoulders as her arms straightened out, pulled by Willard's forward motion. The falling sensation changed instantly to that of weightlessness as she was pulled up away from the pit.

Connelly looked up and saw Willard's body flip over as they moved forward, but Willard never let go. As Willard moved out of view, Connelly felt her speed increase. She was being whipped away from the hole! Suddenly, Willard's grip on her hands released. She reached out for him, but found nothing to hold on to. Her view rotated as she flipped, head over heels through the low gravity.

As she came around, the TES hole came into view again. She had cleared it! But something horrific caught her eye—a pair of booted feet disappearing over the edge! "Ethan!"

Connelly hit the ice and grunted. The impact wasn't hard enough to cause injury, but with the distraction of Willard falling into the pit, it was unexpected. After rolling for a few feet, Connelly leapt to her feet and surged toward the hole, nearly flinging herself back in. "Willard!"

"It's okay, boss," Willard's voice said through her headset. "As long as the big man doesn't lose his grip, I'll be fine."

As Connelly moved to the hole, she could see that Robert had a grip on a thin wire that was stretched out over the edge of the hole. She reached the precipice and looked over. Willard was dangling ten feet down, bouncing against the side.

"Robert," Willard said, "how you doing?"

"Well, you're much lighter in the low gravity, but I wouldn't try anything funny."

"Right. You guys want to pull me out now?" Connelly rushed around the border of the hole, careful not to repeat her folly. After reaching Robert she took hold of the cord and together, they yanked Willard up and onto the TES platform. Willard was exasperated, but smiling. "Extreme..." he said between deep breaths.

Connelly was out of breath too. "Willard...that was...crazy.... We both could...have fallen...in."

Willard laughed. "You *did* fall in."

Connelly smiled.

"Forgive me for not paying more attention to your near death experience, Kathy," Robert said, "But I believe there is a more pressing matter that demands our instant attention."

The information came rocketing back into Connelly's mind. Peterson had discovered life.

On the surface.

12 – EUROPHIDS

"Where did you say these came from?" Connelly said as she bent over one of the several glass containers, each of which held a single sample of the red, gelatinous cucumbers. But the cucumbers were no longer standing tall. All but one lay on their sides, limp and by comparison, lifeless. At the base of each sample was a patch of ruddy soil and a mass of snapped roots where they had been pulled apart from the rest. The largest of the bunch was still erect, balanced on a larger segment of soil.

"From the red streak," Peterson said, looking extremely pleased. "The entire area was covered in them."

Connelly looked flabbergasted. The chances of them finding life in such an inhospitable environment was a statistical improbability. Yet she couldn't deny that the strange organisms spread out before her on the lab tables of the Surveyor's level 5 lab, did not come from Earth.

"We now believe," Choi said, "that all of Europa's streaks are covered with these organisms."

Connelly shook her head, trying to imagine how it was possible.

Willard leaned down close to one of the containers. "They look like they came from cucumber-shaped Jell-O molds. Can we call them Jell-Os?"

Robert flitted Willard aside as he rounded the table, wielding a computer tablet and pen. He made a flurry of notes while moving swiftly from one sample to the next. "How can you even think of Jell-O in the midst of a discovery of this…ah, this magnitude."

Willard crossed his arms and took a step back. "All I'm saying is that they should have a name."

Connelly nodded and looked at Peterson. "You found them."

Peterson stared at the blood-red organisms. "Europhids… Not the technical name of course. I'll let you biology types figure that out. But for now, Europhids."

Harris entered the lab with a bright smile on his face. "Already naming our new friends?"

Connelly hadn't seen Captain Harris since they arrived back on the Surveyor. She felt a new calm fall over the excited crew. "Good to see you, Timothy."

Harris nodded and proceeded to take a closer look at the Europhid samples. "Has the discovery been documented?"

"We took digital stills and video," Choi said. "Each of the…Europhids has been weighed, measured and tagged for future reference."

Connelly stepped forward. "We were hoping to begin taking samples for analysis. We'd like to run the gamut of tests. Cultures, DNA, genetic sequencing. I can't even begin to imagine what these will look like under the electron microscope."

Harris stood up straight, diverting his eyes from the Europhids to Connelly. "All of that is going to have to wait."

Robert stopped his note taking. "What? Why?"

A flurry of anxious questions flooded Connelly's mind and threatened to spill out. She clenched her mouth shut and forced the questions out of her mind. She trusted Harris and if he had come to some sort of conclusion without them, she would abide by it. She couldn't help but fear he was about to order the samples jettisoned. It was true, that having alien biology on board was an immense risk, but Choi seemed certain that as long as the Europhids were contained, risk of contamination was at a minimum. Connelly felt a building fear as Harris opened his mouth to speak again.

"We've run into some kind of interference," Harris said. "All transmissions to Earth are being blocked somehow. Photos, video, audio, nothing's getting through. Solar radiation is normal right now so my only guess is that it's our proximity to Jupiter that's causing the problem. I'm currently running a full diagnostic to rectify the issue."

Connelly's trepidation skyrocketed. Harris was about to drop some kind of bomb.

"In addition, we will soon be on the far side of Jupiter, meaning that even if communications were restored, we still wouldn't have communications until we clear Jupiter again."

"How long will that be?" Willard asked.

"Forty-three hours," Harris said. "Typically we wouldn't make our next move, and that includes the analysis of alien organisms, until we had reported to and received clearance from ground control."

Connelly's heart sank. They were going to be sitting on their hands for forty-three hours!

"However," Harris said, "We did not come to Europa to twiddle our thumbs waiting to hear from mission control."

Feeling hope return, Connelly smiled. "So we can start our analysis?"

Harris shook his head. "No."

Now all the scientists in the room were looking upset.

"Well, which is it," Peterson said. "Can we get some work done or not?"

Robert pushed his glasses higher onto his nose. "This, ah, this is quite possibly the greatest discovery mankind has ever made. We can't just ignore it. There are hours, countless hours of study, research, analysis to—"

Harris held his open palm up. A smile was creeping onto his face. "I understand," he said, his smile growing wider.

"He finds this humorous," Peterson said to Robert, then glanced at Connelly, "He finds this humorous."

"I'm afraid," Harris said in a loud voice, "that there are much more urgent matters that need all of your attention."

Connelly felt her trust in Harris's decision making abilities begin to wane. How could he not see the importance of this work? Nothing else could be as important. Nothing!

"While what we have discovered here already is beyond all predictions and expectations," Harris said. "I'm afraid that this mission cannot be deemed a success until we accomplish what we came here to do."

"And what is that," Connelly said, her heart pounding beneath her ribs.

"I'll pose this as a question," Harris said. "We have discovered life on the surface of Europa, which is, as Kathy reminded us, a statistical improbability. But what we came here for, was not to find life on the surface of Europa, but beneath the surface, in the ocean that we now know exists."

Connelly's mind felt as though a vacuum cleaner had just been inserted and was now sucking out all the confusing, demanding thoughts within. Even the Europhids were beginning to lose ground in the battle for her attention.

"If there is life on the surface of Europa," Harris said, "how much more likely is it that we will discover life within the seas of Europa?"

"What are you saying?" Connelly asked.

"You're going back down," Harris said.

Connelly's jaw dropped. She wanted to ask why, but was afraid it would make her sound like she didn't' want to go. Luckily, the Captain had anticipated the query.

"In space, circumstances can change in an instant," Harris said. "We may round Europa only to discover that a solar storm has arrived, postponing any return to the surface for hours, days or weeks. As far as I can see, we have ten hours of smooth sailing with which to continue our exploration...barring another barrage of charged particles."

Connelly's faith in Harris was restored in full. "When can we go?"

"Three hours," Harris said. "I'll prep the lander and check your PMS suits over. After that, I don't see any reason to delay."

Sighing with relief, Connelly relaxed and leaned back on the lab table. "Then we have a few hours to work with the Europhids."

"Sorry," Harris said. "But I would prefer you all took a three hour break. Go get some sleep. I won't be sending a tired crew to the surface of Europa."

"But—" It was all Peterson could get out before Harris cut him off.

"Not a debate. If you want to work on the Europhids, you can stay here with me while the others go to the surface."

Peterson bit his lip. Connelly knew that everyone would want to go. Of course, it would only be she, Willard, and Robert who took the first ride in TES. But still, the idea of going back to the surface alone was enticing.

The group continued to go over the final details, but Connelly's mind took her in another direction. Their voices faded as she processed what Harris had said. *If there is life on the frozen surface of Europa…what will they find in the warmer ocean?*

And how will they bring it back?

₪ ₪ ₪ ₪ ₪

The blackness that enveloped Connelly was all consuming. There wasn't a sparkle of light anywhere. She could feel her body, but couldn't see it. If it weren't for the comforting warmth caressing her body, she would have thought she'd been blinded and launched into space.

Where am I?

Connelly knew that the words were a thought but they sounded real in her mind, as though she has spoken them aloud.

Then there was another voice…or voices. She couldn't tell. They were muffled, distant, as though several people were speaking on the other side of a thick wall.

She willed herself to hear better.

Nothing.

But there was one voice slightly louder than the rest. It spoke constantly, but the only word Connelly could make out was *relax.* The voice said the word ever few seconds as though it were trying to calm someone down. Unsure why, she had the feeling that the voice was about to break bad news, or speak some harsh words. That's why it wanted someone to relax.

Relax…

Calm…

Slow down…

Connelly felt herself drifting slowly. Her unseen, immaterial body became loose. Her breathing came slowly and steadily. The warmth massaged her as though she were surrounded by hot tub jets. She experienced bliss.

Then the voice grew louder. The smaller voices disappeared.

The voice spoke a long sentence, but she couldn't make out the words. It was still behind an invisible wall.

Again the voice spoke, but this time, a door between the two rooms had been opened and the voice came through clearly. "*Go home.*"

Connelly felt no fear at the voice. It was masculine in tone and feminine in pitch, but had no threatening quality about it. Connelly waited for one of the lesser voices to reply, but silence was all that followed the command.

The voice spoke again. "*Go home.*"

It was more insistent this time, but still calm, soothing even. Connelly realized that the voice might be speaking to her. "Why?"

"*You shouldn't be here!*"

Connelly felt her nonexistent body recoil. The warmth turned frigid. "Who are you?" she said, her voice shaking.

A faint ruby glow emerged in the distant, pulsing with every breath Connelly took, growing larger with every passing second. The pulses came with a rushing whoosh.

Spinning now, the glow became kaleidoscopic. It continued to grow, spinning tendrils out like octopus tentacles. Then it stopped growing. It sat before Connelly, floating in space, continuously spinning and pulsing like a human heart.

"*Go home,*" the voice said again, having regained its previous composure.

"I don't under—"

"*Go home, Kathy. You shouldn't be here.*"

"But—"

"*Go home!*"

With the quickness of lighting the red glow burst forward, shooting out its tendril's. Connelly's world became bright red and searing hot. She screamed.

፱   ፱   ፱   ፱   ፱

Peterson ignored Harris's command to get some sleep. How could he? They'd found the impossible! And everyone, all the world, had his initial discovery to thank for it. He thought back to the day and remembered his sense of wonder upon seeing the meteorite fall from the Arctic sky. Even in those precious moments, he never dreamed it would take him across the solar system. Of course, Benson's death had put a stain on the whole thing. *Stains fade with time*, Peterson thought. Benson's death, as tragic as it was, would soon be an afterthought.

After staying in his room for an hour and forty-five minutes, an idea struck him, that he couldn't wait to try, and couldn't keep to himself. He'd snuck back to the lab, picked up his prize and hurried to Connelly's quarters. After knocking twice, he let himself inside.

Apparently, Connelly could sleep. In the cool blackness of her room, he could barely make her out on the bed. She was still wearing her jumpsuit, but was sound asleep. He thought twice about waking her, but after heading back to the door, he heard her groan. Looking back, he could see that she was kicking her feet slowly and clenching her fists. An expression of deep anxiety covered her face.

Peterson felt sure Connelly would be thankful to be taken away from whatever nightmare was plaguing her slumber. He moved slowly forward, keeping the glass cylinder he'd picked up at the lab, hidden behind his back. "Kathy?"

He stepped closer as Connelly's tension rose. Her movements became more jerky and her face turned sour. "Connelly, wake up."

On the last word of Peterson's sentence, Connelly burst awake with a flail of hands and feet. She was gasping for air and began feeling her body, apparently inspecting it for injuries.

"Whoa, whoa," Peterson said, "It's just me, Connelly. It's just me."

Connelly looked straight into Peterson's eyes and he saw that hers were full of fear. "It was just a dream," he said. "A nightmare."

As her breath began to normalize and her muscles grew less rigid, she said, "Michael...what are you doing here?"

"I brought you a present," he said.

Connelly rubbed her forehead with her palms. "W—What?"

Hoping the sight of their new discovery would wipe the cobwebs from her mind, he brought the glass cylinder out from behind his back and turned on the lights. At first, Connelly shielded her eyes from the bright light, holding her hands in front of her squinting eyes. Peterson moved closer, so she could have a better view.

Connelly lowered her hands and came face to face with the largest of the Europhid samples. It was still in its glass container and still standing tall, like a proud obelisk. It was only a foot tall, but seemed gigantic compared to the others. Connelly's reaction wasn't exactly what Peterson expected.

She leaned away in fear, but quickly became embarrassed. "Sorry," she said.

"That nightmare have something to do with the Europhids?"

Connelly shook her head, no.

"Because they are quite frightening." Peterson held the Europhid sample out and warbled it back and forth. "I'm coming to get you, Kathy! I'm a scary red cucumber from hell and I'm here to steal your soul!"

Connelly smiled. "Enough," she said. "What are you doing with that anyway?" Connelly checked her watch. "We still have an hour before launch prep."

Peterson smiled. "Exactly. I think a two hour nap is sufficient, don't you? There are much more interesting ways to kill time."

Connelly raised a skeptical eyebrow.

"With the *Europhids*, Connelly." Peterson smiled and shook his head. "I'm heading out. You'll have about thirty seconds before I get lost in this maze without you. If you want in, better make it quick." With that, Peterson headed out the door.

Walking slowly, Peterson did his best to hear what was happening inside Connelly's room. He heard what sounded like rushing feet. Then the door opened and he could hear Connelly quickly approaching from behind. "Where are you going? The research lab is the other way."

"We're not going to the research lab," Peterson said, savoring the moment.

"Where then?"

"The bio-lab."

13 – INFECTION

Connelly's awe returned as she stepped into the bio-lab. Its massive size and grand gardens of flowers, vegetables and full sized trees almost made her forget she was floating in orbit around an alien world inhabited by the most unlikely of life forms. The tangy scent of the flowers filled her nose. She took in a deep breath, wondering if this is what the Garden of Eden must have been like…sans the plant incubators.

But her awestruck wonder was suddenly replaced by a sense doom. She squeezed her hands into tight fists when a shooting pain rocketed up her forearm. A tightening knot of tension began to form in Connelly's right shoulder blade, pulsing with pain. Was this anxiety? Had her old enemy returned?

No, this is something more, she thought. *I beat the anxiety years ago.*

She relaxed her grip and made a concerted effort to loosen the rest of her muscles, but it was like trying to soften a stone. Her thoughts returned to the strange dream. The images were still clear; the swirling red colors, the anger, and the message.

Go home, Kathy. You shouldn't be here!

"You OK?" Peterson asked.

"Yeah, sure…I'm fine." Connelly rubbed the back of her neck. "Just get overwhelmed every time I come here." Returning her gaze to the bio-lab greenery, a small sense of peace began to return, but not fully. She remembered her childhood dog, a golden retriever named Sarah, and suddenly wished that the GEC had sent more than flowers to comfort them. Sarah would have been perfect.

A loud clunk and the hiss of a sealing container pulled Connelly's attention to what Peterson was doing. After a moment of confusion, she realized what she was seeing. Peterson had removed a tomato plant from one of the larger plant incubators and had transplanted the Europhid sample.

In an instant, she knew what he was planning to do, and couldn't begin to imagine what the effects might be.

"I don't think that's a good idea," Connelly said. "We don't even really know if that's technically a plant yet. Not to mention how many safety protocols you're breaking."

Peterson smiled. "*We're* breaking."

Connelly crossed her arms and gave Peterson a sour look.

"Fine," he said. "I'm breaking. Your objection is dully noted, blah, blah, blah. We have more samples and Europa is covered in them."

Connelly continued her silent protest.

"Anything that happens, transformations, reactions, augmentations, whatever, will be contained inside the incubator. We're safe."

Connelly didn't budge. She couldn't shake the feeling that this was dangerous.

After taking a deep breath, Peterson stood back and slowly let the air out of his lungs. "Look, if this is a plant, it should have some kind of reaction to the incubator. Why spend hours examining it under a microscope when we can find out in a few seconds by flipping this switch."

Connelly scratched the back of her head and crossed her arms again. "Sorry, you're on your own." She turned toward the door and started walking, though admittedly, not as quickly as she could have. She recognized the sound of the incubator being activated. But her determination remained solid. Her feet carried her toward the door.

Peterson spoke as the automatic doors slid open to allow Connelly exit. "Holy shit, it's working."

Connelly's mind suddenly began a hyper-speed ping pong match over staying or leaving. The match lasted a half second. She spun around and saw Peterson hunched over the incubator. He was looking at the Europhid, which was moving back and forth, swaying as though in the wind—and growing.

Connelly crouched next to Peterson. She watched in amazement as the Europhid not only continued to grow, but spread out new shoots, which became their own, new gelatinous bodies. Within thirty seconds the single organism had grown five new specimens, each now nearing three inches tall. Thin tendrils began squirming out, burrowing down into the ruddy, Europian soil, that Peterson had transplanted along with the Europhid.

"Self replication," Connelly said. "They're asexual."

They watched for another ten seconds as the five Europhids continued to expand. As the flesh of one of the Europhid pushed against the glass, Connelly became nervous. What if the glass broke? "Shut it off," she said.

Peterson snapped back to the here and now and switched off the machine. The light hum of the incubator ceased and the Europhid stopped moving. But something new moved beneath the surface.

Connelly focused on the motion. It looked like a snake slithering beneath the sand of a desert. She gasped as a thin red tendril, like a thick worm, emerged from the soil. It slowly explored the inside of the incubator, feeling the glass shell carefully.

With a confused mix of aversion and awe, Connelly watched in silence.

It's moving!

The Europhids can move!

Or could they? Perhaps they had mutated the Europhid by activating the plant incubator? Connelly shuddered at the thought that the human race was new to this world and had already genetically altered one of the native species, the first alien life ever encountered. She now realized that she should have stopped Peterson before he could activate the incubator. It was a foolish thing to do.

Peterson placed his hand against the glass and the tendril moved toward it. It stopped in front of his hand, hovering like an angry serpent. Peterson moved his hand to the right. It followed. To the left. It followed again.

"Huh." Peterson chuckled. "It seems intelligent...at least enough for motion tracking. Maybe it's an automatic reflex? Like Venus Flytraps?"

"Venus fly traps react to touch."

"So?"

"If the Europhid is tracking your movements...it can *see* you."

Peterson's eyes went wide and he looked to Connelly, meeting her gaze. "See me?"

"Or at least sense your movement. Sensing light and dark…smell, sound, or something entirely new. My point is that it knows you're there."

In a gentle gesture, Peterson reached out and took Connelly's hand. He squeezed tighter as their eyes locked. "Amazing, isn't it?" Connelly felt herself moving closer to Peterson and a wave of nervous energy swept from her toes to the hair follicles on the top of her head. Her eyes began to close as she prepared for—

Crash! A spray of glass exploded onto Connelly and Peterson. In an automatic reaction, both flung themselves away from the plant incubator, sprawling onto the floor. Connelly pulled herself away and scrambled to her feet, shaking the glass from her jumpsuit.

Peterson was still on the floor, holding his right hand in his left, cringing in pain. Connelly moved to him. "Are you all right?"

"Piece of glass got me," he said. "I'll be okay."

Connelly looked toward the plant incubator. Half of the glass tube had been shattered. The single red tendril slowly pulled its way back inside and buried itself in the red soil.

"Oh God…" Peterson's voice was shaky, almost unrecognizable.

Connelly immediately saw that Peterson was terrified. He stared at his hand, which had a red welt, surrounded by a large, white swollen area. At the center was a small puncture wound, the size of a dime.

"It stung me," he said. "I think it stung me. There's a containment lever in the backside of the incubator. Switch it, quick."

Keeping her eye on the Europhid, Kathy rounded the incubator, found the lever and pulled it. A metal casing rose up and around the broken glass. It wriggled violently as the steel sheath rose. Then it was out of sight, sealed inside.

Connelly couldn't believe what she had seen. The Europhid was not only asexual, partly mobile and had motion tracking abilities, but it could also strike out. This seemingly innocent organism had attacked Peterson and whatever foreign elements it contained were now causing Peterson's body to react.

"You'll be okay," Connelly insisted. "We need to get to the infirmary and contact Choi." But Peterson didn't move. He just sat there, staring at his wounded hand, which was swelling larger by the second.

"Michael, you need to get up. If we don't get you to the infirmary, the swelling could get worse, maybe reach your heart.... Are you listening to me?" Connelly was shouting, but Peterson remained frozen.

He looked up suddenly, his eyes full of fear. "Kathy, I don't want to end up like Benson."

Connelly caught her breath. "Who's Benson?"

ת   ת   ת   ת   ת

The hard, metallic floor of the Med-Lab clunked beneath Connelly's feet as she paced, occasionally glancing at Peterson. The man she had come to know as a confident, strong willed and sometimes macho personality now had his forearm strapped to a short operating table, and he was whimpering like a school boy with a skinned knee.

"Ahh! Hurts like hell," Peterson complained, as Choi pinched the festering puncture wound on the back of his hand. A red tinged foam oozed from the gash. Choi added pressure and Peterson began sucking air in between his clenched teeth. Connelly felt sure he would soon let out a scream. But Choi eased up as soon as the liquid draining from his hand began running clear.

Connelly noticed that Choi had all but ignored Peterson's complaint of pain. She also noticed how Harris, who stood behind Choi, his arms crossed tight across his chest, had remained expressionless throughout the ordeal. He was impossible to read, but one thing was for sure, his normally friendly demeanor was gone. Connelly was sure the captain's confidence in her was shattered; that she and Peterson might very well be excluded from the remainder of the mission and banned from the Europhid samples. If she were in change, that's the decision she would make.

Why did I listen to him? she thought.

A typhoon of rage swirled though Connelly's mind. All affection for Peterson dissipated, replaced by anger. But not just at Peterson, at herself as well. While *he* had smuggled the Europhid from the lab, *she* had followed him. He had activated the plant incubator, but she had watched—seduced by curiosity. And now she might lose her position and life's work. All her dreams, all her passion, might have been destroyed by the stupidity of one attractive man and her own foolishness.

"Watch it!" Peterson said in a loud voice that bordered on yelling.

Choi stood above Peterson's hand, clasping a sharp pair of tweezers between her gloved fingers. "Keep your hand still, Dr. Peterson. I wouldn't want to make the wound worse." Choi's voice was controlled and even, but there was no doubting that she would follow up on her veiled threat. Peterson bit his lip and made his body rigid, holding as still as possible.

Peterson's face twisted with pain as Choi slid the needle-tipped tweezers inside his hand. She tried three times, unsuccessfully, to grasp something buried between his metacarpals. Peterson's flesh turned white and his body went slack. On the fourth attempt, Choi grasped something with the tweezers and quickly yanked it out.

Reacting to the immense pain, Peterson yanked his hand back and pulled the small table up into the air. He was about to protest when he saw the centimeter-long sliver, that looked more like a piranha's tooth, held firmly in the tweezers grasp. "God…what is it?"

"The result of your ignorance," Choi said as she looked over the thorny object. Peterson didn't offer a defense. Choi continued, "My best guess is it's a stinger."

Harris was behind Choi now, his expression stern. "Like a bee?"

Choi nodded.

Peterson looked down at his hand, which was covered in ruddy foam, blood and clear liquid. "Then I've been poisoned?"

"We don't know what, if anything, you've been injected with," Choi said. "But it is certain that your body had a reaction to some kind of foreign substance. I would say you're lucky."

"How's that?" Peterson said.

"You are the first human being with which these Europhids have experienced physical contact. I highly doubt that whatever is in your system will accomplish whatever it was designed to do."

"So I'll live?"

Choi placed the stinger in a metal bowl and began removing her rubber gloves. "Fifty-fifty."

"That's not funny," Peterson said as he began to free his injured hand from the straps that held him to the table.

Choi stopped removing her second glove and stared Peterson down. "It wasn't meant to be. We have no idea what kind of toxin is in your system and how it will react. The only information that might relate is the incident involving your deceased crew member."

Connelly's memory kicked in. After Peterson had been stung in the Bio-lab he mentioned not wanting to end up like someone. *What was his name?* But before Peterson could tell her who the man was, Peterson gasped in pain, surged forward and passed out. Twenty minutes later he awoke in the Med-lab and had been strapped down. *What was his name? Benjamin? Bernard?* She knew it began with a "B." "Benson." Connelly hadn't meant to say the name aloud, but everyone heard her.

Harris squinted at Connelly and then shifted an angry stare to Peterson. "That was classified information, mister."

Connelly sensed the water was rising up over her neck and would soon drown her and Peterson. "All he said was the name."

Harris and Choi stared at her, obviously weighing their options, the result of which, Connelly could only imagine. Not wanting to wait to find out, Connelly decided to put the pieces together herself. Benson must have been the crew member Choi mentioned. He had died from similar circumstances to Peterson's situation. Meaning what? Benson had come in contact with Europhids previous to the onset of this mission...on Earth.

Connelly's eyes grew wide. "Why didn't you tell us?" Her question was directed at Harris.

124

The sudden reversal of questioning unbalanced Harris's demeanor. "I, ah, I think you better—"

"I think you better tell me the truth. Withholding information that could have got me or my crew injured or killed is not something I will tolerate."

Harris stood silently. Choi watched him, apparently waiting to follow his lead.

"Okay. You tell me if I'm wrong." Connelly turned her attention to Peterson. "Your discovery in the Arctic, the meteorite, contained a biological sample. Your crew member, Benson, came into contact with the sample and died. But his death didn't stop anyone from moving on, from considering the postponement of this mission."

Peterson looked at Harris, then back to Connelly. "You got one thing wrong."

Connelly crossed her arms.

"Benson's death *inspired* the mission. There were no plans for a manned Europa expedition until after Benson died."

Connelly's face fell flat. Anger vibrated through her body. She wanted to scream at the top of her lungs. The urge to punch Peterson was all consuming. But she knew two truths that kept her in check. First: today's incident was as much her fault as theirs. She shouldn't have encouraged Peterson by staying. What she should have done was report his actions to the captain and been done with it. Second, had she known about Benson's death, she would still have come to Europa. That didn't change the fact that the concealment of this information could have killed her friends.

"Here's what's going to happen," Connelly said. "You do whatever you need to with him." She motioned at Peterson with her head. "But my mission will continue as scheduled. The blame for this incident lies on all four of us and whoever higher up in the food chain decided to keep Benson's death a secret. I am going to tell Ethan and Robert about this, and I expect," Connelly looked into Choi's eyes, "that you will answer any questions Ethan might have regarding our safety."

After thirty seconds of silence, Harris uncrossed his arms and relaxed his tensed up shoulders. "Departure is scheduled for twenty minutes from now. Give us a half hour?"

Connelly nodded.

"What about me?" Peterson asked, as he stood up.

Choi placed her hand firmly on Peterson's shoulder and pushed him back into the chair. "Twenty-four hour quarantine. Standard procedure. Harris will monitor you via the video feed."

Peterson began to complain, but Choi's next words came quick and loud. "While blame ultimately rests on all our shoulders, your actions today could have cost you your life, not to mention the lives of everyone else on board. You should be grateful a day in the Med-lab is all you're getting."

Connelly turned to Choi and said, "See you in a half hour." Then she strode for the door, not wanting to show any concern for Peterson. She knew the lingering feelings for the man were still there, but she wouldn't soon forget what he'd done. How could she trust a man who so easily kept dangerous secrets?

"Kathy," Peterson said.

Connelly paused at the door.

"Be careful down there."

The door whooshed shut behind Connelly as she left without another word.

14 – CHANGES

After meeting with Connelly and being told about the incident in the Bio-lab, Robert had helped himself to a copy of the security feed. He was now watching the replay for the fifth time on his digital tablet. The crystal clear, high def video and impeccable sound allowed him to focus in on visual and audio details that might otherwise be missed.

He played the footage again.

Robert watched as Peterson crouched in front of the plant incubator, waiving his hand back and forth, allowing the Europhid tendril to follow his every move.

How could he be so foolish?

How could Kathy?

Peterson's voice came from the tablet. "It seems intelligent…at least enough for motion tracking. Maybe it's an automatic reflex? Like Venus Flytraps?"

"Venus fly traps react to touch."

"So?"

Robert sighed. *No wonder the man works with rocks.*

"If the Europhid is tracking your movements…it can see you," Kathy said on the screen.

Body tensing for the inevitable, Robert leaned forward. He knew that this was where the first of the two tragedies took place. Robert paused the feed, framed out Peterson and zoomed on Kathy's face. Her eyes were closed, so she didn't see what happened next. But what stood out the most were her pursed lips, which curved up in a slight smile.

"Ugh." Robert leaned back in his chair and frowned. *Why him?* A confusing and nearly overwhelming feeling of jealousy clenched his throat, tightening in to a painful knot. He loved Connelly, but not as a lover.

That's what he told himself, what he'd been telling himself for so long that he now believed it.

Almost.

Zooming out and resuming the feed, Robert watched as the plant incubator shattered. A blur of red struck out, hitting Peterson's hand as he fell back—a perfect shot. The Europhids could not only sense movement, they were damn good shots.

After briefly rewinding, Robert played the footage in slow motion, while zooming in on the Europhid tendril. He watched as Peterson turned his head toward Connelly, and just as he lost sight of the creature, it reeled back and stabbed forward with a quickness that Robert had only seen in rapid striking Earth predators such as the wolf spider or king cobra. The sting had pierced Peterson's hand before the glass hit the floor.

Robert paused the footage and zoomed in again, focusing on the Europhid tendril. Playing the feed, frame by frame, Robert was able to witness what Connelly and Peterson did not. As the innocent looking tendril snapped back, a retractable stinger emerged. It launched forward, broke the glass and stabbed into Peterson's hand. But as it pulled back into the incubator, the stinger was still there. A split second later, the thorny weapon had been retracted, only the tip was missing.

Was the Europhid truly like a bee, only able to sting once? Or would the stinger that was left behind in Peterson's hand regenerate, able to strike again? But that's not what concerned him the most. The tendril and stinger were fascinating, but there was something more to this video…something he couldn't quite place…something that chilled him.

He watched the video again, frame by frame. As Peterson turned his head and the tendril struck out, Robert realized what he was seeing. *The Europhid isn't just seeing, it's thinking. Strategizing.* The Europhid had waited patiently, amusing Peterson, until his attention was diverted and his hand was in striking distance.

The act was deliberate and planned. The Europhids were intelligent.

They were more than just plants.

Robert scratched his head, creating a bird's nest in his hair. His hand stopped moving when he came to a realization.

The tendril and stinger are weapons. Just because we haven't seen them on the other Europhids doesn't mean they're not equipped with similar appendages. If they're all able to attack maybe they're not the harmless plants we've taken them for.

Maybe they're predators?

₪   ₪   ₪   ₪   ₪

After spending five minutes in a blazing hot shower, Connelly felt the confusion surrounding the events of the last hour beginning to fade. She dressed quickly and hurried to the docking bay, where she waited for Robert. Willard and Choi had boarded Lander One three minutes ago. The hum of electricity emanating from the lander told her the ship was prepped and ready to go. So was she.

Where are you, Robert?

Just then, the decon room's doors hissed open and Robert stepped into the landing bay. He removed the PMS hood as he walked, revealing his bushy beard, messy head of hair and thickly wrinkled brow. He strode toward Connelly with sweeping, rapid steps.

Connelly could see that something was bothering her old friend, but had enough stress for one day and hoped to bypass any serious discussions. He had yet to lecture her about the incident involving Peterson and the Europhid, and she was thankful for that, but she knew it would eventually come. Still, she couldn't just ignore his urgent demeanor. "What's got your forehead so wrinkled?"

After coming to an abrupt stop, Robert took a deep breath, let it out slowly and licked his lips nervously. "So I was reviewing the security footage from the Bio-lab."

Connelly held her breath for only a moment, but enough to reveal her discomfort with the subject. "You have?"

Robert nodded slowly. "Yes, and—"

"Hey, boat's leaving," Willard said as he leaned out of Lander One's hatch. His jovial demeanor sounded forced. She had given him a quick rundown on what she'd found out about Benson. His mood had dulled since, but he was trying to remain optimistic. He couldn't help it. His glass was perpetually half full.

"Can it wait?" Connelly said. The words were shoved out with an anxious quickness.

"I'm just the messenger, boss," Willard said. "Choi said to get your asses in here. Well, those weren't her exact words, but—"

"We're coming," Connelly said with an effort not to sound upset. Connelly rolled her head on her shoulders and sighed. "Can we finish this later?" she said to Robert. "Maybe when we have a little more privacy?"

Robert squinted his eyes, expressing his confusion without saying a word.

"I don't want everything that happened in the Bio-lab to be public knowledge," she whispered.

"Ahh," Robert said, a trace of a smile emerging on his face. "Understood."

"Thanks."

As Connelly turned to enter Lander One, Robert squeezed her shoulders and continued to do so, all the way up into the ship. "Don't worry," he said, "if we find anything remotely like what was discovered on the surface, all of the days mistakes will be forgotten."

Connelly chuckled as the lander's hatch sealed shut behind them. Moments later, the hiss of depressurization filled the bay and the docking bay doors peeled apart. Jupiter's great red spot swirled before them. Lander One lifted gently off the floor and glided out into space.

ਿ   ਿ   ਿ   ਿ   ਿ

The silence in the Med-lab began to chew at Peterson's nerves. With no one to talk to, no one to ease his nerves, he had grown increasingly nervous. His palms became slick and his forehead dripped with sweat. He attempted to distract himself by thinking about the chemical composition of the red soil on which the Europhids grew, but his thoughts always returned to the Europhid and its daggered appendage.

He looked at his bandaged hand and noticed that blood had begun seeping through. He willed his thoughts to a better topic.

Connelly.

Kathy.

He wasn't sure she would have anything to do with him after the dust settled, but he hoped so. She was brilliant, strong and could hold her ground—an attribute he valued in women. He had always found himself attracted to independent woman. He wondered if that's why he was still single. He had always thought his bachelorhood had developed as a result of spending so much time in the arctic. But maybe it was just his taste in women.

Peterson's thoughts flashed back to the Bio-lab. He could see Connelly again, closing her eyes, puckering her soft, inviting lips. He wanted nothing else in the world than to kiss her at that moment. All his attention had been focused solely on her. That was when the Europhid struck.

A chill rippled across Peterson's flesh, raising the hairs across his legs, chest, arms and neck. Images of the large Europhid filled his mind's eye. He saw the foam spilling from his hand. He remembered the stinger as it was pulled from the wound. And the smell—foul like feces—from his hand.

Peterson's stomach turned over and he was violently propelled to the floor. A fountain of vomit exploded from his mouth, taking his breath away. Gasping for air and wiping his mouth with his sleeve, Peterson climbed back to his feet. He stumbled to the nearest table and attempted to compose himself.

A series of cold pains rose up his spine, out through his arms and down to his fingertips. Without warning, he lost all feeling in his arms and they flopped uselessly to his sides. "Oh no... No."

This is what happened to Benson!

Peterson ran towards the nearest intercom, desperate to call for help. He knew Harris might see him on camera, but he could just as easily be engaged in one of his many other duties. His arms flailed at his sides with every step. As he rounded an operating table one of his arms smashed into the corner, opening a deep wound. Peterson saw the bloody gash, but he felt no pain.

He ran faster.

Reaching the intercom, Peterson went to push the button, but the hand he was expecting to reach up didn't come. It was as though his arms were no longer attached. "Shit!"

He leaned forward and made several attempts to push the button with his nose, but it wasn't working. He couldn't push the button in far enough. A flash of hope surged when he remembered the medical emergency alarm. He looked across the room and saw the yellow button, which was protected by a pane of glass and labeled "EMERGENCY".

Racing across the room, careful not to smash his useless arms into any more sharp objects, Peterson planned out his next moves. After reaching the glass, he could shattered it with his forehead and push the button with his nose. Then what? He'd have to wait. Harris was the only other crew member on board, but he had medical training.

Half way across the room, Peterson reached his top speed. That was also when his legs gave out. It felt like every sinew of his leg muscles had torn at once. He screamed as he tumbled to the floor, his dysfunctional limbs flapping helplessly. A sickeningly sharp spasm tore into his groin and through his stomach.

He vomited a second time, only now he was unable to wipe his mouth or slide his body away from the acrid smell of his bile. Slithering on the floor like a wounded snake, Peterson did his best to cover the distance to the emergency button. It was only after twenty seconds that he realized he was no longer moving. His head moved up and down, but his torso no longer complied. He was paralyzed from the neck down, like a living statue.

Looking down, Peterson caught a glimpse of his bandaged hand. Crimson foam was seeping through, spilling out onto the floor, mixing with his vomit. Without the control of his muscles, Peterson's body slipped over onto its back. He lay, gazing up at the bright lights of the ceiling, weeping.

"Damn this moon to hell," he said through gritted teeth.

"*Hell is a human concept. You are human.*"

Peterson held his breath. Was there someone in the room or was he hearing things?

"Harris? If that's you, I need help! Harris?"

"*Not Harris.*"

"Willard."

"*No.*"

Peterson's eyes darted back and forth, but all he could see was ceiling. "Where are you?"

"I am everywhere."

"That's not possible."

"Through me, all things are possible."

With that, Peterson felt his will slip away. He watched through his eyes, but was unable to look. He was fully aware, taking in information through all his senses, but it was all he had left. The rest of him was floating inside his mind, like a detached soul, clinging to the body of a dead man.

It was then that Peterson saw his hands rise into the air. His fingers flexed several times. Something had control of his body! An arctic fear froze Peterson's thoughts. He was losing his mind—hallucinating—trapped forever within a useless shell of a body that no longer responds to his commands.

Still…was he speaking with his own deformed psyche? Or was the voice in his mind something more? He decided to ask.

Who are you? Peterson thought.

"Michael…I am God."

15 – INTELLIGENCE

The flight down to Europa's surface had been smooth, touching down on the frozen surface only ten minutes after leaving the Surveyor. While Lander One wasn't an elevator, the view from the window reminded him that if anything mechanical went wrong, Lander One would plummet to the moon's surface. Europa's gravitational pull wasn't nearly as strong as Earth's, but in a descent from orbit, the impact would be enough to transform the ship into a heap of metal, wires and human body parts.

Robert shook his head and focused on the task at hand. Tightening his grip on the support bar, Robert helped Connelly pull the TES sphere to the side of the watery hole, which had already frozen over. The sphere dangled only inches above the platform, held aloft by the three TES cranes. After pulling the sphere up, the cranes had moved it towards its locking position atop one of the TES panels. The final lockdown could have been done automatically, but Connelly insisted on guiding the sphere onto the base by hand. Luckily, the task wasn't as difficult as it sounded. Europa's low gravity made the monster-truck-wheel-sized orb much lighter than it had been on Earth.

Robert squinted to adjust to the new light. Last time they had been on Europa's surface, the area had been well lit by the distant sun and reflected light from Jupiter's gaseous surface. But now they were on the dark side of Jupiter, where all light was blotted out by the massive nearby planet. The portion of space that Jupiter's body consumed was now solid black. Robert couldn't remember a more empty sky. It was haunting. The only proof that something existed in the black space was the occasional flash of lightning from one of Jupiter's storms, a phenomenon not visible on the lit side.

Robert brought his attention back to the sphere as it locked silently into position. Connelly turned to Willard, who had been working the cranes from the control panel on the other side of the chasm. He was starkly illuminated in the spotlights shining from the TES panels. "Nicely done. Go ahead and pop the hatch."

Willard nodded and worked the controls. The upper glass half of the sphere glided open like a clam shell. It stopped at a ninety degree angle. Robert motioned to the open sphere with both hands. "Your chariot awaits."

Connelly stepped inside without a word. Robert wondered if she was feeling the same mix of nervousness, excitement and trepidation. Robert stepped up into the sphere and scanned the interior. It was just as he remembered. Four comfortable-looking chairs sat in the center of the sphere, two facing one direction, two facing the other. The floor was a flat, metal panel, three and a half feet down so that the glass and metal merged at waist level. Three thin stairs leading to the floor marked the only break in computer consoles around the circumference of the sphere's interior. It reminded Robert of a futuristic, alien escape pod.

As soon as Robert took his seat and buckled in next to Connelly, he signaled to Willard with an upturned thumb. "Lock us in."

The hatch slid closed over them. As the sphere's cabin pressurized, Robert became aware of a slight hiss. His heart began to thrum as he thought his suit had sprung a leak, but he quickly realized that with the return of pressurization, also came the return of sound. The hiss was just the cabin being pressurized. But his momentary panic attack was enough to reveal his emotional state. He was on edge. And the ride down to Europa's ocean was going to be a very long elevator ride, ending beneath countless feet of ice. Robert began counting in his head.

One…two…three…

"Start the oxygen feed," Connelly instructed.

"You got it." Willard's voice still rang clear through the sphere's thick outer shell. Through the glass, Robert could see Willard twisting a knob on the side of the TES control panel. A rush of air brushed across Robert's body, though he couldn't feel its coolness through his suit.

"O2 feed is steady and levels are good to go," Willard said. "You may now breath freely."

Connelly glanced at Robert. "You want to go first?"

Robert shook his head. "Beauty before the beast."

Twenty-one…twenty-two…twenty-three…

"Well, Ethan isn't here, so I guess we'll have to go at the same time."

"I can still hear you, you know," Willard said through the headset.

A smile crept onto Robert's face. Connelly always seemed to know when he needed a mood lightener, and taunting Willard always did the trick. He nodded his confirmation and raised his hands to his helmet. Simultaneously, the pair worked through the series of seals and locks that glued their hood-like helmets to the rest of the PMS suit. Two minutes passed before they were ready for the final step. Their eyes met and both removed the hoods, sliding them back over their heads.

Robert sucked in a long breath, letting the cool, dry air flow through his nose and fill his lungs. He held it for ten seconds and let it out quickly. His next breaths were just as deep, but much quicker. With each breath he became more relaxed and more confident that he was breathing good air into his lungs and not just the frozen void of space. He looked up at Connelly. She was already strapping herself into one of the seats. He took his place next to her and buckled himself in tight.

Fifty-eight...fifty-nine...sixty...

After both were settled and comfortable, Connelly switched on the interior com system and spoke, "You there, Ethan?"

"I hear you. How's the old man holding up? He looked pretty freaked when you guys took off the hoods." Willard's voice reverberated all around them, projected from the sphere's speakers, the same speakers that would allow them to hear any sounds flowing through the water below.

"I'm fine," Robert said.

"Air is holding," Connelly added. "All systems green?"

"Green like Kermit."

"Lower us down."

"You got it, boss."

With a quick jerk, the sphere lifted up off the base. Robert strained for a view of the deep hole as they dangled above it, but the seatbelt held him secure. A good thing, too, Robert thought. The sphere warbled back and forth as it stopped above the ice shaft. Seconds later, they were descending.

"Get ready for some steam guys," Willard said. "Looks like we have a few feet of ice to melt again."

The bluish-white walls of the chasm began to pass by all around them. Just as Robert became fascinated, a plume of steam rocketed up around them as the sphere's blazing hot base melted through the ice. Moisture quickly collected on the glass top of the sphere and refroze, obscuring the view in all directions. Robert suddenly felt confined, buried alive in a spherical elevator being lowered into the depths of hell.

His breath caught somewhere between his chest and his mouth, expanding a tightness in his throat he thought would cause his neck to burst, spewing blood all over the interior of the sphere like a Japanese anime cartoon. Robert bit down on his lower lip as sweat began to bead up on his forehead.

A sudden pressure on his knee almost made him gasp. He jerked his head up and came face to face with Connelly, who looked both concerned and amused. "Robert, you stopped breathing."

Robert made a deliberate effort to breath. He closed his eyes as he continued breathing, trying his hardest to ignore the sinking feeling created by the downward motion of the elevator. *Of TES*, he forced himself to think. *Not an elevator.*

"Hey..." Connelly's voice was soft, comforting.

Robert looked opened his eyes and met Connelly's. "Keep counting," she said.

Robert nodded.

One hundred thirty-three...one hundred thirty-four...one hundred thirty-five...

〰 〰 〰 〰 〰

"How's this for privacy?" Connelly said after switching off the com system inside the sphere. "Now what did you want to talk about?" Connelly knew exactly what *she* wanted to talk about and had resisted the urge to bring up the topic for as long as she could. She wanted to get the unavoidable lecture out of the way before they broke the surface of the water. Not because Robert's words of wisdom would sour the moment, but rather, she knew that after taking a dip in the Europa's ocean, Robert would most likely forget what he wanted to discuss. She'd always valued his opinions, welcome or not, and didn't feel right taking advantage of his forgetfulness.

"Think it's safe to undo the belts?" Robert said as he stretched the safety belt away from his belly.

"Not much a seatbelt will do if we fall, right?" Connelly noticed Robert's expression sour. "Sorry."

Robert undid his seatbelt and let it slide back into the sides of the chair. He looked Connelly in the eyes, his gaze expressing the seriousness of the subject about to be broached. "There are security cameras in all the Surveyor's vital compartments, including the Bio-lab."

Connelly had assumed as much after Robert's initial attempt to speak back in the docking bay. "Right…" She tried to sound as casual as possible, like she already knew there were security cameras. "I don't suppose you saw anything of interest?" She couldn't help but let out a nervous chuckle.

Robert scratched his head as his serious tone diminished slightly and his cheeks turned rosy red. "Ahh, you mean other than the budding romance?"

"Exactly." It was Connelly's turn to sound serious.

"I'm not your father," Robert said.

"What are you then? My brother?"

"*Brother*? No, I, ahh… Hey, that's not even what I wanted to talk about."

Connelly felt surprise and relief, but a tinge of disappointment churned within the brew. She wondered if she really did want to hear what he thought. Maybe Michael *was* not good, but she couldn't see it? She'd seen the same thing happen to other women. "You don't?"

"God, no."

"Oh…" Connelly could feel the skin on her forehead bunching up as she tried to figure out where Robert was heading. "What else was on the tape?"

"As you know, the Europhid tracked Michael's movements, displaying that it had senses beyond that of your garden variety vegetable."

"Right."

"I reviewed the tape several times, close up, frame by frame. I'm fairly sure that Europhids, or at least this one, displayed some signs of higher intelligence."

"Compared to garden variety vegetables," Connelly added.

"Exactly."

"What was most intriguing about the footage was the timing of the attack. It played innocent, moving almost cutely back and forth, until the exact moment Michael was completely distracted."

"You're saying the attack wasn't just a reflexive action?"

"More than that. The Europhid, an alien organism that has never come in contact with a human, recognized how Michael perceived the world visually, through human eyes. It understood what his eyes were used for and how they worked. It knew to strike the moment he focused on you. How does a creature that has no knowledge or evolved experience with humanity know how Michael's eyes work?"

Connelly shifted in her seat, not sure if she was uncomfortable with the topic or if she had picked poor padding for the seats. Either way, something was causing her spine to ache. "Have you ruled out coincidence?"

"Barring putting my hand in front of another Europhid and looking away, I'd say the tape is fairly conclusive. Have a look at it when we get back. I think you'll find the video convincing enough." It was Robert's turn to shift uncomfortably. "I would have brought it up publicly if the stinging incident wasn't accompanied by more...intimate matters."

Connelly felt her face flush. Robert said he'd watched the tape several times, close up and frame by frame. How many times had he seen her closing her eyes and reaching out for Peterson? She didn't mind Robert knowing the truth, but it was damned embarrassing. Connelly pushed the topic from her mind and kept to the more urgent, and honestly, more interesting subject at hand. "If the Europhid had a true understanding of human physiology, which would have to be in depth if it really knew when to strike, why did it inject Michael with a poison that had no effect other than to produce a slight infection?"

Robert leaned back in his chair. "Now it's our turn to attempt understanding the actions of an alien creature. We assumed the substance was a poison simply on the basis that on Earth, organisms that inject anything almost always inject toxins or poisons with the intent of paralyzing or outright killing their enemies."

As Robert pursed his lips tightly, they turned. "This is an alien species. The injection could be anything. A pheromone for instance. It could be used to track his movements or attract something to him. Or maybe it's a slow acting poison, meant to kill over time. It could do nothing at all. Or it could just affect his mind, cause him to act irrationally and put the rest of us in danger."

"He *was* acting irrational when he put the Europhid in the incubator," Connelly said with a grimace.

"Your affections can do that to a man."

Connelly shot a fiery stare in to Robert that threatened to broil his brains inside his skull.

"Sorry," he said quickly. Robert regained his composure and continued. "But it's most likely something we haven't even conceived of yet. We have to remember that these are alien organisms. They may not have arms, legs or even mouths, but we know by observing the environment they live in, they're survivors. Of course, I'll be damned before I let a one foot tall, red eggplant outsmart me. If the Europhids can understand the human eye, I'll have them figured out soon enough."

Robert played with his beard for a moment. "The real question is, for what other reason could Peterson have been stung?"

נ   נ   נ   נ   נ

Peterson stood before the Med-lab doors, pushing the button to open them over and over. But the doors were locked. He turned to the security panel and accessed the door mechanism. The lock was password protected.

His head shook. Drool collected at the corner of his mouth. He stared blankly while twitching, his voice making a scratchy click with each breath. Then he typed: Quaren104—the password known only to Harris and Choi.

Stumbling like a stiff legged man in the middle of a grand mal seizure, Peterson made his way through the halls of the Surveyor. He bumped loudly in the walls and nearly tumbled over with each step. What was left of his personality and consciousness was tucked away in the far reaches of his mind, like watching a baseball game from the nose bleed section. His eyes, once deep and brown, were now glazed over with a dark crimson haze.

After a skin-bruising five minute stroll, Peterson's movements became smoother. Along with an increase in balance, his steps became even and quick. With a quick jerk of the head, he stopped moving in the center of the hallway. Twisting with a robot-like rigidity, he looked back over his shoulder, back the way he came, toward a dimly lit hallway.

Peterson's red eyes glowed with recognition. He spun on his heels and pounded toward the hallway. Rounding the corner at top speed, he tipped over. His shoulder hit the smooth wall and his tilted body slid as he continued walking forward. A moment later he sprung back up into a vertical position. With each step, his feet hit the floor harder and harder. His knees began bending and he broke into a sprint.

Three more turns and two long stretches later, Peterson skidded to a stop and peered at a labeled doorway. His lips mouthed the words three times before his lungs provided the air to give them voice. "Bio-lab."

Looking at the doorway, he scanned up and down and eventually turning his red eyes to the button next to the door. He pushed the button and door whooshed open. A crooked, unattractive grin spread on his face. With a wrinkled brow, Peterson lifted his hand and rubbed his mouth, inspecting the smile.

Interest in facial expressions quickly waned as he stepped into the Bio-lab, taking in the scenery. Trees, flowers and plants filled every nook and cranny of the room, except for the research area closest to the door. This is the section that attracted his attention. He stepped forward and bent down to the shielded plant incubator still containing the Europhid. He felt the broken glass on the floor with his finger tips, rubbing back and forth. He smiled again, this time, with more control.

Peterson stood up and turned his head to a yellow closet marked, "Supplies." He shuffled forward, dodging incubators and work benches, but never took his eyes off the double-door closet. Taking the closet door handles in both hands, he threw the doors open, revealing an array of metal gardening tools. Shovels, hoes, trowels, even a pitchfork.

Reaching forward, Peterson took hold of a spiked, metal rake. He brought it out and admired it briefly before tapping his hand on the sharp spikes. He winced and pulled his hand back. A trickle of foamy blood slid out from a fresh wound on the palm of his bandage-free hand. He watched as the blood slowly trickled down his thumb and began dripping onto the floor.

A perfect Michael Peterson grin flashed onto his face and he chuckled lightly. The chuckle grew in fervor, becoming a manic laugh. He stopped suddenly and turned toward the exit.

OCEAN

16 – THE DEEP

Dim light from the sphere's interior dome lamp filtered out through the glass, past the water surrounding the sphere and reflected off the smooth ice walls outside. Variations in the color and texture of the ice revealed millions of years of Europian history. But now, instead of taking core samples by drilling into the ice, Robert and Connelly were gliding straight to the bottom.

Robert had been silent for the past twenty minutes. Connelly could tell he was concentrating on his counting. Elevators alone were enough to throw him, but this was a fully enclosed system with water on all sides, and there would be no sedative to knock him out this time. At least the water dulled the feeling of downward motion. If not for the layers of ice sliding past, she wouldn't even know they were moving.

Seeing Robert had calmed, she decided it was time to conclude their previous conversation. It had been left open ended. It wasn't that she needed a detailed battle plan, just a feeling of where they stood. Would they report their findings and recommend keeping Peterson under quarantine? Would they put Peterson to sleep in one of the impact chairs until they went back home? Several worst case scenarios plowed through her mind and the nervousness began to build inside her stomach like an expanding elastic ball.

"So…" Connelly started.

Robert jolted slightly and then turned to Connelly, his lips still mouthing numbers. Connelly quickly read his lips, "Two thousand fifty-three."

Geez.

"What do you recommend we do about Michael?" Connelly asked.

Robert ran his lower lip beneath his teeth. "Not much we can do aside from wait and see what, if anything, happens to him."

Connelly frowned. "So he's a guinea pig?"

"Of his own design," Robert said. "May I remind you that the experiment involving the Europhid and plant incubator didn't exactly conform to the rules of good science? Sorry if I sound callous, but he brought it on himself."

Connelly felt a surge of embarrassment, knowing that she had played some part in the scientific debacle Robert was referring to. The incident in the bio-lab was not one of her finer moments and had convinced her to put her feelings for Michael on hold. Indefinitely. "You're right," she said.

Robert sighed, relieved she didn't argue the point.

"So," Connelly said, "We wait and see if he grows a third arm. If nothing happens, we'll keep this half-assed theory about little red Jell-O molds having brains to ourselves."

Connelly flashed a smile at Robert and he returned it.

The sphere jerked to a stop and swayed gently in the water.

Robert gripped his knees. "What's happening?"

Connelly leaned forward and flipped on the com system.

"H-e-l-l-o! Can you guys hear me?" Willard's voice boomed loudly from the sphere's interior speakers. "If you don't respond in thirty seconds, I'm pulling you up."

Connelly turned down the volume. "We hear you."

"About time," Willard said, sounding truly annoyed. "You've reached the bottom."

Jerking her head up, Connelly looked through the glass and was surprised to see the ice walls were now gone. They hadn't even noticed the transition from light grey to pitch black. "It's a little dark down here. Hit the exteriors."

After a moment, a dozen lights embedded around the outer circumference of the sphere's glass top blazed into the water. The liquid glowed eerily white, like over-aerated water. The bottom of the ice shelf hung above them, smoothed into swirling rises and falls, like an upside down Zen garden.

Robert was on his feet, staring at the watery haze. "Sure is cloudy."

Connelly joined him by the glass and furrowed her brow. "Could they be microbes? Europian phytoplankton maybe?"

"There would have to be bazillions of them," Robert said.

Connelly smirked. "Bazillions?"

Robert pointed to the com systems microphone. "Don't make me tell Willard about the video," he whispered.

Connelly's smirk disappeared. "See anything yet?"

Robert shook his head, no. There was nothing out there.

Nothing at all.

Five minutes of silent staring was all Robert could take. His disappointment grew with every passing second and the swaying created by sub ice currents began to turn his stomach. "This is hopeless."

Connelly shook her head, conceding, "I thought there would be more. I don't know. I guess we were expecting too much."

Something began to tickle at Robert's memory, something he had forgotten. Robert ignored Connelly and focused on recalling the faded memory...of what?

"This is like trying to explore the United States by looking through a straw," Connelly said. "We need to get a better view somehow; find out what's going on out there beyond the few feet we can see."

"That's it!" Robert shouted, startling Connelly back into one of the seats.

"God, Robert, what's it?"

A smile was stretching on Robert's face. "I just remembered the tech that landed me this gig."

Connelly's eyes widened, remembering Robert's ultra sensitive microphone system. "BUD."

"Ethan, you still listening?" Robert asked.

"Voyeuristic as ever."

"Do me a favor," Robert said, "Run power to the onboard BUD systems and switch control over to the sphere."

"You got it."

"Once BUD is online, we'll lose topside com," Robert said.

"Copy that," Willard said, "Just check back in fifteen. Here come your ears."

Willard's voice cut off and the speakers went silent for a moment. A light static hiss filled the cabin of the sphere as the speakers began receiving data from the onboard BUD system, which was listening to the entire Europian ocean.

Connelly leaned towards the nearest speaker, face to face with Robert. "I don't hear anything."

Robert bent down to the control panel and played with some knobs. "We're taking in too much. It can't process that much in real time. I'm going to reduce the range. How's a one mile radius sound?"

"Let's hear it."

Robert made the adjustments. As he hit the final key, initiating the changes, the cabin filled with a swirl of sounds that hurt their ears. Robert clamped his hands over his ears and could only see Connelly's lips moving, but he knew she was shouting. He quickly removed a hand from his head and flipped the BUD system off.

"What the hell was that?" Connelly asked.

"I, uh, I have no idea." Robert scratched his head. "It was as though the ocean was *full* of sound. On earth you might expect something like this only in highly dense populations of vocal mammals, whales, dolphins, seals, what have you."

"Could BUD be malfunctioning?"

Robert's aghast expression said it all.

"OK, if BUD is working, what *was* that?"

Robert's hand froze on his chin as he rubbed his scruffy beard. He began making adjustments to the BUD system.

"What are you doing?"

"Reducing the radius."

"To what?"

"One hundred yards."

Robert knew it was a long shot, and he could feel Kathy's incredulous look on the back of his neck. If something were within one hundred yards, they should have seen at least a hint of it before. But as far as their eyes could see, nothing was there. Robert reminded himself: *this is an alien world. It will be nothing like my preconceptions.*

Or perhaps they were overlooking the obvious. The sounds could be coming from several sources. Water flowing through the tubes of ice above them, pushing pockets of gas toward the surface. The ice itself, pulled by the gravitational force of Jupiter, could be scraping as massive shelves of ice flexed. Thermal vents from the stone core could be spewing fluids and gases noisily into the ocean. All three scenarios fit the bill and all were more plausible than alien life forms.

Still, he couldn't keep himself from hoping.

After making the final adjustments to BUD, Robert looked back at Kathy. She wrung her hands together and nodded. Robert pushed the final key.

The sound was crystal clear, but in contrast to their last experience, dead silent. Robert and Connelly stood quiet and still, as though they had just turned to stone under Medusa's gaze.

Click, click, click.

The noise was faint, but clear and crisp. Three clicks that sounded like cupped hands clapping.

Connelly shot Robert a glance. He could read the expression on her face. *What was that?*

Robert had no answer and chose to remain silent in case it repeated.

Ten seconds passed.

A vibration filled the inside of the sphere that began at the lowest pitch the human ear could perceive and built higher and higher. It passed in and through their bodies, shaking their very bones. But it wasn't painful. The experience was almost pleasant.

The low tone was followed by four more clicks, three base thumps and another, less powerful tone, which sounded as though it origins differed from the first.

"I can't believe I'm hearing this," Robert said

Connelly pressed herself against the glass wall and tried desperately to see through the murky water. "Dammit! I can't see a thing!"

Three high pitched squeaks zipped through the sphere, followed by two thumps and another deep tone, which lingered and faded peacefully. Robert felt his body relax as the tone faded, taking his tension with it.

"It sounds like they're right on top of us," Connelly said.

"They are," Robert said. "I, uh, I think they are."

With the quickness of a striking eagle, Connelly's hands lurched out and dug into Robert's arm. He flinched and choked back a shout. "What? What is it?"

Connelly smiled devilishly. Robert knew she had come up with the answer. "No sunlight. Extreme pressure. Sound familiar?"

Robert felt all the light switches in his mind being turned on simultaneously. In an instant he knew what Connelly suspected must be true. Robert jumped to the controls, turned off the BUD system and switch on the com. "Ethan, you read?"

"I'm here, but you didn't have to check in for another—"

"Not checking in. Ethan, kill the lights…all of them."

"Interior too?"

"All but the red light."

"OK, say goodnight."

Robert moved quickly, turning off the com and switching on the BUD system before the lights went out. He wanted to hear what he was seeing. Two seconds later they were plunged into near darkness. The only illumination came from the red overhead light, which allowed them to see, but didn't dilate their pupils or degrade their ability to see in the dark.

Through the dark, sounds continued to barrage their ears. Unworldly squeaks, drumming bass beats and powerful pulses of sound filled the interior of the sphere. The sound alone was enough to remind them they were on another world, but the complete darkness that now surrounded them made it all the more real.

Exploring the view from every inch of the sphere, Connelly and Robert looked more like hamsters in a ball than scientists. But Robert could feel his eyes adjusting to the dark. It wouldn't be long until...yes! A pinkish streak wiggled into and out of Robert's vision. It lasted only a second, but it was real.

He hadn't realized he had gasped, but Connelly suddenly appeared at his side.

"Did you see something?" Connelly asked, her voice rushed and breathy.

"Straight out," Robert said. "Don't blink."

The light came again, but this time a little closer and a little brighter. Robert wasn't sure if it was truly brighter or if his eyes were just growing accustomed to the dark, but it was there. Robert clasped his hand on Connelly's shoulder. "You were right," he said.

Connelly never took her eyes off the distant wriggling light. "Bioluminescence. It never occurred to me before. It makes sense, though. This environment closely resembles the deep oceans on earth. It's no surprise that life adapted similarly. But, it looks too small. The noise we heard was large, powerful. That couldn't be much bigger than a terrestrial sea snake."

"I, ah, I don't think it's small.... I think it's far away."

A deep thump pounded from the speakers, five times in a row, followed by a quick, sharp squeak that was louder than anything they had heard before.

Connelly held her fingers up and measured the colorful streak. Her lips moved as she whispered the calculations to herself. "Putting it at the farthest reaches of BUD, one hundred yards, that would make it..." Connelly's eyes widened. "...fifty feet long!"

151

Robert broke from Connelly's stare and continued watching the flowing creature, which he now knew could swallow them whole if it chose too...if it had a mouth at all. Robert began to laugh, but stopped suddenly as he noticed the streak was growing larger. Not only that, five more streaks, then seven more, twelve total joined the first. Thirteen streaks glided through the water, growing larger and heading straight for them.

꼬　꼬　꼬　꼬　꼬

Leaning back in his chair, Harris tried to relax. He gazed up at the clear ceiling of the control center and admired the view of Jupiter, watching as the largest planet's other moons slid past, casting dark spotted shadows on the gas giant's surface. It was a sight no other human beings, outside of this crew, had ever seen before.

He thought about how every landing, every discovery, every meal eaten from the time they arrived until the time they returned to Earth was history in the making. And what they had already discovered dwarfed all of the moon landings.

They had traveled further and had employed new technologies with a degree of success unheard of in any previous space mission. The moon missions had all been marked by near disasters. They were ultimately success stories, but the fates of their crews were often at risk.

Is that where we're headed? Harris thought. The attack on Peterson—and that's what it was, an attack—had him rattled. But Peterson was contained and the mission was back on track.

We're back on track. We'll stay on track.

He willed it to be true, but wasn't completely buying it.

Why?

He'd manned the control center for two landings now and on both occasions had little more to do than confirm the scheduled check-ins from the ground crews. He'd already heard from Choi, who was having great success at harvesting new Europhid samples, and Willard, who informed him that Dr. Connelly and Dr. Samuel's had reached the Europian ocean.

History in the making. And *he* was in charge.

Then why am I worrying?

Peterson.

It had been a little while since he'd checked on him. He brought up the security camera feed from the med-lab and gawked at the empty room. He checked to make sure the feed was live.

Is that vomit on the floor? he wondered.

It was.

Peterson who appeared to be ill, had somehow unlocked the doors and broken quarantine. "Great."

That's when he noticed the ceiling above him. The hull had turned solid again, the view of Jupiter gone.

"I hope you don't mind," Peterson said from the entrance of the control center. "The view was making me dizzy."

Harris felt his muscles tense and a tingle rose up his back from the base of his spine. "You're under quarantine. You better have a damn good reason for coming here."

As Peterson took a step forward, Harris could see he was hiding something behind his back.

"Oh, I do," Peterson said. "I have a very good reason."

17 – THE POD

Connelly winced as Robert's grip on her wrist tightened. The group of shimmering lights warbled closer, expanding in size with every passing moment. Neither of them had acted or said a word since the lights headed in their direction, but now, the pain from her wrist reminded Connelly of her own mortality and that while scientifically wonderful, whatever was coming their way, may also be hungry.

Her imagination ran rampant. The sphere, with its silver bottom and clear top, lit from the inside by a red light looked uncannily like a fishing bobber, dangling at the surface, waiting for something to swim along and bite. Only these creatures, whatever they were, were large enough to eat the sphere whole and yank the bulk of TES, and Willard, down the melted hole they had created.

Her wrist throbbed again. "Robert, we need to do something."

"Not yet."

"What? Why?"

Robert starred out at the pink lights, which now looked closer to a deep maroon. "I want to see them up close."

"We're in danger here."

"Nonsense."

Connelly took hold of Robert's arm and turned him so they were face to face. She noticed how his normally wrinkled forehead was abnormally loose and relaxed. "Now who's being foolish?"

"Kathy, these are alien creatures. They have never, in their lives, seen anything created by human hands. There is no reason to suspect they will view us as a food source. At best they may express some curiosity as to what we are, but they are likely to be more afraid of us than we are of them."

"My mother used to say that about bees," Connelly said.

"And?"

"I got stung."

"Well," Robert said, "I'm smarter than your mother."

Connelly couldn't help but smile. Robert looked over his shoulder, back towards the lights. They had stopped. "Look. They're keeping a distance. We'll be fine."

The coloration of the creatures shimmered from maroon to deep blue, and then lightened. Coinciding with the color change came a whooping call followed by a series of clicks, claps and a long base tone. Connelly smiled. The sound reminded her of a perfectly tuned cello. It occurred to her then that these calls, which were reminiscent of whale calls, though much more complicated, were coming from multiple creatures.

They're communicating!

Just as Connelly's eyes fully adjusted to the darkness and she began to make out other shapes in the deep beyond, the interior of the sphere began to grow lighter. At first, she ignored the light, too captivated by strange creatures lurking in the distance. But as the illumination inside the sphere grew, the view of the watery apparitions began to dwindle. When she saw her reflection in the glass, she could no longer stand the distraction.

In a blur of motion, Connelly launched toward the controls and turned off the BUD system, which plunged the sphere into silence. She flipped on the com and shouted, "Ethan, keep the damn lights down!"

Willard's voice came back after a pause. "Say again? Did you say the lights are on?"

Connelly was fuming. Every second wasted talking was another second the creatures might swim away. Some oceanographers spend entire lifetimes searching vast oceans for creatures like Architeuthis, the giant squid, and never see it living in its natural habitat. Here they were, in an alien ocean, witnessing creatures never seen before and now they might miss out because Willard couldn't get the damn lights right!

"They're leaving!" Robert shouted. "I think they're leaving! But I can't really see them…"

"Ethan, turn off all the lights," Connelly said, her voice as cold as the ice above. "Turn them off, now."

"Boss," Willard said, his voiced forced into calmness, "I'm showing all lights off. If you want me to turn off the red light, I will, but if you're getting light down there, it's not anything I can control from up here."

"If it's not coming from the sphere," Connelly said, "where's it—"

Connelly's breath caught as she spoke the last words. She and Robert had been starring through the glass, out toward the pod of creatures. Not once had either of them turned around. Connelly became acutely aware that the shadows which played across the interior of the sphere revealed that the light source filling the cabin originated from behind them, *outside* the sphere.

With a gentle squeeze on Robert's arm, Connelly got his attention. He glanced at her and reacted to the terror-filled expression on her face by stiffening his entire body. His eyes widened. "Behind us?"

Connelly nodded.

The inside of the sphere filled with a baritone call that vibrated their eardrums and tickled their teeth. It was gentle, probing and lasted ten seconds. After it finished, the sphere filled with an eerie quiet.

It was broken by Willard's voice. "What the hell was that?"

Connelly fought to remain composed. The light was still bright within the sphere and she was too petrified to turn around.

"Creatures—bioluminescent—they're using calls for echolocation, maybe even communication." Connelly noticed how clinical her voice sounded. When faced with the unknown and terrifying, many scientists become detached observers, taking mental notes, instead of tackling the deadly situation head on. It was a defense mechanism that helped several of her colleagues survive the worst, but the same technique had dulled the senses of others, and led to their deaths.

"Are you in danger?" Willard asked. "They must be close for it to be so loud."

"They're still a ways off," Robert said. "We're receiving the sounds through BUD."

Willard's response was immediate and rushed. "The com system is active. BUD is off. The sound we just heard was not from BUD. I repeat, that sound was not from BUD. I'm pulling you up."

"No!" Connelly had to see this for herself. "Wait."

Click, click, click. The noises were loud. Tangibly close.

"Boss, I—"

"Just wait." Connelly turned her head to the side, looking at Robert. She could see the bright source of light in her periphery, just outside the sphere. "Ready?"

"On three," Robert said.

Connelly grasped Robert's hand. "One."

Robert bit his upper lip. "Two."

"Three."

Both turned at once, facing the light source.

Connelly fell back immediately, landing in one of the chairs with her hands clasped over her quivering lips. Connelly's muscles shook with energy. She decided that if this was it, if they died in the next few seconds, she wouldn't regret losing her life or never finishing her work. Just seeing the creature that floated two feet from the sphere's exterior was worth ten lifetimes, because in a thousand generations of humanity, no one had ever seen anything like this.

ꟼꟼ   ꟼꟼ   ꟼꟼ   ꟼꟼ   ꟼꟼ

Brilliant light from Choi's 1000 watt head lamp reflected off the field of crimson Europhids and shimmered on the surrounding mounds of white ice. Choi noticed how, as she moved her head from side to side, passing the light across the field, the Europhids swayed with each pass, as though they were physically touched by the light.

Choi's knees began to ache after a half hour of scooping Europhid samples from the ice. Taking a break wasn't normally something she chose to do, but there was no rush on the sample gathering, and she enjoyed the solitude. After spending so much time with the crew, it was nice to have her thoughts to herself. She was almost glad Peterson got himself quarantined. If he hadn't, he'd be here with her, blathering on excitedly.

Leaning against the ATV's seat, Choi let her muscles relax. The stress brought on by the bio-lab incident had been enough to knot her back into a minefield of tension. She had begun to think that her expertise in rare diseases would be of little use on the mission, but with Peterson's infection, if that's what it truly was, her skills had been called unexpectedly to the forefront of the mission. She believed the alien substance would have no effect—it wasn't designed for human physiology. But if it did, his life would depend solely on her ability to fix whatever ailments the Europhid sting caused.

What bothered her most was the knowledge that only she possessed—if Peterson's infection became deadly, she doubted there was anything she *could* do to save him. The time it would take to understand and study what the alien substance was doing to his body could only be completed post mortem. Her only consolation was that the infection seemed localized. Chances of the substance infecting another crew member were slim to none. Peterson might die, but the rest of them, barring another accident, would survive.

Choi sighed and looked up at Jupiter, watching the pink lightening flash. Every streak lit up a portion of Jupiter's surface, each the size of Europa itself, maybe bigger. She marveled at the raw power of the planet. If she had been anymore entranced by the sight, she may not have noticed the flicker of motion at the edge of the Europhid field.

Whipping around toward the field, Choi's headlamp illuminated the area with a sudden brilliance that the Europhid's seemed to lean away from. But other than that, nothing appeared to be moving.

Maybe they react to the lightning on Jupiter? Choi thought.

To test her theory, Choi extinguished her headlamp. The surrounding area plunged into darkness. After a minute, her eyes began to adjust. The bright stars to her right and left seemed more brilliant and more numerous than ever. But the most astonishing sight was the flashes of light within Jupiter's clouds.

She gazed up through the darkness of space and saw more and more flashes of light. They were dimmer than the others, which she assumed was why she couldn't see them with her headlamp on—like looking at the stars in the city. Her bright light overpowered the distant dim light.

But the brighter flashes, the planet sized ones, were so brilliant that Choi felt herself occasionally squint from the light. She then noticed that the light from the brighter flashes of light, the pink, yellow and blue, all reached the surface of Europa. With each flash the ice and Europhid field were briefly and faintly illuminated.

Throughout a series of these flashes, Choi watched the Europhid field. The motion was faint, but she could see that they reacted to the light. If they react to light this dim, Choi thought, the sun's light must be extremely powerful. Choi wondered if this extreme sensitivity to light was part of how the Europhids survived in such an extreme environment.

The lightning stopped flashing as the storm mellowed. The landscape descended into a ceaseless darkness. If Choi couldn't feel the seat of the ATV beneath her and the warmth of her breath within her facemask, she might believe she'd entered limbo. She forced herself to look toward the horizon occasionally, to focus on the small band of stars visible past the outline of Jupiter. They looked brilliant, but the light they cast on the surface of Europa was imperceptible to Choi's eyes.

But what about the Europhids?

A flash of light, which may have been on par with previous displays, though it seemed brighter, shot through the clouds of Jupiter, momentarily revealing a mass of angry swirled clouds. Choi looked away from the harsh light and down at the Europhid field.

What she saw made her shudder.

Choi gripped the sides of the ATV. *I must have seen wrong*, she thought. *It isn't possible.*

Moving slowly, Choi reached for her headlamp and switched it on. The blinding glow of light shot stabs of pain through her eyes and she had to shield her face from the majority of the view while she readjusted. She only hoped her eyes adjusted before... No.

She was wrong.

She *had* to be.

Choi moved her hands slowly away from her face and looked out over the Europhid field. The majority of the field looked the same. The closest area, only ten feet from her perch atop the ATV, held Choi's gaze. She had taken samples, at least thirty of the Europhids, and sealed them in level five containment units. She had carefully and methodically tagged them and placed them inside the ATV's storage trailer.

But the eight foot swath of ice she had cleared was now covered. The Europhid's were back!

Choi slid off the ATV and moved toward the back of the ATV's trailer. She kept a close eye on the field as she moved. Her breath came slowly, and her head began to pound with tension. She shook her hands out as she reached for the trailer's handle. She took hold of the door and unlatched it. Swinging the door open, Choi jumped back, unsure of what she would see.

She felt a measure of relief when she saw that all the containers were still fixed in their places and secure. At least the Europhids weren't smart enough to mount an escape from sealed containers. Still...

Choi turned her attention to the field, which was as innocent looking as ever. She scoured the area with her eyes, making sure she didn't miss anything, any kind of clue to what really happened here. She continually reached the same conclusion. The new Europhids didn't spontaneously grow to replace the ones she had removed.

It was much worse than that.

When darkness had enveloped the area and blinded Choi to her surroundings, the field—the entire field of Europhids—had inched toward her.

Ω   Ω   Ω   Ω   Ω

An attack never came.

Connelly had expected a violent reaction from the creature. She had no idea why, but the twenty-five foot creature just hung in the water, staring at them through its two charcoal eyes. Connelly wasn't sure who was more curious, this creature or her? It certainly seemed to be watching them.

The beast was the approximate shape of a blue whale, wide and tall at the head and tapering back toward the rear. In place of flippers this creature had undulating "wings" like that of a manta ray, only these ran from the head all the way to the tail. Its black eyes were placed one each side, much like a terrestrial mammal. Its gaping jaw opened vertically, like elevator doors. The creature's gargantuan mouth opened and closed causing its body to expand and shrink—breathing water.

Beyond all of the outstanding features on the behemoth was the single attribute that garnered Connelly and Robert's attention in the first place. Its skin was clear, like a pane of glass and its organs and veins glowed with vibrant colors. A beating blue heart rested at the center of the creature's body, partially obscured by various innards, but it could be seen inside, thumping away.

Connelly thanked God they thought to install cameras on the outside of TES. This was footage she would want to see over and over again.

A deep cry exploded from the creature's mouth, causing a rainbow of colors to ripple across its exterior, from front to back. It was a light show the likes of which Connelly had never seen, not even on the most dazzling of Earth's bioluminescent denizens.

Robert fell to his knees, his hands shaking. "Holy…"

Then the response came.

From behind.

Connelly whipped around. Swimming past, no more than twenty feet away was an entire pod of the creatures. They had snuck up in silence while she and Robert were captivated by the smaller one outside the sphere. Connelly realized the creature they'd had the staring match with was the smallest of the group, perhaps just a baby.

Connelly kneeled next to Robert. They looked like two praying saints, but neither could speak a word. The only sound that escaped their mouths was the occasional gasp as they were simultaneously gripped by awe and fear.

Twenty-odd creatures swept past, gently propelled by their wavering wings. The largest of the group looked to be at least seventy-five feet long. With each roll of flesh, the wings shimmered bright pink. Connelly realized that this is what they had seen from a distance. The colors from the interior of the creatures were beautiful but in sheer brilliance, the light emitted from the outer edge of the wings was staggering.

Connelly's vision blurred from tears, swirling her world into a tie-dyed rainbow. She quickly wiped the tears from her eyes, which beaded on the outside of her PMS and rolled off onto the floor. She didn't want to miss a second.

Another call beckoned, returning Connelly's attention back to the baby. A gentle rocking caused Connelly and Robert to fall forward, but both were able to catch themselves on the console that ringed the interior of the sphere. When they looked back up, the baby's right eye starred at them from only inches away. Only the thick glass of the TES sphere separated them.

Connelly reached out and placed her hand on the glass, wishing to God she could touch the creature, just once. A distant call sounded, followed by three dull clicks. The baby, Robert and Connelly looked toward the source. The pod was moving off. The baby called back and was answered promptly. The message was clear, even to Connelly; *time to go.*

The baby turned back to the sphere and let out a high pitched whine. Then, with a graceful twitch of its wings, floated back, spun around and chased after the pod. As Connelly's vision tracked the baby's retreat, she realized that her eyes had completely adjusted to the dim environment. She could see the bottom, hundreds of feet below, alive with color. Creatures scurried back and forth. Multi-colored plants and coral-like organisms swayed brilliantly in the deep ocean currents. In the water, schools of bioluminescent fishlike creatures of every size, shape and color, darted about. This was a massively intricate ecosystem on par with Earth's.

"Have you ever seen anything so beautiful?" Robert said.

Connelly knew the answer—no—she hadn't even dreamt of anything so magnificent. But she never spoke the word. Her mind was elsewhere. Despite the splendor surrounding them, she couldn't move past the brilliance of the bioluminescent whale-like creatures—bio-whales, she decided to call them. They displayed intelligence equal to a dolphin's, at least, if not more, and she couldn't accept just letting them swim away.

They might never see them again. They had to be observed for as long as possible.

Connelly stood quickly, her body language resolute. She strode to the sphere's main console and worked the keyboard with electrifying fervor.

Robert snapped his head toward Connelly, recognizing the series of keys she just struck. "What are you doing?"

Connelly smiled wide. "Hold on, Robert. We're going for a swim."

18 – PREDATORS

During their previous excursion on the moon, Willard found it near impossible to tear his eyes away from the view above, but with the majority of the sky blotted out by Jupiter's dark side and the remainder of the view obscured by TES's bright lighting, there wasn't much to look at. Willard turned to the control panel and began a series of simple diagnostics on the TES system. Unfortunately, Robert had designed the system so well that, not only was there nothing worth reporting, but the results had come back within seconds.

Willard decided that with twenty minutes before the next scheduled check-in from Connelly, he had time to take a stroll. The hard metal of the TES panel connected solidly with his booted feet and sent him further into the air than the ice. He reached the ice in six large bounds and jumped out onto it. After spending so much time in the Antarctic, the frozen texture of the moon's surface felt familiar to him. Some of the tension wearing at him faded.

He hated being left behind, especially on a mission that was potentially dangerous. He had pleaded his case to Connelly on several occasions, explaining in detail all the problems that could arise, all of the situations that might require his physical presence. But she was hard set in her ways, as usual. She wanted him topside, even insisted he could do more for them from the surface. Willard cringed. He was becoming a grunt on this mission.

Sure, he still wasn't a scientist, but his skills were the ones that kept curiosity from killing the science cat. What was worse about all the waiting was that he knew something was going on down there, and he was missing it. He could hear the excitement in Connelly's voice last time they spoke. And the confusion about the lights being on. And that sound...

What the hell did they find?

Willard stopped and looked back at TES. All was quiet. The cranes sat still, holding the cables in place directly over the melted hole. The bright lights illuminated the black metallic surface of TES, and made the ice around its border glow like a white hot sun. Through the light, Willard could see the green screen of the control console. It hadn't changed. Everything was normal.

Sighing inside his facemask, Willard looked up expecting to see the black nothingness of Jupiter, but instead found himself looking up at a spectacular light show. All across Jupiter he could flashes of light zipping from horizon to horizon. His brow furrowed as he tried to remember hearing anything about this aspect of Jupiter. During their training back at the GEC headquarters, they had been fed an annoying amount of information about Jupiter, Europa and the other neighboring moons, but he couldn't recall any information or images that showed these lights.

Maybe no one knows about them? Maybe I'm the first person to discover them!

Willard's mind began making mental leaps, plotting how the discovery would alter his future. Of course, they'd name the lights after him, Willard's Display or Ethan's Lights. He laughed. *That* would never happen.

He remembered the digital image recorder kept with the TES equipment. He decided to run back, grab it, shoot a few minutes of video and then be ready to receive Connelly's check in.

Willard turned back to TES and squinted as his eyes adjusted from the pitch black above to the glaring light. All at once, Willard's muscles tensed like a twisting rope. He stared straight ahead, watching to see if what he thought he saw—the TES cables moving downward—happened again.

All at once, a spew of worse case scenarios filled Willard's imagination. The TES cables were dangling! Cut loose! The weight of the sphere was no longer pulling the cable down, allowing it to sway back and forth freely. Willard leapt forward, moving too damn slow in the low gravity. *Too damn slow!*

Willard's mind wrestled with the possibilities.

The sphere could have been knocked loose and sunk to the bottom.

It could have sprung a leak and imploded under the pressure.

Something could have eaten them!

As he approached the border of the closest TES panel, the most likely scenario rammed into Willard's consciousness. "Damn it, Connelly."

Willard activated his com. "Connelly, come in."

Thirty seconds past. No response.

Willard reached the control panel and took in the screen, which was now alive with blinking messages. It confirmed his fear that the sphere had detached.

"Connelly, if you are reading me, respond now."

With a tightly clenched jaw, Willard began to pace. He knew Connelly had voluntarily separated the sphere. He wondered if she might try a stunt like this and had warned her not to try it without him present. She swore she wouldn't. Typically, she was honest with him. So what made her detach?

Must be important, he thought. But no matter what it was they had found down there, Connelly was still getting a lecture, if only to make him feel better for all this waiting.

Willard raised the volume on his com and heard a loud hiss. After ten more minutes of waiting, he swore to God he would spare Connelly the lecture if they'd just check in. He walked to the hole TES melted in the ice and looked down. The water was black below, hidden from TES's lights. He was cut off and helpless to help.

Willard tightened his fingers until they hurt. "Dammit, Connelly...What have you gotten yourself into?"

ꑕ ꑕ ꑕ ꑕ ꑕ

Limbs sprawling, Harris dove to the floor of the control center and slid into a nearby console. After quickly righting himself, he looked back to where Peterson stood, still wielding a rake with dagger-like blades. Harris had been immediately wary of Peterson's unsanctioned visit to the control center, but what tipped him off to the ensuing attack was Peterson's unusual stance. It was clear he was hiding something behind his back. And the tone of his voice somehow sounded threatening. When Peterson reeled back and swung the rake around like a sickle, Harris had already flung himself to the floor.

Peterson yanked at the rake, pulling its imbedded blades from the chair's backboard. Harris realized that if he hadn't moved, he would be bleeding to death from twenty stab wounds. Harris climbed to his feet just as Peterson freed the rake and faced off with the captain.

"Peterson..." Harris's tone was authoritative, irritated. He decided that wasn't the best idea. No need to egg the man on. "Michael, put the rake down. Tell me what's bothering you."

Harris watched as Peterson shuffled forward. He could see that his actions were slightly off, staggered and stiff, but just barely. Then he met Peterson's eyes...his *red* eyes. Peterson still had pupils, but the whites of his eyes had gone red, as though the vessels within had burst.

The rake came back, readied for the next assault.

"Michael, wait," Harris said. "Don't do this."

"I do only what must be done," Peterson said, his voice sounded different. Scratchy.

"Peterson...what?" *This isn't Peterson*, Harris thought. *He's not himself. Perhaps the sting he received is affecting his mind, causing hallucinations?* Harris cursed himself. He shouldn't have let Choi go back to the surface. He needed her here.

"You should not have come," Peterson said.

The rake came around like a picket fence caught in a tornado. Harris ducked just in time, feeling the breeze from the farming tool turned weapon *whoosh* over his balding head. "Come where? What are you talking about?"

"You," Peterson said with a deathly gaze that stung Harris's eyes, "are not welcome here. You must be—" A gurgling sound rose up from Peterson's throat. "We must be…immunized!" Peterson lunged forward and brought the rake down hard, smashing the view screen above Harris head.

Harris could see that Peterson had gone completely insane. The reasons for his mental state no longer mattered. It was clear that if Harris didn't fight back, he would die. And with this maniac left alone on the ship, who knows what would happen to the others on the surface.

Peterson swung the rake up over his head, preparing to bring it down again. Just as he began his downward motion, Harris bolted forward like a charging ram. The rake flew through the air and clambered to the floor as Harris tackled Peterson around the waist. Both men fell to the floor, a tangled mess of flailing arms and legs.

Having been in his fair share of fights during his early military years, Harris knew that once the advantage was gained, you should never let your enemy regroup. And right now, Peterson was his enemy. He was the entire crew's enemy. Harris unleashed a flurry of blows to Peterson's kidneys that he knew would cause the man to pee blood for the next few weeks, but he needed to end this fight quickly and that usually did the trick. The effect was instantaneous.

Peterson clutched his side and winced. Harris stood and watched as Peterson's legs shook with the pain. The man was beaten.

Moving to the com console, Harris prepared to call the crew back from the surface. He didn't want anyone out of his sight until they understood what was happening to Peterson. He'd only turned his back to Peterson for five seconds.

"Interesting, the way you feel pain." It was Peterson.

Spinning around quickly, Harris almost fell over backward with surprise when he saw Peterson standing on his feet, looking as though nothing had happened. He wore no expression of pain and aside from the fresh wrinkles on his uniform, appeared just as he had when he first entered in the control center. Peterson charged forward, wildly flailing his fists.

Harris sidestepped, placed a hand behind Peterson's skull and extended his foot. Peterson went down hard, striking his forehead on the nearest console. The crack of bone on metal made Harris wince.

Petersons's body lay still on the floor, a pool of crimson liquid gathering around his head. With a slow jagged movement, Peterson moved his lips. "P…Plea…"

Harris starred at Petersons's lips, utterly amazed the man was still attempting to form words. A flash of movement to the side told Harris that Peterson's failed speaking attempt was all just a clever distraction. But the realization came too late. Looking down, Harris saw the rake swing across the floor in a wide arc. The pole clipped him behind both ankles with surprising force that sent him to the floor.

When he looked up, Peterson was already standing above him.

"Vaccination."

He wasn't sure if the man was just speaking gibberish or if he was pleading for some kind of cure to whatever was wreaking havoc with his mind. It didn't matter. As Peterson raised the rake above his head, Harris realized that he would die above Europa, along with the rest of the crew.

Peterson brought the rake down, smashing into Harris's skull. When Peterson stood back, blood gushed over the sides of Harris's face and onto the floor. Peterson stepped over the body and exited the control center.

נ   נ   נ   נ   נ

The sphere dropped down, falling gently away from the TES cable like a slightly buoyant stone. With a dull pop two panels on opposite sides of the sphere opened and locked into position. They looked like flippers. From the rear, a previously concealed compartment opened. Two propellers extended out into the water and began spinning. Having transformed into a sleek submersible, the sphere launched through the water.

A bolt of excitement shot through Connelly. TES had already performed beyond their best predictions and now the submersible was working flawlessly.

Sitting behind the controls, which looked like those of a fighter jet, Connelly thrust the control stick forward and the sphere sped up. Robert fell back into the seat next to Connelly and quickly buckled himself in. "Warn me next time you're going to do that."

Connelly hardly heard the words. Her thoughts were preoccupied with catching the pod of bio-whales. They had covered a fairly large distance in a short amount of time. Determined not to lose sight of the creatures, Connelly pushed the sphere to its max speed of thirty knots, hoping that the creatures wouldn't mind a snooping tailgater.

Within a minute, they were pulling up behind the pod, gaining on the baby and what must be its mother, a sixty-foot behemoth swimming just above. Connelly eased up on the speed and kept pace with the pod. A squeeze on her arm broke her concentration. She looked at Robert, whose face was pale. "Be careful," he said. "Please."

Connelly grunted an unintelligible response that confirmed she had heard the words, but made no indication of whether or not she would heed Robert's warning. If these creatures wanted to lose them, they could—Connelly felt sure of it. If the bio-whales saw the sphere as a food source, they would have eaten them when the sphere was dangling helplessly from the surface. Twisting her lips, Connelly began a mental brawl, one side arguing Robert's point, the other compelling her to push forward.

With a deep sigh, Connelly eased back on the speed. Robert's advice was usually wise. It pained her to not venture closer. But as she slowed, so did the pod, like they were waiting for the sphere to catch up. As if to confirm Connelly's suspicions, the baby craned its head around, a feat an Earth whale could never do, and called to them. The sound was soft and inviting, like a deep resonating coo. Connelly looked at Robert, her eyes probing for his thoughts.

"Go ahead," he said with a quick nod. "If we're going to die while making first contact with an alien species, so be it."

"We made it this far," Connelly said. "We're not going to die." With that she accelerated the sphere forward, nearing the outer edge of the pod. They bobbed up and down in the wake of the bio-whale's pulsing wing.

Robert gripped the sides of his seat. "So says you."

With the pod of whales surrounding them, the interior of the sphere transformed into a world of glowing colors. Bio-whales swam on every side, some coming closer to take a peek, some paying no attention. Connelly half worked the controls and half gaped in amazement. Sweat beaded on her forehead as she worked to avoid a collision with one of the creatures, an accident which would certainly be fatal.

The light within the sphere suddenly grew brighter and Connelly found herself navigating around the head of the largest creature. Looking back, she could see all seventy-five feet stretched out. She wondered if this was as large as the creatures grew. *Maybe there are other, larger specimens?* she thought.

A large black eye, the size of a cantaloupe stared inside the sphere, watching them. Connelly stared right back into the eye and saw intelligence. A gentle moan vibrated from the creature's skull and vibrated the inside of the sphere. Connelly could feel her organs shake within her body. She wasn't sure what the noise meant. It could have been a warning, a greeting or just a grunt. But as Connelly looked into the giant's eye, she was sure it meant something. They were going to have to figure out what, someday.

"Umm, I feel ridiculous bringing this up now, but ahh, have we had the external cameras running?" Robert's voice sounded nervous.

Tension sprung into Connelly's body and panic set in before she had time to process the question. The sensation was much like the tricks her cousin Tom pulled on her when they were teenagers. He would look at her homework, license or other important document and say as seriously as he could, "You spelled your name wrong." Connelly always fell for it, feeling momentarily panicked while her mind reminded herself that it was impossible, she could never make such an obvious mistake. And even though she knew she had spelled her name right, she always double-checked after Tom left the room, just in case.

Connelly reached forward and checked the status of the external camera array. All were functioning. All were recording. Thank God.

A sudden shriek, louder than any sound Connelly had heard in her life, ripped through the interior of the sphere. Connelly and Robert both fell to the floor, clasping their hands over their ears. Even after the sound had dissipated, a constant ringing plagued her hearing. Connelly rubbed her head, clearing the confusion away. When she refocused her thoughts, something had changed.

It was dark.

Connelly pulled herself up and saw Robert searching the circumference of sphere, peering out into the pitch black water surrounding them. The bio-whales had left. Fast.

"Any sign of them?" Connelly asked.

Robert pointed into the distance. "I, ahh, I think they went that way…but they were moving fast. And that sound…Before I fell to the floor, I saw them swim away. I know there is no basis for me understanding what or how these creatures think, but they looked completely terrified."

"They're seventy-feet long, what could possibly threaten them?"

Click, click, click.

The sound was distinct from those of the bio-whales and came in three second intervals.

Connelly held her breath, listening.

Click, click, click.

"You know what that is." Robert said.

Connelly looked into Robert's glassy eyes. "Echolocation," she said.

Robert nodded. "Something's out there—something big—and as long as we're in the open water, there is no place, and I mean no place, we can hide."

19 – DIVE

Regret wasn't an emotion that Connelly often felt. Her entire life, aside from her bouts with anxiety, read like a textbook example of how to make positive choices. But since joining the Europa mission, it seemed her decision-making abilities were lackluster at best. Thinking about getting involved with Peterson was her first mistake. The experiment gone awry involving the plant incubator was her second. Her third mistake now appeared to be going for a spin in the TES, the consequences of which she and Robert now faced.

The electric glow of the distant schools of fish faded around them, returning the water to its previous pitch black state. Even the sea floor seemed less radiant, as though the tiny creatures and plant life were attempting to draw less attention by dimming their luminosity.

Connelly's eyes shifted to the top of the sphere's interior. The red light, which allowed their eyes to fully adjust to low light while providing enough illumination to see by, glowed brightly in the darkness. They would be easy to see.

We're attracting the creature, Connelly thought.

Click, click, click.

The sound was loud and continuous, repeating every three seconds. The muscles on Connelly's face contracted and tightened with each click until she felt her head would burst, spewing her liquefied mind over the glass of the sphere.

"We need to turn the red light off!" Connelly shouted between clicks.

Click, click, click.

Connelly covered her ears with her hands.

Through the clicks she heard Robert's voice. He was shouting, but she couldn't understand what he was saying. All she could focus on was shutting off the damn light. Then maybe whatever was lurking in the darkness would leave them alone long enough to make a hasty retreat to the surface. Connelly moved toward the red light and prepared to remove the colored glass and extract the bulb. The plan was to perform each move during the three second intervals.

Why didn't we put a light switch in here for that bulb! she thought.

A click of echolocation rang through her hands and into her ears, but it also shook the sphere violently. *The creature must be close.* She had three seconds.

After removing her hands from her ears, Connelly reached for the red glass light fixture. She unscrewed the glass two full rotations in three seconds and then recovered her ears. She waited for the next echolocation to sound out.

It never came.

Instead, she felt an insistent tapping on her shoulder. She turned and saw Robert standing behind her. His face was unusually placid, like he had just received an injection of Botox. "Don't bother," he said, "it's here." Robert stepped aside.

Through the glass, Connelly saw a wriggling worm-like creature, no bigger than a large terrestrial earth night crawler. Glowing brilliant red, the small creature seemed to dance in space like a puppet being dangled by a string. *Like a worm on a hook. Like an angler fish.* The angler fish, which lives in the deepest, darkest portions of the Atlantic and Antarctic oceans, dangles a glowing lure to attract prey towards its massive, dagger toothed jaws.

Connelly's shoulders fell down in defeat. "Oh shit."

Robert ducked down slowly, slid to a side panel and popped it open. He began fiddling with the internal wiring.

Connelly glanced down at him, afraid that any motion, would attract the attention from the creature of unknown size that lurked silently outside the sphere. "What are you doing?"

"Rewiring the lighting controls so we can control the light from down here without being attached to the topside cables."

Connelly gently slid her body down and kneeled next to Robert while keeping her eyes glued on the red worm doing a happy dance outside their window. "And that will accomplish what?"

Robert shifted his body under a bundle of wires. He broke two, stripped them quickly with his teeth and reconnected them oppositely. "I'm assuming that most creatures in this ocean haven't seen anything brighter than what we've already seen. Bioluminescence isn't typically glaringly bright, though it may sometimes seem so in the dark."

"Get to the point, please," Connelly said.

"We'll blind it…if only long enough to escape. Turn on everything we've got and make a run for it. It should be like staring into the sun for these creatures. And if the effect is lasting, we should have plenty of time to—"

Click…

The sound was gentle.

Probing.

"We don't have much time," Robert said.

Connelly tensed her muscles and prepared to spring into action. "I'll handle the controls. You work the lights."

Robert nodded.

"Go!"

נ   נ   נ   נ   נ

Like a stone monolith, Peterson stood before the door to the decon room. He was fully garbed in his PMS and holding his hood-like helmet in his hands. Moving independently of his body, Peterson turned his head to the left. His eyes scanned back and forth left to right in a rapid motion as he read a bright red sign.

WARNING: PERSONAL MULTI-PRESSURE SUITS MUST BE SEALED BEFORE ENTERING DECONTAMINATION ROOM. FAILURE TO DO SO MAY RESULT IN DEATH.

Peterson's eyes lingered on the last word. He reached out and grazed his fingers across the letters, feeling the subtle indentations of the printed word.

"Death," Peterson said, his voice low and distorted.

His eyes moved up, scanning the previous words. He stopped on, "DECONTAMINATION ROOM." Again, he eased his hand across the text. He turned his attention to the sign above the decon room door, which read: DECONTAMINATION ROOM — DOCKING BAY AHEAD.

"Decontamination is death."

As though an electric shock had just jolted through his fingers, Peterson yanked his hand away from the sign. He took one step toward the decon room

174

and stopped. He looked down with wide, red eyes and saw the helmet still in his hands. A gasp escaped his lips and he quickly flung the helmet onto his head and locked it down. His breaths came rapid and deep.

The doors slid open as he stepped inside. He looked down at his hands as the decon room doors closed behind him. They were shaking. The doors slammed shut.

When the exit to the decon room opened up into the docking bay, Peterson burst out, gasping for air. Like frozen fish being flung at a Japanese market, he slammed onto the smooth floor of the docking bay and slid, stopping in a rigid fetal position.

Muscles twitching, Peterson slowly uncurled. Wrinkles of anxiety crisscrossed his forehead. Sounding like a small child coming down from a crying fit, Peterson's voice mixed with each vibrato breath, until slowly, he regained control of his breathing of his body. He stood, inspected the PMS and then struck out in a bold stride across the docking bay.

He stopped in front of Lander Two, which was identical to Lander One. In under a minute he had entered the lander, strapped himself in and started the engines. As the docking bay doors spread open, Peterson caught sight of the flashing lights on Jupiter's cloudy surface. The electrical storms were still raging. The occasional flash illuminated a slice of red on the moon's surface—a vast field of Europhids.

With every show of crimson on the surface of Europa, Peterson's body became more relaxed. He gripped the controls and gently lifted off the docking bay floor. As he guided the craft out into space, he caught a glimpse of a red glow, rippling from a portion of the moon's surface. It was a display never seen from this point of view and a genuine smile creased his lips.

"Come in, Harris, are you reading me? Over." Choi's voice seemed like a thunderous boom in Peterson's ear. He shook and crashed his knee into the console. "If you can hear me, something strange is going on down here. The Europhids...I think there is more to them than we know. I think you should watch Peterson more closely. I'm going to call the TES crew and rendezvous with them back at Lander One unless you tell me otherwise. If you are receiving this, reply when you have coms back. Over."

Peterson squinted and glared at the surface of Europa with the intensity of a coiled snake, ready to strike. Through gritted teeth, he spoke, "Decontamination."

฿   ฿   ฿   ฿   ฿

A dull, constant pain twisted in the sockets behind Robert's eyes. With every movement, the pain cut through his skull. And it didn't help that he was moving as quick as he could. He was working the new lighting controls at a frantic pace, setting them up to all turn on at once. It was more difficult than he thought it would be. Connelly was ready at the sphere's control stick, waiting for the world to glow.

"Robert," Connelly said, her voice stretched with tension, "when I said, 'go,' and jumped up here I thought you were going to turn on the lights?"

"Almost there..." Robert's squeezed his tongue white between his lips. His fingers flew over the keys, finalizing the procedure. "Got it!" Robert slammed down the final key.

Bright white light burst into the water like a flash-bang grenade. But in that blinding moment, Robert refused to close his eyes. He had to see what lurked outside the sphere. When he saw the beast, he wished he hadn't.

Robert scanned from left to right. Hovering just feet from the sphere's exterior were two lips. Each lip was a foot tall and stretched endlessly to each side. Two softball sized, obsidian, eyeballs, only two feet apart, which seemed unnaturally close for a creature of this size, rested just above the top lip. The leviathan's skin had the texture and color of sand, while its two gargantuan lips looked a shade darker.

It took Robert only two seconds to get a full view of the creature—exactly the same time it took for all hell to break loose.

In reaction to the blazing light, the predator lurched back and sunk its eyes back into its head, concealing them from the light. The plan had worked, but Robert quickly noticed a deadly side effect. As the creature reeled from the light, it opened its titanic mouth, which appeared to be large enough to swallow a bio-whale whole, and sucked in. Ocean water, and everything in it, was pulled toward the beast's mouth.

"Dive, Connelly! Dive!" Robert's voice cracked as he pushed the shout out with every decibel his voice box could manage.

Robert was thrown back into his chair as the sphere dropped down. Connelly had the control stick pushed all the way forward, sending them into a rapid and uncontrolled descent. Robert wondered if it would be enough.

The creature was still sucking in. Robert could feel the pull, like gravity. The bottom lip of the beast came into view as they dove down, but they were still approaching the exquisite jaws, which Robert could now see were filled with human sized teeth. The teeth were jagged and crisscrossed, meant for snagging and holding prey rather than chewing. Robert was sure this giant could swallow its dinner whole.

He felt ill as he saw the inside of the creature's throat, wide like a cave, ribbed by a hidden skeletal structure. But the vomit that threatened to free itself from his throat never made it out his mouth. He swallowed it back down as he realized that they were going to crash directly into the creature's lower lip.

"Watch out for the lip!" Robert said.

Connelly pushed harder on the stick. "I'm trying!"

Robert buckled his safety belt a split second before the struck the lip. The collision wasn't as jarring as Robert had expected. They bounced into the creature's flaccid lip and instead of being pulverized, were spun end over end.

The sphere continued its rapid decent as it spun like a cue ball across a pool table. One hundred feet below, the sphere finally came to a stop. Robert leaned forward, head between knees and wretched onto the floor. Without pausing, he wiped off his mouth and looked at Connelly. "We can't outrun that thing down here."

Click, click, click.

The pain behind Robert's eyes became like a quickly repeating explosion inside his cranium. The son-of-a-bitch was hunting them!

Connelly bit her lip and furrowed her brow. "Then we'll have to outsmart it." She thrust the control stick forward and they shot into another rollercoaster drop.

Click, click, click.

The sound grew louder, closer.

Trying desperately not to vomit again, Robert gripped the side of his chair and watched with wide eyes as they rapidly approached the glowing ocean floor. "What in God's name are you doing?"

Connelly stabbed a finger out. "There!" She was pointing to a rocky outcrop, which appeared to hide a large cave. "I saw it while we were spinning."

"We don't know what's in there," Robert said, making no effort to conceal his worry.

"Would you prefer the alternative?"

The clicking grew louder, like tribal war drums.

Robert looked back over his shoulder at a blimp-sized shadow closing in on their position. "Go! Go! Go!"

Dodging the glowing coral, swaying plants and darting sea creatures that lit up the ocean floor like Christmas tree bulbs, Connelly steered straight for the cave. Robert chanced a second glance back. Blackness consumed the view. At first he thought the creature had given up, but then he realized he was starring into the dark void of the beast's throat.

The world suddenly grew bright and brown as the sphere was swallowed by the cave. As the creature pulled up and away from the ocean floor, its body churned water into the cave, surging the sphere forward, down into the hollow. Connelly struggled to regain control, but it was the walls of the cave that ultimately stopped them. A high pitched screech of metal on stone echoed through the sphere. Then they were stopped.

Robert searched for any signs of danger, but saw only brown stone. He felt some comfort at seeing the stone. It looked like any cave you might see on

earth. Just water and stone. Robert let his muscles loosen. "Well, we survived."
Robert noticed that Connelly did not look relieved. "What?"

"I didn't stop the sphere," Connelly said.

"So?"

Connelly pushed the controls forward and backward. A light crackling
sound rang through the sphere, but it didn't budge. "We're stuck."

Robert no longer felt safe, and he became suddenly aware of how foul his
own vomit smelled. He imagined asphyxiating to death in this foul smelling air
and shuddered. He cast a sympathetic glance toward Connelly. "Sorry I threw
up."

20 – HELP

The tension in Willard's back felt as though a vice grip was attached to his
shoulder blades, pulling them closer together with every passing minute. All his
attempts to communicate with Connelly and Robert had gone unanswered.
Since the moment the sphere had disconnected from the cable, he had been
plagued with worry. And without any indication of what had happened, any
action on his part would be foolish. Even though his heart screamed out the
opposite, if Connelly and Robert were already dead, risking his own life in a
totally unknown environment was not an option. With them gone, he was the
next in line for taking charge of TES and he would make damn sure it was used
in a way Connelly would see fit. He could do that much for them, at least.

During the time he had spent waiting for some signal from the sphere, Willard had prepared for every contingency. Extra air tanks lay on the TES platform. A personal propulsion unit, for single person underwater movement, was
unpacked and ready to go. Assorted extra gear, emergency supplies and lights
littered the TES platform next to the hole in the ice.

Normally, Willard hoped to never have to use any emergency equipment. On a good mission, his expertise was never needed. But now, after all this time waiting, he would be happy with a worst case scenario. Anything!

He got his wish three minutes later. "...onnelly to Willard...you read? Over."

Willard snapped to attention, standing quickly from his sitting position against the TES control panel. The motion of his quick stand send him a few feet into the air. He landed, balanced himself on the control panel and near shouted, "Kathy? Is that you?"

"...ank God. Willard, we're in...ave...stuck."

Willard glanced at the TES cable, hoping to see it taut with the weight of an attached sphere. But it gently ebbed back and forth in the water, signifying that the sphere was still water bound. "Your signal is weak, say again?"

"...old on...bert is boosting...OK, how's this? Can you hear me?" Connelly's voice came through loud and clear.

"Boss, where the hell are you two?"

"In a cave system...we're safe for now."

Willard could hear the nervousness in Connelly's voice. He had learned to recognize it, because it didn't show that often and when it did.... Willard took a deep breath. "Tell me the bad news."

There was a pause on the other end. "Listen. We were...something chased us into the cave. We didn't have any other option."

The vice on Willard's back screwed tighter. "And?"

"And we're stuck."

Willard new he had his worst case scenario. Two crew members were stuck in a cave at the bottom of an alien ocean hidden by miles of ice. And he hadn't missed the part about being chased into the cave. "What can you tell me about the something that chased you?"

"It was gargantuan!" Robert's voice came onto the line. "It dwarfed any and all Earthly creatures, prehistoric or current. Bigger than the blue whale and not nearly as docile."

Willard slowly rotated his head on his shoulders. He was beginning to run through a mental check list of everything he needed to do before taking action. "OK...anything else you want to tell me?"

"Yeah," Connelly said, her voice grim and cold, "We're running out of air."

Willard ran through his mental checklist.

Ice...water...high pressure...cold...giant killer predators...low air...and they're stuck...in a cave. Willard ran to the supplies he'd gathered and realized he'd need just about all of it. *Great.* "Connelly, activate your tracking beacon."

"Why?" The question was laced with suspicion.

"Just do it."

"You're not coming down here." It wasn't a question.

"The hell I'm not."

"I'm telling you, you're not."

"Look Connelly, you know as well as I do, when there is an emergency situation, I outrank you. I'm the boss. I'm in charge. You do what I say, dammit, and I say turn on the fucking beacon!" Willard felt some of the tension release from his back.

Dead silence followed.

Willard ignored the silence and began collecting the gear and attaching it to his suit. He felt thankful for Europa's low gravity. He could never carry all this gear back on Earth. And once he entered the water, he'd be weightless.

"Tracking beacon activated," Connelly finally said.

Willard didn't respond. He walked to the edge of the TES hole and looked at the placid water below.

Connelly's voice returned. "Ethan...be careful."

"I always am," Willard replied. He then leapt over the edge and into the alien waters.

ןב ןב ןב ןב ןב

The ATV's headlights glared over the Europhid field, setting them ablaze with blood red shimmers. Choi had kept a careful vigil on the field, waiting for it to repeat its movement, hoping to observe the organisms' mode of locomotion. But nothing moved. Other the gentle sway of the Europhids, nothing budged.

Choi's impatience grew as she sat alone facing the field. She had yet to receive a check in from anyone. The fact that the entire TES crew and Harris had yet to check-in probably meant that something was interfering with the com signals. Most likely a solar storm being pulled through the system by Jupiter's gravity or increased radiation levels from Jupiter itself. Either way, she decided not to worry herself over it.

Throughout her career with the CDC, Choi hadn't been known for her patience. It was part of what made her such a lethal instrument when dealing with infectious diseases. She would persist, beating down every door until a solution was obtained. Sometimes each door opened would reveal part of the puzzle, a hint towards a solution. It was that same persistence—an overwhelming determination—that controlled her now.

She thought on the problems at hand and compartmentalized them in her mind.

First and foremost was her responsibility in handling the situation with Peterson. She was still unsure how the material injected into Peterson's system would affect him. She cursed herself again for leaving, but the truth was, she needed to be on the surface. She needed to understand the Europhids before she could determine their goal.

She knew the others would scoff at her assessment, that the Europhids had a goal, but it was a fact that every living thing, from humans to microbes, had goals. Some people longed to be painters. Elephants on the other hand, lived to eat. It is a simple rule of nature that she often faced when dealing with the microscopic world. The goal of a virus was to multiply and destroy.

Everything in nature acted towards goals. The question now was simple, yet a profound mystery; what do the Europhids want? How does injecting Peterson propel them towards their goal? And if the attack on Peterson was simply a case of mistaken identity, what else lived on the surface that required the Europhids to evolve stingers?

BENEATH

The muscles on the back of Choi's neck tingled and brought her attention back to the Europhids. Were they watching her? She turned around and saw nothing but the ice fields of Europa, covered with crags and spires. Nothing was there. She considered again that something else might dwell on the surface, something that the Europhids needed a defense against. Perhaps the stinger had a use after all?

All the speculation began to wear on Choi's nerves. Without testing, without evidence or new data, all the guesswork in the world wouldn't get her any closer to the answers she sought. She needed to take action.

Choi looked down at her suit, remembering its impregnable capabilities. If Peterson had been wearing a PMS at the time, the Europhid's stinger would have never pierced his hand. Choi stepped toward the Europhid field and stretched her legs.

Time to test a theory.

If all the Europhids had the stinging ability and used it as a defense mechanism, they would defend themselves if attacked. Of course, she realized the flaw in her logic; they had been harvesting the Europhids without incident. But they had been transplanting the samples, not killing them. Choi lined up with one of the largest specimens at the border of the field. She remembered her childhood, playing soccer with her brothers. She could kick better than all three of them. She wondered if she still had the magic touch.

She was about to find out.

Bounding forward, Choi reached the Europhids in two long strides. She swung her leg forward and connected solidly with the large Europhid. The impact was both soft and solid. She could feel the outer layers of the Europhid tearing as her foot severed its flesh. As her kick followed through, Choi saw the Europhid tumble up and float away like a football toward the goal posts—oozing red fluid. It soared nearly one hundred feet before landing in a dense portion of the field.

Choi bent down to the ruined Europhid. Nothing had attacked her during the assault, and as she waved her hand over the site, the Europhids remained motionless. Not one of them showed signs of aggression. "Huh…"

Choi stood up and prepared to kick a second Europhid. She thought a repeat attack might put them more on the defensive. Her muscles tensed as she took her first step forward.

A looming shadow arched across her path for just an instant, but it was enough to make Choi flinch and stumble. She fell to the ice, landing only inches away from the field. Her head pounded as her heart pumped hard. Her subconscious shouted at her consciousness: *you are not alone!*

Choi climbed to her feet, darting her eyes in every direction, searching for the source of the shadow. She realized that the shadow had been cast by the light of the ATV, meaning that whatever created it had passed between her and the vehicle, which was only feet away.

Wishing she could hear, but knowing it was impossible in the vacuum of space, Choi had to rely on her eyes to warn her of danger. She felt entirely underprepared. Sweat beaded on her forehead and rolled into her eyes, stinging them. She blinked to relieve the pain, unable to wipe her eyes through her facemask.

A shadow hovering behind a nearby spire of ice caught her attention. The shape looked darker than the view of space behind. It was absorbing the ambient starlight. Choi's mind struggled to comprehend what she was seeing. Was there really something there? Or was this an illusion exaggerated by her theories of other surface dwelling creatures?

Just before Choi dismissed the shadow as nothing, it moved.

She became rigid, focusing her eyes on the ice spire. She didn't know if she should move or not. Was she in danger? Would the creature attack? Choi had no idea. Alien creatures larger than a microbe were not within her field of expertise.

The black shape moved again, this time shifting forward. Choi eased herself toward the ATV. If she had to flee, she wanted to do it fast, not bumbling on her feet. She knew she'd make an easy target to anything accustomed to low gravity. Choi slid on to the seat and gripped the ignition key, ready to speed away at a moment's notice.

The creature inched forward. It stood on two feet, but appeared hunched and its movements were jerky, strange. Choi struggled to see into the dark and noted that the creature also had two arms. It was humanoid…a completely unrealistic evolutionary adaptation, Choi realized.

This was not a local.

Then who?

She didn't have to wait long for an answer.

The figure stepped into the light. Choi saw the face of Peterson staring back at her through his PMS mask. She couldn't read the expression on his face; it made no sense, like a newborn baby attempting to figure out how to use its facial muscles. And his eyes. They were blood red.

Choi's apprehension didn't fade at the sight of her crewmate. She realized that his presence here was completely unsanctioned by Harris, which meant something had gone very wrong on the Surveyor.

Suddenly, Peterson stood up very straight and smiled wide. "I saw you kick that Europhid," he said, shaking his head. "That wasn't a very nice thing to do."

ת　　ת　　ת　　ת　　ת

Cold bit at Willard's body. He was covered by a layer of thermal underwear, a jumpsuit and the PMS, but it wasn't the temperature making him cold. Temperature-wise, the water was warmer than the gripping cold of space. It was the stark loneliness he felt. As a child he had often wondered what it would be like to fall down a bottomless pit. He'd seen several cartoon characters suffer the fate, but could never quite capture what it might feel like—an endless fall.

The barren walls of ice that surrounded Willard as he swam straight down through the TES hole held little interest. He was sure Robert and Connelly had discussed the different layers, which passed every few feet, marked by a slight change in ice color. But to him, this was a boring and lonely descent.

Not for long, he thought.

Willard wasn't the type to get nervous before taking action. He normally jumped right in and felt at home. But this trek through the deep, unable to see anything beyond the thirty feet his waterproof headlamp could reach... If the propulsion pack on his back wasn't speeding him along, he knew that he might die of starvation before reaching the open ocean. Though he made sure to keep his speed reasonable, too fast and he might lose control and careen into the ice wall.

A black hole appeared below. He could see nothing beyond it.

The cave walls disappeared as he plummeted into the open ocean. Willard came to a complete stop, hovering in space, attempting to get a bearing on his location. Looking up, Willard noticed the gentle waves of ice in the ceiling. Beautiful. But other than that, the water was too cloudy to see anything at all. *How did Connelly and Robert see where they were going?* Willard wondered, *and how did they see anything alive in this milk?*

He thought back to his communications with Connelly while he was topside. What was it she had him do? Switch off the lights? It was worth a try. He would never find them with such poor visibility.

Willard turned off his headlamp and was plunged into a deep, weightless, darkness.

Willard's eyes slowly adjusted to the darkness. He could make out the faint impressions of the glowing world around him. His mouth opened as he saw what had lured Connelly and Robert away from the sphere cable. "Wow..."

A surge of water passed by, causing Willard to spin in place. His gear stretched out away from his waist like a dancer's skirt. When he came to a complete stop he realized that something had just swam past him—close enough for its wake to send him spinning.

Willard gripped the controls of his propulsion pack and prepared to launch himself towards the ocean floor. He couldn't make it out fully, but whatever had passed appeared to be the size of a skyscraper and was quickly turning around. Its dark shape was silhouetted by the slightly brighter waters. As the beast reared around, Willard saw a wiggling creature floating above its head...a parasite?

Click, click, click.

Willard shouted in agony as sound pounded through the water and bounced off his body. Willard's eyes burst open. He was concealed in the water. With no light to give away his position, he was invisible to the naked eyes. But something had tipped this creature off to his whereabouts…and now it knew exactly where to strike.

Willard felt a wave of displaced water suddenly push on him. The creature was charging! As Willard throttled the propulsion pack to full speed, he thought, *this must be the same creature that chased Connelly. Is it waiting for them? Or is this its normal stomping ground?*

Shooting straight down, Willard was sure that a creature of that size wouldn't be agile enough to make the turn and follow him. He turned back to look and was pleased when he saw nothing there—just the black, black water. He turned forward again and saw the glowing ocean floor. He smiled as he noticed it was alive with living creatures and plants.

Confusion gripped Willard's mind as he attempted to comprehend what he saw next. From above and below, massive spikes closed in, blocking his view of the bottom. As the walls closed in, the darkness around him grew more intense.

Click, click, click.

The sounds were so loud that all Willard could do was scream and cover his ears. When the resounding pulses dissipated, he felt an echo of vibration tingling through his body. He looked for the ocean floor. It was gone; replaced by pitch black space.

With a shaking hand, Willard flicked on his headlamp. "Shit." He spoke the word calmly. He knew where he was—in the mouth of an alien predator. And he knew there was only one way out, that is, if aliens had similar digestive tracks to Earth animals. He prayed they did, and that the PMS suit would be strong enough to withstand the beast's digestive juices. Then he would make the most undignified escape of his life…

Well Jonah, Willard thought, *if you're watching this and have any ideas….* No visions came to him, not that he really expected them to. *Fine then*, he thought, *just don't laugh at me after I die.*

The creature swallowed and sucked Willard down its throat and into its 747 sized stomach, where an ocean of acid began to work at breaking down the PMS suit.

21 – PRESSURE

A series of questions sprang to Choi's mind all at once. How had Peterson come down to the surface? He wasn't a trained pilot. What happened to Harris? Why weren't the com systems working? What was wrong with Peterson's eyes? That was just the beginning. But she dared not speak, not a single word. Something was wrong with Peterson.

His red eyes were locked onto her. With flexed arms and clenched fingers, he stalked slowly forward. She kept moving, trying to keep the ATV between them. But Peterson moved in a wide circle, tightening his distance with every step.

Choi had no desire to make a stand against Peterson. He was stronger than she was and very physically fit. And in the low gravity she was clumsy and slow. But running was impossible. In the time it took her to mount the ATV and start the engine, Peterson would be on top of her. She would have to injure or distract him long enough to make her escape.

As she looked into his fiery eyes, she could see nothing but loathing. *What happened to him?* She rounded the back of the ATV, Peterson came around the front, his back to the field of Europhids. It was at that moment that Choi noticed his eye color perfectly matched the red hue of the field.

No...

Peterson seemed to notice the change in expression on her face. He stopped his advance and took on a very unnatural stance. "I understand what you are thinking."

Choi didn't say a word. The voice sounded vaguely like Peterson's, but it wasn't him speaking. Like he was possessed.

Controlled.

"How did we…get inside his mind?" Peterson twisted his lips with an expression that was a poor imitation of deep thought. "The world…all you see…was created by me. By us. All of us. Me. Do you understand?"

Choi stood her ground, but slowly moved her hand to the side of the ATV storage trailer.

"I have seen what he has seen…this Michael Peterson. I know what he knows. You are not my children and you are not welcome here."

Choi slid her hand inside the trailer. "Why are we not welcome?"

"You are a contamination."

Choi shuddered. Whatever had possessed Peterson saw them the way humanity viewed disease, germs, bacteria—the enemy, who could be wiped out without any moral qualms. To the unknown denizens of this moon, they were the foreign invaders, *they* were the disease.

"We only want to understand you."

"Ironic, that in taking this mind," Peterson said as he motioned to his own head, "I now fully understand who *I* am."

Choi waited.

"I am the father of this world. I am the defender, the protector. I give life and I take life."

A growing apprehension about what and who she was speaking to began to churn a stew of vomit deep inside Choi. She was accustomed to the microscopic world; an enemy that could not speak. What she experienced now felt entirely unnatural. It felt wrong.

It felt *evil.*

With the next words out of Peterson's mouth, she knew it was.

"I am that I am," Peterson said"

The words shot through Choi's mind like a bullet and came to a stop at a memory from four years ago. During a weekend excursion to visit in old friend in Montrose, California, she had visited a church with an old friend. The sermon was on the calling of Moses and how he had resisted God's call to save the Hebrews from their Egyptian masters. She remembered the words, "I am that I am," from that story. God had spoken them to Moses, identifying himself as God, the great *I am*.

And now, Peterson, under the control of...something, had identified himself word for word, as God.

Choi's memory snapped back to a few months previous. She recalled a conversation over dinner during their days spent training at the GEC faculty. Robert and Peterson were exchanging personal histories. Both had grown up in the Church, Robert in a Catholic family, Peterson in a Baptist. Whatever had taken control of Peterson's mind must have merged with his thoughts taking on the identity of his memories it most identified with.

He—*it*— believed it was God.

The solid metal handle of a trowel grazed across her fingertips and returned her thoughts to the present. She reached inside the ATV trailer and grabbed the nearest tool, a trowel that she'd used to dig up Europhid samples. She would now use it as a weapon.

She glanced down at the trowel as she gripped it, then back to Peterson. She was relieved to see he hadn't made any further movement, but the look of total confidence unnerved her to the core. "You're not God," she said.

"I am the beginning," Peterson said as he took a step forward.

Choi stepped back, keeping the trowel hidden behind her body.

Peterson jumped and floated gracefully through the low gravity. He landed a few feet from Choi. "I am the end."

"I am everywhere and know everything." He was only a few feet away.

"All you are," Choi said, "is delusional." Before Peterson could respond, Choi brought the trowel around and bashed the side of Peterson's head. A vibration shook through Choi's arm as metal collided with skull. The force of the blow surprised Choi and she suddenly became concerned that she may have killed her crewmate.

Any fear that Peterson was dead dissipated when she recovered from her swing and came face to face with Peterson, who was leaning forward, burrowing into her mind with his eyes. He smiled. "You cannot hurt God with a shovel."

With an amazing burst of speed, Peterson reached forward, clasped onto Choi's PMS and lurched her up into the air. She sailed over ten feet of ice before the world below her turned red. He had thrown her towards the Europhids. Choi watched as the ground approached and wondered if the impact would hurt. She was moving fast and falling hard, but the Europhids would break her fall...or would they?

Choi's body collided with solid ice. The Europhids had moved out of the way. Her head struck the ice hard. Brilliant colors warbled in her view, combined with sparks of white light.

As consciousness faded, Choi became aware of a strange sensation. Something soft touched her body on all sides. It caressed her gently, lifting her up onto a comfortable mattress. Points of pressure undulated against her legs and torso like she was being held up by a crowd at a concert. She was being moved.

She was being taken.

ת   ת   ת   ת   ת

The world was wet and thick. Willard had been thrown down the esophagus of the alien predator. He'd bounced off throat walls like a racquetball and had been repeatedly poked by sharp talons designed to shred prey as they slid to the creature's first stomach. Only the impenetrable skin of his PMS suit kept him from being filleted. Upon awaking, he found himself afloat in a viscous white liquid that reminded him vanilla pudding.

Swimming through the digestive juices wasn't like dogpaddling in water. Moving was slow, tedious and muscle burning work. It took fifteen minutes of pumping away to reach the stomach wall, churned with motion, circulating the stomach fluids. The ribbed stomach wall, which he could see thanks to his still functional headlamp, was covered in splotches of pink and brown. He placed his hand against the stomach wall and felt the bumpy lines across his finger tips.

A surge of motion caused his hand to slide across the ribbed wall. He was being pushed along through the stomach like a piece of food, towards the stomach's exit and into the bowels beyond. Willard closed his eyes, ignoring the images conjured by his imagination. When the surge pulled him forward again, he didn't resist. He knew it would lead him to the exit, which he would never find on his own.

His theory proved correct five minutes later. With a quick surge he felt the floor beneath him open in a pulse. He was yanked down, sucked into another chamber of the beast's intestinal tract. Blinded by the quick movement and entrance into a tight tube, Willard became disoriented. He felt the thick ooze pulled away from his body as he slid, head first, through the conduit. The walls around him rolled with muscle, pushing him forward.

Then he slid into open air and dropped. He fell for several feet and saw a sloshing world of clear liquid below. Within the liquid rested an assortment of partially decayed alien corpses—previous meals that had yet to be fully digested.

Willard crashed into the liquid and thrashed about, panicking, searching for the surface even though all the air he needed to breath was provided by the PMS. He reached the surface and sucked air into his lungs. Twisting his body violently, he searched the chamber for any danger and found only the lonely dead eyes of alien sea creatures. Loose flesh hung from bones. Decaying muscles dripped into the liquid.

This must be where the real digestion takes place, Willard thought as he began to calm himself. Several deep breaths later, Willard became aware of something…a noise.

Splashing.

Beyond the fear of being eaten and digested inside the giant, he now had a sense that he wasn't alone, that the beast's digestion was aided by smaller creatures that lived within the bowels of the larger. Maybe parasitic.

Willard looked into the distance and saw only the dead and the distant grey walls of the grand organ. He ducked beneath the surface and scanned the depths. It was then that he saw his equipment, resting on the bottom. It had been stripped from his body when he was swallowed. The oxygen tanks, the personal propulsion system and the emergency medical supplies all sat on the floor of the stomach.

Forgetting the splashing sound, Willard dove down, knowing that if he had any hope of surviving and saving Robert and Connelly, he needed that equipment. He kicked his way down and clawed past the fragments of endless dead bodies.

As he moved closer to his goal, something nagged at his mind. Something fought for his attention. A sensation he hadn't realized was building began to scream and pound at his intellect.

He was hot.

He was *burning*.

Willard took another look around. The bodies that littered the bottom were awash with tiny bubbles. The liquid seemed to grow hotter...or more acidic the further down he swam. It had become hot enough outside his suit that the cooling system could no longer compensate. Willard wondered at what temperature the suit would reach its limit. If it got much hotter, the PMS would boil him like lobster meat in its shell.

Gritting his teeth, he pushed for the bottom. Every surge brought him closer to his equipment and nearer to death. As his arms and legs slid against the inside of the PMS, it felt as though a hot iron were being gently grazed across his skin. The sweat oozing from his pores stung his eyes and obscured his vision. His vision was all but obscured when he reached the bottom, but his aim had remained true. He felt the hard surface of the equipment strike his hand.

Moving as quickly as he could, feeling that the suit would soon fail him, Willard strapped the propulsion unit to his back, grasped the controls and set the throttle to full. Body parts were liquefied as the propulsion unit burst to life, dragging Willard up. After bashing through a few flimsy bodies, Willard broke the surface. He was exhausted and terrified, but alive and beginning to cool down. Laying on his back and hugging the rescued equipment to his chest, Willard caught his breath.

In the silence that followed his near broiling, he heard the same splashing. He scanned the area for the source of the noise. A ripple of liquid came from behind a large carcass that looked like a whale with a vertical mouth. Its skin was clear, but Willard wasn't sure if that was normal or caused by the digestive process. Willard eased himself toward the body.

As he closed in, the splashing grew louder, more desperate.

"Help me," a voice said.

Willard flinched. Had someone else been swallowed?

"Help me!" The voice was terrified.

As Willard prepared to aid whoever else had become victim to the beast, he realized that the voice was his own...inside his mind.

"Please," it said, "do not be afraid."

Willard felt strangely at ease as he moved around the whale-like creature. On the other side he found another body. It was built like a fish, but its skin was translucent and its internal organs glowed a dull blue. The fish flapped on top of the water, spinning in odd circles—twitching as death slowly claimed it. But what held Willard's attention was a small organism attached to the side of the animal. It had the same shape and size of a Europhid but was blue.

The blue Europhid was limp and motionless. With a final twitch, the dying creature passed away. Willard moved in closer.

"Save me," the voice said. "Save me and I will give you a gift in return."

"Are you...are you the fish?" Willard said.

Silence followed.

"Show me who you are."

The Europhid glowed a gentle blue and then faded.

Willard set his confusion aside. Something...or someone had asked for his aid. As his instincts took over, he responded the only way he knew how. "What do I need to do?"

"Touch me."

Willard felt a stab of distrust. He squinted and said, "And what will you give me in return?"

"Hope," the voice said. "Life."

The last word was weak, fading. Willard reached out with his hand before he could weigh his options. He could sense the creature fading. His finger brushed up against the Europhid and a shock, like electricity ripped through his body. He shook as though claimed by an epileptic seizure and felt his mind, his very thoughts, merge with another's.

When the shaking subsided and his mind cleared, Willard looked back to the blue Europhid. It was withered and colorless—dead. With a hard heart, Willard knew he had failed. But then a new emotion filled his body.

Hope.

"Are you there?" he asked.

No response came. Other than the bubbling of rising digestive gases, not a sound could be heard. Willard wondered if he had had a hallucination brought on by stress.

It felt so real, he thought. But the voice was inside his head, which only supported the idea that his experience had been a delusion. The blue Europhid, which shimmered lightly with life only moments ago now looked decomposed and long dead. Willard concluded without a doubt that the Europhid had not communicated with him.

It was just a damn plant anyway!

Willard focused his thought on the task at hand, escaping from the gargantuan bowels. The feeling Willard couldn't shake, even after determining he'd hallucinated the talking Europhid, was the nagging sense of hope—the knowledge that he knew what to do. Without questioning why, Willard turned to the far wall and gunned the propulsion unit forward. He sped through the digestive fluid, not being able to see any exit, but believing, *knowing*, it lay ahead.

22 – PASSAGE

A polar chill shook through Connelly's body. It had been a half hour since Willard had entered the water, and by her estimations, if nothing went wrong, he should have arrived at their location five minutes ago. She knew that under normal circumstances a five minute delay would be nothing to fret over. But in this strange new world with unknown luminous behemoths and savage predators, five minutes might signify that the worst case scenario for Willard had occurred…and that the worst case scenario for she and Robert would soon arrive.

She looked at the air gauge. They had twenty minutes remaining, but that was only because they had thinned the air by half, making every breath laborious and deficient. A perpetual feeling of lightheadedness permeated Connelly. She and Robert had given up on conserving air by not talking. With the end near, neither wanted to die in silence. They focused on recalling memories from the past.

But the stories soon faded, replaced by an unrelenting sense of doom. Five more minutes passed before either of them spoke again.

"Are we officially giving up on him?"

"Robert." The tone in Connelly's voice forbade him from saying it again.

"What?" Robert said. "He's never this late. Not during an emergency."

"Remember that time in the Arctic?" Connelly said. "You got stuck in the squall and hid under a frost heave for three hours before Willard reached you."

"It was a white out," Robert said, indignant. "How was he supposed to find me faster?"

"You had a GPS tracking device sewn into your gear. He knew where you were."

Robert stared straight ahead working hard to hide his surprise. "Why would he make me wait?"

Connelly smiled. "He was teaching you a lesson."

"What could Willard teach me?"

"A few things…"

Robert raised his eyebrows. He wanted examples.

"Every time Willard's given a storm warning since that day, you hauled ass back to base. He never had to chase after you again." Connelly stretched and took a deep breath, which did little to ease the burning in her chest. "While you were shaking in your boots, we were sipping on hot chocolate and playing checkers."

"That little—I could have frozen to death." Robert locked his gaze onto Connelly. "Wait. You knew?"

"Calm down before you use up all our air," Connelly said.

"I could have died."

"Willard had faith in your equipment. I had faith in Willard." Connelly looked through the sphere's window and took in the view of the barren cave. "I still do."

Robert stood and leaned against the wall of the sphere. "Think this is another lesson?"

"No."

"Why not?"

"Unlike your time in the storm," Connelly said, "Willard doesn't have faith in our equipment."

"What? What do you mean?"

Connelly sighed. "He ran a safety check on TES and the sphere back in the Antarctic. Everything checked out…except for the submersible mode. The GEC made attempts to correct most of what he found, but he was still unconvinced. I think the submersible is fine, but given our current predicament…" Connelly saw that Robert's face had fallen flat and pale. "What?"

He turned to her, his eyes filled with fire. "Why didn't you tell me?"

"I didn't want you to stop the dive."

"I would have."

"I know…I'm sorry."

"Why didn't Willard tell me?"

"He thought you knew."

Robert lowered his head and then glanced at the air gauge. "We have ten minutes of air left, Kathy." Robert's voice was low and gravely. He stood over Connelly and looked down at her like an angry father.

She couldn't bear to look into his eyes. She knew her betrayal by omission would be the cause of their deaths. It was a pain beyond description, worse than any heartbreak she had felt before. Robert's hand took her under the chin and lifted her tear wet face up, so they were looking eye to eye.

Then Robert did the last thing she expected, he smiled. "Seeing what we have seen is a gift beyond my most vivid dreams. I'm glad you didn't tell me about the submersible flaws. I'm glad we're here. And if we die...there is no one else I would rather have by my side."

Staring up into Robert's glossy eyes, Connelly became overwhelmed by the strongest emotion she had ever experienced. She'd known Robert for as long as she could remember. They were the closest of friends, but now she wondered if they were more than that.

Connelly stood up, wrapped her arms around Robert's body and kissed him full on the lips.

Robert melted into her embrace, but then gripped her arms and pulled away.

"What's wrong?" she asked.

"I just realized," Robert said, his eyes wide. "I don't want to die!"

₪   ₪   ₪   ₪   ₪

A pulsing sphincter the size of a monster truck wheel opened and closed with quick bursts. The liquid within the chamber reached the half way mark of the taut muscle, which pulled in the rotting flesh of the giant predator's victims and crushed it with each colossal pinch. The system was painfully efficient and as Willard approached he didn't see any safe way through. Knowledge from some hidden vault in his mind had brought him this far, but it seemed he would go no further.

BENEATH

The digestive juices near the sphincter were thick with thoroughly decomposed bodies and golden, bubbly, froth. A loud slurp accompanied each pulse. Willard had never felt more disgusted in his life. He thanked God he couldn't smell this mess, and then realized that whatever the stomach of the creature smelled like, it would only be worse deeper within its bowels.

Willard watched the undulating circular muscle and began to see a pattern. Three quick twitches, a large crushing squeeze, and then three more twitches. The process repeated consistently. A plan suddenly came together. The idea was simple, yet didn't seem to be his own. He simply saw what would happen and then realized it might work.

Screw where the idea came from, I'm getting the hell out of here.

After turning away from the deadly exit, Willard throttled the propulsion unit and sloshed away, careful not to collide with any carcasses. After moving fifty feet he turned back toward the palpitating flesh and saw a wall of rotten corpses blocking his path.

Willard pushed himself below the liquid and descended ten feet, well below the gassy corpses and foam. Despite being prepared for the sudden acceleration, his head jerked back when the propulsion unit rocketed forward. Rushing liquid surged past his suit. He reached his top speed in ten seconds and had nearly covered the distance to the exit. Arching his back, Willard aimed up, steaming forward at a forty-five degree angle. He watched the sphincter. He counted out the pulses as it continued the pattern.

One. Two Three.

One.

One. Two Three…

Five feet away, the muscle-filled flesh pounded down, crushing a rotted body and pulling nearby liquid through. Willard's body was jerked forward, covering the five feet in a second. Before his face careened into the chamber wall, the sphincter snapped open again. Willard shot through and felt a quick rush just behind his feet as the squeezing process continued.

Relief at being out of the second stomach turned out to be short lived. He found himself in a sewer-sized tube that was covered in sticky mucus and undulating phalanges. A river of thick sludge oozed forward, working its way toward the inevitable exit. Pushing his rising revulsion down into the depths of his psyche, Willard crawled forward on his hands and knees.

The way was lit by his headlamp, but the further he traveled, the tighter his surroundings became. The digested flesh around him was still milky white, but it was growing more compact with every few feet. The tunnel soon closed in and his back slid against the ceiling, scraping off phalanges as he went. A sudden rise in what Willard now knew was feces, blocked the majority of the intestinal track.

Not wanting to wait for nature to take its course, Willard slid up the rise, lying on his stomach, inching forward with one arm and clasping onto the emergency supplies with the other. As the tunnel tightened around him, Willard's ribs began to ache. He could see that the tunnel grew wide again on the other side. Blowing the air from his lungs compressed his chest enough to give a little wiggle room and with a determined shove, he crushed himself forward, then stopped.

Stuck.

He tried to move back, but a wall of fresh feces had already sealed him in from behind.

While Willard's oxygen supply was more than plentiful, he found breathing to be nearly impossible. The dense fecal matter below and tight intestinal wall above had him in an unrelenting grip. Stabbing pains filled his chest as each breath pressed his lungs into his ribs, which threatened to crack under the strain. As dark splotches began to appear in Willard's vision, he became aware of an escape plan.

He slid a hand down to his waist, pushing past the impacted feces and grappled with one of the several spare tanks of compressed air. Though his muscles suffered from severe spasms, caused by lack of oxygen, he worked his fingers as quickly as he could, twisting the cap off the air tank.

As consciousness faded, Willard felt the cap fall into his hand.

You're about to get a serious case of gas, my friend.

Instantly, the tightness around his body loosened. The tube expanded, wider and wider. Willard climbed up the rise and slid to the other side. He looked down the tunnel and saw a wall of white. He knew what it was, and as the gas from his open air canister continued to expand the chamber, he understood what the end result would be.

Figures, Willard thought, *I had to get eaten by a* constipated *alien.*

Preparing for a wild ride, Willard fell to his hands and knees and gripped the pliable fecal floor. And not a moment too soon. Everything began to move, shaking wildly. Willard imagined that the pressure inside the creature's bowels must have become extremely uncomfortable. The travel had so far been even footed, but now the creature must be moving, writhing in pain.

With a sudden burst, like a roller coaster dropping down its tallest peak, everything launched forward. Willard felt himself pulled up, then shoved down. One moment he was impacted in sludge, the next he was being tossed through open air. A sudden decrease in speed pulled at his muscles. Air returned to his lungs. He was free!

A cloud of chalky fecal matter swirled around Willard's body. It rose toward the surface, revealing the colorful ocean floor only ten feet below. *Yes!* Willard looked at the tracking unit strapped to his wrist. It was still functional and the signal from the TES sphere showed brightly on the small screen. He glanced at his watch and felt a twisting pain in his gut. He'd survived the worst hell he could conceive of, but for all his efforts, he might not make it to Connelly and Robert in time to save them.

Click, click, click.

Willard sucked in a deep breath that sent a jolt of pain through his recovering lungs. "I'm not going through that shit again!" Willard shouted and dove down to the ocean floor. Emergency equipment in tow, he entered the nearest cave, hoping…somehow knowing that it would somehow lead to the cave Robert and Connelly were trapped inside.

Since the day Robert met Connelly, he had loved her. But in his mind, it was a platonic love. He now realized that he'd been wrong. Something in his forgiveness of Connelly's actions allowed her to see it first, but when their lips met, all of the barriers that kept his honest feelings for Connelly locked away were torn down. But now that they were down, he felt angry.

"Why did you want to kiss him?" he asked, his voice quietly conserving the last view breaths of air inside the sphere.

Connelly looked up at him. He was sitting on the floor of the sphere with his back against the wall. She was leaning against him, sitting between his legs. She was held tight in his warm embrace, but as he asked the question, his arms loosened slightly. "What?"

"Peterson...in the bio-lab."

Connelly lowered her head. "Oh."

A moment of silence passed between the two of them.

"It was a stupid thing to do," Connelly said. "Very stupid. And if we both knew about...this...about us, I would have never done it."

"I know..." Robert fussed with his hair, twisting it into a bird's nest. "I just don't understand why you actually would pick me over him. For all his obvious flaws, he's the babe magnet, not me."

"You're calling me a babe?"

"A smart babe. I've seen you in your skivvies, you know."

"You said you weren't looking when I changed."

Robert smiled weakly. "There was a mirror."

Connelly elbowed Robert in the ribs, gaining a grunt and a laugh. He squeezed her tight. "You forget the peeking, I'll forget the attempted lip lock."

"I'm sorry."

"I've already forgotten it," Robert said.

"Not about that...I'm sorry it took a near death experience to bring us together."

"I've had you almost completely to myself for years... I wouldn't change a thing." Robert waited for a response, but Connelly remained silent. Robert looked down at her. She wasn't breathing. Robert realized that, though he was still pulling in air, his head was spinning and the world was growing dark.

Time had run out.

Clank! As Robert eased into unconsciousness, a loud metal on metal boom filled his ears. Darkness consumed him. *Boom! Boom!* The sound persisted. Robert's head lulled back and his arms fell away from Connelly's body. He opened his eyes for one last look at their tomb. He saw the strangest thing. Willard was lying on top of the sphere, banging on the exterior and shouting.

What a strange thing to dream of before I die, Robert thought.

Then, along with the banging, came Willard's voice, muffled but screaming. Robert slowly comprehended the words. "Robert! I'm here! Up here!"

Robert returned his gaze to the ceiling of the sphere. Willard looked frantic. With stabbing fingers, Willard pointed towards the control console. He shouted again, this time as loud as he could. "Retract the fins! Blow the ballast tanks!"

The words oozed into Robert's mind as he became acutely aware of a fire burning in his lungs. It felt as though tiny creatures with cheese graters were shredding his chest. But the words finally made sense.

Robert pushed Connelly aside and she slumped to the floor. His muscles ripped with pain from the effort. He stumbled forward and clasped onto the console with both arms. He looked at the screen—a blur of color.

Putting all his effort into focusing his eyes, Robert felt his head spin, threatening to rend him unconscious. Everything became clear for just a moment. Robert worked both arms in separate directions, pushing buttons and working keys. The entire motion lasted ten seconds. Then he'd had enough.

Robert's head fell forward, cracking against the console. He slid back and collapsed on the sphere's floor. His chest, like Connelly's was no longer rose and fell. They lay together, twisted on the floor

Dead.

THE DEN

23 – AWAKENING

A volcano of vomit erupted from Connelly's mouth as she regained consciousness. Her vision flashed in and out like a slideshow. The TES consoles blinked brightly at her. Willard stood over her, his face, free from his helmet, twisted with fear and relief. Robert was there too, leaning over her with a crooked, imperfect grin.

Connelly sat up with some help from Robert. "Did we get drunk?" she said. "Because I have the worst hangover." She wiped her mouth with her suit sleeve.

"Must have mixed your hard liquor and beer," Willard said with a grin.

Connelly grunted and braved a glance at the mess, which was spilled out on the floor next to Robert's drying vomit.

"Well," Robert said, "at least you can't blame the smell on me alone."

A faint smile crossed Connelly's face. "What happened?"

Robert stood from his crouch and slapped Willard on the back. "The boy did his job."

Connelly rubbed her head. The sphere was sealed shut, but something looked different. The cave. Their view had shifted and the water was...gone. They were in an open-air cave *beneath* the Europian ocean! Connelly looked at Willard. "Where...what did you do?"

"Entered a system of tunnels through another cave and made my way here," Willard said. "You were hung up on the fins, which I warned you might be a problem. All Robert had to do was retract the fins and increase your buoyancy. You popped up into the cave without a problem."

Connelly scrunched her forehead. "How did you get in? The sphere was sealed."

Willard shrugged. "Robert popped the hatch."

Robert shook his head lightly. "I don't remember opening the sphere...hardly remember retracting the fins."

"I'm just glad you guys are alive," Willard said.

Connelly extended her hand and Robert pulled her to her feet. She wanted to hold him, to hug him, but she wasn't really sure where they stood. Their relationship had always been safe. They shared all the benefits of a strong emotional bond without the confusion of physical passion. But that had changed. Would it work? She wasn't sure, but she didn't want to let their evolving relationship overshadow the mission...and she certainly didn't want Willard knowing. Not yet. Probably not for a while.

Robert seemed to sense Connelly's reserved body language and made no move to express his affection. She stretched her spine and peered out of the sphere, which had been resealed and filled with fresh air. As she leaned back, a shard of pain sliced through her ribcage. She winced and held her side. It felt as though her ribs, at least two or three, were cracked. She realized what must have taken place, and her respect for Willard's abilities increased tenfold. She had to be sure though. "Was I dead?" Connelly asked, her voice showing no emotions, as though she had just asked the time.

"What—ahh, you...yeah." Willard looked at the floor, hiding his eyes. "You both were."

Robert jumped. "I was?" His eyes were wide, peering over his low hanging glasses. "I was dead?"

Willard nodded. "You revived quickly. Connelly took some work." He glanced at Connelly, hiding his shaking hands behind his back. "Sorry about the ribs."

Connelly took hold of Willard's arm and squeezed. "If you had broken them all, I'd still be glad."

Willard laughed. "You'd still be unconscious."

This brought a small chuckle from them all, only Connelly shuddered with pain with each chortle. After the pain subsided, she returned her gaze to the view outside of the sphere, which was lit by the bright external lights. They were floating in a pool of water, perhaps twenty feet across at the widest point. The smooth stone walls surrounding them were light brown mixed with flecks of red. It some areas, veins of crimson crisscrossed through the stone like streaks of heat lightning. They reminded Connelly of Europa's red streaks when seen from orbit. The cavern was much larger; thirty feet at the tallest dome and at least one hundred feet across. A single tunnel led into the cavern on the far wall. It captured Connelly's attention.

"Is that the tunnel you entered through?" she said, pointing toward the dark hole.

Willard nodded. "Yeah, why?"

Connelly smirked.

"No way," Willard said. "We need to go."

"What are the chances of us ever coming back down here? After what happened we'll be lucky to ever enter the water again. This may be our only chance to explore what lies beneath the ocean. No one even thought to speculate on the existence of a cave system! Willard, I am eternally grateful for you…but this is what we do…we're scientists. We explore."

Willard closed his eyes for a moment and then sighed. "And I have to save your butts every time you guys get in trouble. That's *my* job."

"That a yes?" Connelly asked.

"Promise me we stay together. I don't want to have to chase you down again. I almost didn't make it in time."

Connelly nodded. "Promise…" She paused as a thought occurred to her. "Ethan, don't take this the wrong way…" She wasn't sure if she should ask. But the question would never stop pecking at her thoughts if she didn't. She let a deep breath, doing her best not to reveal the burning pain caused by her broken ribs. "What took you so long?"

Willard laughed lightly and wrung his hands together. "Not sure I want to retell the tale...not now anyway."

Robert adjusted his glasses, propping them higher on his nose. "We'll settle for the abridged version."

"Fine. Long story short...I got eaten by the predator that chased you in here, swam through its two stomachs, hallucinated about a blue Europhid, crawled through its shit-filled intestines and got shat out after giving it gas with an air tank." Willard crossed his arms. He was serious.

"God..." Robert stared at Willard with gaping eyes. "Are you okay?"

Willard uncrossed his arms and leaned against the glass dome. "Hey, I got to use 'shit' and 'shat' in the same sentence." He smiled. "I'm fine."

Connelly watched Willard's bright blue eyes, which seemed bluer than ever, like two sapphires. He looked distracted, edgy, not quite his keen self. But after surviving what he had, who wouldn't be a smidge off target? She decided he just needed time to recover from his experience. Hell, they'd all need a couple of days off after this experience.

"All right," Willard said, adjusting his helmet into place over his head. "Let's take a peek at these caves and then get the hell back to the surface before we all die down here."

₪   ₪   ₪   ₪   ₪

Fully geared in their PMSs, Connelly led Robert and Willard out into the cave. They'd remained close to the sphere for a few minutes, making observations, but after a growing sense of frustration over how little they could actually see, they headed in three different directions, but didn't wander too far.

The barren walls of the cavern looked bright brown under the gleaming sphere lights. Connelly noticed that her shadow was intensely dark as it snaked up the curved rocky surface. But something was off. Her vision seemed blurred, unable to make out the details of the cave. The nooks and crannies, instead of standing out in stark contrast, were vague splotches of color.

"What do you make of it?" Robert asked as he walked across the cave.

Connelly closed in on the wall nearest the tunnel entrance. As she grew closer, the obscure features of the wall began to tighten into a clear picture. "Best guess is that they were formed by high pressure venting gasses or volcanic eruptions a long time ago. That would account for the smoothness of the walls...but there's something else. I'm having a hard time seeing." Connelly came to within a foot of the wall and gasped. A thin coating of...something encrusted the entire wall. It gave the surface a wet look, like a fogged up windshield. Connelly realized that what she was seeing wasn't on the wall at all; it was in front of it, suspended in space. She turned around to report her finding and gasped again. Her thoughts swam with the possibilities...the implications of what she was seeing.

"You know," Robert said as he knelt down to inspect where the floor met the wall. He was leaning in close to one of the glittering streaks of red. "I think there is more to this wall than stone. I think these red veins are the same substance the Europhids on the surface cling to."

Connelly's feet locked solidly to the firm cave floor. "Robert."

"You don't agree?" Robert said without looking away from the wall.

"*Robert,*" Connelly said again, this time with more urgency, "look at me."

Robert paused and then turned around. He shot to his feet, eyes wide. "I can't believe we didn't see it before."

Willard walked into the center of the room. Behind him, Connelly could see the walls blurring in swirls of motion. "Is there something on the wall I'm not seeing?" Willard asked.

"Not on the walls," Robert said.

Connelly waved her hand slowly across her field of vision. Swirls of a light mist curled through the air. "Between them."

Willard paused and repeated the motion Connelly made. "Holy...there's an atmosphere in here?"

Connelly headed for the sphere, nodding. "Oh yeah." She jumped into the sphere, opened a small hatch and pulled out a hand held device that contained a small full color screen, but only one button. Connelly climbed back out of the sphere and headed towards the center of the cavern, where she was joined by Willard and Robert. She held the device in front of her face and pushed the lone button.

A loud beep chirped out as the device began working. A bright blue status bar slide across the screen, displaying the progress made. In ten seconds it reached one hundred percent. Connelly viewed the results, which were displayed as a bar graph. She began to laugh.

Robert caught Connelly's excitement immediately. "What? What are the results?"

"The atmosphere is just about equal in density to Earth's," Connelly said.

Willard crossed his arms. "Don't tell me it's breathable?"

Connelly smiled. "Only if you can breathe methane."

Robert scratched his helmet as though he could reach his hair inside. "A methane atmosphere..."

Connelly nodded. "Methane tops the list at sixty percent. Nitrogen at thirty. Oxygen at five and several other gases make up the rest."

"My neighbors had a cow farm when I was growing up. During the summer, we'd be doused in hot methane," Willard said, "I've never smelled anything so bad in my life."

"What's your point?" Connelly asked.

"Nothing," Willard said. "Just glad I can't smell it."

"Oh..."Robert's voice was barely audible in Connelly's headset, but she could tell he'd just thought of something...something important...something that scared him.

Connelly and Willard turned to Robert, who was staring at the tunnel. His eyes were fixed on it with an intensity rarely seen by anyone other than the souls present. Without taking his eyes off the cave, he spoke. "Are you guys thinking what I'm thinking?"

"Where are all the cows?" Willard laughed at his joke, but Robert did not.

He turned his head toward Willard, his face set with a rock solid expression of sobriety. "Precisely."

ひ   ひ   ひ   ひ   ひ

A smile spread across Choi's face as the massaging hands burrowed into her back, smoothing out muscles and easing tension. The amazing sensation covered the contours of her entire backside, from head to feet. A slight moan escaped her lips and she was suddenly embarrassed. Her muscles tightened like high tensile wires. Her deep bliss was shattered.

But then a calm and soothing voice, deep and masculine, set her at ease. "*Relax,*" said the voice. "*Let go your mind…you're free…floating on a cloud.*"

The analogy was fruity, Choi thought, but accurate. She did indeed feel like she was floating—and moving. The massaging limbs dug in again and she began to calm. It occurred to her that several people must be rubbing her body…but who? And where?

"*Stop thinking,*" the voice said. "*Let go your mind.*"

Choi counted the pressure points on her body, which came and went, as she was moved along. The amount of hands touching her changed from moment to moment, all sizes, from large manly hands to smaller, child-like appendages. And…was she lying on her back? It felt that way. Choi tried to remember what a massage looked like but a fog rolled through her, concealing her thoughts.

"*Your worries are being carried away.*"

A nerve was struck and her stomach tightened. Carried. She was being carried! A rapid strobe of memories flashed into her mind. Europa. The Surveyor. The crew. Europhids…Peterson.

"*Your body is relaxing,*" the voice said. "*You are safe. You are warm. Let go your mind.*"

No, Choi thought.

The voice grew louder. "*Let go.*"

"No!" Choi shouted as her eyes sprung open. Immediately, she could see the electric side of Jupiter blocking out the stars above. She was moving. She could feel it now. She turned her head to the side. A field of red glowing lightly in the dark, looming out at eye level wiggled innocently, almost cutely, as far as she could see. The combined light of the Europhids, the occasional flash of Jupiter's electric storms and the ambient star light was just enough to see by.

Suddenly, the motion below her stopped. She was no longer being moved. Choi screamed as a dark shadow stood over her, looking down with red eyes. It was Peterson.

"Let go your mind," Peterson said insistently as he raised his booted foot into the air above Choi's head. He brought his foot down with crushing force.

Choi felt the Europhids lurch away as she twisted her body out from under the blow. She hit the ice and rolled away. Peterson's foot just missed her head. The Europhid supporting her shoulder at that moment wasn't quick enough and was reduced to a gushing red smear on the white ice.

Choi looked back and saw Peterson's face was twisted in an odd sort of anguish. He stared at the splattered Europhid. He knelt down ton one knee and ran his fingers through the wet remains. Nearby Europhids moved closer, gliding over the ice as though propelled by unseen appendages. They inspected the dead.

Realizing this might be her only chance of escape, she leapt to her feet and staggered forward. Blackness faded into and out of her vision and her head pounded. The memory of her earlier collision with the ice returned and she wondered how far she could run before collapsing.

Choi put all her strength into her legs and sprang forward with high arcing leaps. If she were attempting the run in full Earth gravity, she'd have already hit the dirt, but in the low gravity of Europa, she might have a chance. With every landing, the Europhids at her feet slid away, avoiding a messy death.

She wasn't sure how far she had gone…or if she was moving in the right direction, but she knew she was making good time. As long as Peterson remained distracted by the dead Europhid, she was free to run.

With each ragged breath, a burning sensation swelled in her throat. *Is this just physical exhaustion*, she wondered, *or is something else happening*? She nearly toppled over when she realized she could be miles away from her ATV, from the Lander and from TES, all of which provided the life sustaining electromagnetic shielding. Six minutes…if she were outside the shielded area, she'd only have six minutes to run. She needed to figure out which way to go.

She stopped and scanned the area, looking for any hint of where she was. But the edges of the field were slightly raised and if Peterson had extinguished the lights on the ATV, it would be invisible in the near dark.

Peterson…

She changed her focus and searched the field for any sign of her body-snatched crewmate. He was gone.

A shifting shape fell from the darkness above. The impact struck Choi in the chest and sent her sprawling backwards. She toppled over and landed on a group of Europhids that didn't have time to move. She felt them turn to mush beneath her weight and ooze out from her sides as her weight pushed down.

"No!" Peterson shouted as he landed. He roared loud enough to make his voice hoarse and charged forward.

"What do you want with me?" Choi screamed as she pushed away from Peterson, slipping on the Europhid gut-covered ice. Her chest tore with pain with every move.

"Decontamination," Peterson said, standing above Choi. "You understand the concept."

Choi paused. "Yes."

"You will be studied. With understanding comes efficiency. You understand this as well."

Choi realized that Peterson was expressing the basic concept of, "know your enemy." But he was relating to her field of study and it made sense. The Europhids, the stupid little spongy cucumbers, were going to study her so they could kill human beings better. "Yes," she said, "I understand."

"Then you will understand this as well." Peterson raised his hands to the dark sky and smiled.

Choi watched as a nearby Europhid expanded, opened at the top and then spat out a single golf ball sized orb of light. Within seconds, the darkened domain became lit by thousands, perhaps millions of the tiny luminous globes, all floating towards orbit. She recognized them immediately—the charged particles that had almost destroyed the Surveyor after they arrived in orbit. They were headed for the Surveyor once again, and if Peterson had done something to Harris, there would be no one to stop them this time.

Before Choi could verbally react to the sight, Peterson's foot smashed into the side of her head. Choi fell over sideways as consciousness slipped away again.

They were all going to die on Europa.

24 – THE DEN

"You can't be serious," Willard said with a vigorous shake of the head. "I'll admit that this moon is covered in life, but subterranean Europian cows...c'mon." He looked at Connelly, thinking she would immediately support his objection, but she had quickly become rigid. It was as though Robert's cow comment had set off a silent alarm inside her skull. "What's the deal with you two?"

"Kath," Robert said, as he watched the cave entrance, "Would you mind explaining the significance of a methane rich atmosphere to the boy?" Robert looked at her. "I'll watch the door."

Willard slouched. They *were* serious. He wondered if the stress of their near death experience had further clouded their scientific objectivity. They were setting a record for the number of times a person could jump headlong into the unknown. First detaching from TES, and then chasing a pod of Europian whales, leading them into an encounter with an alien predator and ending in this sub-oceanic cave system—which they now intended on exploring. From a safety standpoint, they were about to cross another line and Willard was beginning to consider reporting their odd behavior to Harris.

Of course, he knew the truth about Connelly's and Robert's actions. They were excited. They were scientists, analytical thinkers at heart, but what they had discovered in the past few days was nearly beyond human comprehension. What made matters worse was that every foolhardy action taken on this mission had only lead to greater discoveries that served to increase the level of excitement and, in turn, increase the number of unsafe calls. At the end of the day, if they survived, their discoveries would be hailed by science as brilliant and brave, but until then, every new wonder brought along a host of unknown dangers that Willard was beginning to resent.

No...more hate.

Ever since his own life-threatening experience in the belly of a massive predator, Willard had felt an unrelenting emotional insistence that they head back to the surface as soon as possible. More than that, he thought they should return to the Surveyor, leave orbit and make haste to Earth without looking back. But that would never happen. Not with this crew.

Willard glanced at Connelly, who had moved closer to speak to him, but had never taken her eyes off the cave entrance.

"Methane gas, as you know, is in abundance around cow farms," Connelly said. She paused and met Willard's eyes. Satisfied that he was listening, she continued. "But it's not the cow feces itself that creates the gas...it's the breakdown of organic material within the manure. This doesn't just happen with cow poop, either. You just notice it because of the high concentrations on most farms."

"Ok, fine," Willard said. "Maybe these caves are filled with methane escaping from the ocean's decomposing organisms. Fish poop, too. And don't volcanoes on Earth spew methane? It could be a naturally occurring gas here."

Willard noticed Robert pause his slow creep toward the cave entrance. "He does have a point."

Connelly nodded. "I'm sure some of the gas comes from natural sources, but the concentration of methane is high enough to suggest otherwise." Connelly switched on her PMS suit's headlamp and aimed it toward the cave. The gentle mist in the cave glowed brightly in the light. The entrance tunnel was empty. She turned to Willard again, lighting up his face. "Methane is created by the decomposition of organic material, *any* organic material."

"Which means that these caves could be filled with little alien rats or some kind of fungus," Willard said.

Robert looked back, shaking his head. "Nope."

"Why not?"

"Too much gas." Robert said. "The amount of organic material somewhere in this cave system must be immense, suggesting a significant population of larger creatures, probably of varying sizes, both plant and animal."

"But this cave is barren, Willard said. "There's nothing here."

Robert smiled. "You've been caving, right?"

Willard didn't want to answer. Robert knew the answer anyway. "Yeah."

"Would you say some of those caves were devoid of life?"

Willard sighed. "I came through about ten different tunnels before I made it to you two. I didn't see anything on the way."

Connelly looked at Willard with a shocked expression. "How did you find us?"

Willard sighed again. "I don't know. All I know is that we need to get the hell out of these caves and back up to the surface."

The seriousness in Willard's voice garnered him the attention of both Robert and Connelly. They stared at him, waiting for him to say more. But that's all he had. Something inside him was urging, pushing him to leave. The message was simple: *run!*

"You feeling okay?" Robert asked.

"I'm fi—" A shadow slid into the cave entrance. Willard blinked and the shadow slipped away.

Robert and Connelly spun towards the entrance. "What is it?" Connelly said.

"What'd you see?" Robert asked, his voice pitched higher than normal.

Conflicting emotions began vying for superiority in Willard's mind. His sense of adventure had kicked in when he saw the shadow. His interest in the unknown began to thirst for more. But he was also responsible for the welfare of Robert and Connelly. His sole job was to keep them alive. On top of all that was the persistent scream inside his brain—run!

Willard replayed the shadow in his mind. It was low to the cave floor. Short. It appeared to have limbs, how many he had no idea. But its size seemed small enough to not be a threat. But it was *something*. He wanted to see it, *needed* to see it for himself.

Willard flicked on his PMS headlamp and stepped toward the entrance. "We mark every turn so we can find our way back. I go first. If anything goes wrong, anything at all, we hightail it back to the sphere and go topside, no questions asked, no complaints." He made eye contact with both Connelly and Robert. "I am understood?"

Robert nodded.

"Perfectly," Connelly said.

Willard opened a small pack that lay with the emergency equipment and took out an ice pick.

"What's that for?" Robert asked.

He gripped the ice pick tightly and headed for the cave entrance. "I'll be damned before I let anything else swallow me today."

ת　　ת　　ת　　ת　　ת

With every light-footed step, Connelly felt her apprehension growing. They were entering the unknown once again. She wondered if turning back might be the wise thing to do. The information they had already amassed during their short stay beneath the surface of Europa was already full of scientific curiosities and amazing new discoveries. Several return missions to Europa would no doubt be scheduled. This moon would become her home for as long as the GEC would let her stay.

Connelly found it peculiar that her goals could have changed so radically over the past months, but she couldn't deny, no matter how much she loved Earth Oceanography, that the ecosystems on and within Europa were endlessly fascinating. She rarely felt more challenged, more rewarded…more alive.

As Connelly took another step forward, she realized that the growing sensation within her belly wasn't just nervousness about facing the unknown, it was

an awakening of her soul. Her mind was enraptured by her recent alien en-
counters and she longed for nothing else. Like a drug addict, she began to look
forward to the next beast, the next fungus, the next predator, no matter how
dangerous…she desired to learn everything there was to know about the organisms on this moon.

Willard stopped his forward motion with a quick jolt. Connelly stopped
behind him. A swell of anxiety drowned her excitement, which now seemed
irrational and foolish. She noticed Willard's grip tighten around the metal handle of the ice pick. He'd seen something.

Light cut across the cave tunnel in a wide swath as Willard peeked around a
curve in the cave wall. Robert eased up behind Connelly and gently rested his
hand on her shoulder. Her anxiety was eased slightly by his reassuring presence.
Her breath came in controlled five second intervals as she suppressed the old
feelings of uncontrollable emotions. The stale smell of her suit mixed with fresh
oxygen further helped repress her rising anxiety.

I will not lose control, Connelly willed herself. *I beat this a long time ago.*

With a cool voice, Connelly said, "What did you see?"

Willard continued his search ten seconds more before answering. When he
finally replied it was with a reticent voice. "Something's been dogging us the
whole way…keeping just out of view. In the shadows."

Robert stepped forward and scanned the area with his headlamp. "I don't
see anything."

"It's there," Willard said, "Just around the bend."

"What's it doing?" Robert asked.

Willard leveled his eyes plumb with Robert's. "I think it's making sure we
follow it."

Robert laughed nervously. "That's, ahh, I think that's probably a bad
thing…" He looked at Connelly. "Right?"

For the majority of her career Connelly had been looked at to make the final decision in different situations. The choices she made sometimes put
people's lives at risk. This was the first time she wished the responsibility be-

longed to someone else. "I don't think we can make any judgment about the intentions of anything living down here."

Willard looked slightly annoyed. "Have we forgotten our little learning experience with the surfboard toothed Shamu?"

She took a moment to breath deep. "Ethan…what we have discovered on this moon is a complete ecosystem full of varied creatures included predators *and* prey. The system works here the same as it does on Earth, we just don't know which creatures are which. We could be following Europa's version of a chipmunk."

"Or an alien Kodiak bear," Willard said.

Connelly caught a sliver of motion in her periphery and jolted her headlamp toward it. She saw a blur of a creature, low to the floor, no bigger than a small dog, scurry quickly away. There was definitely something there, but with their impenetrable suits and the small stature of the creature, Connelly was positive it posed little threat. She looked at Willard. She could see it in his eyes; he'd seen it too. "Still think it's dangerous?"

"Some of the most deadly creatures on Earth are smaller than my hand," Willard said.

"You two…" Robert started. "I swear, you're like brother and sister. I'd like to venture a compromise considering that neither of you are about to agree on anything and standing around doing absolutely nothing is a waste of time and air."

Connelly couldn't help but smile. She loved it when Robert was assertive.

"We continue on—"

Willard opened his mouth to speak, but Robert continued with a louder voice. "However, at the first, and I mean first, sign of danger, I will turn tail and retreat to the sphere. If that happens, both of you will turn and follow me, no questions asked. Can we agree on this?"

Connelly nodded. She knew that she was being over eager and that Willard was being over cautious. Robert would keep them on an even keel and had no compunction over fleeing a dangerous situation. Following his lead was the best way to satiate their curiosity without getting killed in the process.

Willard stood to the side and motioned Robert to take the lead position. "By all means, after you."

Robert took an apprehensive step forward, then paused. He reached back with an open palm. Connelly's face filled with warmth as embarrassment rushed blood to her cheeks. She couldn't believe Robert was openly expressing the desire to take her hand in front of Willard. She felt foolish and slightly disappointed when Willard handed Robert the ice pick.

"Thanks," Robert said and then set off into the tunnel.

Willard followed and Connelly brought up the rear. They moved deeper into the cave system, past several different shades of stone, all streaked with ribbons of red. Connelly noted that the entire trip took them on a slight, almost indiscernible, downward slope. They were delving deep into the stone core of Europa.

Robert paused. He waved a hand back at them. "Turn off your lights." Before she could respond, Robert reached up and switched off her belt and head lamp. Willard complied as well and the cave was plunged into a momentary darkness.

Connelly's eyes quickly adjusted and she realized she could still clearly make out Willard and Robert. The cave was aglow with vibrant, ruby red light from around a bend in the tunnel. Their bright lights made seeing in the dark caves a simple task, but they also drowned out any other light sources. She wondered how far back they could have seen this light if they had had their lamps extinguished.

Robert, true to his word, sensed no danger and continued forward. Connelly felt as though they were about to exit a cave and enter a burning forest. The light flickered and moved across the wall. She couldn't imagine what the source was. When they rounded the tunnel bend and stopped at the exit, Connelly felt her chest-gripping apprehension return. She wasn't sure if what she was seeing was a dream come true or some kind of sick nightmare.

Willard leaned over to Robert without taking his eyes off the intimidating view. "Robert…" His voice was barely a whisper.

Robert's reply was a simple grunt. He wasn't diverting his view either and was too distracted to structure a sentence.

Willard leaned closer and spoke louder. "Robert...why aren't you running?"

ℷ   ℷ   ℷ   ℷ   ℷ

Like a pillar of the Parthenon, Robert stood solidly still for what seemed to be ages, but in reality was closer to three seconds. Craning his head up and around, Robert looked at the cavern. It was three times the size of any sports arena Robert had ever seen. The colossal cavity's highest point, smack dab in the center of the cavern, stood at least five hundred feet above their heads.

But it wasn't the size or scope of the cavern that captured Robert's unyielding attention. Upon entering the cave, Robert's first observation had been that it was bathed in bright red light. As his eyes adjusted to the radiance, he saw the chamber with a new clarity. Covering the floor, walls and ceiling of the cavern were thousands, perhaps hundreds of thousands of blood red Europhids. But unlike the Europhids on the surface, these glowed with the brightness of fifteen watt bulbs—each and every one of them. The radiant, scarlet light filling the cavern made Robert feel as though he were standing inside an oven.

The Europhids on the floor of the cavern were spread out in patches of various sizes and shapes, creating a maze of paths leading from one side of the cave to the other. Scanning from left to right, Robert could see several black specks along the perimeter of the cave, which he assumed were more tunnels into more caverns.

His mind wandered and he began to imagine that the entire moon, surface and subterranean realms, were ruled by the Europhids. The number of individual Europhids could very well outnumber the total quantity of humans on Earth. They were a spectacular organism, completely adapted to their inhospitable environment. A sense of awe and respect crept into Robert's thoughts. He jumped and nearly loosed his bladder when a hand clapped him hard on the shoulder.

"Robert," Willard said, leaning in close. "This really would be a good time to turn back."

"Huh?" Robert looked at Willard with a confused expression. He hadn't heard a word.

Willard sighed, made an adjustment to his com system and spoke again. "Don't respond, don't react, don't do anything to hint at what I'm about to tell you."

Robert's face scrunched into a mush of befuddlement.

"I'm transmitting to you only," Willard said. "Kathy can't hear me. Don't respond verbally to anything I say. Just nod your head inside your mask without moving your body.... You're going to have to trust me."

Robert gave a slight nod.

Willard continued. "I'm pretty sure we're not safe here, but if I point out why, Kathy's only going to continue deeper into the cave system. I know this is amazing stuff, really, but we're going to die down here if we keep making poor choices. Understand?"

Robert nodded again. He trusted Willard enough to feel the first twinges of nervousness enter his stomach. Willard's covert warning meant two things. One, they really were in danger. Willard had never misdiagnosed a dangerous situation. Second, if he was keeping the reason for leaving from Kathy, he had discovered something, something exciting—and dangerous.

Moving slowly, Robert adjusted his com settings so that Connelly could no longer hear his voice. "What did you find?"

Willard glanced down at the nearest path, leading between two patches of Europhids. It was five feet wide and coated in a thin red dust. "On the path, look closely."

Robert gazed at the path and rows of indentations began to materialize out of the cavern floor. Swallowing so hard it hurt, Robert did his best to not physically react to what he was seeing.

Footprints.

The indentations had been made by tiny feet.

Lots of them.

From Robert's vantage point it looked as though the prints were created by creatures with three small toes. Possibly multiple legs. These were mobile, land dwelling creatures. What caused Robert to catch his breath was the small indentations at the tip of each toe, indicating that the creatures that created these markings were clawed…further implying that they were predatory.

"What do you want me to do?" Robert asked.

"Exactly what you said you would do."

Robert looked Willard in the eyes.

"Run," Willard said.

In that instant, Robert realized that he should have turned tail and sprinted back to the sphere already. But the cavern held an almost magical hold on him. That hold had disappeared the moment Willard pointed out the clawed footprints. Robert's muscles were already tightening in preparation for the retreat back to the sphere, but before he could actually move, Willard stopped him.

"Shit!" Willard said, looking past Robert and into the cavern. While they were speaking, Connelly had moved silently past them, hustling forward to inspect some new discovery. Willard readjusted his com and said, "Connelly, what are you doing?"

"Something on the cave floor…" Connelly said. "Some kind of animal…I think its dead."

"Robert and I think it's probably a good idea to head out now," Willard said.

Connelly continued forward, ignoring Willard. Willard and Robert locked eyes.

"Got a game plan?" Robert asked. He didn't look forward to confronting Connelly about leaving, especially now that their newly discovered feelings for each other were out in the open. But if they were in danger, and Robert believed they were, he would risk her anger to save her life.

"If all else fails, I'll take her arms, you take her legs. We'll drag her out kicking and screaming if we have to. Either way, I want us out of the caves and back in the sphere within the next ten minutes."

"You know," Connelly's voice came over the headset. "I can hear you."

"Shit," Willard's curse was quiet but still audible. He looked out over the cavern and saw Connelly kneeling down, inspecting something on the floor.

"You might change your mind after you see this," Connelly said.

Willard made a quick adjustment to his com. "Arms and legs. Don't let her change your mind."

Robert nodded and headed into the cave. The more time he spent in the cave, the more he felt the desperate need to leave it. A presence, like thousands of watching eyes, began crawling up the skin of his back, poking his flesh. Robert quickened his pace while searching for any hidden dangers among the harmless Europhids. He knew that such instincts were most likely the result of his over-active imagination, but the further they voyaged into the cave, the stronger it got.

Minutes later, Robert would learn to trust in instincts.

25 – THE CREEPS

The soft undulations that eased Choi from unconsciousness did little to calm her nerves this time. Memories of her last moment of lucidity returned like a torrent; the Europhids carrying her over the ice, Peterson's attack, the charged particles bounding towards orbit. Her eyes flicked open. With shaky vision, Choi did her best to understand her surroundings. The world was a blur of red, encompassing her on all sides.

She was being transported by Europhids—that much she knew. She could feel the gentle bodies shuffling her along. But as she gazed up, there was no dark sky, just red. She knew her headlamp was still functioning, or the scene would be pitch black. Thinking she might be disoriented and lying on her stomach, Choi rolled herself over. The effort from moving her body sent lighting bolts of pain through her body and into her eye sockets. She could sense that none of her bones were broken, but the soreness gripping her muscles meant her injuries were far from inconsequential.

As the pain subsided, Choi opened her scrunched eyes and took in the view. Things became suddenly clear. Below her eyes, just inches from her nose, Choi could see Europhids pressing their pliable flesh against her clear facemask, pushing her along to the next in line.

Straining her neck muscles, Choi looked up. A long tunnel of Europhids shot up above her, ascending at a thirty degree angle. The Europhids coated every surface of the four foot wide ice tunnel burrowed into the ice, like a cilia-coated bronchial tube.

I'm being swallowed by Europa, she thought.

Choi's mind cleared at the same instant her survival instincts kicked in. She understood the situation fully, that she was being dragged into the ice to be studied, picked apart and analyzed by the Europhids. She had no idea how such complex tasks could be carried out by the malleable beings, but having seen the kind of control they could exert over Peterson, she knew they would find a way. Choi reached out with her hand and squeezed one of the nearest Europhids. For a moment, it seemed her purchase would hold and her descent would be stopped, but the Europhids began squirming, shoving her down with surprising force.

With tightening fingers, Choi felt her grip on the firmly planted Europhid begin to slip away. As her hand slid up from the base of the clenched Europhid, it began to expand like a compressed water balloon. The gelatinous guts of the Europhid were being compressed. The result was an explosion of red swill and spiraled veins that covered Choi's face mask.

Her grip released, Choi was pulled down the tube at an ever increasing rate of speed. She did the only thing that came to mind—flailed. Screaming, she thrashed her arms and legs, smashing Europhids in a savage and uncontrolled assault. Her PMS became coated in Europhid guts, but her downward slide only grew quicker, the ooze acting as a lubricant.

Choi caught her breath and realized that the physical fight had been lost the moment she'd been pulled into the cave. She'd never escape as long as even a

227

few of the Europhids were left to push and pull her down. Setting her mind to the task at hand, Choi closed her eyes and began imagining the solution. What could stop these creatures? What were they afraid of?

With Choi's eyes closed, she did not see the interior of the tunnel begin closing in around her as the diameter shrunk a few inches with every foot.

It wasn't until a tight pressure around her feet that Choi realized her situation had worsened. Abandoning her thoughts of escape, Choi looked down and saw her feet being pulled into a smaller section of tunnel that looked barely wide enough to fit her body. She knew that any hope of escape would be over as soon as she was fully entrenched in the tight tunnel beyond.

As the pressure spread past her ankles and up onto her shins, Choi frantically refocused her efforts. There had to be a way to escape. The Europhids had a weakness. Somewhere in her filing-cabinet-like intellect was a mental note that contained the solution.

Luckily for Choi, not only did she perform well under pressure, she performed exceedingly well. It was like nitrous for her mind. Thoughts came and went faster than she could comprehend and then suddenly, they stopped, focused on a single thread of synapses. She'd found the note.

Decontamination. Her specialty.

At once, she understood why the Europhids wanted her alive. She contained the sum of human knowledge on what the Europhids feared most—infection. Peterson had given the necessary clue when he spoke of decontamination. From experience, Choi knew that such intense fear of infection typically took hold of individuals or populations that were particularly susceptible to disease, especially new, introduced variations. The susceptible hosts naturally adapted a disease to suit their biology, even if it originated in another species. Even among humans, the origins of plagues like AIDS were speculated to have stemmed from an SIV— simian immunodeficiency virus. The original host for AIDS was most likely one of these individuals, whose bodies adapt viruses to human physiology.

The fear of infection exuded by Europhids hinted that they too might be susceptible to foreign disease, whether or not it was originally designed to affect

Europhids. The only path to freedom became clear in Choi's mind. She hoped the reaction would be quick enough.

Choi took a deep breath, filling her lungs with the plastic smelling air inside her PMS. After letting it out slowly, Choi lurched her head back and brought it down like a cannon ball. The Europhid's beneath her head splattered under the force, coating the surrounding Europhids with their innards. Choi noticed a sudden change in her motion. The pressure that had been building around her thighs and moving towards her waist paused.

It was as though the Europhids sensed Choi's intentions.

Not wanting to give them time to react, Choi slammed her face down on the tunnel floor a second time. A wet ooze beneath her nose told her she'd been successful in reaching the first goal in her plan—her nose was dripping blood. She could see it gathering on her facemask, wet, thick and full of Hepatitis C. Her own blood was considered a hazardous material and handled with the greatest of care. She was about to expose the Europhids to it.

There was no way to know what effect her poisonous blood would have on the alien creatures, but other options did not exist. She smashed her head into the ice one more time, with all the force she could muster. A loud hiss signified success. A small crack had been opened in her facemask, and as her air was sucked out into the vacuum of space, her blood—her personal toxin—went with it.

Choi held her breath and closed her eyes tight. The vacuum of space stole her air at the same time it extracted her blood. Her chest burned with the need for oxygen. The hiss of escaping air became higher pitched as the self healing facemask resealed. An abrupt silence followed.

The mask had mended.

Choi let her lungs fill with air as she opened her eyes. She couldn't see her blood sprayed across the surface of Europhids, but she knew it was there, coating them in a thin mist. Not wanting to spur the Europhids into action, Choi waited without moving. The tunnel had become still. The undulating creatures had stopped moving.

The change came so slowly that Choi wasn't sure if she were seeing things or not, but as the effect spread, she knew it was a reaction of some kind. The Europhids were expanding. Swelling. The confines of the tunnel began to expand around her, exerting a painful strangle on her lower body. Her upper body became ensnared as well, and she feared being crushed to death.

Then the reaction grew. The swollen Europhids began pushing and pulling at Choi's body once again, but this time action seemed more like an uncontrolled frenzy—a panic. More importantly, the direction had changed. She was moving up. The Europhids were working as a group, perfectly synchronized, even in their hyperactive state. The result was that Choi's acceleration up the tunnel increased rapidly. Within seconds she'd been vaulted forward to the speed of an Olympic sprinter.

She rocketed towards freedom. As her body continued to accelerate, her mind came to a screeching halt. She was about to be launched out of a thirty degree tunnel at nearly forty miles an hour and would be entering the low gravity atmosphere of Europa. Her eyes widened as she neared the exit.

She was about to be launched into space.

ꠃ   ꠃ   ꠃ   ꠃ   ꠃ

An indistinct shadow emerged around Connelly's kneeling form, revealing that something large had loomed over head, blocking out the red light cast down by the Europhid-coated ceiling. Looking up, she saw Robert and Willard looking down at her, arms crossed.

"What's it going to be, boss?" Willard asked. "You can go on your feet or over my shoulder. Either way, we're leaving now."

Connelly knew he was serious, and that ultimately, she should listen to him. What she'd discovered on the cave floor only reinforced the idea that they were in a dangerous environment. But she couldn't leave without taking the body. It was a perfect specimen, and it was already dead. She was sure they'd agree once they saw it.

As though revealing the latest car model, Connelly shuffled to the side and swept her hand over the dead creature. Upon seeing the small beast, Robert and Willard's eyebrows sprang up. Connelly returned her eyes to the creature and made mental notes as she examined it.

Four double jointed limbs tipped with serrated edges grew from the creature's sides. They were either very good at climbing or killing...or both. The coloration of the beast's smooth and tightly stretched skin was pale green. Unlike the other creatures they'd observed so far, this had opaque skin, like a frog's, but tougher. She imagined that while standing on all four limbs, the creature's height would hover around a foot tall, while its length, if including the ten inch tail, stretched out two feet. It had no mouth, nose, ears or eyes to speak of.

Two syringe tipped, retractable tentacles extended from the front of the creature's triangle shaped head. While retracted, they might look like fangs, but they were more like flexible straws, most likely for sucking in a liquefied food source. Connelly imagined that the appendages would make efficient weapons when speared forward, like an iguana's tongue tipped with a spider's fang.

Starting at the center of the creature's head and moving down the back in a straight line were four red humps of flesh that appeared to be growing right out of the beast's back. Connelly found it odd that the humps color and texture appeared identical to the Europhids. *Perhaps the Europhids are also parasitic?* Connelly wondered. She felt suddenly glad to be wearing an impenetrable space suit.

Connelly reached out slowly, taking hold of one of the creature's legs.

"Umm. Kathy...." Robert didn't have to finish his sentence. Connelly knew he was telling her not to touch the creature.

She ignored him.

With a quick flip, Connelly turned the creature over onto its back, revealing bloated stomach.

"All right, that's enough," Willard said. He knelt down next to Connelly and clenched her arms. Looking into his eyes, Connelly could see that he meant business. "You have ten seconds before I drag you out of here."

Connelly nodded and gently took hold of the creature, placing her hands under two of the limbs. She stood and held it up for Robert to see. "I don't think this could be classified as either mammal or a reptile." Her excitement was palpable, but Robert was unaffected.

"Better put it down," Robert said.

"What? Why?" Before Robert answered, Connelly noticed that his eyes were not on her, they were locked on the back wall through which they had entered the cavern. Something was behind them, blocking their exit.

Connelly turned around slowly, hoping that what she was about to see wasn't nearly as bad as the horrified look on Robert's face indicated. As the embankment came into view, Connelly dropped the dead creature, letting its body fall to the hard cavern floor. The spectacle before her was like a nightmare. Unlike the other cave walls, the back wall was completely free of Europhids. The stone was full of holes, thousands of perfectly cut holes, each a few feet in diameter. She immediately saw the wall for what it really was—a nest.

Willard leaned over and in the most serious voice Connelly had ever heard him use, he said, "From now on you do exactly what I say when I say it. You debate, you get left behind. *Am. I. Clear?*"

Connelly nodded, but she was sure there was nothing Willard could do to save them. Not if the horde of alien creatures, each a clone of the one she had found dead on the floor, became violent.

Connelly pushed the image from her mind. She'd found years ago that imagining her own gruesome death was a sure fire way to trigger an anxiety attack, and the one building pressure in her chest was already about to explode.

ש   ש   ש   ש   ש

If a crowd of circus fans had been flown into orbit along with the Surveyor they would have been cheering madly when Choi rocketed out of the Europhid filled tunnel like a futuristic human cannon ball. Only there was no net to catch her when she inevitably fell back towards the hard ice surface. If she returned at all.

Choi fought waves of dizziness as she looked down at the fading landscape. She'd never been afraid of flying, but this was different. Floating free above the moon's surface was as close as anyone ever got to flying, really flying. Europa's faint gravity was barely holding her from the cold grip of space. She had no wings to alter her trajectory and no air resistance to slow her down. She was a helpless projectile.

The surface of Europa seemed to glare brilliantly at her, as though she had just stepped out of a dark movie theater and into the light of day. She noticed a radiant spot on the horizon, like a double bright but half-sized Earth moon.

Ganymede, Choi thought. *It must have cleared the dark side of Jupiter, reflecting the sun's light.*

The largest of Jupiter's moons, Ganymede's surface was a thick sheet of ice. It was the perfect surface for reflecting sunlight, which it did now, brightly enough to illuminate the surface of Europa.

Looking down, Choi wished Ganymede had waited to cast its light on Europa. Passing below, the field of red Europhids spilled out in every direction—for miles. She'd be lucky to ever find TES or her crew again.

Before she could delve deeper into worrisome thoughts, Choi noticed a violent chain reaction reshaping the Europhid field. A growing darkness expanded below her, spreading out from the epicenter where she had been launched. Her infection had been fully adapted, with disastrous effects and was spreading like wildfire. The Europhids, all of the Europhids below her, were dying.

A twinge of guilt wrenched her chest into a tight knot. She may have inadvertently destroyed Europa's entire ecosystem. Already, thousands of organisms had been killed by her single act, and for what, to save her own skin? Even if the Europhids were evil, did saving her own life justify wiping them out completely? As Choi watched the Europhid-covered ice pass by below, she doubted she'd even succeeded in saving herself.

A warmth, like a giant hot compress, squeezed her body. In an instant, she knew she hadn't come close to saving her own life. If anything, she'd be better off back in the ice tunnel with the Europhids. Cruising across the lower atmosphere, far from the ATV, Lander and TES left her out in the open, unprotected from Jupiter's deadly radiation. Six minutes…that's all she had. If she didn't crash to the ice and snap her neck in the next six minutes, she would be cooked alive inside her space suit.

The warmth turned uncomfortably hot and her muscles began to ache. Her insides began to revolt, twisting within her like a dying snake.

She knew the first step to surviving the next six minutes was to get back to the surface. If she could find another ice cave or thick overhang, she might be able to wait until the others found her…if Peterson didn't get them first. Choi had forgotten all about Peterson and the charged particles. Her feeling of hopelessness spread like a plague. It took all her mental focus to push her thoughts beyond the worsening circumstances and physical pain she was enduring.

One step at a time.

Choi extended her arms, fighting the urge to curl into a fetal position. Simultaneously, she spun both her arms in a counterclockwise motion, putting her body into a spin. She needed to be facing away from the surface, but there was no way to stop spinning once she had started. Her vision became a confusing swirl of the gently glowing Europhid field, the horizon, Jupiter's blackness, the horizon, the Europhids, Jupiter…over and over again.

A spew of vomit exploded from Choi's mouth, brought on by the spinning and the radiation poisoning her system. With her facemask covered in bile, she couldn't see which direction she was facing. Held in place by centrifugal force, the vomit didn't budge from the face mask. Choi was blind.

Precious seconds were passing by as Choi panicked. Her plan was to release a burst of the compressed oxygen from her spare tank attached to her belt, but if she had it pointed in the wrong direction she might launch herself into space. Left with little choice, Choi reached down, felt for her spare tank and detached it.

Holding the small air tank in both tanks against her torso, Choi prepared to open the valve. Just before opening the valve, she pointed the tank to her right and let out the faintest of bursts. She didn't feel any change in motion at all, but within a few seconds she saw the result of her modified plan.

The vomit on her face mask oozed onto her face. The warm wretch and acidic stinging smell made her want to puke again, but she managed to hold it in, concentrating on seeing what was outside her facemask. As the mask cleared, Choi saw a jet black nothingness in the sky above. She was facing up.

Twisting open the valve, Choi let the compressed air fly. She immediately began descending towards the moon's surface. Using the compressed air as a guidance system, she rotated herself around so that she was facing the Europhid field again. She was shocked to see that the Europhids were still dying off. It was like a wave of death spreading out in a perfect circle. The field was vibrant with red one second, ash black the next.

She descended toward the field, hoping the soft Europhids would cushion her impact. If the Europhids in her landing zone had died before she arrived, she would smash into solid ice.

It seemed like an eternity had passed and that she should already be dead. The pain pounding throughout her body supported the idea. But she'd only been exposed to the radiation for two minutes now. She still had four to find safe shelter.

Her thoughts returned to the Europhids. She watched as the black death consuming the field spread out towards her. As she fell it appeared that the dying Europhids were racing ahead to meet her.

Forty feet from the ice, Choi witnessed an unbelievable act of sacrifice that saved her life and the lives of millions of Europhids all across the surface of the moon. A ring of Europhids, perhaps five feet across and twenty feet from the spreading infection, suddenly swelled to the breaking point and burst, sending plumes of red guts arcing high in the low gravity. Choi splashed through a geyser of entrails and continued toward the surface. As she passed by the barrier of exploded Europhids, Choi noticed that the infection had stopped at the edge. The violent gambit had worked. The Europhids stopped the infection by quarantining the area. Choi realized that if faced with the same circumstances, she would have made the same choice. The Europhids were smart.

The force of returning to the surface knocked the wind from Choi's lungs, but as she had hoped, the still living field of Europhids cushioned the impact.

She stopped moving after sliding thirty feet. She sat up and looked at the thirty foot swath of crushed Europhids that had taken the brunt of the impact from her fall. Beyond she saw a black expanse of dead Europhids, perhaps a mile around.

Choi's body shook with a violent chill. If the Europhids experienced emotions like people, they were going to be pissed.

26 – ANXIETY

Choi's muscles twanged with pain, but the malicious flu-like symptoms caused by radiation exposure had all faded. This didn't mean her body wasn't being irradiated, just that she was so far gone already that her nerves were no longer transmitting her internal discomfort.

Desperate for security, Choi crawled through the Europhid field, crushing a number of them as she did. On her hands and knees, her view was just over the top of the tallest Europhids. She was headed for what looked like clear ice.

Pushing and shoving her way through the red forest, the hopelessness she felt while cruising over Europa's surface returned. She knew what dying from radiation exposure would be like. Six minutes was the time you had to escape radiation...not because you'd die in six minutes, but because you'd pass the point of no return. You wouldn't be dead, you'd be dying...and short of a bullet in the head, there was nothing anyone could do to stop it, or ease your suffering.

Choi charged, head down, casting Europhids aside like a bull running the streets of Pamplona. With her eyes cast downward, Choi didn't see the field clear and tumbled forward over the empty ice. She lay still for a moment, gasping for air. Four minutes. The number ran through her head, telling how long she had been exposed to the radiation. Two minutes to go…two minutes until the real torture began. She hadn't realized she'd been keeping track.

The countdown spurred her on. She pushed up on her arms and rose from the ice. Her muscles protested the motion, but in the low gravity, it wasn't too hard. She got to her feet and looked out over the Europhid field. A perfectly round patch of darkness revealed where she'd unleashed her toxic potential. Extending straight toward her was a smooth, crushed line in the field where she'd slid to a stop. From there, a mash of crushed and fallen Europhids lay askew, revealing her mad crawl to the edge of the field.

With all the changes to the field, Choi never realized how familiar the view was…not until she turned around.

Not ten feet from where she emerged sat the ATV, lights out, but still emitting its protective electromagnetic shield. She was safe…and had been for at least the past minute. Choi ran to the ATV, plugged her com system in to the onboard transmitter, hoping to boost her signal.

"TES team, this is Choi. Do you read me? Over." Choi waited ten seconds for a response and got none. "TES team, come in." Choi's voice took on a desperate tone as her voice was projected on multiple channels across the surface of Europa. "TES team, if you can hear me, the Europhids…they're dangerous…violent…and they have control of Peterson. I think he's on his way to you. Do not trust him. I repeat, do not trust Peterson."

Choi continued transmitting. She thought about racing across the ice in an effort to overtake and subdue Peterson, but she was nowhere near a physical match for him and she had no idea how long she'd been unconscious. For all she knew, they were already dead.

She wouldn't accept that. "Connelly, this is Choi. Do you read? Respond, dammit!"

Choi looked up as she spoke and remembered that things were only going to get worse. The cloud of charged particles were still gliding slowly toward the Surveyor. Even if they survived further attacks from the Europhids and Peterson, if the Surveyor was brought down with Harris unable to correct the situation, they might all be trapped on the moon's surface with no hope of rescue.

"Please, God, someone respond."

₪   ₪   ₪   ₪   ₪

The muscles in Willard's back became taut to the point of nearly snapping. So far the mass of creatures clinging to the nested wall had paid no attention to the three of them, but he wasn't sure that would last, especially if they tried to exit the way they came in. Their best bet might be to slip out another exit without being seen and try to make it back to TES another way. He found his way through the cave system before. He could do it again.

He relayed his plan to the others and they both agreed, but before they could execute the scheme a crackling voice interrupted his thoughts. It was faint and full of static. "Choi…"

Connelly glanced at Willard. "What? Are we leaving?"

They hadn't heard it. "Stop talking and boost your com volume. I thought I heard Choi."

All three made the adjustments, moving slowly so as to not attract attention from the wall of beasts. Choi's voice came through again, this time much clearer. "Please respond…TES team…If anyone can hear this…respond. Over."

"Reading you now, Choi," Willard said. "Over."

"Thank God." Willard had never heard so much emotion poured into Choi's normally reserved voice. Something was wrong.

"What's your situation?" Willard asked. "Are you okay?"

The com crackled for a moment and then cleared. "…fine. But you're all in danger."

Tell me about it, Willard thought.

"The Europhids," Choi said, "stay away from them."

Willard squinted and glanced from side to side. They were surrounded by Europhids. "Why?"

"They're…they're dangerous."

"Outside of our experiment with the plant incubator they haven't shown any signs of malicious behavior," Connelly said. "They can't even move."

"Wrong on both counts, Dr. Connelly," Choi said. "They Europhids *are* capable of movement, though limited. And I've seen signs of human level intelligence and strategic thinking."

Connelly became rigid. "That's not possible."

"They nearly killed me," Choi said, her voice flat. "And they have control of Peterson."

Robert began to fidget. "Ahh, can you elaborate on 'have control of Peterson.' He's on Surveyor…in the Med-lab, right?"

"Peterson is topside and headed towards TES. I don't know what he did with Harris, but I suspect the worst. Listen, if you are not topside, you need to get there ASAP. I think Peterson might try to sabotage TES. Where are you?"

"We're in a cave system below the Europian ocean," Willard said. "And we're in a bit of a bind. Might be a while before we make it back to the surface."

There was a silence on the other end. When Choi spoke again, her voice was hard, borderline furious, but she didn't express her feelings in words, simply assimilated the information and moved on. "I'll see if I can slow him down. Get to the surface. That is your number one priority."

Willard shot Connelly a stern look. "Has been for a while."

"Once I get moving," Choi said, "I won't be able to transmit at this power level. We will be cut off again. Contact me upon reaching the surface. If I do not respond, assume I'm dead, return to the lander and head for the Surveyor. If she's still in orbit, dock and wait for my signal."

"You got it," Willard said. "Anything else before we cut off?"

"Yeah," Choi said, "If the Europhids can control Peterson, its logical to assume they can control creatures of lesser intelligence. If you run into anything down there, avoid it at all costs. If they're under Europhid control, they will respond violently to your presence."

Willard's eyes trailed up the living wall of creatures. "Un-fucking-believable."

"What?" Choi asked.

"Nothing," Willard said. "We'll see you topside, but we need to move. Now."

"Good luck," Choi said. "Over and out."

Willard knew the warning came too late. During the conversation he had secretly watched as several shadows dodged in and out of Europhid patches, making their way toward their location. He reached over to Robert's hand and slowly took the ice pick.

"What are you doing?" Robert asked, his eyes still on the wall of alien nests.

Willard tightened his grip around the ice pick, yanked it out of Robert's hand and swung it up towards Robert's head. He missed Robert's skull by inches and connected with one of the aliens that had launched out of a nearby Europhid patch. The ice pick punctured the creature through the chest. It squirmed and shrieked for several seconds and then fell limp, hanging from the end of the improvised weapon.

Moving slowly, Willard placed the creature on the cave floor, planted his foot on top of it, and pulled the pick from its back. A blackish liquid chugged from the wound, pooling around the small body. Willard returned his eyes to the nest wall. Every one of the creatures had stopped moving. He could barely see them on the wall, but he knew they were there.

Willard was thankful that he didn't have to speak to Robert or Connelly to get them moving. They both turned tail and started running for the far wall. Three more of the creatures jumped out and began to pursue. "Keep running," he said. "I'll be right behind you."

Willard glanced over his shoulder to make sure they were listening. They were. Willard turned back in time to deflect a launched alien. The second attacked with its fangs, shooting them out on the ends of two long tendrils. He wasn't sure if they could pierce the PMS, but didn't feel like finding out. He jumped to the side dodging the attack.

The third creature appeared at his feet. Without thought, he lifted up his foot and brought it down with a crushing force. Whatever bone or internal structure the creature possessed was pulverized by the force of the blow. Its legs twitched madly before it died. The other two creatures pressed the attack again.

Moving quickly, Willard struck out at one of the creatures and severed one of its four legs. It squealed as it ran in circles, oozing black liquid. The last of the three leapt at Willard's head, shooting out its dart-like tendrils. Willard leaned back, avoiding the attack while at the same time reaching up and catching the beast by the ribs. He cupped the creature in one arm, spun around to gain momentum and let it fly like an Olympic discus thrower. The creature flew away from him in the low gravity.

Willard's heart hammered like an eight cylinder engine, coursing adrenaline-laden blood to his muscles. He was ready for more. Looking down, prepared for another attack, he found the creature with the severed limb lying at his feet, dead. They were done.

Willard turned to chase after Connelly and Robert, but before leaving chanced a glance back at the nest wall. He could clearly see the thousands of creatures again. They were streaming down the wall like a water fall. After reaching the floor, they leapt forward in packs, giving chase.

He still felt ready for more...but not this much more. Willard turned and ran as fast as he could, knowing that outrunning these creatures, which were adapted to traveling in low gravity would be all but impossible for the three slow moving, clumsy humans. His only hope was that the beast's best attacks couldn't damage the PMS's protective skin.

ॼ ॼ ॼ ॼ ॼ

Replacing her rising panic with concentration, Connelly ran for the opposite end of the cavern as quickly as she could. She'd seen the approaching swarm and wanted nothing to do with them. She'd had entirely enough of alien creatures trying to make a snack of her crew. No more distractions, no more wonderment, they were getting the hell out of these caves.

The Europhids on either side of the path that lead to the nearest tunnel slowly closed in, narrowing the space through which they could run—or franticly bobble in their case. A barrage of stingers launched from either side of the Europhid patches, swiping across the PMS suit's impervious skin.

Connelly realized that all Europhids were equipped with such weapons. The sample they'd put in the incubator had simply grown. No mutation had occurred. It also meant that what had happened to Peterson could happen to any of them if the Europhids found a chink in their armor.

As the pathway continued to constrict, the number of swiping stingers increased to the point where from her feet to her elbows Connelly felt a constant sharp rubbing. If her body hadn't developed on Earth, where muscles grow stronger to compensate for the increased gravity, the net of Europhid limbs might have held her tight. But she and Robert plowed through the mass of scratching arms, now only feet from the nearest exit.

As they grew closer to the exit, Connelly felt a pain in her chest. It felt like what most people imagine a heart attack feels like, but she'd felt the pain before. Her anxiety was mounting to the breaking point. The onset was so subtle that it went unnoticed, especially during stressful situations when her mind was distracted by other events. She might be able to deal with the situation like any normal person, but when other people reached their emotional cap, her psychological pressure point continued to rise, even after the stressful situation had subsided.

The ache in her chest was the first warning sign. If things didn't calm down soon it might be days before she felt the anxiety subside. A surge of anger pushed the pain away.

I've gone years without having an anxiety attack, Connelly thought. *I won't have one now!*

"How are we doing, guys?" It was Willard. She hadn't looked back since she and Robert started running. She was glad to hear he was still there.

"Okay," she said. "We're about to enter the cave system."

"I know," Willard said.

A shape landed next to Connelly, catching her off guard and squeezing a shriek from her lungs. Her eyes opened wide with fright and she twisted her head toward the figure.

"Whoa, boss," Willard said as he took Connelly's arm. "It's just me."

A surge of pain like someone driving a railroad spike into her heart tore through her chest. The attack was growing worse.

"Guys," Robert said. "We might have a problem."

Connelly looked ahead. The Europhids had closed in from either side, sealing off a ten foot swath, cutting them off from the exit. A heart palpitation echoed in her chest. They were trapped.

"Don't stop, Robert." Connelly felt a measure of reassurance from Willard's voice. He was calm and in control. "These things are like Jell-O and the stingers can't pierce your suit."

Robert listened. He was still moving; vaulting towards the wall of Europhids.

"Ever notice how they kind of look like bowling pins?" Willard asked. Connelly didn't look, but she could see the smile on Willard's face. "Be the ball, Robert. Be the ball."

Connelly almost laughed through her anxiety as she watched Robert launch himself forward, plowing through the wall of Europhids. The small red bodies ripped away, exploded or simply mashed onto the cave floor. Willard dragged Connelly by the arm. She was trying to move fast, but her anxiety was telling her body to lie down.

Do nothing.

Give up.

Without Robert and Willard, she'd have been dead already.

After clearing the destroyed wall of Europhids, they entered the cave system. Connelly gave a quick glance back and immediately wished she hadn't. No more than fifty feet away was a tidal wave of ravenous alien creatures. Some were launching themselves through the air. Others were scurrying along the cave floor, across direct routes opened up by the Europhids.

The next stage of the anxiety attack hit her with a suddenness that took her breath away. Her chest tightened and her throat and nose swelled. She was still able to breath enough air, she'd learned that long ago, but it certainly did not feel that way. The effect mimicked an asthma attack. The physical changes were minimal, but the mind believed they were real. Connelly began taking deep breaths in an effort to ease the discomfort.

The cave system glowed under the light of their headlamps, but Connelly quickly wished they couldn't see anything. Scurrying shadows skimmed across the floor, moving to meet them, no matter which of the cave systems they decided to flee through.

Willard's voice continued to be calm. "These things can't get through the suits. If you're attacked, just keep moving. I'll keep them off."

Willard moved to a nearby tunnel that was free of the approaching shadows. Robert entered the tunnel without a word and kept moving. Connelly knew he must be petrified, but was acting brave. She reached the tunnel and paused at the top. "Ethan, this goes *down*. We need to go up!"

"Boss, this is the right way. You need to trust me."

"Ethan…"

"I haven't been wrong yet."

One of the creatures slammed into the side of Willard's face mask and clamped on. Willard hit the floor. "Go, Connelly! Go now!"

Connelly watched as Willard struggled to remove the creature from his head. The beast shot its stingers at Willard's facemask and was actually managing to scratch it. Connelly screamed as she lunged forward, wrapped her hands around the creature and yanked it off Willard's head. She held the creature out away from her and in a single violent motion, slammed the creature down on her bent knee. Its chest split open and oozed black blood. Connelly dropped the creature to the ground. Willard hopped to his feet. "Thanks, boss."

Connelly leaned forward on her hands, breathing hard. Willard's hand on her arm pulled her up and shifted her mindset back into survival mode. He pulled her into the tunnel, moving quickly downward, toward whatever new hell hid beneath Europa's surface.

27 – STALKING

Connelly stumbled down the steep incline, following Robert, and fighting to keep herself upright and moving. Through the com system she could hear the panting breaths of Robert and the occasional verbal spur from Willard. It was their presence that kept what little logic remained in her mind locked down. They had always been her secure anchor. And she had never needed them so much in her life as now, when her anxiety was threatening to take over and remove her will to fight.

They'd been bumbling through the tunnels for nearly a minute and the small creatures had yet to overtake them. While agile and mobile in the open cave, they had trouble negotiating the rapid turns of the cave system. But they were there, waiting for one of them to stumble, to slow. Then they would pounce.

She glanced over her shoulder, watching for the tiny predators. Her head-lamp cut through the darkness. Willard was feet behind her and off to the side, giving her a perfect view of the tunnel behind them. She could see a mass of creatures surging towards them like water forced through a tube.

"Keep going," Willard shouted. "We're almost there."

"Almost. Where?" Robert asked between wheezy breaths. It was the exact question Connelly wanted answered. Had Willard explored more of the cave system than they knew? Maybe that's why he was really late in rescuing them at the sphere? Maybe he'd already been here? Connelly's mind cleared slightly as new thoughts slipped past her growing anxiety.

Choi had mentioned that the Europhids had taken control of Peterson. Maybe the same thing happened to Willard? If he were under Europhid con-trol, this could all be a ploy to get them deeper into the cave system. She felt a pain like a baseball being forced through her chest and into her throat. Her broiling anxiety devoured her remaining logic.

Connelly felt her body fall away from her. Consumed by the pain in her body, she found it impossible to focus on her footing or even care if she was eaten alive. She bounced into one wall, skipped across the ceiling and careened into the opposite side of the cave.

She could hear Robert and Willard shouting in her ear, but other than her name, it sounded like a mix of forgotten languages. Something struck her side and two long…things…like elephant trunks wrapped around her waist. She felt the ground slip away and suddenly, she was flying. Her view of the world blurred further.

Pain and confusion warped Connelly's mind so much that the following five minutes could never be recalled. When her thoughts began to clear, she slowly became aware of her new surroundings. She was leaning against a solid wall. The numbness on her backside told her she was sitting on a cold stone floor. Seeing was still a challenge. Tears had begun to solidify around her eyes becoming goopy clumps on her eyelashes. She blinked them away, wishing her hands could reach inside the space suit and wipe her eyes. As Connelly's vision unclouded her first impression was that the red world of the inner cavern had turned sunflower yellow.

The stillness in the new setting also caught her attention. They were no longer moving. She could hear breathing in her com, but it wasn't labored. They'd been stopped for a few minutes at least. She became embarrassed by her anxiety. She couldn't recall how they had got here or what she had said or done on the way.

At first, Connelly thought her vision was still screwed up, because everything around her appeared to be yellow. She looked to the left and saw Robert sitting next to her, staring at her with wary eyes. Her vision wasn't wrong, everything really was yellow. Even Robert.

"It's a fungus," Robert explained. "Well, as close to a fungus as an alien species might get. I really have no idea what it is, but that's my closest guess. It glows yellow…but you already knew that."

Connelly could sense his nervousness, but it wasn't for his safety, it was for her sanity. She knew the look. She'd seen it before. "I'm all right," she said.

"You're back?"

Connelly nodded. "How bad was I? I didn't hurt Willard, did I?"

"Hurt Willard?"

"He carried me here, didn't he?"

Robert shook his head and stretched back. He winced slightly as he moved. Connelly realized the truth. "*You* carried me?"

Robert gave a smile and a nod. "Nothing a few days with an ice pack and a hot pad won't fix. Can't let Willard do all the work, you know…besides…"

She took his hand. "I know." Connelly furrowed her eyebrows. She felt Robert's hand tighten on hers.

"What?" he asked.

"Willard…where is he?"

"Went for a little recon trip while I caught my breath. Don't worry, those little guys don't like these yellow caves much."

Connelly remembered her fears about Willard being controlled by the Europhids. It seemed strange that Willard would leave them. She quickly wrote off her paranoid thoughts. She didn't want to descend into a full blown anxiety attack again.

"Where are we?" she asked.

"Deep in the cave system. Very deep."

"And the creatures?"

Robert motioned with his head toward one end of the tunnel. "Around the corner. They stopped at the yellow growth like old men at a stop sign. They're not moving."

Connelly looked to where Robert had motioned. She couldn't imagine that just around the bend was a wall of monstrous creatures just waiting for her to show herself. And then what? Would they slice through her mask and peel off the space suit? Would they crush her to death under their collective mass? Connelly felt her chest tighten as her line of anxious thinking continued.

Thankfully, Robert could still read her thoughts. "We're safe here," he said. "Willard will be back any minute, and he'll have a way back to the surface."

"I'm back now," Willard said as he entered the tunnel. "But I'm afraid we're not quite safe, and I have no idea how to get back to the surface."

Connelly's throat began to seal off.

"But," Willard said with emphasis, "The tunnels ahead are large and move at an upward angle. If we can find one that goes up and around that giant den, we might be able to backtrack to the sphere. Our air is limited, so we're going to have to move fast. No more rests." Willard looked into Connelly's eyes. "No more panic attacks."

Connelly turned her eyes to the floor.

"Sorry, boss," Willard said, "I don't mean to be harsh. But if Robert hadn't turned into the incredible hulk back there, we wouldn't have made it."

For a moment, Connelly wished she could see Robert in action, but decided it was better to have no memory of the event. "No more panic attacks. Got it…. Let's get the fuck out of here."

This brought a smile to Willard's face. He patted Connelly's shoulder and chuckled. "You're almost as crazy as I am, boss."

Connelly grinned, remembering the last time he'd used that phrase, the day all this insanity began in Antarctica. "Crazier."

Willard turned and began walking down the tunnel, moving at a quick pace. Before taking three steps, he stopped and turned around. "I almost forgot. The tunnels up ahead are populated."

Robert stumbled. "Pop—populated?"

"By what?" Connelly asked, feeling her grip on reality tighten.

"Can't say for sure…but they're big."

"How big?"

"Ever seen a rhino up close?" Willard asked.

Connelly didn't want to answer, but did. "Yes."

Willard sighed. "Bigger."

The temperature inside Connelly's space suit seemed to be climbing. Sweat dripped down her forehead like rain off a windshield. Of course, the perspiration had nothing to do with heat and everything to do with her emotional state. Even if her body had begun to overheat, the finely tuned body temperature system in the PMS would have cooled her before she registered feeling hot.

Ever since her breakdown while being chased by the "creeps," as Willard had come to call them, she had struggled to reel in and control her emotions. At first she felt back to her stable self—cool, collected and in control. But every few feet they climbed into the new cave system, the more her anticipation had increased. She wished Willard had never told her about the large creatures dwelling in these caves. Sometimes ignorance really was bliss. If she didn't know the danger existed, she wouldn't be starting to panic, and if they were attacked, she might be able to handle the stress. But now…now she was spiraling down that dark path again and her fears were getting the best of her.

Willard's description of the creatures he'd seen didn't help her anxious imagination either. He described them as large, bipeds, maybe quadrupeds and hard to see—like they blended in with the surrounding cave wall colors, which had varied from cave to cave. The bright walls were the only distraction Connelly found from her sense of impending doom. The tunnel they were moving through now was a deep violet, so rich it looked as though it might taste like blueberry pie.

Robert's steady pace broke at the end of the cave, where the tunnel opened up into a large, dark cavity.

"What is it?" Connelly asked.

Robert stood to the side. "The tunnel ends here. There's a path moving down the face of the cavern. I can't see the bottom."

Willard joined them at the mouth of the opening. "Switch on your headlamps," he said. They had shut them off to conserve battery life. The caves had been bright enough to see by so far. Since leaving the first tunnels, this open space was the first completely dark area.

Willard snapped on his light. Connelly and Robert followed suit. The three lights did little to trim away the darkness. "Boost the juice," Willard said. "Just for a minute."

All three turned their lights up, which glowed with three thousand watts. The enormous halo of light was enough to illuminate the bottom of the cave, which looked like a graveyard. Phallic stones, rising up from the cave floor cast deep shadows and created a maze with several exits to the other side of the cavern. The opposite wall glimmered lightly in the distance. A path of switch backs rose up the wall and into a tunnel on the opposite side. There was no other way to go.

Connelly couldn't help but notice the purposeful switchback trails. They resembled those leading to the bottom of the Grand Canyon. These trails had been created by living creatures, and from the width of the paths—six feet minimum—they were designed for creatures much larger than human beings. Connelly swallowed hard. They had to cross through the maze.

"Let's get a move on," Connelly said, trying to put up a tough front. She might crack again, but she'd be damned before she let Robert and Willard see it happen.

They headed down the steep path, which dropped three hundred feet to the floor. The low gravity made the descent easier on the knees, but Connelly found it difficult not to overcompensate with ever step. A normal step forward meant drifting for several long moments as gravity pulled her slowly back to the steep path. She only made the mistake once and nearly spilled over the edge when the path reversed directions. If not for Willard's quick grab at her boot, she would have toppled over the side and fallen all the way to the bottom.

After reaching the bottom of the cave, Connelly could see the tall stones clearly. They were fifteen feet in height, each and every one of them. They reminded her of the statues erected on Easter Island, standing tall and noble, like eternal watchers. It was then that she realized it was more than the stones watching her.

With a quick turn, she was facing the stone wall that they had just descended. Standing flat against the wall was a massive creature. Connelly's voice caught in her throat, keeping her verbal warning locked inside her throbbing ribcage. But the creature did not move. It simply watched. Robert and Willard stepped forward, leaving her a few feet behind. They had no idea the creature was there.

The creature stood on two, three toed feet. Each toe was spread wide, displacing the creature's weight and increasing its gripping surface area. Its legs were built like tree trunks, but single jointed like a humans. That's were the physical similarities ended. The upper torso was hunched slightly, pulled forward by the creature's large, domed head. Its eyes looked like blue teacups. Its translucent skin gave an eerie peek into the inner workings of the creature's internal organs. Connelly didn't recognize any portion of the creature's exposed physiology. The strangest aspect of the creature was its two arms, if that's what they were. The appendages were built like a squid's two longer tentacles. The tips looked like soft diamond shaped spear heads. Rising up from behind the creatures head, they hovered in the air, wavering back and forth as though moved by a slight breeze. Connelly was more than twenty feet away but felt the creature could easily lurch out and snag her if it desired.

Before Connelly could will herself to react, the creature appeared to grow wet, as though liquid were being excreted from hidden glands. As the moisture spread, the creature's body absorbed the darkness of the cavern. Within seconds, the entire alien had vanished, save for its cobalt eyes, which stared at Connelly with an intensity she had never felt before.

During that single moment of connection, Connelly felt her anxiety wane, her nervousness disappear, and her fear about life and death, Robert and their mission, fade to nothing. She saw peace in the monster's eyes…until it closed them and disappeared completely.

Connelly's thoughts and emotions returned in a torrent when her connection with the creature ended. She realized that with the ability to blend into the surrounding environment, these creatures could have been tracking them the entire time. A lightning bolt of worry struck her. She had to warn the guys. She turned to where they had been and squinted as her head lamp glared off a nearby rock.

She swept the area with her light, cutting through the darkness. She moved from side to side, over and over again, until she came to the conclusion she dreaded most. Robert and Willard were gone.

They had left her behind.

A glint of metal on the floor caught Connelly's attention. She knelt down and cast her light on the floor. Willard's ice pick lay among a flurry of dusty footprints.

They hadn't left her.

They'd been taken, and she hadn't seen or heard a thing.

ᛈ   ᛈ   ᛈ   ᛈ   ᛈ

The cavern twisted around Connelly like a living thing. She'd begun running in a blind panic. Images of Robert and Willard's demise flashed through her mind. They had been kidnapped, she knew that, but if they were still alive…she had no idea.

Before she could pause and think the situation through, her body had reacted on instinct alone. The muscles in her upper back twisted with tension as she remembered the creature hiding in the darkness somewhere behind her. She could feel it growing closer, moving in for what? The kill? She didn't know, but had no intention of finding out. If the guys were still alive, she'd have to find out *after* she saved herself. Connelly gripped the ice pick and bolted into the maze of alien obelisks.

In an effort to lose anything following her, Connelly swerved in and out of stones, following a rapid and chaotic path. In the end, she only succeeded in tiring her lungs, wasting some air and confounding herself beyond recovery. She had no idea which direction lead to the switchback trail. She quickly attempted backtracking by following her boot prints, but soon realized she had crossed her own path several times during her mad sprint.

The surrounding darkness closed in around her, compressing her with a claustrophobic tightness. She forced her breath to come slowly…calmly. Robert wouldn't carry her this time and Willard wouldn't catch her if she fell. She was on her own.

Leaning against one of the lanky boulders, Connelly let herself slide down onto her backside. She pulled her knees up close and strained her muscles as she squeezed her arms around her legs.

Connelly had always thought of herself as an independent woman. She'd never relied on a man for anything. That's what she had thought anyway. On her own now, she realized that her self-image was slightly askew. Robert and Willard had become so much a part of her life that she'd come to depend on them for certain things. She realized now that their support, their encouragement, had been one of the contributing factors in keeping her anxiety at bay over the years...but now...now they were both gone. No one would tell her to get up. No one would encourage her to press on.

It was then that she realized the guys depended on her for just as much. Strength. Leadership. Determination.

"Get up," she said loudly to herself. "Get up, now."

After standing, Connelly rolled her neck on her shoulders and set her face into an expression of raw determination. It was Robert and Willard who needed her now. Anxiety be damned. She'd function through the tears and closed throat. She'd ignore the paranoid images that assaulted her mind. Never, in all her years of battling anxiety, had one of Connelly's anxious premonitions come to pass.

She focused on that thought as she prepared to set out. She'd head in one direction until finding a wall, then would follow the perimeter until she found the switchback trail. It might take some time, but she had no other options. Her light alone did little to pierce the darkness of the cavern and the tall stones blocked her view.

Connelly turned in the direction she thought, for no real reason, the switch back trail was located. As her light cut through the blackness, three objects filled her vision: the stone path, the obelisks, and a tall, tentacled alien, standing calmly in front of her. For the first time in all her life, her feeling of doom had been right. If only she'd listened to her inner voice and run again. If only...

Raising the ice pick over her head, Connelly prepared to attack the beast. In the time it took Connelly to poise the ice pick over her head, the creature leapt onto the side of one of the tall stones, gripping on to it with thick toes, and launched a tentacle towards Connelly. The appendage shot towards her head like a spear. Just before connecting, the tip of the long arm spread open like a beaked jaw, revealing a sticky, froth covered surface. The light from her headlamp was blocked out as the alien clamped onto her facemask.

Connelly let out a scream, but it caught in her throat as she felt her feet leave the floor. She was yanked up and continued to rise for what seemed a full minute. During that time, trapped in the darkness, limbs dangling helplessly, Connelly felt her anxiety return. But this time it was masked by the cancerous despair. She'd failed Robert and Willard. And she was about to share in their morbid fate.

IMMUNE SYSTEM

28 – TOPSIDE

A flashing yellow hell greeted Harris as he came to, hours later. Wailing electronic screams rang in his ears like tortured souls. The stench of smoke and blood assaulted his nose. He really was in hell. Hadn't he lived a good life? If a child dropped a toy, he'd pick it up. If an old woman needed help carrying groceries, he'd help. He'd been a regular Boy Scout all his life, but he ended up heading south for the long winter?

Someone began shouting at him as he floated free, feeling neither floor beneath or ceiling above. The words were just beyond him, meshed with a loud rumbling—the fiery embers of Hades being stoked. Harris gritted his teeth as he began to sort through the chaos. The voice droned on. Insistent and toneless. Electronic…

The devil is a robot, Harris thought.

The ridiculousness of the thought snapped Harris into a fully aware state. The voice sounded clear, "WARNING…ORBIT FAILING…WARNING…"

The warning systems on the Surveyor were designed in tiers, increasing in severity with every passing minute. It began with a flashing light. This was followed by a text message on all the ships video screens. The text on the screen would then begin flashing, accompanied by a loud beep. The beeping would become a loud wailing throughout the ship. Anyone onboard would be hard pressed to ignore it. And finally, the ship's computerized voice would announce exactly what was going wrong, repeating over and over, until the situation was averted, the system was reset, or the entire crew and ship had been destroyed. The fact that the voice was chanting the same message over and over again meant that whatever had happened to the Surveyor occurred several minutes ago, at least.

"WARNING...ORBIT FAILING...WARNING..." The ship repeated. Harris bit down harder as the message sunk in. The Surveyor was headed towards Europa's surface. They were going to crash.

Harris focused all his energy on understanding his surroundings and situation. He was in the control center still. Peterson had left him for dead. Harris could see the blood stain on the floor. The wound on the back of his head was crusted over. He squinted. Something wasn't right.

Focus...

I'm floating, he realized

Artificial gravity was out.

Harris stretched his legs up and away. He connected gently with the ceiling and glided towards the floor. He latched onto a chair and dragged himself over to the command console, where all the ship's systems could be attended to. Fearing sabotage, Harris ran a preliminary status check. There was no internal damage to any of the ships systems, though several were shut down or malfunctioning. What caught Harris's eye were the external sensors. They were lit up like the Los Angeles Lights Festival.

The hull was taking a pummeling.

Harris worked the manual controls for the ceiling, turning it clear without the need for one of the remotes. The view was beautiful at first glimpse, but it quickly turned sickening as Harris remembered what he was seeing.

A plume of charged particles spread out before the Surveyor. He knew in that instant that he was in the middle of a frappe-thick cloud of the little bombs. He had no doubt that the thousands of mini explosions wracking the hull pushed the ship out of a stationary orbit. He had yet to determine how long the Surveyor had been falling and how far. The answers to those questions would tell him if he would live or die in the next few minutes.

He sent his query to the computer. As he waited the few seconds it took the system to work the thousands of variables affecting the ship, he did his best to block out the screaming alarm, which pulsed in synchronized beats along with the pain in his skull. When he saw the text flash on the screen, he got the one answer he didn't expect: results unknown.

What the computer was telling him was, you can get out of this if you do absolutely everything right. Under normal circumstances, Harris would feel confident in his training and knowledge, but in his current condition…. As Harris rubbed his hand over his head, an automatic reflex, he felt the thick glob of dried blood on the back of his head. The wound made him think of his humanity, of his crew—they were in danger too. They were his responsibility. He was the captain. If *he* died, they all died.

"Not acceptable," he said.

He had just minutes to formulate and implement a plan. Step one, shut off the damn alarm.

In ten seconds, he had the alarm system shut down. As the lights ceased flashing and the alarm went silent, his mind did the one thing he couldn't afford it to do, went blank.

ת   ת   ת   ת   ת

Choi's arms shook like she was performing a handstand during a 7.0 magnitude earthquake. She had the ATV pegged to full speed and was cruising across the rough Europian terrain. Even without the sample trailer, which she had left behind, the ATV held sufficient weight to keep it planted firmly on the moon's surface. But at her current speed, even the weight of the modified four-wheeler would do little to keep her on the ground for long.

Rounding a spire of ice, Choi eased up on the throttle. The turn was tight, and for a moment she rode on two wheels, skirting the edge of danger like a carnival trick car. She moved her weight to the opposite side, knowing that if she fell over sideways the ATV might come down on top of her. All four wheels returned to the ice, just in time. A wall of ice, too steep to climb, blocked her path. Worse than that, the area was full of ruby red Europhids.

Choi hammered the brakes. The wheels caught, but the vehicle's speed was too great. The ATV slid into the Europhid coated area, plowing a red smeared path as it skidded over the ice. After ten seconds of sliding, the ATV came to a stop. With a quick jerking motion, Choi looked at her surroundings. She searched for Peterson, watching for an ambush. It never came.

She noticed the Europhids again. They had closed in around her, moving so subtly that she hadn't noticed their approach. She had no intention of repeating the bloodletting that allowed her to escape the cave. Her nose still stung and breathing was difficult through her congested nostrils.

Choi revved the engine in an attempt to frighten the Europhids, but it had little effect. Choi then realized that the roaring engine made no noise at all while in the vacuum of space. As the Europhids continued inching forward, propelled by unseen rows on phalanges on their underside, Choi realized there was another way she could use the ATV against them.

Squeezing the front brakes, Choi locked the front wheels in place. With her other hand, she twisted the throttle to full, sending the back tires into a mad spin. Vibrations from the wheels swirling across the frozen ice reverberated up Choi's spine and into her skull. She knew the tires would do much worse to the Europhids.

With a quick jerk, Choi turned the handle bars of the ATV. The vehicle spun around, its back end swinging out, while its two front tires spun in a rigid circle. As the ATV came around it caught the edge of the approaching Europhids, shredding and splattering them across the others. The violent act seemed to spur the others into action.

The Europhids sprang forward all at once, leaping up in the low gravity, and descending towards Choi.

Leaning to the side to maintain her balance, Choi saw the incoming assault and smiled. She knew the flaccid creatures didn't stand a chance. As the first wave hit, a geyser of crimson guts exploded into the low atmosphere like a brilliant firecracker. Choi was slightly surprised to see the Europhids continuing their fruitless assault. They kept coming—a constant barrage of rubber flesh spewed up and around, like frogs in an open blender.

As the ATV continued its shredding revolutions, Choi noticed that each consecutive spin had less power. She was slowing down. She tried twisting the throttle, but it was at full speed. Choi glanced down at her rear wheels and noticed a mash of red flesh and oozing innards gumming up the axles.

"Shit," Choi said as she realized what was happening. If the internal workings of the ATV got any more gummed up, it might not run at all. The Europhids weren't attacking, they were stalling.

Buying time.

For Peterson.

Choi eased up on the gas and slid to a stop. The Europhids immediately went for the wheels, clinging to them like blood starved leeches. Choi threw the ATV into reverse and hit the throttle. The wheels spun in the opposite direction, sending a spray of Europhid remains into the air. The ATV lurched backwards, plowing through the crowd of Europhids.

Satisfied that enough of the gelatinous creatures had been dislodged from the axles, Choi shifted into drive and launched forward. In fifteen seconds she was at top speed. In twenty she had cleared the remaining Europhids, swerving onto clear ice. As the remaining red ooze cleared from the ATV's system, Choi felt a jolt as the vehicle's speed jumped.

With clenched fingers, Choi worked her way around the wall of ice that had blocked her original approach. Feeling like a pin ball, Choi dodged in and out of ice heaves, bounced over small rises and spun around sharp corners. She was running a one woman race and had no idea if she winning.

A clearing opened up in front of her, allowing the ATV to reach higher and higher speeds. Choi realized too late that the clearing was actually a massive ice sheet that had long ago lifted from the flat surface of Europa and refrozen at an angle. Her rapid approach to the edge, which dropped thirty feet straight down, made it impossible for her to stop in time. If she attempted a stop she would simply topple over the edge and land in an uncontrolled crash.

She did the only thing she could; held on tight.

For the second time in her life, Choi felt what it was like to fly; only this time, the solid ATV beneath her body gave her a slight measure of relief. If she were able to land wheels down, the ATV would absorb the brunt of the impact.

At the height of her long arc over the ice, Choi was able to see TES in the distance. Even in the dim light cast by the sun's reflection on Ganymede, TES was easy to make out. Its solid black surface stood out in stark contrast against the pure white ice.

Choi nearly let go of the ATV as she saw Peterson. He was a hundred yards from TES and closing fast. If she didn't intercept him in time, the TES crew didn't stand a chance. Choi kept the ATV's wheels spinning at full speed. All she had to do was control the landing and she'd be able to continue the chase without missing a beat.

I can do this, she thought, as the ATV began descending towards the surface.

"Round two, Peterson," Choi said. "Round two."

ℶ ℶ ℶ ℶ ℶ

Peterson—the *real* Peterson—realized he'd become a consciousness without a body. The things he'd seen—that he'd watched *his own hands* do—he could never have done. After losing control of his bodily functions, he had watched helplessly as he clubbed Harris and left him for dead. He could only observe as he appropriated a lander, stalked Choi and ultimately attacked her.

The long minutes as he hauled Choi's motionless body to a hole in the ice were among the most torturous of his life. He had no idea what had become of her since he shoved her inside and watched her be swallowed down.

It was the Europhids. All of it.

He couldn't begin to comprehend how they'd rendered his mind inert or how they were controlling his limbs, but they were. And that's what kept him from going insane. Blaming the Europhids gave him direction, focus, something to think about other than the horrific deeds he had done. What he wanted, more than anything, more than regaining control of his body, was revenge.

Revenge for Harris.

Revenge for Choi.

Revenge for whatever the Europhids would do with his body next.

He would kill every last one of the little shits until they were wiped off the face of Europa.

"*That is why you must be destroyed.*"

The voice had returned. Peterson clearly remembered his previous encounter with the voice that claimed to be God. He knew it wasn't true. God wasn't a fucking red cucumber.

"You're not God," Peterson said inside his mind.

"*No?*"

"No."

"*Then who?*"

"Europhids."

"*A ridiculous name. I* am *God.*"

"Why bother speaking to me?"

"*To understand.*"

"God understands everything."

The silence that followed inside Peterson's consciousness could have lasted seconds or minutes. In his current state, time had lost all meaning for Peterson. A deep sense of discomfort filled his thoughts, distracting him. It wasn't painful, but the feeling of dread generated within his psyche was intense. Knowing he was under some form of attack, Peterson stubbornly pressed on. "God does not need this body. God does not need me to kill. And God does not *fear* anything."

"*I am not afraid of you.*"

"I felt your fear…before you went through decon…you stopped. You were afraid."

"*I see all there is to see. I know all there is to know. I have power to do all I please. You are insignificant to me. I am—*"

"Delusional."

"Silence!"

"*You* silence me." Peterson had no voice. The mocking tone of his thoughts could not be concealed. The Europhids could *not* silence him. Apparently, they could control his body and chain his will, but they could not delete him entirely. "You have seen my thoughts. My memories. You now know that I come from a planet far from here. You know there are billions of others, just like me. You know that you are not God."

Again, the silence in Peterson's mind lasted for several moments. When the voice returned it was softer, less rigid. *"I am not. I am we. We are billions too."*

A breakthrough! Peterson allowed a tinge of relief to build.

"We understand God now...saw God in your mind...the limitless power.... We have always been defined that way. We were...confused. But you have brought us clarity. You would destroy us. Decontamination must be accomplished."

Peterson wanted to shout out a rebuke, but he felt neither his lungs nor his jaw. In an instant he felt the connection with the other consciousness fade away. It had broken off the dialogue. Refocused on its grim task. Decontamination. The Europhids were intelligent, he knew that, but their grasp of reason held a little to be desired.

As Peterson's mind filtered through the conversation, he became aware of his new surroundings. While distracted by the voice, he had failed to pay attention to what his still functioning eyes were seeing. Spread out before him, like a futuristic chip and dip plate was TES. The sphere was still lowered beneath the ice and he was steadily approaching the control panel.

Peterson's mind convulsed. The others would share the same fate as Harris and Choi, and their deaths would be on his hands. Pushing his will with all the determination he could render, Peterson attempted to will control of his body back to himself. The attempt was fruitless.

The only response he received echoed through his mind.

It was the voice again.

Laughing.

29 – BLUE

As anxiety welled within her, Connelly found herself reacting in a way she never had before. Her body fell limp. She was helpless as a rag doll in a laundry dryer. She could feel her body being pulled through a series of tunnels. The entire trip was masked in darkness as the creature that had taken her kept a firm grasp on her face plate.

The only hint that she was experiencing severe anxiety was her thought process. She recognized the rapid thought transitions, moving from one horrid topic to the next, seeing every gruesome detail of friends' deaths, imaginary dangers and painful memories exaggerated to the point of hysteria. But she felt no pain in her chest. Her throat never closed.

This anxiety attack was something new. Something she had never experienced or even heard of before. She wasn't sure if it was the extraordinary circumstances that had brought on the attack or the unusual stress of the last few days, but something was affecting her mind in a wildly different way.

Catatonic anxiety.

In many ways, what she experienced seemed a welcome change to the panic she normally felt. This was more subdued. A motionless lump would be hard pressed to make a fool of itself; like she had earlier, when she had turned into a sobbing, hysterical harpy in front of Robert and Willard.

For the first time since her attack began, she felt pain. It streaked across her chest like a razor's edge. And then it was gone.

As though waking from a dream, Connelly's world transformed. A brilliant blue light filled her eyes. After the long minutes of darkness it was like staring into a brilliant azure star. She clenched her eyes shut as her body hovered in mid air for a moment. Then she collapsed onto what felt like a thick rug.

Her first glimpse of the surreal new surroundings left Connelly feeling oddly far from home. True, she had never been further from home, but she couldn't find a single Earthly reference to describe what she was seeing. The floor, which she saw first, was thickly padded with sunflower yellow filaments that looked like billions of bright caterpillars standing on end. The growth covered every inch of the chamber's floor, like wall to wall carpeting.

It was the walls of the room that caught and held her attention next. Every inch of every wall, minus the three exits, was coated in gently undulating Europhids. But these Europhids were unlike any she had seen. They were immense, four foot long rods of gelatinous flesh. Their size alone wasn't what impressed Connelly the most, it was their color. Each Europhid radiated a cerulean glow. The blue coloration varied from organism to organism, giving the walls a varied and stunning texture. "Comfortable" was the only word Connelly could think of to describe the walls. She wanted to crawl into them and fall asleep.

As though a drain had been pulled on Connelly's anxiety reserves, she felt swirls of tension slide down her body and exit through her toes. She felt her muscles relax to the point of not being to hold her torso away from the floor.

The draining anxiety became dammed up instantly when Connelly caught a glimmer of shifting light in the glow of her head lamp. A subtle shift of color that appeared and then faded away again.

She was not alone.

The hunched creature that brought her here had lingered, remaining cloaked.

Connelly believed her thoughts must be an open book to the creatures as one by one, ten of the hulks shimmered into view. Their long appendages were folded down in a nonthreatening way and their eyes glowed with the same blue light as the Europhids coating the walls. They stood still and silent, like guardian statues. But Connelly knew better. They were brutishly strong and agile. She would be dead already if they desired. Her PMS may protect her from lacerations, but they could just as easily pummel her to death. She understood it would be effortless for the creatures. So why were they delaying? What did bringing her here accomplish?

Without thinking about communication problems that inherently existed between species that developed on different worlds, Connelly spoke rhetorically. "What do you want with me?"

The creatures remained motionless, silhouetted by the blue light emanating from the Europhid walls.

Connelly pushed herself onto her knees, waiting for some kind of attack. "Why am I here?" she asked.

Two of the creatures moved, causing Connelly to shirk away. They were going to pounce. This was it…

But they simply stood to either side, opening a path to a section of the Europhid wall. Then they were motionless again.

Connelly stood to her feet and looked around. The creatures stood all around her. It was clear they wanted her to move through the open space, to walk towards the wall, but why? Lacking options or the means to plead her case, Connelly moved slowly towards the wall. She stopped a foot away, looking into the glimmering blue flesh of the fragile Europhids.

A smile crept onto her face. She took another step forward, peering at the internal workings of the translucent Europhids.

Amazing.

Connelly didn't have a chance to scream or react as a barrage of blue tendrils snapped out of the wall, wrapped around her body and pulled her into the wall. Connelly sank deeper and deeper into the wall. A jolt, like an electric shock, paralyzed her. There was no pain, just immobility.

Like jellyfish tentacles, she thought. Even humans weren't immune to the effects of jellyfish, whose tendrils caused severe burning and immense pain. The effect of the Europhid tentacles on Connelly's body was overwhelming, even with the PMS on.

As Connelly was swallowed up by the wall, the view through her facemask became stark blue…like she was floating in the sky. She felt her mind slipping away. Her thoughts became jumbled, tired, like sleep induced by a sedative. A blanket of total and complete peace had been laid over her. Her anxiety had been reduced to nothing. Here she was, about to face a death unlike any human had experienced before and she felt better than she had in all her life.

The void that enveloped Connelly was all consuming. She attempted to look at her hands. They were gone. She tried to turn her head, hoping for a better view, but she lacked a neck. In fact, she had no body at all. For a brief moment she thought that maybe she had been killed and the Catholics were right all along, there was a purgatory and she was there. She'd always thought of purgatory as all white.

Why not blue? she thought. It's not the most extravagant color…but it wasn't bad either…just somewhere in the middle. In limbo.

But the blue void began to change. Light filtered down from above, the beams reflecting off of a cloud of tiny bubbles. The light shimmered and shook. There was a surface above her. As the density of her surroundings increased, Connelly felt that she was underwater and that the illumination from above was sunlight glimmering through the surface.

The world around her became real. She was in a tropical lagoon. Snorkeling. She was seven years old.

A memory.

Her parents had taken her to Hawaii on her seventh birthday. Not really for her birthday, but she had always pretended the vacation was in honor of her birth. After a day seeing the smaller islands from the air on a helicopter tour, her mother, father and two brothers had retreated to a small beach, hidden inside a cove on the big island. Her father had bragged that discovering its location had only cost him fifty dollars. While her brothers built a sand castle out of the fine grey sand and mom and dad laid out to tan, she had taken to the ocean with snorkel in hand.

She was an avid and skilled swimmer, but she had never used a snorkel before. She'd seen it done, though, and needed no lessons on how to use the device. The feeling of freedom the snorkel had given her was like nothing she'd experienced in her seven years of life. For the next half hour, Connelly had swum in circles, circumventing the small cove, admiring the snails, crabs and multicolored fish, and never once had to come up for air.

Thirty-one minutes in the water marked the point where her experience changed drastically. Her insistent splashing had attracted the attention of a small tiger shark, a dwarf at only three and half feet long, but still more than a match for a seven-year-old girl in the water. Connelly had heard her father give warnings about sharks, about what attracted them: constant splashing, blood, and waving white skin on the palms and soles of feet. It was the first and last of the three that Connelly had been tempting the shark with for the past thirty minutes. It was the middle of the three which the shark would add to the mix.

Connelly saw a dim shadow swish past her off to the left, deeper in the lagoon. She'd already seen the light play tricks on her, though. Every time a cloud passed in front of the sun, the light would change, causing shapes to emerge and swirl through the water. The first few times caused her to catch her breath. But by now, she was so used to it, she didn't give the new shadow a second thought.

What happened next became a blur in her waking memory, something she had never fully recalled. But now, she was seeing it all as though the day were repeating itself in full detail. First came a horrible burning on her left calf. It was followed by an intense pressure that shot the air from Connelly's lungs as she screamed through her snorkel tube. She spun in the water as the pressure decreased and saw the black eyes of the small shark turn white as its protective eyelid snapped shut in preparation for a second attack.

Gripped by the pain lancing up her leg Connelly could only watch as the shark opened its jaws again and lunged at her face. The water above her head exploded as a fist broke through the surface of the water and connected solidly with the shark's snout, causing it to thrash and bolt away. The hand clasped onto Connelly's wrist and pulled her up out of the water. As she cleared the ocean waves, she looked up and saw the silhouette of her father standing above her like a statue of a Greek god. He was amazing. He was her hero.

Her father yanked her up out of the water, onto the backside of a boat.

Connelly became confused. Her father had been on the shore. He had pulled her onto the beach. They never even owned a boat!

She looked to her father again, expecting to see his scruffy face, dark eyes and tan skin, but instead she was met by an awkward smile, thick glasses and an explosion of hair. Robert...ten years ago. The day they first met.

Echo One, her first research ship, was little more than a decked-out pleasure boat. She and Robert both worked as consultants for Environ-O, an ocean conservation unit dedicated to studying the ocean and lobbying for a change in maritime laws that would protect Earth's endangered species. The job this time around had been laborious and time consuming: crab counting in the Florida Keys. Crabs were difficult to keep track of, most looked alike and there wasn't time to map out each individual's minute differences. More than that, crabs didn't always want to be found. It was the daunting scope of the task that caused Environ-O to hire both scientists at once. Connelly had always been glad they did. Robert saved them days of work by using a mathematical equation to estimate the number of crabs throughout the Keys by extrapolating the data from three separate islands, the closest to the mainland, one in the middle and the one furthest from shore.

The survey was completed in four days. It would have taken three weeks. They spent the following weeks vacationing together on board Orca One. It was the beginning of their bond...one that would eventually lead to more. Connelly felt slightly sad as she looked into the younger Robert's eyes. His attraction to her, even then had been obvious. But they had both been blind to it.

This was the second to last day of their vacation and Connelly had just been snorkeling for two hours. She'd been hooked on it, on the entire ocean and all its creatures, since that fateful day in the lagoon. She didn't fear or hate the shark for what it had done, she loved it for its perfection—*Galeacerdo cuvier*—the perfect eating machine. And she devoted her life to the study of all water dwelling creatures, even the microbial.

Connelly remembered the rest of this day in a flash. She and Robert drank a few beers, grilled a few fish, played a few rounds of chess and then sat on the deck, staring up at the stars until both fell asleep, side by side. She knew what Robert was about to say. She had been wearing a very skimpy bathing suit and one of her breasts was beginning to slide out as she was pulled from the water. Robert, seemingly unaffected by the view said, "You're slipping out up top." He had turned away as he hoisted Connelly onto the back of the boat and gave her ample time to adjust her suit.

She was shocked when events didn't play out as she remembered. "My God," Robert said. "You're just as stunning as I remember." And then he didn't turn around. His eyes lingered on her slipping bikini top, which was just beginning to reveal the top of her nipple. She stood on the deck and quickly adjusted her suit.

Robert chuckled. "You know, I kicked myself for years for not waiting to see if you fell out of that thing. Looks like it was all for nothing."

Connelly smiled, feeling as relaxed as she did on that day ten years ago.

"Could have fooled me. You hid your interest well."

Robert looked surprised. "Wait a minute. You didn't say that."

"And you didn't gape at my boobs."

"Then you're you? You're really you?"

Connelly realized that she was talking to the real Robert. She wasn't sure how, but she knew it was him, the current version. She wrapped her arms around him and planted a kiss on his young lips. It was the first kiss they should have had, but never did.

"Hate to break up the party, guys, but where the hell are we?" Connelly jerked away from Robert and looked toward the source of the familiar voice. Willard, looking just like Willard, was sitting behind the steering wheel, looking back at she and Robert. He was wearing shorts and a gaudy Hawaiian shirt. "And why did I just relive my eighth grade class portrait?"

₪ ₪ ₪ ₪ ₪

The small door that accessed Orca One's inner cabin opened from inside. A woman dressed in a flowing, see through, white skirt and a matching tube top stepped onto the deck. Her golden hair hung down past her shoulders and seemed to reflect the blue water rippling around the boat. She stood sensually

271

next to a stunned Willard, yet her brilliant cobalt eyes revealed an intelligence beyond her years.

Connelly didn't recognize the woman and she certainly hadn't been on the Orca One with her and Robert. When Willard finally found his tongue, it was apparent *he* knew the woman.

"Ms. Tamworth?" Willard's eyes were wide. His lips spread in a wide smile.

The woman nodded and flashed Willard a smile that seemed to paralyze him. He slowly shook his head. "But…"

"A friend of yours?" Robert asked, scratching his bare, curly haired chest.

Connelly noticed that apart from the amazement on Willard's part, neither she nor Robert felt threatened by the woman's sudden appearance. In fact, everything felt fine. This ranked at the top of Connelly's weird events list, but she was taking it all in stride. Even the realization that she felt no fear or anxiety failed to spur some kind of negative emotional reaction.

"It's Ms. Tamworth…Heather Tamworth…my eight grade teacher," Willard said as his eyes followed the outline of her scantily clad curves. "But I never saw her like this."

"Why are you here?" Connelly asked. She may be experiencing some kind of bliss, but she still knew how to get down to business.

Heather turned to Connelly and said, "You have all experienced defining moments in your life. You have just experienced them again. I was watching…to understand."

"Ms. Tamworth," Willard said, "Are you…were you an alien?"

Heather laughed loudly. "Ethan…I was your first love. When you think of me, even to this day, you feel a real, physical pain in your chest. You're feeling it right now."

Willard leaned away from Heather. "How?"

"The Europhids," Connelly said, "They're doing this."

Heather nodded and looked at Willard. "I am the consciousness that you rescued from the belly of the oceanic predator. I was on my way to the surface, to attempt direct contact with your crew. The predator, whose mind is too feeble to control, did as nature commanded, ate me as it later did you. But you, in your act of mercy, saved me."

"You're a Europhid?" Willard asked.

Heather nodded again. "That is the name you have given my species, yes."

"Why do you look like Ms. Tamworth?" Willard asked.

"After sensing your feelings for this woman...I wanted to repay your kindness by fulfilling the desires of your heart." Heather leaned towards Willard, took him by the back of the head and laid her lips upon his. Willard's rigid body soon went slack and he enveloped Heather in a tight embrace. When they separated, Willard slouched back on wobbly muscles. His face was gleefully relaxed.

Heather turned to Connelly, who had watched the entire event as though it were a Broadway play. When she met Heather's other-worldly blue eyes, she remembered that this was a real experience.

"I have questions," Connelly said. She crossed her arms as if to accentuate she meant business. It was hard to do considering how wonderful she felt.

Heather sat in the seat opposite Willard and crossed her smoothly tanned legs. She smiled and bounced her foot back and forth. She was waiting for Connelly.

"You're speaking English," Connelly said.

"We're communicating directly mind to mind," Heather said. "Pure thought has no language. You hear my words as English, because it is the language of your thoughts. My species has no language. We do not speak at all." Heather shifted in her seat and leaned forward, elbows on knees. "Let me clarify. I am what you would call a blue Europhid. We have no name for ourselves, so Europhid is appropriate for your understanding. We are conscience. We are logic. We are thinkers. Like you, we seek to understand. We value life. All life."

"We've been attacked continually since arriving on Europa," Robert interjected.

Heather looked at Connelly with an intensity that almost broke through Connelly's misty sense of joy. "We sent a warning."

"My dreams," Connelly said.

273

Heather nodded. "Unfortunately, you did not understand the origin of the message."

"But why attack us at all?" Robert asked.

"The attacks on you and your crew have been and *are being* carried out by what you call red Europhids. While we represent the mind of Europa, intelligent as they are, the red Europhids represent instinct. They are the protectors of this sphere and their work has kept our world alive."

"Can't you stop them?" Connelly asked.

"Can you stop your white blood cells from acting when a germ enters your body?"

Connelly didn't answer. She didn't need to. She understood perfectly now. Europa was like a living creature, a body unto itself. The blue Europhids were the brain. The red Europhids were the immune system, reacting to perceived threats as they had been programmed to do by millions, perhaps billions of years of evolution. They attacked, and would continue to do so until the invaders has been wiped out. She and the crew of the Surveyor were simply germs invading a body.

Germs that needed to be exterminated.

"Yes," Heather said, "You understand. While we recognize that you mean us no harm, the others sense that you are a threat...and to be honest, after seeing into your minds, I believe they are correct."

30 – ESCAPE

If fear, outrage and defiance were emotions Connelly were capable of feeling at that time, she would have been filled with all three. A blue Europhid in the form of Willard's eighth grade teacher had just accused her of being a threat to the denizens of Europa. Few things made her angry more than being falsely accused. She wanted to deny the accusation, but she couldn't bring herself to say a word.

Instead, she thought about things from the perspective of the Europhids. Her crew had come from space, landed on the surface of Europa, taken and killed sample Europhids, even genetically altered one in a plant incubator. They had unintentionally committed atrocities against sentient beings.

Europhid Heather was right.

"I'm sorry," Connelly said quietly. "We had no idea...we didn't understand what you were. We thought...we thought you were—"

"Vegetables," Heather said. "I know. And the mistake is forgivable given your ignorance. Knowing what you know now, *you* would never repeat those mistakes." Heather stood and walked to the starboard side of the boat, her taut frame bobbing up and down with the motion of the ocean waves. "Your world is beautiful and full of creatures as spectacular as those on our world...but your people must never learn of our existence."

Robert huffed lightly. "We can't just hide what we've discovered from the world. This is our first contact with an alien species."

"This is our first contact as well," Heather said. "I would say it's not going well, wouldn't you?"

"We can learn from our mistakes," Robert said.

Heather crossed her arms across her breasts. "Neither species is ready for prolonged contact."

Robert took a step forward, "But—"

And then he was gone. He simply vanished as though he had never been there. Willard quickly protested, placing his hand on Heather's shoulder. "Eighth grade crush or not, you better tell me what you did with—" In a blink, Willard ceased to exist.

Even with the disappearance of Willard and Robert, Connelly felt no fear or ill will to or from Heather.

Turning to Connelly again, Heather's eyes took on a seriousness that locked her into a forced staring contest. "I have seen into your hearts and minds and know your crew has the best intentions, but your people do not always."

After mulling over the statement, Connelly nodded slowly, ominously. "We would destroy your world for resources, in the name of science and..."

"For pleasure," Heather finished, a hint of sadness in her voice.

Connelly agreed. She could see the hunting excursions that would bring Europian species to the brink of extinction, the territorial wars fought between humans over parcels of ice. They had put Europa in danger by coming here.

"But that's not the worst of it, is it?" Heather asked.

"War?" Connelly said.

Heather nodded. "You've seen the defense system of this world. The only way to exploit Europa would be to exterminate my species. There would be casualties on both sides, but ultimately, I fear we would be eradicated."

Tears brimmed in Connelly's eyes. It seemed she was still able to experience despair, or the Europhid was allowing her to experience it. Either way, Heather was right. Humanity could never know about what they'd found on Europa. It would inevitably lead to the destruction and exploitation of all life on Europa. It was the same sick pattern played out on Earth time and time again. When a new resource, biological or mineral, was discovered on Earth, it was consumed until it ceased to exist. The cycle was threatening to continue on Europa, and Connelly had brought it. She cursed herself for it.

Heather took Connelly by the hand. Her skin was unusually soft and warm. "The burden is not yours to bear alone."

"You don't understand. I can't stop what's begun. If we survive, if any of us survive, Earth will learn about you. I might not tell anyone, but the others...I don't think they will be convinced." Connelly's eyes opened wide. "That's it, isn't it? You wanted me to realize this before you killed us. Our deaths are the only way to protect Europa...to ensure your survival."

Connelly looked down at the floor of the boat. Her jaw became tight and her fingers gripped down. "Do what you need to do. I understand."

"I knew you would," Heather said. She took Connelly's other hand and squeezed it. Heather leaned her face in close to Connelly's. The warm breath from Heather's lips slid across Connelly's cheeks. "Before you go...I give you a gift." Heather pulled Connelly forward and brought their lips together in a soft embrace.

The kiss was like nothing Connelly had ever felt before. Raw energy coursed through her body and into her mind. It felt like Heather was breathing fire into Connelly's soul. A bright light formed at the apex of Connelly's vision and exploded with the violence of a nuclear blast. Connelly screamed as her world turned scorching white.

ᚱ   ᚱ   ᚱ   ᚱ   ᚱ

The transition from boating in the tropics to the starkness of a stone cavern cast in blue light took Robert's mind several moments to process. He realized he was back in the cave system beneath Europa's ocean a second before Willard toppled down next to him. Robert slid over and inspected him.

He was breathing.

He was alive.

Sitting up came as a challenge. His stomach muscles felt oddly numb, as though he'd done a marathon of sit ups. He propped himself up, leaning back on his wobbly arms and found himself, once again, confused. A wall rose before him, as massively tall as it was wide, coated in blue Europhids that blanketed the smooth stone cavern in a soft, comforting glow.

Willard stirred. Robert looked down at his companion and then back to the wall. Had they both been inside the horizontal field of giant blue Europhids? He shook his head, determined not to focus on the eerie details. The events of the past few hours were almost beyond comprehension. He really only had two questions that needed answers.

Where is Kathy? And how do I get her back?

He needed help. "Ethan, you awake in there?" Robert gave Willard a shake.

Willard grunted and rolled from his side onto his back. He shrugged away from Robert's touch like a grumpy teenager taking refuge in a cozy morning bed. "Ugh, just trying to get my thoughts to make sense."

277

Willard pushed himself up into a sitting position. That's when he saw the wall. "Whoa." He looked at Robert. "Were...were we in their?"

Robert shrugged. "Best I can figure, everything we just experienced was up here." Robert tapped his head with his index finger. "And I can't remember how we got here."

"Something grabbed us back in the caves," Willard said. "I think it was the creatures I told you about. They came from above."

"That cavern was hundreds of feet tall," Robert said. "They couldn't have just jumped down from above."

Connelly landed between them, a motionless heap. After jumping back in fear, Robert realized it was Connelly and dove to her side. He rolled her onto her back and looked at her face. Her color looked good and there were no signs of injury. "Thank God."

Robert jumped a second time when Connelly's eyes snapped open and she sucked in a lung full of air. Her breath came in gulps as she blinked several times to clear her vision. "We...we have to get out of here," she said.

"We will," Robert said, holding Connelly by the shoulders. "But you need to catch your breath."

"There's no time," Connelly said, her voice barley a squeak.

"Boss," Willard said, "we don't even know how to get out of here."

"There's only one way out," Connelly said.

Robert felt an explosion of fear burst in his stomach. "The way we came."

Connelly nodded and struggled to her feet. "The only way out is through the creeps in the other cavern. We can fight our way through. The PMS's will protect us from the brunt of the attack, but the TES sphere needs to be guarded. Without it, we'll never reach the surface."

"What do you propose we do?" Robert asked.

"I'll take care of that when we get there."

"*How* will we get there?" Willard asked. He did little to hide his annoyance at bringing up the subject again. "We don't know where we are or how to get back."

"I know the way back," Connelly said.

"How?"

Connelly looked at the wall of blue Europhids. "They told me.... Besides, if we get lost, we have guides." Connelly adjusted her view towards the cave's only exit. Two of the hulking, long armed aliens slid into view.

Robert shuddered, realizing that the creatures had been standing there the whole time.

Connelly gazed into Robert's eyes and the oddness of her stare struck Robert. Something was very wrong...but he couldn't place it. Was it the blue light playing tricks, or...

"No more arguing. Let's go," Connelly said. She turned and headed for the exit. She took only two steps before Robert reached out and took her arm. He pulled her around. "Robert, what—"

"I just realized what's different about you," Robert said. "Your eyes...they're blue."

ᕪ   ᕪ   ᕪ   ᕪ   ᕪ

For the first time since showering on Surveyor before leaving for Europa's surface, Connelly saw her own face in the reflection of Robert's face mask. He activated an unnecessary feature of the PMS that would only need to be utilized in Earth orbit—solar shielding. The external surface of the face mask became highly reflective, which distorted the bounced image, but functioned well enough for Connelly to look into the eyes of a stranger...her own.

"My eyes..." Connelly looked at Willard. A moment of hope squirmed through. "Your eyes are blue, too."

Willard shook his head. "My eyes have always been blue."

Connelly knew that. But had hoped the brilliant blue she had seen in his eyes earlier was still there. It wasn't. The solar shield retracted and Robert's frowning face appeared behind it. "All I need to know," Robert said, "Is that you are you."

"I am," Connelly said.

"That's not good enough."

279

Time was short and the pressure was building. If they didn't escape soon, they and the rest of the Surveyor's crew would die. "What do you want me to do, Robert?" Her voice was loud and forceful. She'd never used a voice like that with Robert, but it came naturally now.

"Prove it, Kathy!" Robert's voice was just as strong.

She was angry because the delay was putting his life in danger. He was angry because he didn't know if she was safe or not.

Connelly placed her hand on his facemask and stared into his eyes. She leaned in, placing their heads together. Close up, their eyes were locked on each other. "Look at my eyes. Look past the color, Robert." She took his gloved hand and squeezed. "I'm me. And if we don't move now, there will never be an *us*."

Willard clapped his hands on each of their shoulders. "Awesome. That's great. Seriously. Let's go now."

"An us?" Robert asked.

Connelly nodded. "If we live."

Robert stepped back from her. "Lead the way."

Connelly turned to the two aliens who were standing like sentinels by the entryway, their arms undulating gently. "Follow them."

The group was led through a winding series of tunnels that ranged from wide open to congested squeezes. The creatures moved through the tunnels with a grace and speed despite their bulk. Stretching their sticky-tipped arms out, they'd clasp onto a distant wall or outcrop and then lifted their thick toed feet from the ground. They propelled themselves forward in a constant and never ending slingshot motion. Connelly and the others struggled to keep up, and several times the creatures stopped and waited patiently. They moved through the yellow tunnels that Connelly recognized from their previous travels.

After clearing the yellow tunnels, the two aliens stopped dead and held a more guarded stance.

"What do they want?" Willard ask.

"We're taking point from here," Connelly said. They're not coming for the whole trip. Connelly moved to the front with Robert and Willard close behind. She led them through three more tunnels, which were blessedly vacant of any creeps. At the end of the third tunnel was a bright red glow.

The cavern.

Connelly paused twenty feet from the exit. Robert was next to her, his eyes trained on the tunnel opening. "Why haven't we been spotted yet? We're in creep territory."

"The blues are blocking our presence from the creeps. But it won't hold once we enter the cavern," Connelly said.

Willard crouched next to them. "I think you're right about that territory theory. I don't think the big guys are supposed to be here either."

Robert glanced at Willard. "Why's that?"

"They bugged out."

Robert looked back. The two aliens were gone. He could feel Connelly's smile before he saw it. "They're still there, aren't they?"

Connelly nodded. "But we're on our own from here. Ready?"

Robert nodded.

"Last one's a rotten egg," Willard said.

"Hold on," Connelly said.

Robert crinkled his nose. "For what?"

A pressure wrapped around the three of them. Two shimmering appendages struck out and clasped onto the end of the tunnel. The realization of what was about to happen struck Willard and Robert simultaneously.

"Oh crap," Willard said.

"Damnable hell," Robert managed to say before the nearly invisible alien lifted its feet from the cave surface and catapulted them into the cave.

They were half way across the cave before they landed in a patch of red Europhids. The little red creatures broke their fall, but the sudden crushing of fifty or so Europhids put the wall of creeps on high alert. They streamed out by the hundreds, scurrying down the den pocked wall.

"Move!" Connelly shouted, but Willard and Robert were already on their feet and headed for the exit.

Connelly looked back over her shoulder. She saw the two aliens, looking very small now, reach up to the wall above the cave entrance. They latched on with their tendrils and pulled the stone down, collapsing the roof and sealing the chamber. There was no going back and only one way out.

The first wave of creeps hit, but they were thin and no match for the fast moving bulk of the three fleeing crewmates. They plowed through the creatures, flinging them to the sides and crushing them underfoot.

They came within ten yards of the exit, Connelly chanced a look up. She saw a creep army dislodge from the wall and fall toward the floor. It was obvious they couldn't pierce the suits, so they were going to crush them under the weight of their immense numbers.

She dove forward with all the momentum she could gather and tackled Willard and Robert into the cave. The cascade of creeps hit the cave floor and became a jumbled mass of writhing bodies, all squirming to enter the cave and continue the pursuit. The chaos gave the crew precious time to pick themselves up and move into the cave system.

Connelly led the way and in minutes they reached the cave where their adventure had started. The TES sphere was still there and appeared to be intact. They ran for it. "Get inside," Connelly said. "They're coming." Willard and Robert climbed inside while Connelly lingered on the outside.

Robert reached out and offered his hand to Connelly. She ignored it. "Willard, give me your spare air tank and the propulsion pack."

Willard had left both on the floor of the sphere before they departed. He looked down at the equipment. "Why?"

Robert's eyes grew wide. "Connelly...you can't."

"I'm not going to argue. Give me the equipment or I stand here and we all die." Connelly's voice was sharp. It was clear she was taking charge again. In fact, she never felt so confident, so in control. The Europhids had given her more than knowledge of how to escape. They had also removed her anxiety. She was seeing the world with a new clarity. Her actions were well thought out and perfectly timed. What she was about to attempt was insane, but she was coolly confident. The wound to Europa's body would be minor. More importantly, it would provide a distraction that would allow them to get out of the ocean and off the moon's surface. Once the red Europhids recovered from the break in their world-wide connectivity, the hunt would continue.

Willard handed the equipment to her. She strapped the propulsion pack to her back. "Robert, give me the wrench from the toolkit." Robert opened a small compartment, removed a wrench and handed it to Connelly.

"Retract the fins and get the hell back to the surface. I'll be right behind you."

Willard couldn't hide the concerned look on his face. "Boss, what are you planning?"

"Methane gas," Connelly said. "All it's going to take is a spark."

31 – IGNITION

Choi swore she could hear an ancient tribe pounding on drums in preparation for a battle. But she was the only warrior around and the drumming pulse was her rapidly beating heart. She clung to the ATV, steering through the maze of ice spires, cracks and divots. Moving fast, each turn and obstacle threatened to throw her from the vehicle. But she didn't let up. She *couldn't* let up.

She'd been barreling across Europa's surface since she'd seen Peterson approaching TES. Rounding a large chunk of ice, she entered a clearing and could clearly see Peterson, silhouetted by the TES flood lights. She set the ATV on a ruler straight course, heading for Peterson.

She covered the distance in a minute flat and was approaching the vehicle's top speed. As she closed in, she could see that Peterson had yet to begin tampering with the equipment, but he was moving towards the control panel.

Then he stopped and turned, as though he could sense her silent approach. *Maybe he felt vibrations in the ice?* Choi wondered. Figuring out how her surprise attack had failed would have to wait.

It was time for plan B.

Plan A had been to run Peterson down. It was a brutal tactic that was sure to kill her crewmate, but there was also no doubt it would work. She'd felt Peterson's enhanced strength first hand and knew she couldn't face him in hand-to-hand combat and win. Plan B would be slightly less effective and much more painful.

Choi pushed down on the foot rests and rose up in to the air. She planted her feet on the ATV's seat and rode it like a daredevil. She was only feet from Peterson. He was dodging to the side, moving slowly in the low gravity, but fast enough to avoid the straight shot ATV. Taking careful aim, Choi tightened her muscles and then launched herself off the ATV.

Choi curled into a tight ball, hoping to put all of the energy created by the impact into a smaller area, boosting the amount of damage done. As she flew forward, she couldn't see where she was going and prayed her aim was true. If it wasn't…if she missed, she'd plunge straight into the hole melted by TES.

A shot of pain burst in her legs as her feet connected solidly with Peterson's back. Her feet remained in contact with Peterson's arched back even after the blow. She pushed her legs out straight and sent Peterson tumbling forward. The action also slowed her own motion enough for her to make a smooth landing. Choi watched as Peterson toppled over and slammed his facemask into the corner of the solid control panel. He slumped to the metal floor of TES. When Peterson turned to face Choi his eyes were wide with panic and he was gasping for air.

Her attack had gouged a huge hole in the facemask. But she could already see the self healing materials kicking in. She couldn't reach him to press the attack before the mask was healed, so she stood her ground and prepared for the worst. Peterson held onto the side of the control panel and pulled himself up. His face was covered in dense sweat that trickled over his skin. He was suffering from more than the blow Choi had just given him. She was sure of it.

"We felt what you did to the others," Peterson said, his voice wavering slightly. "Twenty thousand three hundred and five of our kind. Destroyed by your plague." Peterson began a steady advance toward Choi. "Their deaths and sacrifice will pale in comparison to the suffering you will experience before you are decontaminated."

Choi clenched her fists. "You brought me to them. It was you who passed the plague on. You broke quarantine. You are to blame for their deaths."

Peterson snarled and lunged forward. Choi attempted to dive away, but one of his hands caught hold of her boot. He pulled her to the ground. In the next instant, Choi was pulled up by her legs and tossed toward the TES pit.

He's trying to throw me in! she thought.

She landed just short.

Choi regained her footing as Peterson reached her. She swung at his head and connected solidly, but the pain in her hand far outweighed the jolt Peterson received. Not conceding defeat, Choi ducked low and swung three left hooks into Peterson's side. Her punches had no effect. Peterson brought his arm up and caught Choi under her chin with his forearm. She sprawled backwards, closer still to the hole melted in the ice.

Peterson reached her before she made it to her feet.

"Time to feel real pain," Choi said through her blood soaked mouth. Balanced on one knee, she took careful aim and snapped her fist out like a striking snake. She connected dead on with Peterson's crotch. It was a blow that would have sent even the most disciplined man to the floor.

Peterson reacted like a castrated man. He smiled.

"I have disconnected the pain sensors in this mind," Peterson said. "You cannot stop what I am about to do."

Peterson swung his leg out and punted her into the TES hole. She descended ten feet before bouncing off the frozen wall. The impact knocked her unconscious. She didn't even feel the water envelop her body as she entered the Europian ocean and sunk into the frigid depths.

ᚱ   ᚱ   ᚱ   ᚱ   ᚱ

Robert and Willard had left the cave a full minute ago, moving quickly after learning Connelly's suicidal plans. Robert had put up a momentary fuss, but she squelched it quickly. Their feelings might be out in the open, but she was in charge and ultimately, he respected her decision. They'd retracted the fins and sailed easily out of the watery cave and into the open ocean.

They should be half way to the surface by now, Connelly thought. *Far enough.*

Connelly shined her headlamp into the cave entrance and saw dancing shadows rushing towards her like flood water. That was her cue. Connelly raised the wrench over her head and brought it down on the oxygen tank's cap. The metal on metal impact shook her arm, but the cap remained solid. Connelly repeated the action several times and began wondering if she lacked the physical strength to break the top off. Just as she began loosing track of the number of strikes the top blew off with an explosion of air and launched the oxygen tank in the tunnel.

The first of the creeps had just reached the caves entrance and were shattered by the projectile. Limbs were still scattering across the cave floor when the first of the creeps dove into the cave and hopped madly toward Connelly.

The air tank rocketed through the cave system, straight for the central cavern. It pummeled past every creep in its path. But the desired effect—a spark—never occurred, the stone walls were coated with advancing creeps and their bodies served as a buffer, metal and stone never connected.

Connelly swatted away the first creep to lunge at her, but the second was too quick. It launched onto her face mask and began scratching at it, using its forelimbs like jig saws. She felt a pressure grow around her legs as more of the creatures latched on and began probing for chinks in the PMS armor. Oddly, she felt cool and collected.

She reached up and yanked the creep from her face mask and quickly snapped its relatively fragile limbs. The creature writhed and let go its hold on her facemask. She could now see that five creeps were busy at work, gnawing at her legs, while a constant stream of the creatures poured out of the entrance. Connelly's fear wasn't of the creeps. Her own self made bomb, which was still careening through the cave system was much more of a threat to her life than the army of creeps.

The idea of tearing through hordes of attacking enemies appealed to some primal instinct deep within her, but there wasn't even time to remove the creatures from her legs. She hopped twice and then dove into the water.

Instantly, the creeps attached to her legs let go and flailed as they sank to the bottom and drowned. Connelly took aim at the mouth of the cave and kicked the propulsion pack into overdrive. With a snap of her neck, Connelly launched forward, out of the cave and into the brightly decorated open ocean. She squinted back at the luminous colors of the bioluminescent world. She'd forgotten how beautiful it all was.

For the first time since her encounter with the blue Europhids, Connelly felt a twang of sadness. She knew it got through whatever emotion filter the Europhids had given her because it was an authentic and appropriate. Live or die, she would never see the Europian ocean or its rare beauty again. Connelly turned up and headed for the surface.

Back in the cave system, the oxygen tank rounded the last of several turns, crushing a swath of creeps as it slid at breakneck speeds. With a burst of creep bodies, it entered the massive cavern housing the creep colony and patches of red Europhids. Understanding the metal projectile's intention, a flurry of tendrils shot up like fans doing the wave at a baseball game. They reached out for the tank, but all that connected met the same limbless fate as the creeps.

After sailing fifty feet, the tank fell to the floor and smashed through a patch of Europhids. The impact knocked the tank up and over a second patch. Spindly red limbs stretched out for the tank, but missed. When it landed again, its jagged metal top, which Connelly had severed with the wrench, struck the stone at twenty miles per hour, creating a shower of sparks.

In the methane filled atmosphere, it was enough.

As though God had just created a new star within the confines of the cavern, every particle of methane trapped inside combusted. The outpouring flames incinerated every living thing in the cavern and quickly expanded through the only exit, frying the army of creeps in its wake. When the expanding explosion reached the outer edges of the cave system, it did the only thing it could, pushed up and through the mantle and burst into the open ocean. The caverns flooded in seconds. A shockwave and chaotic stream of bubbles raced towards the surface.

Towards Connelly.

ﬡ   ﬡ   ﬡ   ﬡ   ﬡ

"Can't we go any faster?" Willard said

Robert wished he could say yes, but going faster was not an option. The sound of a massive explosion had roared past them as they ascended through the Europian ocean. After the sound had passed, Robert felt as though his mind had been scrambled with a wire whisk, but he also knew the worst was yet to come. The devastating effects of an underwater explosion rose up through the depths like a leviathan. The TES sphere would be shaken apart and swallowed into the depths.

"We're approaching the cable," Robert said as he worked the controls. "We have to slow down to attach."

"Well, don't miss."

Robert shot Willard an annoyed glance. "I'll do my best." The cable appeared above, encircled by the large melted hole. "Choi must have stalled Peterson. The hole isn't frozen over."

The sphere approached the cable. Robert held his breath as he delicately maneuvered the sphere into position. A loud clunk echoed through the sphere as it was jolted by contact. Three loud clicks sounded out, one at a time, as the locking mechanism engaged. A green light flashed on the console.

"We're locked in!" Robert shouted. He quickly popped open a panel, which revealed a red switch and the label, EMERGENCY RETRACT. "Hold on." Robert flipped the switch.

Like an amusement park ride, they launched up through the hole, passing strata of ice so fast that the ten foot layers became a blur of color. Robert let the air in his lungs slowly seep out, allowing himself the slightest reprieve. He knew they would safely outrun the shockwave now that they were headed topside, but Connelly...

Robert looked up to say a silent prayer. He didn't know if there was a God, but he believed in covering all his bases, and with Connelly's life on the line, he didn't have anything to lose. But as he looked up, he saw a dark shape approaching from above. "What's that?" he said.

Willard looked up. "Don't know...but we're going to hit it." Willard looked at Robert. "Will the sphere hold against an impact at this speed?"

Robert paused. "I have no idea."

As they grew closer to the object the shape became distinctly human. "Oh no..." Robert said. "Who is it?"

Willard shook his head. "Better brace for impact. If this egg cracks, we might be able to swim to the surface."

"Doubtful," Robert said, gripping the arm rests of his chair. "We lack the buoyancy."

"Thank you for the optimism," Willard said.

As the sphere came within ten feet of the body, a pressure wave of water, pushed up by the ascending sphere, saved their lives. The body was pushed up and around the outside of the sphere. As they passed it, Robert clearly saw Choi's face, alert and panicked. She was reaching out for the sphere, but the pass was so quick, she didn't have a chance.

"That was close," Willard said.

"That was Choi."

Willard looked into Robert's eyes.

"She was alive," Robert said.

Willard remained silent for a moment, his face becoming gravely serious. "Then he's still up there."

Robert nodded. Peterson had sent Choi to a death no person deserved. If she wasn't killed by the shockwave, she'd asphyxiate on the ocean floor...or perhaps be eaten by an alien predator. Either way, her death would be solitary and very uncomfortable. The Europhids had to be stopped. That meant Peterson had to be stopped...by whatever means necessary...if they reached the top.

Robert's only hope was that the control panel would confuse whatever intelligence had consumed Peterson. Even if the Europhids had absorbed every bit of Peterson's mind, they still wouldn't know how to operate TES. He had never been trained. And the command to disengage the sphere was buried under so much protective protocol, he was sure it wouldn't be found in a short span of time. As long as Peterson didn't think to stop the ascent—that could be done with the push of a button.

32 – BALLISTIC

The oceanic world became a blur of color as Connelly shot toward the frozen ceiling like a torpedo. She had the propulsion pack pounding out more speed for longer than it was designed to handle. It had been created for undersea exploration, which was normally very slow and methodical, not for drag races. A tight vibration tingled Connelly's back. The pack was nearing its breaking point.

Just another minute, Connelly thought.

But a propulsion pack failure wasn't the only danger she faced now. The PMS suit had an uncanny ability to handle multiple extreme pressures, from the vacuum of space to the compression of the deep sea. But Connelly's rapid ascent was testing the limits of how quickly the PMS could adapt to significant pressure changes. The higher she climbed, the more quickly the suit had to compensate for lesser amounts of pressure. And once Connelly reached the top of the hole, the PMS would endure the ultimate test as it exited the pressurized water and entered open space.

With the shockwave booming up from below, Connelly sensed danger on all sides. By all rights, she should already be dead. But she zipped forward on a direct course for the hole above her head.

As she approached the hole, which was illuminated only by the bright lamp on Connelly's helmet, something fluttered out.

A body.

Connelly feared that it might be Robert or Willard. Perhaps Peterson had found a way to destroy the sphere on its way to the surface? She was relieved to see that whoever it was still had life in them. Arms and legs pulled and kicked at the water in an attempt to slow the descent, but the body continued down at a steady rate.

Adjusting her course to a slightly less steep angle, Connelly maneuvered in to intercept the sinking victim. She reached the body quicker than anticipated, still cruising at full speed. The impact knocked the breath out of her and caused whoever it was to flail. Probably thought an alien predator was having a go. Connelly wrapped her arms around the person's shoulders. She arched her back and resumed her vertical rise.

Connelly felt the hand of whoever she was carrying searching across the side of her body. The hand stopped on Connelly's com system, adjusting the settings. Connelly had a sneaking suspicion about who she was holding. Only one person could be so in control after a near death experience. The suspicion was confirmed when a voice echoed in her headset. "I adjusted your com to the emergency channel."

Choi.

"What's our situation?" Connelly asked as they surged headlong into the tunnel.

"Peterson's still on the surface. His strength has been enhanced and he's still under Europhid control, but appeared to be suffering from a fever. He was covered in sweat. Can I ask why we're rising so quickly? These suits need time to adjust to pressure changes."

Just as Connelly was about to reply, she no longer had to. The first effects of the explosion reached them. A swarm of rapidly rising bubbles roiled toward the surface, pushed upward by the outer edge of the shockwave. "Just hold on tight," Connelly said.

A pulse of compressed water, squeezed up the ice tube, enveloped them from below. They were immediately propelled to the full speed of the shock-wave.

Connelly looked up and saw a clean white hole above. The sphere was nowhere in sight. The guys had reached the top and had already locked the sphere down. The path was clear. Using the propulsion pack to guide their speedy ascent, Connelly kept them directly centered. She did her best to squeeze Choi even closer. The next part of their journey would be the most risky, especially for Choi. If Connelly let go of her, there would be nothing to stop Choi from being launched straight up into space.

₪   ₪   ₪   ₪   ₪

The Surveyor was shook so violently that Harris's vision became a blur. He was forced to work the controls by memory, which became a more and more difficult task as the Surveyor's descent became maddening.

When he'd first sat down, he discovered the primary systems were no longer functioning. He'd had to manually switch to a backup system. After pushing himself across the command center several times in an effort to reach the back-up system switches, he finally reached it. He had yanked open the door and fought with the ten tight switches that looked like circuit breakers. Once all ten were switched, he flung himself back across the room. He'd struck the ceiling as the ship pitched forward, but the impact flung him towards his chair, which he was able to grab. He'd succeeded in switching to the backup system, but the effort had exhausted him.

He had managed to strap himself into the command console seat, but he was having trouble focusing.

One step at a time, Harris thought.

The alarm had been shut off. That was his first step. Number two…

The pounding of thousands of charged particles blasting the outer hull was like a Fourth of July celebration, amplified through a loud speaker. The gash on his head throbbed with every concussion.

Restart the system! The thought snuck through the chaos. Harris reacted instantly. His shaking fingers sped over the controls. A series of colorful control screen flashed past as Harris accessed and reset the ship's system. With a final strike of a button, the command center went black.

After several seconds of waiting in weightlessness, the screen in front of Harris blinked back on. Text scrolled down the screen. He recognized it from their previous encounter with the charged particle bombs. He held his breath, hoping that everything would check out.

System reboot...
Life support systems engaged...
Main electric engaged...
Gravity engaged...

Harris felt the weight of his body pulled down into the seat. Blood rushed from his skull towards his feet, relieving some of the pressure from his head wound and clearing his thoughts slightly. The text continued to roll across the screen.

Status check in 3...2...1...
Optimal atmosphere...
Optimal pressure...
Optimal gravity...
All systems functional...

Harris glanced up through the clear hull above...when he realized that above was actually below. To him, he was right side up, but Surveyor was actually upside down over Europa. As the descending ship cleared the lower rim of the charged particle cloud, Europa came into view.

The frozen moon was uncomfortably close. The Surveyor had been created for space exploration and high speed travel. Harris knew that the evasive maneuvers it would take to avoid crashing into the moon were not in the cards.

The speed and bulk of Surveyor was too much. Crashing was inevitable. But surviving the crash—that might be possible.

Surveyor was the most expensive vessel ever created by mankind with a price tag in the high billions. The grand total was classified, but Harris thought it most likely surmounted the combined total income of the globes second and third world countries combined. It was no wonder Surveyor had been equipped with the very finest crash survival protocols.

Of course, they had never been tested. How could they be?

"First time for everything," Harris said.

Working through the series of commands that only he and Choi knew, he prepped the Surveyor for a crash landing. After typing in the final command, he watched as the ship's computer extrapolated all the information it needed. Descent rate, surface density, angle, everything was taken into account.

Harris didn't like sitting back and letting the computer do the work for him, but there was no way he could manage the hundreds of factors involved in landing a gigantic spacecraft on a frozen ball of ice.

A warning flashed on the screen in front of him:

EMERGENCY LANDING PROTOCOLS ACTIVATED...
SYSTEM ENGAGE IN 3... 2... 1...

Harris clung to his arm rests and watched through the clear ceiling. A jolt pounded him as the ship violently pitched to the side and then rolled, propelled by external thrusters. The computer was doing things fast.

Must be closer to the surface than I thought.

The Surveyor's spin snapped to a stop as thrusters on the other side of the ship slowed the rotation. Had he been unbuckled, Harris might have become a stain on the wall.

The dark side of Jupiter and stars filled the view above him. The ship was now bottom down. Several explosions similar to those of the charged particles rocked the ship from below. But Harris felt no fear as section by section of the ship shook from the outside. He knew the concussions were created by the emergency protocol's secret weapon. Thousands of ten by ten panels lined the base of the ship. Hidden beneath each panel was a massive balloon, capable of absorbing tremendous amounts of energy and displacing untold tons of weight. The panels were separated from the lower hull by tiny explosive charges and launched downward.

The final piece of Surveyor's emergency landing protocol was about to kick in, and Harris knew this would be the most grueling. The ship, pushed out of orbit by the charged particles and pulled down by Europa's gravity, would slow itself as much as possible.

Harris felt all of the Surveyors down-turned thrusters kick on at once. He was pushed into his seatbelt. It dug into his chest, squeezing his ribs. Harris gritted his teeth in determination. The Surveyor had taken a beating and pulled through. Now she had to survive worse.

"C'mon, baby," Harris said. "Get your nose up. Get it up or we're both going to rot on this moon."

ﬡ   ﬡ   ﬡ   ﬡ   ﬡ

As the sphere edged over the top of the ice, Robert felt as though he had experienced a rebirth. He had believed, several times, that his life was coming to an end. Back on the surface, he felt renewed. Regardless of the fact that an entire alien species felt the need to exterminate all human life on Europa, he felt his fear ebb.

Then he saw Peterson.

As they rode the sphere towards the surface, Robert had imagined all the possible scenarios. There were hundreds of ways a creative intelligence could have killed him and Willard while they were helpless in the sphere. But nothing had happened. Their ride up had been smooth and fast. With Choi meeting her fate in the depths of the Europian ocean, there was nothing to stop Peterson from acting. So why hadn't he?

After reaching the surface, docking the sphere and searching the TES platform with Willard, Robert had his answer—part of it anyway. They found Peterson face down on the ice, ten feet from TES. Robert noticed that TES's control panel had been accessed, but no commands had been successfully entered. Perhaps whatever was controlling Peterson attempted to disrupt the sphere's ascent, but having failed, threw a temper tantrum on the ice?

Doubt it, Robert thought as he approached Peterson's still body.

"Careful," Willard said.

"Playing possum?"

"Could be. Are his hands clear?"

Robert inspected Peterson's nearest hand, while Willard checked out the other. "Nothing," Robert said. "Looks like he passed out."

"Let's roll him over," Willard said. "Nice and slow."

The dead weight and stiffness of Peterson's body confirmed that he was either dead or unconscious. Robert grunted as they pushed Peterson onto his back. "Oh my," Robert said.

Peterson's face was bright red and pocked with hives. His skin and what was visible of his hair was soaked with sweat.

"Looks like he's burning up," Robert said.

Willard nodded. "He's alive. Look at his chest."

Peterson's chest was undulating like an eight cylinder engine. Robert was about to comment on the possible causes for Peterson's condition, but a growing tremor in the ice distracted him. He met Willard's eyes. "Take an arm."

Grabbing the ragdoll body of Peterson, they dragged him away from TES as quickly as they could. Seconds later, they were thrown to the ice as a wave of pressure burst from the melted hole. Robert landed on his back and watched as a geyser of ocean water spewed into space, rising one hundred times higher than Old Faithful. As he watched the climbing water freeze and drift away, he was overcome with a deep and sudden sadness. He hadn't seen a body come out with the water…Connelly never made it to the hole. She never had a chance.

Robert's head hung low. He'd never see her again. He clasped his hands on the back of his head and shook his head. Willard's hand rested on Robert's shoulder.

A shrill beeping stung Robert's ears as his headset blared out. He jumped back and looked around for the source of the noise, completely confused.

"Emergency channel," Willard said.

Robert quickly adjusted his com.

"If you guys can hear me, better move your butts." It was Connelly! "You've got incoming."

Robert looked toward orbit and saw a dimly lit object falling at him among the frozen snow and ice floating gingerly to the surface. He rolled to the side as Willard yanked Peterson back. The object hit the ice more gently than Robert thought possible, as though it had slowed its descent. Robert's eyes adjusted and he saw two PMS dressed bodies standing in front of him. But they weren't standing for long. Both slumped to the ice, exhausted.

Robert stepped forward. "Kathy?"

Connelly flipped onto her back and shot Robert a bright, but weary smile. "Hi, big guy."

Laughing, Robert threw himself on top of Connelly and squeezed her tight. She reciprocated his embrace.

"Thought I'd lost you," Robert said.

"Couldn't let that happen," Connelly said. "You just found me."

"Umm, guys?" Robert looked away from Connelly's smiling face and found Willard staring straight up. "Somebody mind telling me what the hell *that* is?"

Robert climbed off of Connelly and set his own eyes to the sky. Fluttering above him, beyond the frozen water that had been spewed from the TES hole, was a newly created star field, blinking in and out of existence. Robert squinted at the objects. He'd never seen anything like it. "I have no idea."

Thousands of glittering diamonds floated between Europa and Jupiter. What bothered Robert more than not knowing what he was looking at was that they were getting larger. Fast. He was about to offer a theory when the ice shook violently. He turned toward the source of the impact and saw a ten foot square of solid metal stabbing into the ice like a giant Chinese star.

"It's Harris," Choi said coldly as she stood on wobbly legs. "He's activated the emergency crash protocols."

Peterson sat up straight, suddenly revived. His eyes were wide. He glanced at the vertical sheet of metal gouging the ice, and then back up at the twinkling sky. "I know I've done some awful things, and my opinion might not matter to anyone anymore, but I'd like to make a suggestion."

All eyes were on Peterson. He was back to normal, but seriously on edge, and as far as Robert could tell, with good cause.

Peterson grunted as he climbed to his feet. "Run," he said.

Robert looked up. Running would be useless. There was no escape. The swath of falling panels covered an area larger than any of them could run. "There's no running from this," Robert said. "There's too many."

As though to reinforce Robert's observation, two more of the panels struck the ice, both within fifty feet.

"Not from them," Peterson said. "The Europhids. They're going to kill us! They're going to kill us—ack!" Overcome by some kind of paralysis, Peterson twisted his body into a sick position and fell back onto the ice. His breathing regained its rapid pace.

Connelly's voice filled Robert's ear. She had the voice of a commander again. "Everyone get down!"

Everyone quickly obeyed, diving to their stomachs. All Robert could see was the ice below his face. "What's going on?" he asked.

"Just stay down!" Connelly had an edge to her voice that told Robert there was a damn good reason for her insistence. Still, he had to see for himself. As soon as he did, he wished he hadn't. The Surveyor was crashing down towards them, its bottom covered in giant balloons, its thrusters spewing jets of blue flame towards the ice. Invulnerable space suit or not, they were about to be smeared on the ice.

33 – THE RETURN

Connelly looked to the left.

Willard and Choi were there, lying face down on the ice. Choi had one leg extended and bent, while her arms were spread in a sharp "Y". Willard's body was held tightly together, flat as can be, hands over head.

She looked to her right.

Peterson lay next to her, unconscious again, his body limp. Robert was just beyond Peterson, face down, arms clenched beneath his chest.

Connelly cursed herself for being dim witted. Out of the five of them, she was the only one to lay down face up. She had no way of knowing whether death would come in a quick crushing blow or whether it would be a slow drawn out suffocation under the weight of the Surveyor. But she knew one thing—

She'd see it coming.

And what she saw made her cringe. Even her Europhid altered emotional state was no match for the sheer terror of being crushed by a skyscraper sized starship.

As Surveyor closed in, Connelly could see that the thrusters were having an effect. The nose was turning up, but nowhere near fast enough to pull up from the surface and avoid a collision.

A shadow fell over Connelly as the Surveyor blocked out the reflected sunlight. It was almost on top of them. Connelly closed her eyes and waited for death. After five seconds, Connelly realized she was still alive. At the speed Surveyor was traveling and how close it appeared, she should have been crushed to paste by now. Connelly opened her eyes and gasped.

Two inches from her face, a blur of gargantuan balloons raced past. She felt like she was standing at the edge of a hover train track leaning out, tempting death. Only this experience was different in every way. She could see the flash of movement, but there was no physical sensation to accompany the image. No rush of wind. No roar of engines or whine of brakes. The vacuum of space made the ghastly crashing ship appear to be nothing more than an apparition. But Connelly knew better. With every passing second the Surveyor was descending. In moments one of the balloons would snag her helmet and snap her neck or catch her boot and fold her in half.

A fear of death no longer clutched her throat or ached her heart. This time, she kept her eyes open. The blur got closer and closer, she could see the thick stitches of the balloons moving back and forth across her vision like a pulse line.

Then the line disappeared, replaced by black space. Connelly's focus adjusted to the emptiness. She could see stars in her periphery...including a bright moon. The majority of the sky was black, blotted out by Jupiter's mass.

"Are we dead yet or can I pick up my head?" It was Willard.

"Surveyor missed us," Connelly said.

With a suddenness that surprised all of them, the ice shook. Surveyor was crashing.

Connelly yanked her body around and watched in horror as the Surveyor made contact with the ice, several hundred yards beyond their location. Shards of ice exploded into orbit as the weight of the Surveyor pummeled every vertical clump in its path. Surveyor lurched slowly to the starboard side as it slide across Europa's frozen surface on a sheet of balloons, which held the Surveyor aloft on a cushion of air. Surveyor slid to a stop nearly a mile away, leaving a smooth trail of ice its wake.

Connelly sat up and leaned back on her hands, trying not to remember the closeness of the balloons, the haunting silence. She pushed the disturbing thoughts from her mind and took charge again. "What's our situation?"

If they had seen how close to death they had all come, Connelly felt sure not one of the crew would act so effectively as they all did in the next few minutes.

Robert leaned over Peterson's body and gave him a few gentle smacks. "Peterson's out again," he said, "but he's still alive."

Willard took the defensive route. "Not a Europhid in sight, creep or otherwise. I think we made a clean getaway."

"What about the Surveyor? Could she have survived a crash like that?"

Choi didn't answer. Connelly looked at her. She was standing on her feet, scanning the horizon. Connelly stood next to her. "Choi?"

"We have concerns other than the functionality of Surveyor," Choi said.

"What is it?"

Choi stopped searching the horizon and looked Connelly in the eyes. "How's your stomach feel?"

The question struck Connelly as oddly out of place, but with all the confusion and excitement of the past minute, she had completely ignored her physical pain. She focused on her body. She was struck by a sharp pain in her broken ribs, a sore back and a headache worse than any hangover she experienced during her college days. But there was something else, and it was getting worse. A nausea began twisting in her stomach, slowly gaining momentum.

The sickening sensation grew doubly worse when Connelly realized what was causing it. "Radiation."

Choi nodded.

"But TES has an electromagnetic shield."

"As does the ATV I was driving…but both were destroyed by Surveyor."

Connelly spun around, taking in their surroundings. A smear of debris caught her eye. She could see a mass of black twisted metal that used to be TES's three cranes. A loose string of cable was stretched out over the ice like an oil pipeline. Connelly imagined that the sphere had been punted like a kick ball when Surveyor struck it, dragging the cable out behind it. All that was left intact of TES were the three diamond shaped panels and the melted hole that led into the Europian ocean.

"She's gone," Connelly said.

A moment later, Connelly felt Robert's hand on her shoulder. "We can build her again," he said.

Connelly looked up into his kind eyes. "No…we can't."

"Found it!" Choi said, and before explaining herself, began hopping into the distance. "The lander's still intact. We have six minutes to get within range of her shielding or we're going to wish Surveyor had landed on top of us."

ꕔ   ꕔ   ꕔ   ꕔ   ꕔ

The run back to the lander took only two minutes. Choi had just about left them all in the dust as Willard and Robert dragged Peterson between them. Half way across the ice, Connelly picked Peterson up by the legs and the three of them lugged him to the lander. By the time they arrived, out of breath and twisted with discomfort from the growing nausea, Choi was in the command seat, prepping for takeoff.

Connelly sat down next to Choi as Willard and Robert strapped Peterson in and took their seats. With the effects of radiation exposure wearing off, Connelly focused on her annoyance. "Where were you?" she said to Choi. "We could have used your help with Michael."

Choi worked the controls. The lander's hatch slid closed and the internal atmosphere and pressure adjusted. Choi removed her helmet and turned to Connelly.

With a brief gasp, Connelly sat back in her chair. "What happened to you?" Choi's face was covered in small lesions that looked like burnt flesh. "I spent a few minutes in the open radiation earlier. You had six minutes...I had three."

Connelly frowned. "Sorry."

"I'll be fine with some treatment," Choi said. "Right now, we need to get back to Surveyor, assess the damage and get the hell off this ice ball."

Connelly was constantly amazed by Choi's control in the face of impossible odds. Since Connelly's alteration by the blue Europhids, she'd discovered that same level of control within herself, but with Choi, it was natural.

The lander lifted off the surface of Europa with a relaxing smoothness that made everything feel normal again. The flight was just as easy. If Surveyor were still in orbit, and not lying out on Europa's surface, Connelly would have felt like everything was okay. But a dark foreboding filled her. They had survived the worst this moon had to throw at them. They'd all survived, every one of them. But still, something nagged at the back of Connelly's mind...a slight tickle that whispered: *run!*

ꔛ   ꔛ   ꔛ   ꔛ   ꔛ

Communications between the landing team and Harris commenced a minute later. Harris had a head wound that needed tending, but he was otherwise intact. The Surveyor had similar wounds, lots of topical injuries, but all major systems were operational. Harris guided them into the TES cargo bay. The landing bay doors had been fused shut by the charged particle barrage.

Within twenty minutes they had all congregated in Surveyor's med lab for patching up and debriefing. Connelly spoke very quickly about their suboceanic adventure and the encounter with the massive predator, the creeps, the blue Europhids and ultimately, their explosive escape.

After Choi related her end of the story, Harris scratched his newly stitched head and winced. "Ugh...So basically," he said, "Europa is like a large living organism?"

Connelly nodded. "Just as a human's made up of several separate parts that function as a whole. The red Europhids are a primal force acting like an immune system for the moon. They repair injuries, purge the weak and defend the body with their lives. They have an amazing ability to adapt to new threats. Just as humanity actively seeks to wipe out disease, the Europhids sought to destroy us. We're the foreign invaders. We're the disease."

Harris stood over Peterson's unconscious body. "And him?"

"They took over his mind...adapted to our species," Robert said. "They, ahh, they're really amazing creatures."

Harris shook his head. "Well, it almost worked."

Willard stood from his seat in the corner, "So what's his story?" he said to Choi as she checked Peterson's vitals.

"Ironic," she said.

"Peterson's vitals are ironic?" Willard asked with a smile. "I don't think that's a medical term."

Choi turned to Willard. "His immune system eventually routed out the Europhid infection. The fever and spasms were the result of the internal battle he was fighting. The Europhid that invaded his body was undergoing the same assaults from Peterson's immune system that we were experiencing from Europa."

"So the human immune system is better, then?" Willard said, standing next to Peterson. "How did he beat them?"

"Eventually, the fever did them in. His body found their weakness and turned up the heat. Used to living in a frozen world, his temperature was too much for them to handle. That's my theory anyway."

"So, he'll be okay then?" Robert asked.

"He's in a deep sleep, no doubt recovering from his battle with the Europhids. I'm going to keep him out until we return to Earth."

Connelly heard the conversation as it played out but she'd been distracted by the voice in her head. It was growing louder, simply more insistent.

"Amazing how the human immune system can adapt."

Connelly couldn't recall who made the comment, but it started a chain reaction of thoughts within her mind that ended with a one word expletive that alerted the entire crew to her concerns. "Huh."

Robert was at her side in an instant. "What is it?"

Connelly turned to the others. They stood around her, wounded and beat up, looking defenseless…weak…fragile. They were sitting ducks. "We need to get off the ice. We need to leave now."

As Connelly's final word slipped from her flush lips a gentle vibration shook her feet and slowly moved up her body, increasing in violence.

With a jolt, the vibration became a powerful shaking. Something was breaking through the ice. Harris was already moving to the exit. "Strap Peterson down and buckle up!" He was out the door and headed for the control center. Choi was at his heels.

"Take care of him, guys," Connelly said before rushing out the door after Harris and Choi. She felt slightly guilty for leaving the guys like that, but she had to see it. She had to see what the Europhids were sending to finish them off.

Connelly sat down to the right of Harris and buckled herself in, pulling the strap as snug as she could manage. The outer hull of the command center was still clear and she had a clear view of the swath of ice laid out before Surveyor. It was a jumble of crags, nooks, towers and humps, far from smooth. A chill shook Connelly's body. This was their airstrip.

"Thrusters to maximum," Harris said as he worked the controls, prepping the ship for lift off, something it was not designed to do...especially not in a rush.

"Thrusters at maximum," Choi replied. She was a model of cool efficiency, as usual.

The shaking grew worse. Connelly could feel her teeth clattering together. She clenched her jaw tight and kept an eye on the view. A slight distortion in the ice crust caught her attention. She watched, waiting for it to repeat.

Then it did. The ice rose subtlety as something from below pushed up. A thick crack began to spread towards them. "It's coming!" Connelly shouted. "Get us in the air!"

Harris slapped a few more buttons and switched on the internal com system. "Emergency lift off in ten seconds. Robert, Willard, buckle up or hold on. Five...four...three...two...one..." Harris activated the engines and then slammed the rear thrusters to full speed. They shot forward, sliding across the ice.

The shaking produced by Surveyor's balloon coated hull sliding over the tumultuous ice concealed the tremor created by whatever was coming up through the ice. But Connelly could see the ice rising and splitting directly in front of them. Their path was being blocked.

The weight Connelly experienced as her body was pressed into her chair was intense and she found it difficult to breathe. It was hard to believe that this acceleration was just a fraction of what would eventually propel them through the solar system and back to Earth...if they survived that long.

"Vertical thrusters!" Harris shouted over the cacophony of jolted metal joints and tumbling equipment throughout the ship.

"Vertical thrusters!" Choi returned.

Connelly saw Choi move as a blur. The thrusters engaged with a sudden upward motion that lifted them off the surface of the moon. The smoothness of frictionless travel instantly quieted the ship. The shaking was gone. The noise was gone. Peace had returned to the interior of the Surveyor, but outside—on Europa—was something else entirely.

The ice split open like a festering wound, a streak of red lunged out, launching toward Surveyor. The massive tendril had the thickness of a 747 and God only knew how much strength. Connelly was sure it would be strong and flexible enough to wrap around Surveyor like an anaconda and crush the life from her before dragging them all back into the Europian ocean below.

Connelly was about to scream, but Harris's voice cut her off. "Jettison the balloons!"

Choi didn't bother responding. She just acted. Connelly felt a sudden surge of upward motion. She was feeling the Surveyor blast up, pushed by the detaching balloons. Each explosive detachment provided more lift to the Surveyor...and there were thousands.

As the Surveyor lifted further off the ice and away from the tendril, the balloons rolled forward across the ice like a horizontal avalanche. The tumbling balloons distracted the tendril. It snapped back down toward the ice, impaling one of the balloons and bursting several others beneath its weight.

The blackness of open space came into view as the Surveyor pulled up into the sky, approaching orbit. Proximity sensors revealed that the tendril had lunged up again, but missed the Surveyor's back side by thirty feet.

But there was no time to celebrate. "Incoming!" Choi shouted.

A cloud of charged particles shot out in front of Surveyor. It was just the beginning of a thicker, impenetrably thick mass that was sure to tear the ship apart. Harris yanked the controls to the left and the Surveyor leaned and continued to climb. "Damn this moon!" The first of the charged particles shattered against the outer hull, echoing concussions throughout the ship, but Surveyor continued to rise, pulling away from the barrage.

In less than thirty seconds, they were through the worst of it. Complete silence enveloped the ship. Connelly let her breath out. Not only had they traveled further than anyone had before...not only had they made the most important scientific discovery of all time...not *only* had they been attacked by a raw and powerful alien intellect.

They had also survived.

34 – HOME

The face looking back at Connelly was a stranger. A thick bruise on her cheek glowed purple. A scrape across her forehead might leave a scar. Connelly's face, reflected in her private bathroom mirror looked nothing like it had a day earlier. But more than the injuries, which would fade in time, Connelly couldn't stop peering into her own deep blue eyes. She had taken her dark brown eyes for granted and could now hardly remember what they looked like.

Her corneas had been transformed from the color of rich soil to that of the endless ocean. Connelly decided she liked the change. Images of her strange visit with the blue Europhids filled her mind. The research boat, the kiss with Robert, the strange explanations...her mind drifted back...back to the tiger shark. It had bit her with such force, such raw power.

Connelly let her hand drift down her naked leg. She felt the staggered scar run across her calf and around to her shin. Odd, Connelly thought, that an incident which should have caused her to fear the creatures of the ocean, instead invoked a love of them. She realized why the Europhids were interested in the memory. It was that single moment in time that redirected her life and eventually brought her to Europa. Connelly snickered. If that shark had passed her by for a fish, she might have ended up a supermarket cashier.

Stepping back, Connelly inspected her naked body. She had bruises from head to toe, but was otherwise intact.

A knock at the door made Connelly jump. "Who is it?"

"Robert."

"Give me a second," Connelly said as she slid into her underwear and strapped on her bra.

"Don't trust me not to look any more?"

"Not a chance," Connelly said. "There's too many mirrors in here."

Connelly threw on her grey jumpsuit. "Coast is clear."

The door slid open and Robert entered, dressed in a similar jumpsuit that fit slightly less flatteringly. He entered and walked past the bathroom where Connelly was still fixing her hair. "Enjoy the view while it lasts," she said.

Connelly had left the exterior wall of her quarters clear. Outside was a close up view of Jupiter. Surveyor had been orbiting Jupiter on the opposite side of Europa since their escape. The red, orange and yellow swirling clouds filled the entire view. Connelly wondered how long it would be before mankind returned. She hoped never. Returning to Europa would be disastrous for anyone foolish enough to return. The Europhids had grown more and more adept at defending themselves from the human threat. They'd probably continue to refine their abilities until they were effectively immune to the human disease.

"Ready for our farewell dinner?" Robert asked.

"Just about," she said. "A girl needs to look pretty you know."

Robert appeared in the doorway, his face stretched in a grin. "Hairdo or not, Jupiter has nothing on you."

Connelly let her hair fall, wrapped her arms around Robert and kissed him hard on the lips. He moaned with ecstatic pleasure. She pulled away and quickly put her hair up. "You mentioned dinner?"

"It can wait," Robert said with a wry smile.

"But the ship can't," she said. "We head home in a few hours. This is going to be our last meal for three months."

"I suppose we will be waiting for each other on the other side." Robert wrapped his hands around her waist.

Connelly kissed his forehead, took his hand and pulled him toward the door. "C'mon, let's go eat with the others. The fact that we all survived is miraculous. I think it's fitting that our last memory of this voyage should be with the entire crew."

 נ   נ   נ   נ   נ

The crew sat around the table enjoying a meal of fettuccini alfredo and blackened chicken, served with spinach salad, garlic bread and ice water; all compliments of Harris, who was as good a cook as captain. The conversation was relaxed and full of laughter. Even Choi had let herself go. Connelly had heard that near death experiences could bring people together. It appeared to be true. Though she had met some of these people only months ago, they all felt like family now.

Only Peterson remained distant. Connelly wasn't sure if he was still groggy from his long sleep or if he was feeling guilty for the crimes he committed while under Europhid control...but she knew it wasn't either of those. Upon waking, he had requested to see Connelly. When she entered the med-lab, he reached out to embrace her. Connelly had dodged his advance and quickly said, "What happened between us was a mistake."

That's when he had noticed Robert waiting outside the door, his arms crossed tightly across his chest. "Moved on while I was out?" Peterson asked.

"Just opened my eyes," she replied.

Connelly left Peterson alone to lick his physical and emotional wounds.

"Pass the greens, please," Willard said, bringing Connelly back to the present.

"On a diet?" Robert asked and handed the salad to Willard.

"I don't trust those impact chairs to give me all my vitamins." Willard heaped a large portion of the salad onto his plate.

309

"The impact chairs are flawless and they were not damaged," Choi said. "You'll be fine."

"As long as you're tucking me in again," Willard said with a grin.

"Whatever it takes to get the job done," Choi said with a straight face, then broke into a smile.

Harris shook his head at the antics of the crew and stood up, reaching out for a collection of empty plates. "You guys seem more like...sib...lings... than...."

The world around Connelly froze. Everyone had stopped moving and talking in the same instant, as though they were animatronic puppets and someone had pulled the plug. "Guys?" No one moved.

Connelly stood, but before she could take action, her head burst with a flash of pain so brilliant she thought it might blind her. After the brightness faded, she began to see things again, but her vision was tinted blue. She thought about moving to Robert, but her body had other plans. She watched as her arms fell to her side and she slowly walked for the door. She could her the crew stand and shuffle out the door behind her, following her lead like the Pied Piper's mice.

For several hours, Connelly had no control of her body. She could only watch as she and the rest of the crew scoured the ship's labs, eradicating every single sample of Europian life. In one fatal burst, all the samples were blown out the airlock. Next, the crew set to work on the computers, erasing all data, video, images, personal files and logs. Their entire trip from beginning to end was erased.

Connelly realized that this was the blue Europhids. Somehow, they had left behind enough of themselves in Connelly to exact their will on the crew. Their intentions were not violent, but self preservative. By erasing the files and samples, the crew had no evidence to support their claims of life on Europa. But she knew the word of every crewmember would be enough to convince the world of life on Europa and a second mission would eventually be launched.

But Connelly intended to refute the crew's claims. She knew such an action would make her extremely unpopular with Harris, Choi and Peterson, but she also felt confident that Willard and Robert would back her up. The existence of life on Europa would become a long standing debate...she hoped...and humanity's return to the frozen moon would, at the very least, be delayed.

To further refute the claims of the crew, Connelly and the crew wrote corresponding personal logs about the journey. Subjects ranged from a damaging solar storm funneled through the system by Jupiter's gravity, to TES malfunctions and ultimately their failure to find any life on the moon. The logs mentioned the physical realities that could not be hidden; TES was destroyed and one of the landers was lost on the surface. The story ended with them retreating from a second solar storm that caused them to crash on the surface of Europa. After losing communications, they decided to return home before the storm finished them off. The entire story was incredibly detailed, fit the physical evidence and was corroborated by every single crew member. The written accounts would prove any verbal testimonies to be false.

Still unable to move, Connelly watched as the Surveyor was set on autopilot and programmed to make the jump back to Earth. Countdown, ten minutes Slowly, calmly, the crew all returned to their quarters, stripped nude and climbed into their impact chairs.

As the liquid metal of the chair oozed up over Connelly's eyes, the last thing she saw was a blue tinged view of her quarters.

Her vision turned from blue to black as she fell asleep.

ﬠ　　ﬠ　　ﬠ　　ﬠ　　ﬠ

Three months later, Connelly woke. A nightmare of constriction held her in place. Recalling the events that brought her to this point was difficult...almost impossible. She remembered Europa and the Europhids. She remembered their near death escape. Worst of all, she remembered her body being controlled by an outside force, while all she could do was watch.

But the darkness that consumed her was all enveloping, physically pressing on her on all sides. It reminded her of the time she spent within the wall of blue Europhids, how they had swallowed her whole and entered her mind. A pang of concern swept through her as she thought she might still be in the wall, that the last events she remembered were all an illusion created by the Europhids.

The pressure loosened around her. She had room to move, and instinctively pushed forward. A thickness slid off her body and she pulled herself from the viscous womb. The outer skin popped and Connelly slid out, falling on to a cold, hard surface. She opened her eyes, of her own volition, and took in her surroundings.

She was in her quarters still on board Surveyor. The last minutes of her time spent in orbit around Jupiter returned, fresh in her mind. The Europhids had erased all physical evidence that they or any life existed on Europa, and they'd used the crew to do it.

Rather than focus on past events, Connelly turned her thoughts to the future. A pulse of hope beat harder and harder inside her chest as she realized how desperately she missed Earth—the blue oceans, the golden deserts, the abundant life that only occasionally posed a threat to people.

Connelly climbed to her feet, shivering and dripping gel. Her body cried out for a warm shower, but she had to make sure her high hopes were justified. She found the remote control and pushed the single button that rendered the out wall clear. The skin of the wall turned milky white and slowly, steadily became as transparent as water. Glowing brightly below was Earth, hanging in space like a dazzling oasis.

They were home.

Connelly placed her hands on the clear wall. It shimmered under her touch. Tears filled her eyes for just a moment…until she realized she was standing stark naked in front of a very large window on a spacecraft that every space enthusiast with a telescope was probably watching like a horde of hawks. She covered herself and ducked back away from the window. Rather than return the wall to its opaque state, she headed into the bathroom and ran the shower.

Twenty minutes later Connelly was free of gel. She quickly toweled off and dressed in a blue jumpsuit. Somehow, being so close to Earth made the fabric feel softer and warm. She smiled at the comfort.

A familiar knock at the door drew her attention from the bathroom. "Come on in, Robert."

The door whooshed open and Robert stepped in, dressed in a tan jumpsuit. His hair was neat and his beard newly trimmed. He'd spent some extra time in the bathroom.

Probably trying to impress me, Connelly thought with a smile.

"How'd you know it was me?" Robert asked.

"You knocked on my door just like that before dinner back at Europa."

"I, ahh, I did?" Robert scratched his neat head of hair, messing it up. "I don't even remember dinner.... Must be a side effect of the impact chairs."

Connelly expected Robert to greet her with a hug, or a kiss if he was still feeling bold, but he strolled right past her and admired the view. She followed him to the window, feeling much more secure now that she was fully clothed. "Didn't happen on the way out," she said.

"Maybe they were affected by the solar storms," Robert said. "God, it's beautiful from up here."

"What did you say?"

Robert looked at her. "The Earth…it's beautiful."

"Not that."

"What? The solar storms? We're lucky they didn't strand us on that lifeless ice ball."

Connelly just stared into Robert's eyes. In that instant she knew that the rewrite of history the Europhids had performed on the collected data and logs had been duplicated in the crew's memories as well. The fact that her memories remained intact must be the gift—or curse—mentioned by the blue Europhids. It was an expression of trust that Connelly would never share the story with humanity.

"You okay?" Robert asked. "You look...stunned."

Connelly shook her head. "Just still shaking off the fog of sleeping for so long." She turned her eyes back to the bright blue orb spinning slowly in front of them. A sudden sadness struck her. Robert remembered *nothing* of their trip. He had no recollection of what they had survived together and the feelings they had unearthed. In fact, he hadn't commented on her now blue eyes, meaning the Europhids had altered his memory going back years. Her new, blue eyes were old hat. The emotional dread dissipated slightly when she came to the conclusion that the events they had experienced merely brought their feelings for each other out. It wasn't the impetus of their affection, just the release.

"Robert?" Connelly said, turning towards him.

"Yup?" Robert's voice was relaxed and jovial. He adjusted his glasses and looked into her eyes.

She kissed him hard on the lips.

After being released, Robert physically stammered backward. "What...ahh, what?"

"I've wanted to do that since our time on Orca One." Connelly took his hands.

"But...how..." Robert's breath escaped him and his shoulders fell slack. A smile crept onto his face. "I...me too."

It was Connelly's turn to smile. "I knew you did."

"But—"

"Robert," Connelly pulled him close so that their bodies were flush against each other and hugged him tight.

Wrapping her arms around Robert made her trip home complete. The crew had escaped with no permanent damage. No one remembered what had happened or what they had discovered. The human race would have no idea the Europhids existed and both species would be better off because of it.

As Connelly felt her muscles loosen within Robert's embrace, she thought about how she had grown, how her opinions had been so radically challenged and changed by their voyage. In all her years exploring for new life forms—in Earth's oceans, in Antarctica, and now on Europa, she always believed her quest for understanding and knowledge was the right course of action, the right thing to do. She had never considered whether the life she uncovered would *want* to be found. They had lifted the proverbial stone concealing the angry snake and it was only the mercy of the blue Europhids that saved them. But now she knew better...and would teach humanity to know better. After all, how would humans have reacted if the tides were turned, if it was the Europhids who came to Earth?

Robert broke from their embrace and said, "Have I ever told you how beautiful your blue eyes are?"

Connelly smiled. "Not once."

ABOUT THE AUTHOR

Photo by Aaron Brodeur

JEREMY ROBINSON is the author of seven thrillers including *Pulse* and *Instinct*, the first two books in his exciting Jack Sigler series. His novels have been translated into eight languages. He is also the director of New Hampshire AuthorFest, a non-profit organization promoting literacy. He lives in New Hampshire with his wife and three children.

Connect with Robinson online:

Twitter: www.twitter.com/jrobinsonauthor
Myspace: www.myspace.com/sciencethriller
Facebook: www.facebook.com/sciencethriller
Website: www.jeremyrobinsononline.com

Lightning Source UK Ltd.
Milton Keynes UK
17 January 2011

165832UK00002B/57/P